The way Noah watched the parking lot, sweeping his gaze over the area, made Maddy nervous.

The minutes ticked by with excruciating slowness, but then a large black K-9 SUV pulled into the parking lot, the twin headlights bright amid the dusky shadows.

Maddy headed for the door. Noah moved lightning fast, grasping her arm, halting her progress.

"Hold on a minute, Maddy." He pushed her behind him. "I'm going first, just in case."

She didn't want Noah in harm's way, but he was wearing the vest that had saved his life once before. She grasped the back of his utility belt, determined to follow close on his heels.

Outside, her gaze centered on the SUV. The driver-side door opened and a man climbed out. Her brother turned and the moment she saw his face, the missing puzzle pieces clicked into place.

She let go of Noah and rushed around him in a hurry to reach her brother.

"Get down!" Noah shouted just before the boom of a gun echoed through the parking lot.

Laura Scott has always loved romance and read faith-based books by Grace Livingston Hill in her teenage years. She's thrilled to have been given the opportunity to retire from thirty-eight years of nursing to become a full-time author. Laura has published over thirty books for Love Inspired Suspense. She has two adult children and lives in Milwaukee, Wisconsin, with her husband of thirty-five years. Please visit Laura at laurascottbooks.com, as she loves to hear from her readers.

Terri Reed's romance and romantic suspense novels have appeared on the *Publishers Weekly* top twenty-five and NPD BookScan top one hundred lists and have been featured in *USA TODAY*, *Christian Fiction* magazine and *RT Book Reviews*. Her books have been finalists for the Romance Writers of America RITA® Award and the National Readers' Choice Award and finalists three times for the American Christian Fiction Writers Carol Award. Contact Terri at terrireed.com or PO Box 19555, Portland, OR 97224.

Deadly Christmas Memories

USA TODAY Bestselling Author

Laura Scott

&

Terri Reed

2 Thrilling Stories

Christmas Amnesia and *Identity Unknown*

LOVE INSPIRED
INSPIRATIONAL ROMANCE

LOVE INSPIRED®
INSPIRATIONAL ROMANCE

ISBN-13: 978-1-335-42993-3

Recycling programs for this product may not exist in your area.

Deadly Christmas Memories

Copyright © 2022 by Harlequin Enterprises ULC

Christmas Amnesia
First published in 2017. This edition published in 2022.
Copyright © 2017 by Laura Iding

Identity Unknown
First published in 2016. This edition published in 2022.
Copyright © 2016 by Terri Reed

For questions and comments about the quality of this book, please contact us at CustomerService@Harlequin.com.

Love Inspired
22 Adelaide St. West, 41st Floor
Toronto, Ontario M5H 4E3, Canada
www.LoveInspired.com

Printed in U.S.A.

CONTENTS

CHRISTMAS AMNESIA

Laura Scott

This book is dedicated to my niece Brianna Umhoefer.
Always remember you are strong and smart.
Reach for your dreams!

Answer me when I call to you, my righteous God.
Give me relief from my distress;
have mercy on me and hear my prayer.
—*Psalms* 4:1

Chapter One

Assistant district attorney Madison Callahan hesitated on the concrete steps of the Milwaukee County Courthouse, shivering in the cold breeze coming off Lake Michigan. Had she heard something? Or was she letting her imagination run wild?

Working late and leaving at nine o'clock at night wasn't unusual, but for some undefined reason she hesitated. Giving herself a mental shake, she continued down the stairs, careful to avoid any icy patches.

When she reached the bottom of the stairs, she instinctively headed toward the reassuring streetlight, digging in her purse for her phone. Normally she walked the three-quarters of a mile to her condo, but since the hour was late, she decided to pull up the ride-sharing app on her phone.

She was moments from confirming her pickup location for her ride when strong arms yanked her backward, causing her to drop the phone. She sucked in a breath to scream, but the arms tightened crushingly around her. The sharp edge of a blade pressed painfully against her throat.

"Drop the case or you will all die, including the two old ladies in the house on the hill."

Maddy froze, her mind grappling with what was happening. *Two old ladies* had to be referring to her mother and grandmother, but how did this guy know where her family lived?

She forced herself to speak. "Did Alexander Pietro send you?"

The blade pressed deeper, causing her to suck in a harsh breath from the sharp pain. Something warm trickled over her skin. Blood? Was this man going to slit her throat right here?

Headlights swept over the road, brightening as a vehicle approached, but before she could be relieved that help had arrived, the man holding her suddenly gave her a hard shove, causing her head to crack soundly against the solid steel of the light post.

Pain exploded in her temple and she felt herself falling, arms flailing as she sought to break her fall. Her last fleeting thought was that she needed to find a way to keep her mother and grandmother safe. If anything happened to them, she'd never be able to live with herself.

"Ma'am? Can you hear me?"

She moaned and blinked, the light overhead painfully bright. Her head was pounding so hard she thought she might throw up. "Yes," she croaked. "I can hear you."

"That's good." An older guy, with salt-and-pepper hair and thick black-rimmed glasses, filled her field of vision. He was blurry initially, but then became clear. "Can you tell me your name?"

"Huh?" Moving her head hurt too much, so she stared at the man. He was dressed in green scrubs, a stethoscope wrapped around his neck.

"Your name," he repeated patiently. "There wasn't any ID found at the scene."

She opened her mouth, then shut it again. Of course she knew her name. Didn't she? The pain in her head quadrupled and she winced, closing her eyes and swallowing hard, willing the contents of her stomach to stay put.

Panic gripped her throat, making it impossible to breathe. Why couldn't she tell this man her name? What was wrong? Could it be that the pain was making her confused?

Forcing her eyelids open, she stared at the stranger looming over her. Concern darkened his gaze.

"We need to get a CT scan of her brain," he said to someone nearby. "Make sure there isn't any intracranial bleeding."

If pain was a good way to judge potential bleeding, then she was all for the brain scan. But even as the hospital staff wheeled her over to the radiology department, she couldn't ignore the strange sense of urgency that weighed heavily on her chest. She needed to get up and out of here; there was something very important for her to do.

But what? There was nothing but a dark void where her sense of self should have been.

Not just her name, but all of her memories were missing, lost in the swirling vortex of black pain.

Thankfully the scan didn't take long. As she was being wheeled through the hallway back to the ER, at least what she assumed was an ER, a handsome man wearing a navy blue police uniform caught her gaze.

"Maddy? You're the mugging victim? What happened?"

She stared at him for a moment, hoping she'd recognize him. For some weird reason, the dark navy blue MPD uniform was reassuring.

Wait, MPD? Milwaukee Police Department? How did she know what the initials stood for? Why not Minneapolis or some other city?

No clue.

"Maddy," he said again, crossing over and reaching for the side rail of her gurney. "What happened? Are you all right?"

It took her a long second to realize this man seemed to know her. "Maddy?" she echoed with a frown. "Is that my name?"

The officer's face paled with alarm and he kept pace with the orderlies who were currently pushing her through the hallway. "You don't know your name? Do you recognize me?" he asked.

"I'm sorry," she murmured, feeling as if she was letting this guy down. She hoped he wasn't her boyfriend or someone she'd once dated. He was attractive, with his short blond hair and deep brown eyes, and she could easily imagine herself dating a guy who looked like him. "My head hurts."

"Officer, you can't come into her room," the orderly said.

"Just try and stop me," the cop said, his features etched in a fierce scowl. "I'm here to take her statement."

"I'm getting Dr. Wagner." The orderly disappeared, leaving her alone with the officer.

"Who are you?" she asked.

"Noah Sinclair," he said, his gaze expectant as if the words would spark some sort of memory.

They didn't.

"You're with the Milwaukee Police Department, aren't you?" she asked.

"Yes. Maddy, I need to understand what happened. Who did this to you?"

"I don't know what happened." Boy, was she sick and tired of saying that! "All I know is that I woke up here, in the hospital with a skull-splitting headache."

"Listen, how about I call your brother? I'm sure once you see Matt, your memory will return."

Brother? It seemed wrong that she couldn't remember a brother. Although maybe she wasn't close to her family. For some reason she couldn't explain, she didn't want this cop calling anyone on her behalf.

"No. Please, don't." Reaching up, she managed to grasp his wrist, the warmth of his skin oddly reassuring. "I— Just give me a few minutes, okay? I'm sure I'll remember everything soon enough."

Officer Sinclair's deep brown eyes held indecision. She tightened her grip.

"Please. I need some time."

He glanced down at her hand on his arm, then lifted his gaze back to hers. "Okay, I'll hold off for now. But I hope that doctor comes back soon. I have a few questions."

"Thank you." Her hand slipped from his arm and she closed her eyes in an attempt to clear her mind. Her poor brain cells were scrambled like eggs. All she needed was a little rest.

She concentrated on breathing, in and out, allowing her muscles to relax. Someone, maybe the cop, turned the overhead lights off, leaving her alone.

Oh, that was much better. She had no idea if she normally did this type of relaxation technique, but it seemed to come automatically.

In and out. In and out. *Slow your breathing and your heart rate.*

Ignoring the vague sounds coming from the hospital staff, she concentrated on keeping her mind clear. Was it always this easy to think of nothing in particular?

She must have dozed a bit, because someone suddenly bellowed, "Hey! What are you doing in there?"

Prying her eyes open, she saw a deeply tanned man hovering close to her bedside. For a moment, his pale eyes held an angry malevolence, but then he turned away. "Cleaning," he muttered, pushing past the cop and the doctor and then hurrying away.

"Did he hurt you?" Noah demanded.

"No. He's just one of the cleaning staff."

"Maybe," Noah said in a low voice, his gaze following the tanned man as he made his way into another room. "I don't like it, though. I think it's best to get you out of here as soon as possible."

She looked up at Noah, searching her memory for anything that would help her remember. But there was only a vast emptiness. No name. No memory.

Nothing.

A horrible sense of helplessness tightened her chest. She'd asked for some time, but so far, that hadn't helped much. She still didn't remember anything. And then another terrifying thought hit her squarely in the gut.

What if her memory was gone forever?

Noah leveled the doctor with a hard stare. "Does she have bleeding in her brain or not?"

The ER doctor, Daniel Wagner, shook his head. "No, her scan was clear."

"Then I'd like to take her home." Noah had been upset to find out that Maddy Callahan had been mugged near the courthouse. But what was even more disturbing was that she didn't remember her own name. Or anything about her family.

The only thing working in his favor at the moment was that Maddy didn't remember him, either. Which meant she wasn't glaring at him or telling him to get lost in that lofty tone of hers.

Noah knew she blamed him for her brother Matt being stabbed in the stomach eighteen months ago. Matt and Maddy were twins, and truthfully she had a right to be angry. Noah had hesitated a fraction of a second too long, allowing the female drug addict to lunge at Matt, sticking the blade deep.

At least Matt hadn't been injured too badly; the tip of the knife had managed to miss his liver by a fraction of an inch. Matt claimed the assault wasn't Noah's fault, yet right after the injury, Matt had abruptly decided to pursue becoming a K-9 cop.

Noah knew the real reason was that Matt didn't trust him to be his partner any longer, and he couldn't shake the guilt that clung to him like a soggy woolen sweater. After all, Matt wouldn't have been hurt in the first place if Noah had reacted instantly to the threat.

Old news, he reminded himself. Time to get over it.

His radio went off, and he quickly turned away to answer it. His latest partner of just over six months, Jackson Dellis, was asking if he needed assistance to question the mugging victim. He assured the younger man he had it under control. Since their shift was officially over, he told his partner to go home and that he'd file the report on the mugging victim himself. Jackson didn't hesitate to agree.

Noah turned back to the doctor. "I'm a friend of the family and I'd like to take her home now," he repeated.

"Well…" The doctor hesitated, obviously not happy with the thought of letting his patient go. "She still seems to have some cognitive issues."

"More like amnesia, don't you think?" Noah countered. He crossed his arms over his chest. "Are you trying to tell me she has to stay in the hospital until her memory returns?"

"Not exactly," Wagner backtracked. "But she needs to be watched closely for worsening signs and symptoms."

Yeah, he could understand that. "Listen, Doc, I promise I won't leave her alone. But since we don't know what happened to her, I think she needs to be taken someplace safe."

That made the doctor bristle. "Our hospital is safe," he protested.

Noah wasn't in the mood to argue. When he swept another gaze over the ER, he noticed the mop that the tanned guy had been using was lying on the floor as if it had been dropped and abandoned. The man himself was nowhere in sight.

Maybe he was being paranoid, but Noah couldn't help but think that Maddy's injury was related to the case she was scheduled to take to trial in less than a week.

Noah knew all about Alexander Pietro's drug-running business; he was one of the cops who'd helped arrest him. They had plenty of evidence, but Pietro had serious mob connections in Chicago, and Noah wouldn't put it past them to attempt to free Alexander by doing whatever was necessary.

Even threatening to take out the assistant district attorney handling the case.

The fact that Maddy was still wearing a pair of black slacks, topped with a dark gray blazer over a blue blouse that matched her eyes, confirmed that she'd been working late down at the courthouse.

"I'll check with my boss," Dr. Wagner said. He left Maddy's room and Noah remained where he was at the foot of her gurney. As far as he was concerned, no one was going to touch Maddy without his permission.

He glanced back at her, noticing once again the long slice along the front of her neck. A small portion of the scratch had been deep enough to require a few stitches. Imagining the way the mugger must have held a knife to her throat brought a flash of anger.

Nope. No one was going to touch Maddy Callahan again. No way, no how.

"Is there a problem?" A female physician entered the room. She was tall and beautiful with long curly red hair and it took him a minute to recognize her as Dr. Gabrielle Hawkins, the infamous trauma surgeon who'd saved the lives of numerous cops on the force. She was the best trauma surgeon on staff at Trinity Medical Center.

The prettiest one, too. Married, of course, to Deputy Shane Hawkins.

"Dr. Hawkins, I'm Officer Sinclair." Noah held out his hand and she gave it a firm shake. "This patient is Maddy—"

"Callahan," Dr. Hawkins finished, her eyes on the

patient lying on the gurney. "I recognize her from when I took care of her brother Miles after he suffered a gunshot wound last April."

Noah figured he shouldn't have been surprised; rumor on the street was that Dr. Hawkins was exceptionally smart and never forgot a name or a face. "Yes. I have reason to believe she's in danger, so I'd like for her to be discharged into my care as soon as possible."

"Hmm." Dr. Hawkins skirted around him to approach Maddy. "Ms. Callahan? Can you open your eyes for me?"

Noah gripped the edge of the side rail as Maddy struggled to comply. Dr. Hawkins used a flashlight to examine Maddy's pupils and then had her follow a few basic commands. When she finished, she questioned Maddy about what she remembered.

"I don't remember anything," Maddy said, her brow deeply furrowed with obvious distress. "I don't understand, why can't I remember?"

Dr. Hawkins's smile was gentle. "It may be that you've suffered some sort of traumatic experience. I suspect that your memory will return on its own, but I'd like you to follow up in the neurology clinic in a week if the memory loss continues, okay?"

"All right," Maddy agreed and Noah knew then she really wasn't herself. The Madison Callahan he knew would never agree to a doctor's appointment in the middle of a trial.

Then it hit him. Until Maddy had her memory back, there wouldn't be a trial.

Oh, sure, maybe another ADA could pick up the case, but he knew from personal experience that getting ready for a trial took hours and hours of preparation. Maddy had grilled him about his testimony for a full eight-hour day and he was just one of the officers involved. What about the others? He couldn't imagine going through all that prep again.

Would the DA ask for a continuance? And if so, for how long? It wasn't as if they could just tell the judge to wait for Maddy's memory to return. Victims had a right to a speedy trial. What if they were forced to let Pietro out on bail?

The thought of Alexander Pietro being back on the street filled him with dread. Not just because the guy had threatened to kill every cop who'd participated in the bust, but more so because months of hard work would be lost forever. They'd have to start from scratch to build another case against him.

Placing more innocent lives at risk.

Noah curled his fingers into fists, knowing that he was taking the entire drug-trafficking case too personally. Because of his younger sister, Rose, who'd died of a heroin overdose when she was a senior in high school.

Another death that was mostly his fault. First Rose, then his former college girlfriend, Gina. One guilt piled on the other, with Matt's injury sitting at the top of the lopsided guilt cake.

He shook off the depressing thoughts and focused on the immediate issue at hand. Maddy hadn't wanted him to call Matt, but he'd called his former partner's cell number anyway. Matt didn't answer, so Noah left a vague message asking for a return call. Hopefully, Maddy's memory would return by the time Matt called back.

"I'll write the discharge order, Officer Sinclair, if you promise Maddy won't be left alone," Dr. Hawkins said.

"I promise I'll stay with her until someone from her family takes over."

Dr. Hawkins nodded. "Done. I'll have the nurse come in to explain what you should look for."

The nurse, a plump blonde with a cheerful smile, came into the room rattling off a list of signs and symptoms to be on the lookout for. Noah was glad when she handed him a packet of paperwork listing everything she'd just told him.

"Thanks," he said, folding the papers in half and sticking them in his back pocket. "Maddy? Do you need help sitting up?"

"I can do it," she said with a wince. She gripped the rail, pulling herself upright. She swayed, and he quickly moved closer and placed a steadying arm around her shoulders.

"Easy now," he said. "Take your time, there's no rush."

"I'm okay," she said, and the familiar stubborn edge to her voice made him smile. This was the Maddy Callahan he remembered.

The same woman Matt had warned him to stay away from the first time he'd laid eyes on her. Matt didn't want his baby sister, born a few minutes after him, to be in a relationship with a cop. The way Matt had lost his father, who'd happened to be the former chief of police as well as being murdered while visiting a crime scene, had made Matt overly protective. Noah had completely understood where his former partner was coming from.

The warning hadn't been necessary since Noah had no intention of being in a relationship with anyone, especially not Madison Callahan.

Maddy swung her legs over the edge of the bed, placing her feet on the floor, then frowned at her stocking-covered toes. "Where are my shoes?"

"Here." Keeping a hand on her arm, he used his feet to bring the flats into position so she could slip them on.

"Thanks." She stood, then reached out to grab his arm. "Whoa. The room spins when I move too fast."

A flash of guilt assaulted him. Was he causing more harm than good by taking her out of here? Maybe he'd be better off asking for her to spend the night at the hospital so he could sit at her bedside, keeping an eye on her.

Then his eyes fell on the discarded mop. A tall man with thinning hair stood beside the mop, arguing with a middle-aged lady. There was still no sign of the man with the tanned skin, and the hairs on the back of his neck lifted in alarm.

No way did he believe the guy who'd been looming over Maddy was a hospital employee.

"Are you sure you're okay?" Noah asked. "I can probably convince Dr. Hawkins to admit you upstairs."

Maddy looked puzzled. "Who?"

"The red-haired doctor."

"You know her?" Maddy asked.

It was on the tip of his tongue to explain how she knew Dr. Hawkins, too, but he decided that would only make her feel bad. "Yeah, she's married to a cop, a deputy from the sheriff's department."

"Oh, I see. No, I don't want to stay here. I'd rather go home." She frowned. "I must not have a purse or a phone, huh?"

"Unfortunately not. It appears the mugger took them." He bent over to grab her long coat off the chair. "Here, let me help you with this."

"Thank you." Maddy slid her arms into the sleeves as he held the coat for her. "Your mother must have taught you manners."

"Yeah." He didn't bother to elaborate since his mother had died a long time ago, and what was left of his family was scattered all over the globe. He and his siblings weren't at all close. In fact, he couldn't remember the last time he'd seen his older brother. Three years? Four? Rose's death six months after losing their mother to cancer had torn their family apart and, like the famous nursery rhyme, there hadn't been a way to put the pieces back together again.

He knew the Callahan clan was a tight-knit family and he wondered again why Matt hadn't returned his call. Should he start calling her other brothers? The only problem was that he didn't know their numbers and obviously Maddy couldn't help. Right now, she didn't realize she had five brothers—Marc, Miles, Mitch, Mike and Matt—every one of them older than her.

Wrapping his arm around Maddy's waist, he matched her slower pace as they made their way out of the emergency room. She stopped, looked surprised to see the Christmas tree in the lobby of the ER, as if she hadn't known the holiday was near. When they were outside, he gestured to a squad car in the small parking lot across the street. "That's our ride."

"Okay."

She ducked her head against the cold wind, walking alongside him down the sidewalk toward the parking lot. As they reached the road, a car came out of nowhere, heading straight toward them.

"Look out!" Noah grabbed Maddy around the waist and leaped out of the way, landing in a snowbank on the other side of the road. The car came close enough to clip the back of his legs, then careened from view.

Noah stared at the retreating taillights, knowing that he wasn't imagining things. This was the second, maybe even the third, attempt on Maddy's life—if you considered that the tanned guy who'd been in Maddy's room wasn't a hospital employee—all in the span of a few hours.

All these incidents were related, he was convinced, to the upcoming trial of Alexander Pietro. And the thought of Maddy being in danger, not to mention having lost her memory, gave him a desperate sense of urgency.

Right now, he was the only one who could keep her safe.

Chapter Two

$\sim$

"Are you okay?" The cop—she searched her memory; Noah?—helped her upright, brushing snow off her pants and coat.

"I don't understand. What's going on?" In the second she thought the car would hit her, she'd found herself praying for safety. Was that something she did on a regular basis? Must be, and for some reason, knowing that slight bit of information, that she believed in God and prayed often, helped calm her frayed nerves.

Thankfully Noah had reacted with lightning-fast reflexes, or she was sure she'd have ended up back in the ER with worse injuries. The hammering in her skull was bad enough, and it hadn't lessened one iota.

"You're in danger," Noah said in a grim tone. He put his arm around her waist, urging her toward the squad car. "I need to get you someplace safe."

"Why?" She braced herself with a hand on the squad car when he released her long enough to open the passenger-side door. "You think the mugging and this close call are somehow related?"

"Yes. I'll explain once we're somewhere safe," he said, his voice clipped.

She gingerly slid into the passenger seat. Noah shut the door, then came around to climb in behind the wheel. She latched the seat belt, then rested her head back against the cushion and closed her eyes, swallowing hard against the increased pain.

Noah didn't break the silence, and she felt the car moving down the street. It wasn't until he took several turns, heading away from the hospital, that she opened her eyes and grabbed his arm, seized by a sense of panic. "Wait! I—I don't know where I live."

He flashed a reassuring smile, gently covering her hand with his for a long moment before letting go. "Don't worry, I do. You share a condo with a woman by the name of Gretchen Herald; she's a flight attendant for Airstream Airlines."

It seemed so wrong that this cop, this man, knew more about her than she did. Ignoring the pain in her head, she continued pressing him for information. "Tell me more, specifically why I'm in danger."

"Okay." His smile faded, his expression turning serious. "Maddy, you're an attorney, working in the DA's office."

His statement should have brought forth a flood of memories, but didn't. She stared at him, feeling stupid and not at all like a lawyer. "I am?"

"Yes. You have a big trial starting next week. A man by the name of Alexander Pietro is facing serious felony charges related to drug trafficking and gun running. Thanks to your impressive track record of winning guilty verdicts, you're the lead prosecutor on his case."

She stared at Noah's profile, straining to remember.

Did the name Alexander Pietro sound familiar? Yes, it did, but she couldn't picture what he looked like. Was she remembering him from the case? Or because of something she'd heard about in the news?

Why couldn't she remember?

The deep sense of urgency returned with a vengeance. There was something important she needed to do. But what? The pain in her head intensified as she struggled to push past the haze in her mind.

"Don't, Maddy," Noah said in a low voice, reaching over to take her hand in his. "I don't think you should try so hard. Dr. Hawkins mentioned you need to rest, and relax. She believes your memory will return on its own."

"But when?" She couldn't help feeling as if she were standing on the precipice of a cliff, where one strong breeze would blow her over. "If what you're saying is right, that I'm working on a case, then I don't have time to wait around to see if my memory returns. I need to get back to work. Or call my boss, whoever that is, so he or she can assign someone else to the case." Then another thought hit her. "How do you know so much about this Alexander guy, anyway? Especially my involvement in the case?"

"I helped bring him down," Noah said, his tone matter-of-fact. He pulled up in front of a large brick building, gesturing to it. "I don't know if your roommate is home or not. Since your purse is gone, I'm assuming you don't have your keys."

Instinctively, she patted her coat pockets, surprised when she felt the distinct bulge. "I do have keys," she said, pulling them out of her right-hand pocket with a frown. "That's odd. I wonder why they weren't in my purse. Isn't that where I usually carry them?"

"I don't know, but right now I'm glad they weren't." Noah took them from her fingers. "That makes things easier for us, especially if your roommate isn't home."

She stared at the building, searching for something, anything that looked familiar. There were a few Christmas decorations in some of the windows, but overall, the place looked impersonal, as if it could contain anything from offices to apartments, no different than any other building they'd passed along the way. Of course, it wasn't easy to see clearly in the darkness. She couldn't imagine living there, yet Noah had no reason to lie to her, either. Was she crazy to trust him, just because he knew her and her brother?

Who else could she trust?

"Are you ready?" he asked.

She ignored the sense of dread. "Of course."

"Give me a minute," Noah said. She couldn't help but be impressed when he came around to open her door. Why was she so impressed with Noah? Was it possible the men she dated didn't have these kinds of manners? "Here, take my hand."

"Thank you." His hand was warm and strong around hers, and she was struck again by how handsome he was. It was inappropriate to focus on something like that, considering she didn't remember her own name, but still, she couldn't deny she was grateful for his strong, reassuring presence.

The inside of the building was very modern and nicely decorated, but didn't look at all familiar. Noah pushed the button on the elevator, and the doors instantly slid open. There were six floors and apparently she lived right in the middle on the third level.

She followed Noah down the hall to room 304. There weren't many doors, indicating the dwellings were spacious in size rather than piled one on top of the other.

"Stay here," he said, using her key to access the condo. He pushed open the door and flipped on the lights, looking around before gesturing for her to come inside.

She crossed the threshold, hoping, praying that the holes in her memory would begin to fill in enough to create a picture she could latch on to. But while the inside of the condo was nice and neat, it still didn't seem familiar. And worse, it didn't instill a sense of home.

There was a tiny Christmas tree in the corner, but it wasn't lit up. A detail that also seemed wrong, somehow.

"You're sure this is where I live?"

"You and Gretchen," Noah said. "Although I'm assuming that since the doors to both bedrooms are open, Gretchen must be traveling. If I remember correctly when I helped you guys move in, you have the room on the right, Gretchen's is on the left."

Swallowing a pang of disappointment, she walked around the living room, searching for what? She had no idea. There was a laptop case on the counter, so she crossed over and peeked inside. The computer didn't look familiar, but then again, why would it? Nothing personal about a machine. There was a paper file folder inside labeled Pietro. Hmm, that was interesting. Something to review in more detail later.

She turned away, searching for something personal. She headed toward the bedroom off to the right, thinking that she probably had family photographs since Noah had mentioned a brother. She'd only taken two steps when the soft dinging sound of the elevator door reached her ears.

"Wait," Noah said in a hushed tone, plastering himself up against the wall near the door, quickly twisting the dead bolt into place and shutting off the lights. "Get down."

When she saw the gun in his hand, Madison ducked behind the kitchen counter, her heart thudding painfully in her chest. He doused the lights, and for several long minutes they waited, the silence thick and oppressing.

The door handle rattled as someone tried to gain entry. Maddy found herself holding her breath, wondering if this was her roommate returning home from a late flight. But then she quickly dismissed the idea, knowing a roommate would simply use her key, the same way she and Noah had.

Another rattle of the doorknob caused the tiny hairs on the back of her neck to rise. Someone was trying to access the apartment.

To get to her?

More jiggling noises—what could the person in the hallway be doing? Picking the lock? She wished she could see Noah's face.

After what seemed like a lifetime, the noise stopped. She didn't move, waiting for some sort of signal from Noah.

The minutes passed slowly. When her leg muscles began to cramp from crouching, Noah came over to stand beside her, resting his hand on her shoulder. "Are you all right?" he whispered.

No, she wasn't all right. She couldn't remember anything about her past, her job, her life—plus someone had tried to hurt her not just once, but twice. She swallowed hard and pushed past the wave of anxiety. "Yes."

"We can't stay here," Noah continued in a hushed voice. "Whoever was out there might come back, or worse, hide someplace nearby to watch the place. I need to take you far away from here, someplace no one will know to look for you."

Her condo wasn't safe. The idea was terrifying, but then again, everything seemed surreal, as if this was happening to someone else, not her. Was that because she couldn't remember her past?

"Okay," she agreed, because really, what else could she say? She wasn't in a position to argue. She had no idea where to go or who to turn to for help.

Only Noah Sinclair, her buoy in a rough sea.

"Is that your computer case?" Noah asked.

"I think so. There's a file labeled Pietro inside. Although it's odd that it would be here when I was supposedly working late. Wouldn't I carry my computer with me?"

"I don't know. You could have been doing prep work with a witness. Regardless, let's take it with us," Noah said, releasing her to snag the strap of the case off the counter. He swung it over his shoulder, then reached for her hand. The moonlight shining in through the windows provided enough illumination for her to see his dark frame now that her eyes had adjusted to the darkness. "Come on, we'll need to take the back staircase down to the first floor."

She wanted to ask how he knew about the back staircase, then realized he'd mentioned helping her move in. Ironic that he knew more about the place she lived in than she did. In fact, it was clear Noah knew everything about her, which once again made her wonder about their relationship. Were they friends? Something more? Had they dated at one point? Sneaking another glance at his handsome profile, she thought that if he'd asked her out, she'd have said yes.

Then again, maybe she already had a boyfriend. There were no rings on her fingers, which made her feel slightly better about being attracted to Noah.

Enough. Stay on track, she admonished herself. Her headache must be making her loopy. There were more serious issues facing her right now than wondering about her personal relationships or lack thereof. "Can I pack a suitcase?"

"No time. We need to get out of here right away." His hand tightened around hers.

"Okay." She closed her eyes for a moment, sending up a prayer for safety, before following Noah to the door. He cracked it open, peering in the hallway to make sure the coast was clear.

"Let's go." He slid through the opening, using his broad shoulders as a shield in front of her as they made their way to the exit sign at the end of the hallway.

The stairwell was brightly lit, causing her to screen her eyes with her hand, wincing at the pain ricocheting through her skull. She followed Noah down the stairs, trying to mimic his soft, stealthy movements.

The way he paused at each floor, opening the doorway and looking down the hallway as if searching for anything out of place, caused her muscles to knot with tension. What if the door-handle rattler came back and found them?

She trusted in Noah's ability to protect them, but the thought of him putting his life on the line bothered her.

And as they made their way to ground level, Maddy couldn't help but wonder if she'd ever feel safe again.

The stark fear in Maddy's blue eyes made Noah grit his teeth against a surge of anger. This wasn't right. Maddy was a lawyer doing her job; she didn't deserve to be stalked by Pietro's goons.

Yeah, there was the remote possibility that it was someone else who held a grudge against the assistant district attorney. Maddy had assisted in putting other criminals away. Rumor had it she was one of the up-and-coming ADAs with an impressive conviction rate. Yet the timing of the assault against her was suspicious. Noah firmly believed that Alexander Pietro was the mastermind behind these recent attempts on Maddy's life.

Pietro had the most to lose. Maddy was the ADA standing in the way of his ability to beat the charges against him. The idea that Pietro might actually succeed in getting away with his crimes was unbearable.

For a second, his younger sister Rose's face flashed in Noah's mind. He remembered the way he'd last seen her—pale and lifeless, lying on the floor of her bathroom, with a needle and syringe still embedded in her skinny arm.

Dead from a heroin overdose.

Then there had been Gina, the girlfriend he'd broken up with because of her relentless partying. She'd later died from alcohol poisoning.

He stopped so abruptly that Maddy bumped into him

from behind. He automatically reached out to steady her. "Sorry."

"What's wrong?"

The way she gazed up at him, as if she actually cared about how he was feeling, made him cringe. He felt like a fraud. If Maddy's memory was intact, there's no way she'd be here with him right now. In fact, she'd likely demand Noah stay far away from her.

But she didn't have her memory and the danger surrounding her was all too real. He told himself to focus on the immediate threat. They were on the ground floor and unfortunately, he had left his squad car on the street directly in front of the building.

Smart, Sinclair. If the guy inside the apartment building was the same one who tried to run her over, he knows you're here. Idiot!

Too late to do anything about that decision now. He eased the door leading outside open a bit, looking out to be sure that no one was waiting there for them.

He didn't see anyone, but hesitated, unwilling to make another mistake, especially with another Callahan's life hanging in the balance.

If anything happened to Maddy, her twin brother, Matt, would never forgive him.

Noah wouldn't be able to forgive himself, either.

"What are we waiting for?" Maddy whispered.

Good question. Was he overreacting? Maybe the person outside Maddy's door wasn't trying to hurt her at all, but simply had the wrong apartment.

Then again, that wasn't a risk he was willing to take. He could call for backup, too, but he didn't like the idea of anyone with a police scanner knowing where they were. For all he knew, the guys working for Pietro could be listening in. "Stay behind me. I need to be sure that the coast is clear before we return to the squad car."

He could feel Maddy's fingers grabbing on to his belt and her simple trust had him deepening his resolve to protect her no matter what. "Whatever you say," she whispered.

The icy wind greeted him as he pushed the door open. Moving outside, he stayed close to the wall, grateful they were both wearing dark clothing that would help them blend into the night. He swept his gaze over the area, seeing nothing out of place as Maddy let the door close softly behind her.

They were on the south side of the building, and the street where he'd left his squad car was in the front facing west, so he edged closer to the back side of the building.

There was a narrow alley there, the darkness impenetrable. Noah considered their options. They could circle the building, making sure it was clear before making a run for the squad car. Or they could leave the car, making their way on foot until they could flag a taxi or car service for a ride.

He'd rather have his own set of wheels. While taxi and service drivers needed to pass criminal background checks, he knew the checks weren't foolproof. Decision made, he crept through the narrow alley between buildings until he reached the north side of the condo.

Peeking around the corner, he still didn't see anything out of place. Feeling better, he made his way up to the street where he'd left his vehicle.

"Ready?" he asked, glancing over his shoulder at Maddy.

"Yes."

"Here's the plan. I want you to stay behind me. I'll protect you until you're safely inside the car."

"I don't think—" she began, but he shook his head.

"Not open for discussion. I'm wearing a vest beneath my uniform."

"Fine." She didn't look happy but kept her hand on his belt. "Let's go."

Noah held his weapon ready as he cleared the corner of the building. The squad car wasn't as far away as he'd anticipated, so it didn't take long to reach the passenger door. Yanking it open, he swept his gaze over the area as Maddy ducked into the passenger seat. He shut the door, then quickly jogged around to the driver side.

He jammed his gun into the holster and then cranked the key, bringing the engine roaring to life. Pulling away from the curb, he made a quick right-hand turn and headed east toward the lakefront.

"We made it," Maddy said softly.

He didn't say anything, keeping a keen eye on the rearview mirror for a possible tail. The hour was approaching one thirty in the morning and he was grateful traffic was light this time on a Monday night.

"Thank you, Noah."

He wanted to tell Maddy not to thank him, that if she knew who he was and how many people he'd let down, she'd never thank him for anything ever again, but he held back. For one thing, her memory loss was hardly her fault. And for another, it was easier to keep her safe when she was cooperating with him.

Headlights flashed behind him, the high beams blindingly bright. He was on Lake Drive now, following the shoreline of Lake Michigan, when the headlights grew closer and impossibly brighter.

"Who is that?" Maddy asked, grabbing for the door handle as Noah took the curve faster than the speed limit recommended.

"Hang on," he warned, pressing the accelerator.

There was a loud bang as the car behind them rammed into the back of his squad car. Noah wrestled with the steering wheel, straining to keep the car on the road.

He reached for his radio to call for backup when the car rear-ended them again.

This time, his police cruiser skidded sideways off the road, heading straight for the icy waters of Lake Michigan.

He hit the brakes, but the car didn't slow down. He tried again, desperate to avoid the freezing cold lake. If they went under, they'd surely die.

Chapter Three

❧

"No!" Maddy screamed as Noah yanked on the steering wheel, doing his best to keep the car from going into the water. They spun, but then hit something hard, bringing the vehicle to a stop.

She was thankful Noah had gotten things under control, but then the vehicle abruptly tipped backward, the rear tires dropping over the edge of the embankment lining the shore. There was a hiss as something hot, maybe the muffler, sizzled, the back end of the car sliding into the freezing cold water.

She fumbled with her seat belt, the car teetering precariously on the ledge. She knew that if she and Noah ended up in the lake, they risked severe hypothermia and possible death.

"Maddy!" Noah must have already unlatched his seat belt, reaching over to help her. "Hurry! We have to get out of here."

"I know." The hood of the car was raised up at an angle, the back end submerged. She gasped in alarm as the car slid backward another inch. No doubt the trunk was filling with water, and she had no idea how much longer they had before the rest of the vehicle would sink silently beneath the inky surface.

Hurry! Hurry!

The restraint fell free and Noah grabbed the computer case that was nestled between her feet. He looped the case over his shoulder, accidentally knocking the police radio off his collar in the process. Using both hands, he pushed open the driver-side door, then reached down to grab the radio before jumping out of the car.

"This way," he said, keeping his arm wedged beneath the heavy door. Maddy climbed over the console, sucking in a harsh breath when she cracked her elbow against the computer mounted on the dash. The space from the floor of the car to the ground was farther than she anticipated.

She lightly jumped down, but the uneven terrain caused her to stumble against Noah. He caught her up against him, holding her close and preventing her from hitting the ground. But she accidentally hit the radio draped over his arm, sending it down into a pile of slush. She knew water and electronics were a bad combination and Noah must have agreed because he didn't bother attempting to retrieve it.

Headlights pierced the night, pointing directly at them. She averted her gaze from the blinding glare, searching for someplace to hide.

"Hold on to me," Noah said, keeping his arm anchored around her. "See the rows and rows of boats stored up on blocks? That's where we're going."

She didn't answer, concentrating on following his lead as they quickly ran, slipping and sliding over to the closest row of boats.

The sound of a car door slamming shut caused her

heart to leap into her throat and she imagined the driver of the car was already running after them. She clung to Noah, grateful for his support as she struggled to keep up. The boats were large and provided some cover from the bright headlights, but not enough that they wouldn't be seen.

Fear tightened around her throat. Did Noah believe they could outrun the guy behind them? Maybe if he was alone, but she knew her being here was an added liability.

If only she was wearing her running shoes.

Did she have running shoes?

This wasn't the time to worry about her lost memory. With the threat before them, the throbbing in her temple had lessened a bit, and she tried to ignore it. Pushing the ridiculous thoughts from her mind, she focused on following Noah as he moved from one boat to the next. He seemed to be checking them out, for what she had no idea. Plastic shrink-wrap covered most of the boats, protecting them from the harsh winter weather.

When they reached the middle of the sea of boats, Noah stopped. She leaned against a fiberglass frame, using the opportunity to catch her breath. Noah was doing something with the boat next to her, unlatching bungee cords holding a tarp in place, rather than the usual shrink-wrap. Peering through the darkness, she could see that two of the boats had tarps in lieu of plastic, and Noah worked on both of them.

She hoped he didn't plan on using one of them as a hiding place. Considering most of the boats were covered, it wouldn't take a genius to figure out that they'd take refuge in one of the two boats not shrink-wrapped in plastic.

Straining to listen, she attempted to pinpoint where the guy following them might be located. For a long moment she heard nothing but the gentle lapping of the waves against the shore. She was about to whisper to Noah that they should keep going when she heard the distinct sound of a muffled thump.

Noah froze, turning toward her. She stared at him, wondering if the noise was from the guy on their tail or from the squad car falling the rest of the way into the lake.

She reached for Noah's hand, needing his reassuring strength. As if he knew what she was thinking, he pulled her close and lowered his head so that his mouth was next to her ear. "We're going to be okay."

The tightness around her chest eased, enabling her to take a deep breath. Noah gently tugged on her hand, indicating they needed to keep moving. When she passed the two boats he'd been fiddling with, she realized he'd unlatched several of the cords holding the tarp, leaving a slight gaping hole.

Why on earth? Then it occurred to her that Noah had done that to make it look as if they'd chosen to hide inside the empty boat. If the attacker believed they were inside, he might waste time searching for them inside the boats.

Good thing she was on the run with a smart cop. One she trusted to keep her safe, no matter how steeply adversity was stacked against them.

Dear Lord, thank You for bringing Noah Sinclair into my life when I needed him the most. Please continue guiding us and keeping us safe in Your care. Amen.

The whispered prayer formed in her mind without

conscious thought and she immediately felt a sense of peace and hope wash over her.

Noah was right; they would be okay.

When they reached the edge of the boat storage area, she tightened her grip on Noah's hand. Now what? This area of the marina was brightly lit, without offering many places to hide.

Surprisingly there was a boat still in the water, anchored to the pier. It looked as if the motor was running. The water around the engine was swirling. There was no sign of the boat's owner, but that didn't mean he— or she—wasn't nearby.

But they didn't have time to waste searching, either.

"See that boat?" Noah asked in a hushed tone. "That's our target."

She resisted when he tugged her forward. "We can't," she hissed. "That's stealing!"

"Borrowing," Noah corrected. He pulled his cell phone from his breast pocket, showing it to her. "I'll call it in as soon as we're safe."

She didn't like it, but then again, allowing the guy on their heels to capture them wasn't a good option, either. "Okay, let's go."

Leaving the shadows to step into the light took a tremendous amount of courage. She hunched her shoulders, trying to make herself a smaller target as they approached the dock. Walking along the pier was just as treacherous, the moisture from the lake mixing with the snow to create a slick surface. She walked as fast as she dared, following Noah as he approached the boat.

She glanced around, expecting the owner to be somewhere close by. Why else would the motor be running? Then again, the guy could be on the boat, too.

The lapping waves caused the boat to rock against the buoy in a rhythmic pattern. Noah braced his palms on the edge of the boat, really more of a small yacht, and used the flashlight on his phone to peer inside.

"Hurry," he urged, gesturing for her to come over. Maddy swallowed a wave of apprehension, putting her trust and her faith in Noah.

"You first," he whispered. After slipping his phone back into his shirt pocket, he held the boat steady while assisting her aboard.

The rocking motion caused her to stumble, and she accidentally yanked on Noah's hand, tugging him forward. She widened her stance, trying to find her balance. The fact that her head still ached didn't help, although pain was the least of her worries.

Noah leaped into the boat, then leaned over to unleash the ties. The boat immediately drifted away from the pier, so she hurried over to assist. Her arms weren't long enough, so she could only watch helplessly as he stretched out to unhook the second tether.

Leaning over the way he was, she shouldn't have been surprised when his phone slipped from his pocket and landed in the lake with a soft *ker-plop*.

She closed her eyes against a stabbing frustration but there wasn't time to worry about the submerged device now. The boat was loose in the water, so Noah quickly disappeared inside the pilothouse to take control.

The sound of the engines revving to life seemed incredibly loud, giving away their location to anyone within a hundred yards. She stumbled inside the pilothouse mere seconds before she heard someone shouting at them to stop, followed by the sharp retort of gunfire ripping through the night.

* * *

Noah hit the throttle, sending the boat surging out from the marina into the large lake, praying for the first time in years that none of the bullets would hit the vessel.

"I can't believe he's shooting at us," Maddy said, coming up to stand beside him. The enclosure of the pilothouse helped keep the stiff breeze away, but the cold December air still surrounded them.

"Don't worry, he can't follow us." Noah divided his gaze between the buoys on the water and the boat's navigation system. He hadn't sailed on Lake Michigan in four years, but basic geography made it impossible to get lost. If he hugged the shoreline, he could head south all the way to Chicago or go due east to Michigan.

Heading north would take them toward Green Bay, but he didn't want to go that far. He turned the boat south. His partner, Jackson Dellis, lived near the border between Milwaukee and Racine, and he was fairly certain there was a smaller marina in that area, too.

"Is there a radio on this boat?" Maddy, so cold that her teeth were chattering, asked. "We need to call for help."

"There is, but I don't want to alert the Coast Guard," he said. "I'd rather find a way to contact my partner."

"Wh-why not the C-Coast Guard?"

Noah glanced over at Maddy, knowing he should have done a better job of protecting her. Dr. Hawkins had ordered rest and relaxation, and the past few hours had been anything but. At this rate, her memory might never return.

"Because right now I don't want the entire world to know that you're suffering from amnesia," he explained.

"Alexander Pietro is going to be tried by a jury of his peers starting next week, but we know he still has a lot of guys working for him. We need to make sure nothing related to your situation leaks into the press."

"Police reports are open to the public," Maddy said, her expression thoughtful.

"Yeah. Of course, the Milwaukee Police Department can limit the information that gets out, but your name has been linked to Pietro's case a lot already. Even the merest hint of an attack on you will have the media swarming all over it. I think it's better for now that we keep this quiet."

Until your memory returns, he added silently, refusing to consider the possibility that it might be lost long enough to derail the trial.

No way. He couldn't bear the thought of Pietro getting away with his crimes.

"And your partner will stand by your decision?" Maddy asked with a frown.

"I hope so." Jackson was his third partner in the last eighteen months, and so far he seemed okay. At least the younger guy hadn't dropped any hints about needing a partner that would back him up, the way his previous partner had. Matt hadn't held him responsible for the stabbing, but other cops hadn't been shy about sharing their opinions, especially Lynda. When Jackson had replaced her as Noah's new partner, Noah had been secretly relieved. Yet if he were honest, he didn't know Jackson Dellis very well yet. He couldn't say for sure if he'd agree with Noah's decision to keep the series of incidents surrounding Maddy quiet.

He didn't plan on giving him an option. Jackson was

only in his second year of being a cop, so Noah would pull rank if he had to.

"I hope so, too," Maddy agreed. She shivered and moved closer. He put his arm around her in an attempt to share his warmth. "How are we going to get in touch with him without a phone?"

Good question. It was already past two thirty in the morning; even those places that catered to the nighttime crowd would close down soon, if they hadn't already. "I'm not sure," he admitted. "We'll think of something."

Maddy fell silent and he wondered if she was second-guessing her decision to go along with him. It hadn't been an easy last few hours for her. Although he hated to think about what might have happened if she'd gone off on her own. From the near miss outside the hospital, to being rammed off the road toward the icy lake, to being shot at as they sped away on a borrowed boat, the bad guys, no doubt hired by Pietro, had remained one step behind them.

Too close for comfort.

Noah cranked the wheel of the boat into a sharp right, toward the much smaller and not as brightly lit Racine Marina. When they were a nautical mile away, he pulled back the throttle so that they drifted quietly toward the pier. Sweeping his gaze over the area, he didn't see anyone lurking around, but he refused to relax his guard.

"I need you to hold the wheel steady," he instructed Maddy. "Then when I give the signal, put the engine in Reverse, see here? Just enough to prevent us from ramming into the dock, okay?"

"No problem." She placed her small hands near his, taking over the wheel the way he'd showed her. Fighting the instinct to hold her close, Noah moved away and headed out to the deck. He grasped the edge of the pier and quickly looped one of the boat's mooring lines over it.

"Now," he said and she instantly pulled the lever down, sending the engine into Reverse. "Off," he said, as he quickly secured the second rope. She turned off the key, and he waited for her to come over to join him.

"Ready?" He helped her step off the boat onto the pier first, then came up behind her.

"What's next?" Maddy's voice sounded weak, betraying her exhaustion.

The area was far more deserted; only a few boats were stored here for the winter. He spied an old building off to the left. "This way." He headed in that direction, relieved to see that the place was a snack bar used during the sailing season. It was boarded up for the winter.

Banking on the fact that there would be a phone inside, he examined the door. It was locked up tight and the windows were covered, as well. Refusing to give up, he checked every bit of plywood, finding one that wasn't secured as tightly as the others.

"Are you breaking in?" Maddy asked, sounding horrified.

"We need access to a phone."

"Even if there is a phone inside, that doesn't mean it will work," Maddy argued, sounding so much like her old self that it made him smile. "If they were smart, they'd shut down the phone line over winter."

"Yeah, but there's a chance they didn't bother. The sailing season extends beyond just the summer months."

"I—I guess it's worth a sh-shot." Her teeth were chattering again and Noah hoped that his instincts were right. Prying the plywood away, he managed to reveal a broken window.

Using his leather jacket–clad elbow, he knocked the rest of the glass out of the way and then poked his head inside. There were boxes stored beneath a counter, and thankfully a phone hung on the wall near the door.

"I'll be right back." He didn't like leaving Maddy alone, but this wouldn't take long. He handed her the computer case for the time being, then levered himself up through the window. It wasn't easy—his shoulders were stuck momentarily—but then he was inside. Lifting the phone receiver, he closed his eyes with gratitude when he heard a dial tone.

He punched in Jackson's number. The ringing seemed to go on forever and just when he was afraid he wouldn't answer, he picked up.

"H'lo?" His partner's voice was slurred with sleep.

"Jackson? It's Noah. I need your help."

"Noah?" Now he sounded more awake. "Do you realize it's almost three o'clock in the morning?"

"I know, I'm sorry, but I'm in a jam. Can you meet me down at the Racine Marina?"

"Now? Seriously? Is it important?"

"Yes."

Long silence, then, "Yeah, okay. Give me fifteen minutes."

"Thank you." He replaced the receiver then checked the door. A giant padlock hung through the latch, so he gave up and crawled back out the window. Maddy was huddled against the building, her arms crossed and her chin ducked into the collar of her coat.

After taking the computer case from her, he didn't hesitate to gather her into his arms. "Jackson will be here soon. I need you to hang in there for a little while longer, okay?"

"I—I can't get warm," she whispered.

"I know." He rubbed his hands up and down her back, hoping to ward off the possibility of hypothermia. She had a winter coat on, but no hat or gloves or decent boots. No wonder she was shivering. He tucked her head into his shoulder and tried not to be distracted by the cinnamon scent of her hair.

If Matt knew what a terrible job Noah was doing in protecting Maddy, he'd be furious. Which made him wonder why Matt hadn't called him back. The only thing he could imagine that would keep Matt from returning his call was if he was out on a case. Of course now that his phone was in the bottom of the lake, it didn't matter much.

He should have mentioned Maddy being in danger; then for sure nothing would have stopped Matt from returning his call. But back when he'd made that initial contact, he hadn't realized just how serious Maddy's situation was.

For a moment, Noah debated going back inside the building to make another call to Matt, but decided against it. He didn't want to leave Maddy alone and Jackson would be here soon. He could easily borrow his partner's phone to make the call. This time, Noah would be sure to give Matt the specifics on how many attempts had been made on Maddy's life.

"Headlights," Maddy whispered, her body going tense, her breath warm against his throat.

"I'm sure it's Jackson," he assured her. They stood in the shadow of the building, a spot that provided them a broad view of the parking lot while keeping them hidden. He knew his partner drove a large pickup, so he waited until the vehicle pulled into a parking space to make sure. Yep, the truck looked familiar, so he felt certain Jackson was the one behind the wheel.

Sure enough, the driver-side door sprung open, revealing a short redheaded guy. Jackson climbed out and stood for a moment, glancing around expectantly, his expression irritated that Noah wasn't anywhere in sight.

He released Maddy and tried to step away, but she tightened her grip. "No, wait. I don't like this."

"That's my partner," he reminded her. "I'm sure we'll be fine."

"Noah, please…" Her voice trailed off.

"We don't have another option," he told her. "We need to get someplace warm."

She hesitated for a moment, then capitulated. "All right."

Before they could step out from the shadows, there was a loud crack and Jackson Dellis crumpled to the ground in a heap.

Noah sucked in a harsh breath, horrified to see his partner shot before his eyes, thinking, *Not again, not again!* But then he focused on protecting Maddy, dragging her deeper into the shadows, trying to comprehend what had happened.

Their only escape route had been effectively cut off, leaving them stranded at the mercy of a hidden shooter.

Chapter Four

"Stay down," Noah said, pushing her behind him. Maddy huddled close to his back, holding on to his utility belt, shivering at the realization they were vulnerable here, near the back edge of the building.

She'd known something was off, but hadn't expected this.

Another shot rang out and the truck's windshield shattered into millions of pieces. Noah's partner didn't move, but there was a large pool of blood on the ground around him and she suspected the poor guy was dead.

Maddy's heart was lodged in her throat. "We need to get out of here," she whispered. She knew it wouldn't take the gunman long to figure out they were hiding in the shadows of the small structure. "We don't know where the threat is coming from."

For several long moments, he didn't say anything. "I believe the gunman is up on the hill." Noah's soft voice held a steady calmness she envied. "Let's stay here in the shadows for a moment."

She drew her coat up over her face and twisted around to look up at the snow-covered hill looming above the parking lot. Her stomach knotted, because if Noah was right, they had to assume that being up so high gave the gunman the advantage. He would see them if they left their hiding place to run toward the boat.

But what choice did they have? For all they knew, the gunman wasn't alone. He could sit up there picking them off while sending someone else down to find them.

"Okay, here's the plan," Noah whispered. "The minute I return fire, we run for the boat. I want you to use a zigzag pattern while trying to stay directly in front of me so I can protect you."

Maddy didn't like leaving Noah exposed, but nodded, trying to take comfort in the fact he was wearing a bulletproof vest. "Okay."

"If anything happens to me, I want you to keep going for the boat. Use the radio and call the Coast Guard and insist on being connected with either Miles or Matthew Callahan. They're both cops with the MPD. Don't talk to anyone else until one of your brothers shows up. Understand?"

Two brothers? He'd mentioned one earlier at the hospital, but two? And they were both cops? Somehow, that part didn't surprise her. Maybe that was why she'd subconsciously recognized Noah's uniform.

"All right," she whispered. "But here's the deal. I don't want anything to happen to you, either. We're both going to get out of this alive, understand?"

Noah flashed a grim smile, then waited for another long moment, the night air eerily silent. Maddy wanted so badly to leave this place, wishing they'd never come here. Or that they'd called Noah's partner here. What if the gunman was making his way toward them right now?

She wrestled the panic under control, sending up a silent prayer for assistance.

Dear Lord, protect us from harm!

The boom from Noah's gun was so unexpectedly loud, her ears rang and the pounding headache intensified. But she didn't let that stop her. Instantly, she whirled and ran around the corner of the structure. Moving as fast as she dared, she ran across the open space, heading toward the boat bobbing up and down in the water.

She could feel Noah behind her. Knowing he was placing his life on the line to protect her made her run faster. Gunfire rang out behind them and she swallowed a sob, jutting one way, then the other in an attempt to make it more difficult for the gunman to hit them.

"Oomph," Noah muttered.

"Are you hit?" She wanted to turn around to see what was wrong.

"I'm fine, keep going," he whispered.

The pier was growing closer. She juked left, then abruptly turned right. Ten yards. Five. She pushed for more speed, leaping onto the pier and then diving into the boat.

Thankfully Noah was right behind her, stopping long enough to remove the lines keeping them connected to the dock. Without waiting for him to tell her, she went to the pilothouse and started up the engine.

"Go!" Noah shouted, jumping into the bow of the boat just as another round of gunfire echoed through the night.

She didn't need to be told twice. Hoping she didn't wreck the boat engine doing something she shouldn't, she pulled the throttle into Reverse. The boat shot away from the shoreline, rocking dangerously on the water.

Praying the bullets wouldn't render the boat useless, she did her best to get control so she could command the boat farther out into the center of the lake. A few minutes later, Noah came over to join her.

"We need to go farther south," he said, reaching around her to turn the wheel, pointing the boat southeast.

"What if the gunman follows?" she asked, grateful they'd managed to escape.

Noah kept his hands on the wheel, his arms bracketing her on both sides, and she was comforted by his strong, reassuring presence. "Don't worry, we'll stay far enough from shore that they'll soon lose sight of us."

She hoped he was right. Turning her head, she looked up at him. His face was set in grim lines. "Are you sure you're all right?"

He didn't answer right away, and she belatedly realized he was grieving over his partner.

"I'm sorry about your partner," she said softly. "We need to call the authorities, send them to the Racine Marina. Maybe he's still alive."

Noah shook his head. "He was hit in the chest and went down like a rock. I doubt he was wearing his vest. I should have warned him..." His voice trailed off.

She covered his hand on the wheel with hers. "You didn't know there was a gunman hiding on the hill."

Noah didn't respond and she could tell that he was beating himself up over his partner's death.

"If this is anyone's fault, it's mine," she tried again. "The only reason you called him is because you were stuck protecting me. I'm the real target here, right? This Pietro guy is after me."

He glanced down at her, and she wondered if it was just her imagination or if there was a softness in his expression now. "Yes, but trust me, Pietro would love nothing more than to kill me, too. In fact, there's a chance he's put a price on the head of anyone who helped get him arrested."

Maddy swallowed hard, trying not to show her horror. It was bad enough that she and Noah were in immediate danger from this man, but knowing there might be other targets he was going after made it much, much worse.

She needed her memory to return. Before more innocent lives were lost.

Noah ignored the pain spreading throughout the right side of his back. As long as he could move, he wasn't going to waste time stopping to inspect the damage.

The vest he was wearing had saved his life, and Maddy's, too.

But not Jackson's. The image of his partner threatened to send him to his knees and guilt choked him.

When would the deaths stop?

The boat lurched to the side, and he realized he'd loosened his grip on the wheel. This wasn't the time to feel sorry for himself. He needed to stay focused, to clear his thoughts. To find a way to keep Maddy safe.

Nothing would bring his partner back. All he could do was keep moving forward. Find a way to bring Pietro's henchman, if that's who was behind all this, which was the only thing that made sense, to justice.

But his partner's unexpected shooting begged the

question about how the gunman had found them in the first place? Had Jackson's phone been bugged? Or had his partner been followed to the marina? If the guy who'd rammed them into the lake was working for Pietro and had figured out Noah's name, it stood to reason that they'd assume he'd go to Jackson for help. The gunman might have staked out Jackson's place and when he figured out they were headed for the marina, went over to pick his spot on the hill.

Was it possible someone from within law enforcement was involved? As soon as the idea entered Noah's head, he pushed it away.

No, he wasn't going there. Besides, he had no evidence that these attempts against Maddy were the result of an inside job.

Maddy settled back against him. He told himself not to read into her gesture; she was likely freezing cold and seeking warmth. Even if she one day decided to forgive him for causing her twin brother's injury, there would never be anything but friendship between them.

He didn't do relationships. Losing his sister and then Gina had taught him that love hurt. He wasn't about to open himself up to that again, and especially not with Matt's twin sister. She was off-limits in every way.

The cinnamon scent of her hair was distracting and he kept his eyes on the water, making sure there weren't any vehicles that seemed to be tailing them.

Should he turn around and head back to Milwaukee?

He considered the cities and towns north of Milwaukee. There were a few areas that would serve as a good hiding place.

But there was the temperature to consider. Maddy had already been exposed to the elements for too long.

Dr. Hawkins had told him she needed rest and relaxation. The sooner he could find them a safe place to spend what was left of the night, the better.

Heading north was out of the question, so he focused on finding a place that was within walking distance of the southern shore of the lakefront.

Easier said than done.

Maddy shivered, accentuating the need to get her someplace safe and warm. He eyed the fuel gauge. Was there enough to take them to Chicago? Then again, maybe just getting across the Illinois border would help.

Five minutes passed, then ten. He was beginning to give up hope of finding anything close by when he caught a glimpse of a neon sign.

Vacancy.

Perfect. But where was the motel? Objects in the distance could look deceiving. What appeared close was likely farther away than he'd like.

He cranked the wheel, pointing the bow of their boat toward shore. The vacancy sign grew brighter and he was relieved to see that the small structure was adjacent to what looked like a truck stop.

Sweeping his gaze over the area, he stumbled across a small boathouse next to a pier. It looked private, but he didn't care. They needed safe access to shore, and from there he would let the boat drift away, hopefully taking anyone working for Pietro far away from their hiding spot.

Maddy didn't say anything as he steered the boat toward shore. In fact, she took over the wheel, leaving him to guide the vessel to the pier, as if they'd done this together a hundred times, instead of just once.

"Now," he called. The engine immediately went into

Reverse and he looped the line over the pylon. "Cut the engine."

She did. Within seconds, she joined him in the bow.

"Take my hand," he instructed, hiding a wince when his back muscles screamed in protest.

Maddy stumbled, her movements sluggish, and he knew hypothermia was beginning to set in. They didn't have any time to waste. He needed to get her inside the warmth of a building as soon as possible.

"Come on, Maddy, we're almost there," he urged, taking more of her weight so that he could get her onto solid ground. When she was standing on the pier beside him, he quickly lifted the line off the pylon and gave the boat a firm shove with his foot.

"Wh-what are y-you doing?" He took it as a good sign that her teeth were chattering again. At least her body was still attempting to stay warm.

He needed her to fight for just a little longer.

"If Pietro's men are watching, they'll hopefully assume we're still on board." He wrapped his arm around her waist. "The motel isn't far, see the vacancy sign? Warmth is just a few yards away."

"I—I see—it."

Was it his imagination or were her words coming slower and more slurred? He urged her forward, anxious to get to their destination. Dividing his attention between Maddy's precarious health and searching for signs of danger, he took the shortest possible route to the motel.

The lobby of the motel was dark except for a small lamp he could see at the front desk. As they approached, he didn't see anyone standing there and when he tested the door, it was locked.

Since the truck stop café was open and likely serving coffee, he gestured to it. "We'll stop in there, get something hot to drink."

This time she didn't respond and it appeared she was having a hard time putting one foot in front of the other. The light shining from the café was like a beacon.

After what seemed like forever, but was less than a few minutes, they reached the building. He opened the door and practically shoved Maddy inside. When the door closed behind him, the interior warmth hit him like a welcoming embrace. He found himself closing his eyes and praying.

Thank You, Lord, for giving me the strength to get Maddy to safety.

As they dropped into the closest open booth, it struck him that praying for Maddy was instinctive and much easier than praying for himself.

Maddy cradled the mug of hot chocolate in her hands, taking tiny sips to warm her belly. She hadn't realized just how cold she'd been until she'd stumbled into the warmth of the café.

She glanced over at Noah, who was sitting beside her, rather than across the table. Maybe it was her imagination but she thought she could feel warmth radiating from his hand that was resting on her knee.

Shivers racked her body, which made it difficult to drink the chocolate. In some tiny corner of her mind, she understood how dangerously close she'd been to succumbing to hypothermia.

"Thank you, Noah," she whispered.

He stiffened. "You shouldn't be thanking me," he said in a flat tone.

"Yes, I should. Without your help, I'm fairly certain I'd already be dead," she said, knowing she owed her life to this man, this officer who'd put his own life on the line to protect her. "I wish I remembered—well, everything, but especially you. I'm sure we were friends before this."

Noah shrugged. "Friends might be pushing it. We were acquaintances, nothing more." He cleared his throat, obviously uncomfortable with the topic. "Since we're here, we may as well order breakfast. When the motel opens up, we'll grab a room."

She couldn't bear to let go of the steaming mug long enough to open the menu, so she rested her cheek against Noah's shoulder and looked at his. "I'll have a veggie omelet and a side of hash browns."

A wry grin tugged at the corner of his mouth. "You still don't eat much meat, do you?"

That observation made her frown. Had she ordered the veggies because of a buried memory? And if so, were there other memories that might begin surfacing? She sincerely hoped so. "I guess not," she said. "Is there anything else you know about me? You mentioned two brothers, earlier. Do I have parents, too?"

Their server chose that moment to approach their table, refilling Noah's coffee mug and asking if they were ready to order.

Noah ordered a sausage-and-mushroom omelet rather than the veggie, but they both requested hash-brown potatoes as their side. After the woman hustled away, he turned to look at Maddy, his deep brown eyes, the color of melted chocolate, serious.

"You have a large family, Maddy. Five brothers, a mother and grandmother. Your father was killed in the line of duty almost two years ago. If you want me to call your brothers, I will. I don't like the idea of using an unsecured phone in the motel, but if that's what you want, we'll find a way to make it work."

A large family? Her breath caught in her chest. How was it that she'd completely forgotten everyone in her family? A mother? Brothers? Grandmother? It didn't make any sense.

Thinking made her head ache. "I don't know what to do," she confessed softly. Logically it would make sense for Noah to call her brothers, handing her over into their care, but the idea of leaving him to go off with men she didn't know wasn't appealing. Granted, he'd been a stranger at first, but now she felt comfortable with him.

Scary how much she'd come to depend on Noah.

"Listen, let's eat, get some sleep and see how you feel in a few hours," he suggested. "It's still pretty early. No reason to raise the alarm right now, and maybe by then your memory will have returned."

She nodded, trying to ignore the lingering headache. "That sounds good to me. I'd rather not risk anything happening to my family, the way—" She stopped just short of mentioning his partner.

Noah's expression turned grim. "Then we're in agreement," he said. He gently squeezed her knee, then removed his hand. She immediately missed the warmth of his touch.

The food arrived with surprising speed. Maddy bowed her head and murmured a quick prayer before digging into her breakfast. By the time they'd finished their respective meals, and a second hot chocolate, Maddy noticed the main lights had been turned on at the motel across the street.

She'd finally stopped shivering, and she didn't relish the thought of heading back out into the biting cold, even for a short trip across the road. Yet sitting in the booth made her realize how exhausted she was. Her eyelids drooped and she wished she could lean again on Noah.

"Ready?" Noah asked, as she drained the last of her second hot chocolate. He'd paid the server in cash, leaving a nice tip.

"Sure." She forced a smile.

He slid out of the booth first, then offered her his hand. She took it, glancing up at his face as he helped her stand. A flash of pain darkened his eyes, making her frown.

"Are you sure you're okay?" she asked. From what she could tell, he wasn't bleeding anywhere.

"Of course." He didn't say anything more, and she shrugged it off, thinking her tired mind was playing tricks on her.

He opened the café door for her and she sucked in a harsh breath as the biting cold hit her face. Instantly the shivers returned.

"I'm here, and we'll be inside again soon," Noah said, wrapping his arm around her waist.

She nodded and fixated her gaze on the single light in the lobby and the loops of garland hanging around the window. Within moments they were inside, sheltered from the icy wind.

Noah requested two adjoining rooms and used his badge to convince the manager to allow him to pay in cash.

The rooms were nothing fancy, but clean. Noah knocked on their connecting door, so she went over to unlock her side.

"I know you need privacy, but humor me by leaving your side unlocked and ajar, okay? Just in case."

After everything that had transpired over the last several hours, she knew his request was more than reasonable. "Of course."

"Get some rest," he said with a gentle smile.

"You, too." She left her door open an inch, then quickly washed up in the bathroom. When she returned, she heard a muffled groan from next door.

"Noah?" She pushed open the connecting door. Noah was wearing a white T-shirt and was bending over to pick up the bulletproof vest from the floor.

"It's nothing," he said, but the paleness of his skin and the beads of sweat gathering at his temples belied his words.

She crossed over and took the vest from his hands, running her fingers over the surface. The gear was heavier than she'd expected and it didn't take but a moment to find the bullet lodged three inches to the right of center.

She felt her own color draining from her face at the evidence she was staring at with her own eyes. A bullet. Smashed beyond recognition embedded in the material. Noah had almost died tonight, protecting her. If he hadn't been wearing his vest...

The consequences were unthinkable. She barely knew Noah Sinclair, didn't remember anything about him, or her own history, but at this moment she couldn't imagine her life without him.

Chapter Five

Noah mentally berated himself for being loud enough to draw Maddy's attention. Unfortunately, bending over had caused a sharp pain to lance through him, which meant he may have cracked a rib or two.

He reminded himself that Maddy had been injured, too, worse than he had. So he sucked it up. "I'm fine, Maddy, the vest did its job."

She tossed the vest over the back of a chair. "You're bruised, though, aren't you? I know that the force of a slug still packs a punch, in spite of wearing protective gear."

Bits of her memory were coming back to her, which both gave him hope and filled him with dread. He forced himself to focus on the former. Maddy needed her memory in order to try the case against Pietro; his personal feelings didn't matter.

"Yes, but I'll survive. It's not the first time I've been hit."

Her blue eyes widened in horror. "It's not?"

Oh, boy, that was the wrong thing to say. He tried

again. "I'll be okay. The bruises will fade in a few days. Please try to get some rest."

She stared at him for so long, he had to fight not to squirm beneath the intensity of her gaze. "You should take some ibuprofen for your back," she said. "There's a convenience store adjacent to the gas station. I'm sure they have some."

"That's a good idea," he said, even though he had no intention of leaving her alone. "They'll have toiletries and other items there, too. Get some rest and we'll check it out, later."

She frowned and crossed her arms over her chest, tilting her chin defiantly. "You need the ibuprofen now, Noah. I'm not leaving until you go out to get it."

The familiar Maddy stubbornness made him smile. She was so tired she was practically swaying on her feet, but he also knew that she wouldn't budge until she got her way. He considered taking her with him, then decided he could be there and back in a matter of minutes. Faster, really, than if he dragged her along.

"I'll go if you stretch out and relax. Deal?"

"Deal."

He dragged his jacket back on and crossed over to head outside. Walking swiftly and ignoring the pain, he purchased the ibuprofen along with two toothbrushes, toothpaste, a hairbrush and two warm fleece sweatshirts, one for each of them. If she was going to insist he shop, then he'd make sure to take care of her needs, as well.

When he returned to his room, he was relieved to see that Maddy had indeed stretched out on her bed and was already fast asleep.

Moving silently, he set the personal items he'd purchased for her on the dresser in clear view for when she woke up, before returning to his room. He downed the ibuprofen, and then sat on the edge of his bed. The computer case caught his eye, and it occurred to him that he might be able to find a picture of Maddy's brothers to show her when she woke up. It was something productive he could do now, since he wasn't about to risk using the motel phone.

Jackson's dead body flashed in his memory, and he closed his eyes, willing the image away.

There was nothing he could do about his partner; right now, his priority had to be keeping Maddy safe. Which meant helping her to recover her memory as they stayed hidden.

Shoving his exhaustion aside, he pulled out the computer and turned it on. He silently groaned when he discovered the device was password protected.

Of course Maddy would be sure not to leave her work unsecured. He considered guessing her password, but didn't want to risk locking it up for good.

He turned off the computer and turned his attention to the manila file labeled Pietro.

He carried the folder over to the bed and stretched out with the pillows propped against his sore back. The ibuprofen barely took the edge off, but he hadn't expected it would help much anyway.

But a hot shower might. He rolled off the bed and headed into the bathroom. When he emerged twenty minutes later, the soreness in his back muscles had loosened up.

He dressed in his uniform pants and the sweatshirt, then began reviewing Maddy's file. Maybe there was something in there, some detail that would help him uncover a clue as to who might be working on Pietro's behalf.

It didn't take long for the words to swim on the page. The next thing Noah knew, he was blinking at bright sunlight shining in through the window.

The clock on the bedside table read eleven thirty in the morning. He'd slept for almost five hours, and while his brain felt clearer as a result of his nap, the muscles in his back had grown stiff from lying in one place for so long.

Swallowing a groan, he awkwardly rolled into a sitting position. There were muffled sounds coming from Maddy's room, indicating she was up, too.

Sure enough, in less than a minute she knocked lightly on his side of the connecting door. "Noah?"

"Come in," he said, making an effort to hide the level of discomfort he was feeling.

She entered his room, looking adorable in the navy blue sweatshirt he'd purchased for her. "How's your back?"

"Sore. How's your memory?" He thought for sure it would have returned by now.

"Still vacant, like a wide-open empty field." Her gaze zeroed in on the Pietro file with the precision of a laser beam. "What are you doing? You can't read that." She came over, scooping up the papers and shoving them back into the file. "What were you thinking? You're a key witness for the prosecution—reviewing my notes jeopardizes my case!"

"I guess your legal memory is back," he said. Her scowl deepened and he raised a hand in defense. "Relax, I don't remember reading anything before I conked out. I haven't compromised your case, I promise."

"You better not," she warned, hugging the file close to her chest. "If—*when* my memory returns, I'll have a lot of catching up to do."

He rose to his feet and crossed over to Maddy. "I had a thought about how to spur your memory to return." He gestured toward the computer. "You might have photos of your family on there, but it's password protected so I can't get in."

She stared at the device. "I'm not sure I know my password, either," she admitted softly.

"It's worth a try," he said, injecting confidence in his tone. "Your memory about what you like to eat and about your job seems clear enough. Maybe you'll instinctively remember."

"Maybe." Her tone lacked certainty. She dropped into the chair next to the desk, set the Pietro file aside and turned on the computer. Resting her fingers on the keys, she appeared to wait for some deeply rooted instinct to kick in.

After a few seconds, her hands dropped to her sides and she slowly shook her head. "I don't know. *I can't remember!*"

He immediately regretted putting her on the spot. "Hey, it's okay. It's not important. I'll call your brother Matt, okay? I'm sure when you see him, your memory will return."

"No!" She twisted in the chair to glare at him. "I don't think that's a good idea. I don't want to place my family in danger."

Her words were something that he could easily imagine her brothers saying. Being protective of their family was truly a Callahan trait. So different from what his family was like. "Maddy, listen." He pulled up a second chair and sat beside her, taking her hands in his. "You need to trust me. Matt is a good cop. I won't tell him where we are, but I'll suggest a meeting place, somewhere public with a lot of people around. He'll want to be there for you."

"But Jackson— You said yourself, whoever is after me knows who we are. They must have tapped Jackson's phone. How else would they have known he was coming to help us?"

There was nothing wrong with her ability to perform deductive reasoning, that was for sure. Noah was impressed that she'd made the connection.

"And that means they know my family, too. I refuse to put any one of them in danger."

"Maddy, we need help. We can't do this alone, especially since your memory hasn't returned yet. We need disposable phones, additional clothing and a vehicle. I don't have enough cash, and we can't afford to leave an electronic trail."

"But…" Her voice trailed off and soon he could see resigned acceptance in her eyes. "I wish we could use a pay phone, instead of the one here at the motel."

"I didn't see one at the convenience store, or the diner, either. But the best way to keep Matt safe is to provide a meeting place in a populated area. I doubt the gunman who followed Jackson to the Racine Marina would have taken so many shots if it had been daytime in a crowded place."

She closed her eyes for a moment. "You don't know that for sure. If he was well hidden and had an escape route planned, he may have taken the chance."

Realizing there wasn't anything he could say to ease

her mind, he let it go. No point in making rash promises he might not be able to keep.

"Go ahead and make the call." She pulled her hands out of his, and rose to her feet, as if needing to put distance between them. Guilt, his familiar companion, rested heavy on his shoulders.

What else could he do to ensure Matt's safety?

The woman at the front desk. He could offer some money to use her cell phone. It wasn't foolproof, personal cell phones could still be traced, but it would take longer. Possibly giving them the head start they needed. "I'll be right back," he said, reaching for his coat.

"Why? Where are you going?"

He briefly explained his plan, then rushed back out in the cold air. The sun was up, but the temperature surely wasn't. Ducking his head against the icy wind, he walked to the lobby.

The woman behind the desk looked to be in her mid-fifties and he hoped she'd be sympathetic to his cause. The lobby was also empty, so there wouldn't be anyone listening in.

"Ma'am, would you be so kind as to allow me to borrow your personal cell phone?" He set his badge on the counter along with a ten-dollar bill. "I need to make a long-distance call and I can't use the phone in my room."

She looked at him with suspicion, but then shrugged and scooped up the ten-dollar bill. "Why not?" She pulled the phone out of her purse and entered her pass code. "Stay where I can see you, sonny. No funny stuff."

"Yes, ma'am." Noah quickly entered Matthew's phone number—thankfully he'd memorized it from their time together as partners—and listened to the ringing on the other end of the line.

After ten long rings, Matt's voice mail came on. Noah turned a bit so that his back was to the woman at the desk, and spoke in a low, urgent tone. "Matt, it's Noah. Maddy is in extreme danger related to a case she's working on, and we really need your help. It's vitally important that you meet us this afternoon at four o'clock at the Rosemont bowling alley. Please finish up whatever you're doing to meet us there. We'll be waiting for you."

He disconnected from the line and then deleted Matthew's number from the phone's memory so the woman couldn't see what number he'd called before handing the device back to her. "Thank you very much."

She checked the phone, seemingly disconcerted by the lack of evidence related to the call. "You're welcome, officer."

Should he try Miles Callahan? He didn't know Matt's older brother very well and didn't know his personal phone number, either. He could try to get the information from dispatch but there was no guarantee they'd give it to him. Since Maddy was closest to her twin, he decided to leave it alone. If for some reason Matt didn't show, then he'd have no choice but to move on to plan B.

As he returned to the motel room, he hoped and prayed he and Maddy wouldn't need a plan B. Noah had purposefully used four o'clock in the afternoon, not just because that was when darkness began to fall, but also to give Matt plenty of time to finish up whatever he was doing to meet them. He couldn't imagine Matt not rushing to his twin sister's aid.

Unless he was physically hurt, or worse. A remote possibility he had no intention of relaying to Maddy.

She'd suffered enough already.

Maddy shoved the computer out of the way to make room for the Pietro file. Her lack of memory was starting to make her mad, and it occurred to her that reviewing the details of the high-profile case she must have lived and breathed for weeks on end might help.

To her dismay, the notes didn't feel at all familiar. Panic tightened her chest and she forced herself to slow her breathing. In and out. In and out.

She focused on reading the entire report she'd included in the file. The names didn't help spur any recognition, but she pushed on.

The door opened, bringing a rush of cold air as Noah returned. She glanced over. "Did you talk to my brother?"

He grimaced and shook his head. "No, but I left a message. I'm sure he'll meet up with us at four o'clock this afternoon at the Rosemont bowling alley."

The place didn't sound familiar, either. "Noah, maybe you should take me to my office. I'm sure someone there will restore my memory."

"I'm not sure about that. Besides, returning to your office is too dangerous. Not just related to your personal safety, but what if your memory doesn't return? People will greet you and expect you to know who they are. No, the risk of your amnesia leaking to the press is too great."

He had a good point. She gestured to the file. "There's nothing in here about Pietro's known associates. I must have that information on my computer."

Noah shrugged off his jacket, then came over to sit beside her, his woodsy scent a soothing balm on her ragged nerves. She thought again how fortunate she was to have him there, protecting her.

"Let's try to figure out your password," Noah said. "You're closest to your brother Matt, so try a combination of your names."

She tried MadMatt and a few other variations without success. "Wait, what's my birthday?"

"April 4," Noah said. "Same as Matt's, you're twins. Matt was born a full three minutes before you."

Twins? No wonder they were close. Maddy tried more variations of their names along with their date of birth. Then she typed in *Twins44ever* and instantly the computer screen opened, revealing a beautiful landscape of fall leaves in full color.

"Autumn is your favorite season," Noah said.

She smiled weakly. Once again, Noah knew more about her than she did. Clicking on the file explorer, she was stunned to discover she had several documents listed under the name of Alexander Pietro.

"Wow. This must include everything I have related to the case," she said, overwhelmed by the amount of information she possessed. She was about to open one of the files, but then hesitated, glancing at Noah. "Maybe you should let me look through this on my own first."

"Maddy, if your memory doesn't return, there may not be a trial," he said with clear exasperation. "I think finding the man who's trying to kill you takes priority over your worry about me seeing something I shouldn't."

She minimized the screen, but remembered the date in the lower right-hand corner. "Today is Tuesday, right?

It's only been a little over fourteen hours since I lost my memory. If I can get it back later today or tomorrow morning, then there's still a chance I can bring the case to trial. Putting Pietro behind bars for the rest of his life is my top priority. Finding the accomplices working for him has to be secondary."

"Not if they find you first," he argued.

She swallowed against a lump of fear. It was unacceptable to allow Pietro to scare her away. She lightly grasped Noah's arm. "Please, Noah. Just give me a little time alone to review the files."

His dark brown eyes clung to hers, then dropped to her hand, pale against the tanned skin of his forearm where he'd shoved the sweatshirt sleeves out of the way. His arm was warm and strong.

"Fine." Noah abruptly shot to his feet and she let him go, feeling the anger radiating off him. "But I don't think keeping me out of the investigation is the best way to get this case to trial."

She hated to admit he might be right. Still, the need to keep the integrity of her case intact overrode all else. Noah crossed over and turned the TV on to a local news station and she took her computer back to her room, doing her best to ignore him.

She clicked on a document labeled "Pietro's known associates." When the file opened, she noted that she'd neatly listed names followed by whatever information she'd uncovered about them.

Unfortunately, the names didn't mean anything to her. She could have been reading a recipe for cabbage soup, instead of identifying someone who might have come after them.

Not just once, but several times; killing Jackson, and shooting Noah in the back.

Remembering the slug she'd found in his vest made her shiver. Noah had placed his life on the line for her, over and over again. She stared at the list of names.

It was no use. She needed Noah's help with this. He'd been a part of the team who'd arrested Pietro, so it was possible that he knew many of these known associates already.

"Noah? Would you mind taking a look at this?"

The television went silent and he came through the connecting doorway to lean over her shoulder, peering at the screen. He whistled softly between his teeth. "That's some list you have there."

"Does anything jump out at you?" she pressed. "I'm sure you know some of them, but you may not know them all. I need to know if anyone from this list jogs your memory."

He was so close she could feel the warmth of his breath against her hair. The woodsy scent was stronger now, and she had an insane urge to throw herself into his arms.

"This one," he said, reaching around her to tap gently on the screen. "Lance Arvani."

Her pulse quickened and not just because of Noah's nearness. "What about him?"

"He was in my class at the police academy. We graduated together, seven years ago. Are you sure he's a known associate of Pietro? Last I heard, he was working for the Chicago Police Department."

No, at the moment she wasn't sure about anything. She stared at the name, wondering how or why she'd connected Arvani to Pietro. Why hadn't she left additional notes?

Was it possible that this was the link they were looking for? Noah thought it was likely the shooter at the marina had ties to the police, but this? A cop who was still active on the force?

She tightened her fingers into fists, battling a wave of helplessness.

Why couldn't she remember?

Chapter Six

Noah stared at Lance Arvani's name, trying not to be distracted by Maddy's nearness. He hadn't liked Arvani much; the guy had come across as arrogant and in-your-face.

But not liking a guy was a far cry from accusing him of being involved with a known drug trafficker like Pietro.

"You don't remember seeing him at all during the drug bust?" Maddy asked.

He straightened and shook his head. "No, and I'm sure I would have recognized him if he was around." He gestured to the computer. "Do you mind if I do a little searching for information on him?"

She didn't hesitate to turn the computer so he could access the keyboard from the chair beside her. "I'd love to see a picture of him."

"That part is easy." He found their academy graduation picture. Lance was on the opposite side of where he'd stood, and the image of his own serious yet youthful face made him wince. His father hadn't come to the ceremony, and neither had any of his siblings. Noah remembered standing there, thinking about how he was going to work hard to make the city a safer place, so that kids like his sister Rose wouldn't have such easy access to drugs.

He'd been naive, really, to think that one person could have much of an impact.

"Oh, look how handsome you are!" Maddy tapped her finger on his picture. "I bet your parents were so proud."

"My mom passed away just before Thanksgiving my first year of college, and my dad, well, he wasn't impressed with my career choice." Noah didn't like talking about his family, so he quickly changed the subject. "This guy standing on the end here is Lance Arvani."

Maddy leaned closer to get a better look. "He doesn't look familiar," she said. "Of course, no one looks familiar at this point, right?"

He felt bad for her. Not having a memory, good or bad, had to be difficult. "Speaking of which, did you look in the pictures folder to see if you have any of your family on here?"

"No, I didn't think of that. I was focused on Pietro."

Clicking on the photos folder revealed it was empty. He frowned. "That's weird. You're very close to your family. It seems odd you don't have pictures of them on here."

"Maybe it's a work computer."

He glanced over at her. "Yeah, probably. At least you'll see your brother later today. I'm sure seeing your twin will restore your memory."

"I hope so," she agreed. "Back to Arvani, what else can we find out about him?"

Noah took control of the keyboard, searching on Arvani's name. "His last known address is in a suburb north of Chicago."

"That doesn't help much," she groused.

He tried several other searches using different key phrases, but still nothing came up. He sat back in his seat. "I wonder if Arvani's working undercover."

"What makes you think that?"

He glanced at Maddy. "Consider the theory that Arvani was working as an undercover narcotics officer. Maybe he got greedy and turned dirty. Or maybe that's just his cover, a way to get close to working with Pietro."

She pursed her lips, considering the angle. "I thought undercover cops didn't use their real names? If he was known to be a cop, why would anyone from Pietro's organization trust him?"

"Good point," he conceded. "Going undercover usually involves a new name and cover story. But there's always the possibility that Arvani did something, or got caught with product owned by Pietro, so the organization is using that information to blackmail him."

She turned to face him, her knees pressing against his. "You want him to be a good guy, huh?"

"Not particularly," he argued. "We weren't friends or anything. I'm trying to understand why a cop's name would be linked to Pietro as a known associate."

"Would help if I could remember," Maddy said with a glum expression. "I really thought my memory would have returned by now."

"It will," he said reassuringly. He reached out to take her small hand in his. "In a few hours we'll meet up with Matt and I'm convinced he'll help you to remember."

She smiled and tilted her head. "Noah, do you mind if I ask you a personal question?"

Personal? His heart thudded against his rib cage with such force, he was surprised the cracked ribs didn't give way. His mouth was dry, but he managed to return her smile. "Of course not. What do you want to know?"

"Do you have a girlfriend?" The words came out in a breathless rush. "I'm only asking because you've been with me all night and I think she'd want to know you're okay."

For a moment, his mind flashed back to the last time he saw Gina, how upset she'd been when he'd broken up with her.

How she'd gone out to party, using prescription drugs and alcohol, and had been found unresponsive and ultimately brain-dead.

"No." He pushed the word past his tight throat. "I don't have a girlfriend. I'm not good with relationships."

Her expression turned sympathetic. "Someone hurt you badly, huh?"

"No, you have it all wrong." He pulled away, leaping to his feet with such force his chair toppled over backward. "*I'm* the one who hurts *them*."

She looked surprised by that, and he could tell she wanted to ask more questions.

Not happening. He needed to go. To get away. "Excuse me," he said, making a beeline for the connecting door.

He dropped down on the edge of his bed, cradling his head in his hands. The memories of his sister's death, followed two and a half years later by Gina's passing, would never go away.

In truth he didn't want them to. If he'd been a better brother to Rose, a better boyfriend to Gina, maybe things would have turned out differently.

Once Maddy regained her memory, she'd remember how much she didn't like him. But even if her feelings had softened toward him, it didn't matter. Better for her to understand that no matter how much he cared about her, there could never be anything but friendship between them.

Maddy watched with dismay as Noah bolted to his adjoining room. She hated that her lack of memory had caused him pain.

No way did she believe Noah was the type to hurt women, especially not physically. Emotionally? Maybe, she didn't know him, or remember enough, to say for sure either way.

Yet his claim didn't make sense when he'd been nothing but kind to her since he'd come to see her in the ER. More than kind. Sweet. Compassionate. Supportive. Protective.

No, she wasn't buying it. There had to be more to the story. Unfortunately, Noah had made it clear he wasn't going to clue her in.

Her back went ramrod straight as a horrible thought hit her. What if Noah was talking about the two of them? That he'd done something to ruin their relationship? After all, from the moment she first saw him, she'd been struck by how handsome he was.

As if he was the type of guy she normally was attracted to. Was it possible they were seeing each other?

No, surely if there had been something more than friendship between them, he would have said something? Her memory was nothing but pea soup anyway. Why not give her a high-level but condensed version of what had transpired between them?

None of it made any sense, so she told herself to focus on the case.

A case she couldn't remember.

Frustrated tears pricked her eyelids. She quickly blinked them back, refusing to wallow in self-pity. Her headache was better after her brief nap, but staring at the computer screen seemed to make it worse, so she quickly shut it down.

"I'm sorry."

Noah's quiet words had her spinning around in surprise. "For what?"

"Walking away like that. It's something my dad used to do when he got angry and I promised myself I wouldn't be like that." Noah stepped across the threshold of their connecting rooms. "Please accept my apology."

She rose to her feet. "I think I'm the one who should apologize for poking my nose into your personal life. But I want you to know, Noah, I'm here if you want to talk."

He dropped his gaze as if embarrassed. "Thanks, but we have bigger issues to worry about. If you're feeling up to it, I'd like to head out and pick up a couple of prepaid phones."

The thought of heading out into the cold held little appeal. Through the window she could see the sun was shining, but at the truck stop across the street people were bundled up against the cold, their breath steaming in front of their faces. She shivered just thinking about the cold. "Do you really think there's something within walking distance?"

"I was thinking of calling a taxi. I'd rather use a car service because they're much cheaper, but I can't do that without a phone and credit card. Still, it can't cost too much to get to the nearest big-box store. And if there's anything else you need, we can get everything in one fell swoop."

"Are you sure you have enough cash?" He'd purchased a toothbrush and hairbrush for her already, along with the warm fleece she was currently wearing. Offhand, she couldn't think of anything else she desperately needed. But she understood why he wanted a phone.

"Just enough, but I'll need more, soon."

"Sure, I'm glad to go."

"All right then. Be ready to leave in five."

She used the time to freshen up in the bathroom, before donning her coat. Maybe if there was enough cash left over, they could pick up a couple of hats, gloves and a nice warm scarf, too.

"Ready?" Noah stood waiting by the door. She noticed he had his uniform back on, including the vest that had saved his life.

"What about the computer and the rest of our things? Isn't it better to take everything with us, just in case?"

He hesitated, then nodded. "You're right. In fact, it's probably better if we don't come back here at all."

Leaving the warmth of the motel room for good hadn't been her intention, but she couldn't deny that moving from one place to the next was smarter than staying put.

Stuffing their meager items into the computer case and the convenience store bag didn't take long. She carried the plastic bag, leaving Noah to sling the computer case over his shoulder.

Before they left the room, though, he crossed over and picked up the phone. He dialed a number, then spoke quickly.

"Milwaukee Police Officer Jackson Dellis was murdered at the Racine Marina." He paused, listening, then said, "No, I'm sorry but I can't give you my name. Trust me, send a squad to the marina."

He hung up the phone, capturing her gaze. "I had to call it in," he said defensively. "I waited till now, so that we'll be long gone before the cops trace the call."

"I'm not arguing with you, Noah."

"Thanks." He led the way outside without saying anything more.

Noah hailed a taxi and soon they were on the road, the motel growing smaller behind them. The driver seemed a bit intimidated by Noah's uniform, judging by the way he kept glancing at them in the rearview mirror, but he didn't say anything.

After sliding out of the back seat, she glanced at Noah. "Do you think he'll call the police?"

Noah smirked. "Why would he? I am the police."

His teasing tone made her smile. "I know that, and you know that, but he probably thinks you're pretending to be a cop. Otherwise, why would you need a taxi?"

"Because my squad car is in Lake Michigan," he said, tucking his hand beneath her elbow. "I'm not worried about the driver calling anyone. He has no reason to be suspicious and won't want to cause trouble. Come on, let's get inside."

Having Noah beside her was nice, and she noticed several people glanced at them curiously as they entered the store. Because he was in uniform? Or because he was so attractive?

Both, she decided.

The store was playing Christmas music and there were dozens of shoppers milling around. Noah headed for the electronics section first, choosing two disposable phones. "I'm not sure I need one," she said in a low voice. "Can't call people I don't remember."

"You'll remember soon," he said, tucking the packages into their cart. "Are you sure you don't want anything else?"

"Maybe gloves and a scarf, if we have enough cash left over."

"Not a problem. This way." He wheeled the cart down another aisle, taking her past the craft section.

A large glossy book on knitting caught her eye. She stopped, reaching out to touch the cover. It looked familiar.

The memory fragment was there, hovering just out of reach. She knew she'd seen this book before, but where? She pressed her fingertips to her temples, willing herself to remember.

"Maddy? Something wrong?"

The foggy image of this book sitting on a coffee table faded away, leaving behind a frustrated sense of urgency.

She had something important to do. Related to the trial? She didn't know.

"Maddy?" Noah lightly grasped her arm. "What's wrong? Is your memory returning?"

"Not really. For a moment I had an image of this book sitting on a coffee table, but that's it. Nothing helpful."

He slid his arm around her waist, giving her a hug. "I'm sorry, but let's take this as a good sign. Fragments of memories are better than nothing. This may be just the beginning."

She leaned her head against his shoulder for a moment, breathing in his reassuring woodsy scent. "Yeah, I hope so."

He surprised her by pressing a kiss to the top of her head. "Maybe we should wander around the store some more, see if anything else looks familiar."

She smiled and shook her head. "Doubtful. Let's find those gloves and scarves, okay?"

The items were fairly picked over, maybe because Christmas was only three weeks away. She didn't care if the items were mismatched as long as they were warm.

After paying for their items, she ripped the tags off the gloves, hat and scarf and put them on. Noah did the same, and the few items helped her feel warmer when they went back outside.

"How about we get a bite to eat over there?" Noah gestured to a family-style restaurant. "We have an hour or so before we need to head over to the bowling alley."

"Sounds good."

The place was busy, maybe because of the holiday season, but they only waited a few minutes before being seated in a booth near the window. She felt self-conscious carrying all their stuff, but then realized that it probably looked as if they'd been out Christmas shopping.

Their server was a young woman who smiled and introduced herself as Cindy. Maddy ordered coffee and Noah raised a brow questioningly, even though he asked for the same. The menu was basic fare, so she opted for a veggie burger while he requested beef.

"What?" she asked, when their server went to enter their order. "Don't I like coffee?"

He shrugged. "There's a coffeemaker in your condo, but I can't say for sure if you use it or Gretchen does."

Cindy returned, filling both of their mugs with coffee. Maddy didn't hesitate to add cream and sugar, before taking a sip. "Aah, that hits the spot."

"You ordered hot chocolate earlier," he said, cradling his own mug. "Did you remember liking coffee?"

"I wish. No, earlier hot chocolate sounded good, but this time, I wanted coffee." She shrugged. "I'm still tired, could use something to help wake me up a bit."

"Or maybe, subconsciously, your memory is starting to return."

She stared down at her cup for a moment. Was Noah right? Were little pieces of her previous life instinctively coming back to her? First the knitting book, avoiding meat and now adding cream and sugar to her coffee?

The small flicker of hope burned brighter. She knew that with God's love and support, anything was possible.

"More coffee?" Cindy asked. "Your food will be ready shortly."

Maddy nodded. Their server wasn't kidding. Five minutes later, she brought out two sandwich plates, one veggie, both with a mountain of french fries. Maddy placed her napkin in her lap, then reached for Noah's hand.

"Let's pray," she said.

His warm fingers wrapped around hers, and he bowed his head, waiting for her to start.

"Dear Lord, we thank You for this food we are about to eat. We also ask that You continue healing our wounds, Noah's bruises and my lost memory. Amen."

"Amen," Noah echoed. He raised his head and looked at her, continuing to hold her hand in his. "That was nice."

She smiled. "I'm glad."

The food was delicious, although there was no way in the world she could eat that many fries. When they finished, Noah paid Cindy, including a tip.

"Maybe we should have skipped breakfast. How

much cash do you have left?" Maddy asked, winding her new scarf around her neck.

"Less than eighty bucks," Noah admitted with a wry grimace. "But I'm sure Matt will bring some with him."

Matt. The twin brother she couldn't remember.

This time, it took longer to grab a taxi but the bowling alley was only ten miles away. Maddy watched as Noah paid, feeling bad that she was unable to contribute.

"Let's head over to the coffee shop. We can see the entire parking lot from there."

She nodded in agreement, then put her hand on his arm, stopping him from walking away. "Noah?"

He met her gaze. "What? Is there something you need?"

"You're going to think I'm crazy, but I need a hug."

His mouth dropped open as if stunned speechless, but then he covered his reaction by wrapping his arms around her and pulling her close. "Hey, everything is going to be fine, you'll see."

She wanted desperately to believe that. But deep down, she was afraid that her twin would arrive and she wouldn't remember anything.

After several moments, Noah loosened his grip. "Okay now?"

She tipped her head back to look up at him. Being held in his arms was so nice—she couldn't remember feeling like this before. His gaze held hers questioningly, but instead of telling him, she did what she'd wanted to do since she saw him in the emergency room. Lifting herself up on her toes, she pressed her mouth against his.

Chapter Seven

At first, Noah was taken aback by Maddy's unexpected kiss, but then his instincts took over and he crushed her close, deepening the embrace. She felt so right in his arms, tasting like a mixture of coffee, cinnamon, sunshine and juniper.

Like Christmas.

If he were honest with himself, he'd dreamed of kissing her, since way back when he and Matthew first became partners. But he didn't do relationships, even back then, and regardless he'd known she was off-limits.

Off-limits!

Reality kicked hard and he broke away, breathing heavily. "Uh, Maddy, we shouldn't be doing this," he managed.

"Why? You said yourself, you don't have a girlfriend."

"I don't." But then again, she might be seeing someone. The thought was sobering. She hadn't mentioned dating anyone during the trial prep, but she'd also been focused solely on the case. "And I explained why. I don't do relationships."

"Could have fooled me with that kiss," she responded tartly. "And don't bother handing me that line about how you're the one who hurts others." She angled her chin in that stubborn way she had. "Because I'm not buying it."

"Trust me, you won't be happy about this once your memory returns." He resisted the urge to pull her back into his arms, instead forcing himself to take a step back, putting more distance between them, at least physically.

Mentally was another story. There was no way he'd be able to get her out of his head; at least, not anytime soon.

"Noah," she started, but he cut her off.

"Let's get inside. Your brother should be here in less than twenty minutes."

Hopefully, he added silently. *Please, Lord, please send Matt to help.*

Maddy walked ahead of him into the café, her head held high. He reminded himself how terrible he was at relationships. How he was responsible for Gina's death. And how even if Maddy might be interested now, she surely wouldn't be once she remembered everything.

Yet her taste lingered on his mouth, taunting him with what he'd never have.

He'd been knocked off balance since the moment he'd recognized her in the ER. And if anything, they'd only grown closer as they fled from danger. He'd always admired her dedication to her career, but being with her like this had shown him another side of her. Her strength, even when she was exhausted. Her caring and compassion, when she'd realized his vest had stopped a bullet. Her sweetness when she'd kissed him.

And especially the way she'd prayed with him in the

restaurant. He'd been humbled by her instinctive faith, remembering the way he'd often attended church services with the Callahan family.

After Matthew had been stabbed, his former partner's decision to attend K-9 training instead had eroded the closeness they'd once shared. Oh, sure, Matt had reached out a few times, asking Noah to join his family at church followed by his mother's famous brunch, but the thought of sitting around the dining room table with them, knowing they had every right to blame him for Matt's injury, had kept him far, far away.

Until now. Being sent to the ER to take Maddy's statement about the assault must have been God's way of protecting her. Noah firmly believed Matt would show at the bowling alley. And if he couldn't, Noah was certain he'd send one of the other Callahans in his place.

Any one of Maddy's brothers would likely restore her memory. Which would be a good thing, since he wanted—no, needed to know she'd be safe at last.

The Callahans always protected their own.

"Are you interested in more coffee?" she asked, breaking into his thoughts. "I think we should buy something if we're going to sit here."

He nodded. "What would you like?"

"Chamomile tea," she responded. "I think I've had enough caffeine for the day."

The request for tea surprised him. Then again, he truly didn't know what Maddy usually ate or drank. She assumed they were closer than they were, and he needed to tell her the truth, regardless of the fact that doing so would ruin the camaraderie they shared.

Feeling grim, he placed their order and paid, grimacing at his dwindling cash reserves. One of the Callahans better show, or they'd be in trouble. He didn't have enough cash to pay for another motel room. Especially if he needed to pay for a taxi ride to get there.

Carrying his coffee in one hand and her chamomile tea in the other, he joined her at a two-top table near the window overlooking the parking lot.

"Tell me about her," Maddy said, holding on to her tea with both hands.

"Who?"

"The girl who broke your heart."

His sister's face flashed into his brain. Losing Rose to a heroin overdose had been heartbreaking, but he knew that wasn't what Maddy meant. She was talking about Gina. He stalled, taking a sip of coffee, only to burn his tongue with the scalding hot brew. "I told you, it was the other way around. I was the one to break things off."

And Gina had died as a result of his rejection.

"Noah, the pain in your eyes tells a different story," she said gently. "Maybe she didn't break your heart, but she still hurt you."

"No, actually, she hurt herself. I broke up with her on a Friday night and she was found dead the next morning."

"No," Maddy said with a gasp and he grimaced, realizing he should have tried to soften the blow. His stomach knotted, but he continued sitting there, figuring it was better she knew the truth. "Suicide?"

"Accidental prescription-drug overdose mixed with alcohol or suicide. What's the difference? Dead is dead. Either way it was my fault."

Maddy rested her hand on his upper arm, her expression earnest. "Noah, you can't seriously believe you're responsible for her actions."

He couldn't sit there a moment longer. "Excuse me," he said, sliding off his chair. Her hand fell to her side and ridiculously enough, he immediately missed her touch. "I'm going to use the outlet over there to charge up and activate one of the phones."

Thankfully, she didn't try to stop him. At least now, Maddy knew the truth. There would be no more hugging or kissing, regardless of how much he yearned for that closeness.

Once Matt arrived, he could extricate himself from his role of her bodyguard and focus his efforts on finding out who had killed his partner and was trying to hurt Maddy.

Maddy watched Noah deal with their new phones, reeling from the news of his girlfriend's death. He was right, accidental overdose or suicide, the end result had been the same.

But why did he feel responsible? Couples broke up all the time for a variety of reasons. Growing apart and wanting different things from life, or maybe infidelity.

She sipped her tea, enjoying the soothing effect it had on her nerves. Noah didn't seem like the type of guy to cheat on his girlfriend; then again, maybe he'd broken things off because he'd found someone else. That was the sort of thing that could send a woman over the edge of despair. Although taking drugs and alcohol had been a conscious decision on her part, not Noah's.

Their mutual response to their kiss had convinced Maddy there was definitely something between them. Attraction at the very least.

There was no denying she'd hoped that kissing Noah would cause a spontaneous return of her memory, but it hadn't. Because they'd never kissed before? Possibly.

She stared out the window, watching cars coming and going. Would she instinctively recognize her brother when he arrived? How embarrassing if she didn't.

Propping her elbows on the table, she pressed her fingertips against her temples. Her headache had never truly gone away, but at times like this, when she tried to concentrate on remembering the past, the intensity of her pain increased exponentially.

She closed her eyes for a moment and silently asked for God's blessing.

"Are you okay?" Noah asked, his voice near her ear. He wrapped his arm around her shoulders as if afraid she'd fall off her stool. "What can I do?"

She looked up at him with a soft smile. "I'm fine."

"You don't look fine," he said bluntly, his brown eyes mirroring concern. She liked having his arm around her and allowed herself a moment to lean against him, soaking up his strength. "I still have that bottle of ibuprofen. You should take some."

"I can do that," she agreed. He moved away from her, so she straightened her shoulders, determined not to be weak. Watching as he dug through their bag of belongings, she knew this was exactly why she didn't believe he'd intentionally set out to hurt anyone. He'd been upset about her probing into his past, but the moment he thought she needed help, he'd come rushing over to offer assistance, putting her needs before his.

"Here." He opened the bottle and shook a couple pills into her palm. "This should help."

"I hope so." She tossed them back and took a sip of her tea. "Of course it might also help if I stopped trying so hard to remember."

His smile was lopsided. "Have faith, Maddy. Your memory will return when your brain is ready."

"My brother won't appreciate me not remembering him," she pointed out.

"Your brothers love you, Maddy. You're very close to them. I promise, they're not going to hold a bit of amnesia against you."

"So tell me, Noah, how is it that you know so much about me and my family?" She held his gaze, hoping he'd fill the gaps. "You and I haven't dated, have we?"

His eyes widened comically. "No! Of course not."

She couldn't help but wonder why. Especially given this underlying attraction that relentlessly simmered between them. "But you helped me and my roommate move into our condo," she pressed. "So we must be friends."

He hesitated, then nodded. "Yes, we're friends. In fact, your brother Matt used to be my partner."

Hearing that surprised her. "Used to be? What happened?"

He paused for so long she thought he wasn't going to answer. Then he finally let out a heavy sigh, and met her gaze. "A little over a year ago now, Matt was injured on the job." His tone was full of resignation, as if this story was somehow painful to tell. "He was stabbed during a drug bust. When he recovered, he decided to pursue his dream of K-9 training."

She sensed there was more he wasn't telling her, but decided not to push. "What kind of dog does he have?"

A smile tugged at the corner of his mouth. "A German shepherd named Duchess. He's done an incredible job with her. The two of them are amazing to watch."

"Maybe he'll bring Duchess along today," she said, glancing at her watch. Ten minutes until four o'clock. "I'd love to meet her." Then she flushed. "Well, I guess I've already met her, huh?"

"Yes," he said gently. "But you need to stop beating yourself up about your memory loss. This isn't your fault."

"I will if you will," she countered.

He frowned. "If I will what?"

"Stop beating yourself up for the choices your girl-friend made the night she died."

Instantly his face turned to stone. "You don't seem to understand that I am responsible. My actions caused her reaction. Your amnesia is the result of an assault. Two completely different scenarios."

She didn't agree, but apparently Noah wasn't inter-ested in further discussion on the topic. So she let it go, turning her attention to the parking lot.

Dusk was beginning to fall, the days growing shorter and shorter as the winter solstice approached. A black sedan pulled in and she straightened in her seat when she noticed a dog in the back of the vehicle.

"Is that him?" she asked, pointing toward the car.

Noah frowned. "I don't think so."

"Maybe you should call him."

Noah picked up the phone he'd just activated and punched in a series of numbers. He placed the call on speaker, and they both listened as it rang. She was glad he knew her brother's number by heart, since she, of course, had no idea.

"Yeah?" A male voice answered.

"Matt? It's Noah Sinclair."

"Where's Maddy? Are you both okay?" Concern edged Matt's tone.

"Don't worry, we're fine. Are you coming to meet us? What are you driving these days?"

"Should be there in less than five. I'm driving a black SUV." There was a pause, then Matt asked, "Maddy's with you, right?"

"I'm here," she said, speaking up for the first time. The sound of her brother's voice didn't bring on a tumble of memories, the way she'd hoped. "Noah has been doing a great job of protecting me."

"Good. Glad you're getting along," Matt said. "I'll see you both soon, okay?"

"Okay." She smiled gratefully at Noah, watching as he disconnected the call. "He sounds nice."

"Nice?" Noah chuckled. "I'd like to hear you say that to Matt's face. You'll always stick up for each other, but at the same time, you can squabble worse than a couple of five-year-olds."

Noah's description filled her with yearning. She wished so much that she could remember.

Her tea had gone cold, but she finished it off anyway. Noah had barely touched his coffee. The way he watched the parking lot, sweeping his gaze over the area, made her nervous.

Surely he didn't think they'd be ambushed here? No, it was more likely that he was just being a cop.

The minutes ticked by with excruciating slowness, but then a large black K-9 SUV pulled into the parking lot, the twin headlights bright amid the dusky shadows.

She couldn't get a good look at the man behind the wheel. After wrapping her scarf around her neck and pulling on her gloves, she slid off her seat. Noah had already grabbed their stuff, so she headed for the door. Noah moved lightning-fast, grasping her arm, halting her progress.

"Hold on a minute, Maddy." He pushed her behind him. "I'm going first, just in case."

Remembering how Jackson had been gunned down, she swallowed hard and nodded. She didn't want Noah in harm's way, either, but he was wearing the vest that had saved his life once before. She grasped the back of his utility belt, determined to follow close on his heels.

Outside, she barely noticed the cold air, her gaze centered on the black SUV she could see parked in a spot that was facing the bowling alley. The driver-side door opened and a tall, lithe man with hair so dark it looked black climbed out. Her brother turned and the moment she saw his face, the missing puzzle pieces clicked into place.

Matt! She let go of Noah and rushed around him in a hurry to reach her brother. "I remember you, Matt! I remember everything!"

"Get down!" Noah shouted just before the boom of a gun echoed through the parking lot.

Her brother reacted instinctively, covering Maddy and shoving her down to the ground. Noah ran over, crouching beside them.

"Where did the shot come from?" Matt asked, his voice tense.

"The three o'clock position. Get around to the front of the vehicle," Noah rasped. "Hurry, I'll cover."

"No, wait!" Maddy shouted, but it was too late. Noah turned to fire in the direction where the gunshot came from at the same time Matt yanked her around the open door, to the relative shelter of the front of the SUV.

Thankfully, Noah joined them a few seconds later. She pushed past Matt to check Noah for signs of injury.

"We need to call for backup," her brother said in a low voice.

"Not yet. There must be some sort of bug on your phone," Noah pointed out. "I'm positive we weren't followed and I called you with a brand-new disposable phone."

Matt's expression turned grim, and Maddy glanced between the two men. Oddly enough, there was no more gunfire, and she once again felt the sense of urgency.

"We need to get out of here," she whispered.

Matt and Noah exchanged a long look, ignoring her.

"Give me your keys," Noah said. "I'll get behind the wheel first. See if I can draw his fire."

"I'll do it," Matt said. "Duchess is in the back. She doesn't know you."

"I'm wearing a vest," Noah pointed out.

"I'll be fine." Matt didn't wait for Noah's response, but quickly rolled beneath the door, coming up and diving into the front seat. The move was quick and unexpected and no gunfire erupted as a result.

Noah grasped Maddy's hand. "Matt is going to slowly back up and turn around so that the truck is between us and the gunman," he said in a low voice. "Once he's turned, we'll get in the back of the cab, okay?"

"Got it," she agreed.

Matt already had the SUV rolling backward, angling to the side so that the front of the truck was pointing toward the exit. She and Noah moved as one, keeping pace with the vehicle while staying crouched down.

"Now," Noah said when the SUV was perpendicular to the parking spot.

She yanked open the back door and crawled inside. Noah tossed their stuff in, then clambered in behind her. He'd barely shut the door when Matt hit the accelerator.

Still no gunfire. Had Noah's return fire scared them off? The seconds stretched into a full minute before Matt said, "We're all clear."

"Thank You, Lord," Maddy whispered, relaxing back into the seat, grateful to God for keeping them safe. Then her eyes flew open. "Matt! We need to check on Mom and Nan."

Her twin, his face now as familiar as her own, caught her gaze in the rearview mirror. "Why?"

She swallowed hard. "I was attacked outside the courthouse. The man who grabbed me told me to drop the case or everyone I cared about would die, including the two old ladies living on the hill." The words came out in a rush. "Don't you see? Mom and Nan live in the old colonial house on the top of Brookmont Ridge. They're both in danger."

"They were fine when I spoke to them yesterday," Matt said. "But I can call to check on them now."

"No, don't use your phone," Noah warned. "Not until we figure out how in the world Pietro's men knew our meeting place."

Maddy pressed her hand against her stomach, feeling sick. She needed, desperately, to know her mother and grandmother were safe.

If they were harmed in any way, she'd never forgive herself. *Never.*

Chapter Eight

Noah was thankful they'd gotten away from the parking lot, but his instincts were still screaming at him about the level of danger. He twisted in his seat to keep an eye out for anyone who might be following, only to come face to face with Matt's K-9 partner, Duchess.

"Hey, Duchess. Remember me?" He put his hand near the crate bars for the dog to sniff. Looking past the animal, he could see several pairs of headlights behind them.

Could one of them be the shooter?

The dog sniffed his hand, then wagged her tail. He turned his attention back to the issue at hand. "Matt, there's a chance the shooter has your license plate number."

"I know." Matt didn't sound at all happy about the possibility. "It's not as if a K-9 SUV is easy to disguise, either."

"Noah, I need to use your new phone to call my mom," Maddy said. "I can't bear the thought that Pietro's goons have their house staked out."

Noah hesitated, not because he wanted to deny Maddy's request—he certainly understood her need to know her mother and grandmother were safe—but because he'd used his phone to call Matt. Disposable cell phones weren't easy to trace, but he knew it was possible. Especially if Pietro had someone working for him within law enforcement.

"Noah, please!" Maddy's voice rose with agitation.

"Hold on, Maddy," Matt said. "Don't call Mom directly. It's better if we call Miles and send him over there to check on them."

"Why is that any different?" Maddy asked, clearly frustrated.

"Because Miles is a homicide detective," Noah reminded her. "We can call Dispatch and ask to have the call sent directly to him. If the call is traced, they'll know only that we called the police, not specifically who within the department."

"Fine. Call Dispatch, then. But hurry," Maddy said.

Noah made the call, requesting to be connected to Miles Callahan's number. Unfortunately, the detective didn't pick up. He left a message telling Miles to go directly to his mother's house to ensure their safety. But he knew Maddy wouldn't be satisfied with that.

"Send a squad over there," she demanded. "I want a wellness check."

"Okay." Noah made the second call, wondering if the terseness of Maddy's tone was related to her memory return. She'd been antagonistic toward him at the hospital after Matt's injury, standing at her twin's bedside as if she was his personal bodyguard. Two days earlier, she'd profusely thanked him for helping her and Gretchen move into their new condo, so he knew her icy attitude had been because she blamed him for Matt's injury.

"Officer Matt Callahan is requesting a wellness check on his mother and grandmother," he told the dispatcher. "Please send a squad to the premises ASAP."

"Will do, officer," the dispatcher responded.

Noah didn't bother to correct her assumption that he was actually Matt. Right now the important thing was to make sure that Matt and Maddy's mother and grandmother were safe. Besides, he wasn't so sure he wanted the dispatcher to know who he was. He'd left the anonymous tip about Jackson's murder, but did they also know about his squad car being submerged in Lake Michigan? He had to believe they would put the two issues together and realize he was either in trouble or had gone rogue, killing his own partner.

After all, it wasn't a huge leap. His reputation related to keeping a partner safe was already ruined. Jackson's death would be the final nail in that coffin.

His career was likely so far down in the gutter there was no hope of recovery. His chest tightened painfully and he struggled to draw a deep breath.

What would he do without his career? He had no idea.

"Thank you, Noah," Maddy said, derailing his thoughts by resting her hand on his arm. "I appreciate your sending the squad to check on Mom and Nan."

"Ah, sure." He was nonplussed by the note of sincerity in her tone. "I completely understand. I want them to be safe, too."

She squeezed his arm. "I know you do."

He stared at her pale fingers, wondering why she was being so nice to him. Maybe for Matt's benefit? That was the only thing that made sense, now that her memory had returned.

"Where to?" Matt asked, interrupting them. "I'm

doing my best to make sure I'm not being followed, but it would be nice to have a destination in mind."

"I'm not sure," Noah admitted. Maddy let go of his arm and he had to curb his desire to reach out to clasp her hand in his. "A motel would be best. It's likely that the police are searching for me, so I don't think it's smart to head back to my place. Too much has happened, I'm worried they'll arrest me first and ask questions later."

"Why would they arrest you?" Matt's questioning gaze met his. "What's really going on here?"

"My partner, Jackson Dellis, was murdered earlier this morning. He was shot because I called him and asked him to pick us up at the Racine Marina."

Matt whistled between his teeth. "That's not good. Although it's strange, I didn't hear anything in the news about a murder victim being found in that area. Usually the reporters are all over that kind of thing."

In Noah's opinion, the media were bloodsucking leeches, but hey, all in the name of freedom of speech, right? He'd never forget how relentlessly awful they were the day after his sister died. "Maybe you missed it. Trust me, it's probably being broadcast as we speak. In fact, we were fortunate to get away from the marina in one piece."

"Noah took a bullet in the back," Maddy chimed in, once again coming to his defense. "Thankfully, he was wearing his vest."

Matt's expression darkened for a moment, then he gave a terse nod. "Thanks for saving Maddy's life, Noah. I owe you for that."

He shifted in his seat, uncomfortable with Matt's gratitude. "It's nothing. But I'm sorry to tell you I'm out of cash. I hope you'll lend me some."

"There's no lending involved," Maddy interjected. "You've already paid for our meals, clothing, phones and the rooms at the last motel. I need to pay my fair share."

"I have plenty of cash," Matt said. "No need to worry about who owes whom. The important thing is to keep Maddy safe while we figure out who Pietro hired to kill her."

"Yes, I know he's the one behind this, but don't forget, I have a trial to prepare for," Maddy reminded him, a stubborn edge to her voice. "So really, the most important thing is to keep Mom and Nan safe. I need to get to my office."

"I don't think that's a good idea," Noah said, striving for patience. "Pietro already made one attempt on you at the courthouse. Why would you give him access to a second attempt? What if he succeeds next time?"

Maddy drew away from him as if he'd hurt her. "Why on earth would I cave in to his pathetic attempts to derail the trial? Prosecuting this case has only gotten more important in the past twenty-four hours. I won't let him chase me away from doing my job."

Noah inwardly groaned at the way she folded her arms across her chest and thrust out her chin. Stubborn Maddy was back.

At least Memory Loss Maddy had agreed to follow his lead in keeping her safe. Now, protecting her from harm would only be more difficult.

If not downright impossible.

Maddy turned away from Noah, staring sightlessly out the passenger-side window. She'd expected Matt to give her a hard time about moving forward with the trial, but not Noah.

She'd thought they'd connected on a deeper, more personal level over the past several hours.

Since their heated kiss.

Then again, Noah had been the one to pull away from their embrace. Her cheeks went pink with embarrassment at the memory. Kissing him in the first place had been out of character for her. Now that her memory had returned, she knew just how much she'd avoided men since the night four months ago she'd been groped by one of her colleagues, who'd thought he was the catch of the century.

Yeah, so *not*.

She hadn't told anyone, especially not her brothers, about that night, about how scared she'd been deep down in her heart that Blake Ratcliff would force her against her will. He'd had her pinned against the desk in his office, blocking the doorway, holding her against him. Fortunately, a security guard had come on his rounds outside Blake's office. He'd knocked sharply on the door, asking if everything was all right. Blake had let her go, and she'd used the opportunity to escape unscathed.

Mostly unscathed. For weeks afterward, she'd had trouble putting the event behind her, doing her best to focus instead on her career.

Alexander Pietro's case had been a good distraction, but she'd continued looking over her shoulder, afraid she'd find herself targeted once again by Ratcliff.

"I have to agree with Noah," Matt said from the front seat. "You can't just stroll into your office, Maddy."

She tossed her head, glaring at him. "Oh, really? As if you or any of our other brothers would ever let something like this stop you from doing your job. Just because you happen to be in some area of law enforcement doesn't make you bulletproof. Miles and Marc were shot last year while protecting their witnesses. And you were stabbed just a few months before Marc's injury."

Noah flinched beside her, and for a moment she regretted adding that last part. Not that it wasn't true, because it was. And yeah, she'd blamed Noah for Matt's injury for weeks afterward. Until Matt confronted her, asking why she couldn't forgive him the way God taught them to.

So she'd done her best to do just that.

"Matt's wound was my fault, not his," Noah said. "And that's not the point. Neither one of us goes into dangerous situations without being prepared. Matt's right, you can't just stroll into work as if none of this happened."

They were ganging up on her, two against one. But they'd forgotten that she'd grown up with five older brothers and knew how to hold her own. "Then we'll find a way to prepare," she said. "I'm sure one of you can get me a vest, and between the two of you, provide round-the-clock protection. We need to find a way to make this work. If Pietro walks, all of this will have been for nothing. Including Jackson's murder."

Silence filled the vehicle, broken only by Duchess's movements and breathing. It seemed like hours, but was likely only a few minutes, before Noah spoke up.

"She's right, Matt. We can't let Pietro get away with this. In fact, there's no guarantee that he wouldn't continue to come after Maddy or the rest of your family, even if she did drop the case."

Her twin let out a heavy sigh. "Yeah, okay. But first we find a motel."

"And a new ride," Noah added. "I'm sorry, but I don't think we can safely use this one."

"I know." Matt took another turn and Maddy was surprised to see they were in front of a low-budget motel on the opposite side of town from where her mother and grandmother lived. Was that a good thing? She wasn't sure. She'd rather be close by, in case something happened. "I'll drop you off and return later with another vehicle."

"Thanks, Matt," Noah said. "Don't forget we need cash, too."

"I got it." He pushed out of the car and dug in his pocket. Noah slid out to join him, offering a hand to Maddy. She took it, allowing him to help her, struck again by his manners. Had Noah always been this courteous? To be fair, she'd always thought he was a nice-looking guy, but she hadn't been interested in getting involved with her brother's partner. And then, after the stabbing, she'd distanced herself from Noah even further.

Then Blake had put her off men, completely. Or so she'd thought.

Looking back over the time they'd spent together since Noah had come to her rescue at the hospital, she realized she'd never really known him on a personal level. The man who carried the guilt over his girlfriend's death like a yoke across his shoulders.

She gave herself a mental shake as she followed Matt inside the motel lobby. Noah had been nothing but kind and protective of her, but that didn't mean anything had changed between them. He still didn't want to become involved and frankly, she wasn't interested in a long-term relationship right now, either. The incident with Blake Ratcliff still bothered her, and her priority had to be on winning the case against Alexander Pietro, sending him to prison for a long, long time.

"They have adjoining rooms available," Noah said in a low voice. "So I told Matt to take them."

She nodded, thinking that it would be good to have her own space. Strange how being close to Noah hadn't bothered her when she'd had amnesia, but now she was a little relieved to have some separation between them. Not that Noah had ever acted the way Ratcliff had.

Still, remembering the way Blake had accused her of sending out vibes that she was interested in him made her wonder if maybe she had.

After all, she'd initiated the kiss with Noah, hadn't she?

When they were finished in the lobby, they headed back outside. "Here you go," Matt said, passing respective room keys to them. He also handed Noah a wad of cash. "It's ten minutes past five o'clock now. I plan to return no later than eight."

"Where are you going to get a spare ride?" Noah asked.

"Not sure," Matt admitted.

"Your friend Garrett is back from his deployment, isn't he?" Maddy asked. "So using his truck is probably out of the question."

"Garrett's a great guy. He may be willing to help out. If not, we have other friends. I'll find a way."

"I know you will," she agreed.

Matt stepped in and wrapped her in a bear hug. She clung to him for a moment, tears pricking her eyes. How could she have forgotten her twin? Her family? Her mother and grandmother?

"Stay safe," Matt whispered in her ear. "And be nice to Noah."

"I will." She hung on for another long moment, then released him. "See you later."

"Back at you." Matt slapped Noah on the shoulder. "Take care of my baby sis."

"Of course. Come on, Maddy, let's get inside." Noah gestured for Maddy to precede him toward their rooms, but she waited until Matt slid into the SUV and started up the engine, watching as he drove away.

Their rooms were nothing special; they were clean but smelled musty enough to make her wrinkle her nose. Still, it was warm and they were safe, so she wasn't about to complain. As she turned up the heater, there was a knock on the connecting door between their rooms.

She crossed over to unlock it. Noah stood there, holding out the plastic bag containing their personal items. "I took out my sweatshirt and toothbrush. The rest is yours."

"Thanks." She took the bag, then gestured toward the computer case. "What are you working on?"

"Nothing yet, but now that you have your memory back, we should review your notes again. We still have Lance Arvani as a key suspect."

She winced. Under normal circumstances, Noah shouldn't know anything about Arvani. Although clearly there wasn't anything normal about being rammed into a lake or being shot at, not just once but three times. She needed to figure out a way to salvage the case, and how Noah had gotten dragged into the recent events, as well. "Give me a few minutes, okay?"

"Sure." Noah stepped back and closed his door halfway.

Maddy carried her personal items into the bathroom, using the time to freshen up. There were dark circles beneath her eyes; the restorative effect of the measly five hours of sleep she'd managed to grab was fading fast. The only good thing was that her headache wasn't nearly as bad as it had been, the level of pain such that it was easily ignored.

Ten minutes later, she entered Noah's room to find him searching the internet on the computer. "Find anything?" she asked, dropping into the seat beside him.

"No, and I don't like it."

She raised an eyebrow. "Okay, what exactly are you looking for? Something on Arvani?"

"No, on Jackson's murder." Noah cleared his current search and tried again, typing in the words *Racine Marina.*

She leaned in close, trying not to let Noah's masculine scent distract her as she watched various results fill the screen.

"I don't understand," Noah muttered. "The news of Jackson's death should be all over the place by now. A dead off-duty cop lying beside a car in a pool of blood wouldn't be overlooked."

She agreed. "Do you think it's possible that the police found him first and kept the whole thing under wraps?"

Noah shrugged, trying different key phrases in the search engine. "I left an anonymous call about it, so I guess it's possible, but I don't see why they would. After all, they probably already know about my squad car being in Lake Michigan, too. Surely they linked the two incidents."

"Maybe someone else moved the body?" Maddy said.

"And cleaned up all the blood? Not likely."

"Try searching on the squad car falling into Lake Michigan?" she suggested.

He did as she asked, and immediately several hits came up. Noah clicked on the top story with the headline Abandoned Police Vehicle Submerged in Lake Michigan.

Silently they both scanned the article. The reporter described the vehicle as being mostly submerged in the water before it was found and that foul play against the officer assigned to the vehicle was suspected. Strangely, the article didn't mention Noah Sinclair by name.

"It doesn't make sense," Noah said again. "They obviously have the story here on my squad car being found in the lake, but nothing related to my murdered partner? That's the bigger news story here. Not an empty police car. A man's death should be taking priority."

"Here, let me try." Maddy turned the laptop computer so that it was facing her directly. She tried several different search engines, along with different phrases, but without a single result.

It was as if Jackson's murder hadn't happened.

How was that possible?

She twisted toward Noah. "What if the shooter came down the hill and stuffed Jackson back in his car?" she asked. "A parked car might not raise anyone's suspicions. What if he's still out there?"

Noah's mouth thinned. "Anything is possible, although I still think someone would have gone searching for him by now. And if they'd found his home empty but his car gone from the garage, they would have put out an APB."

A chill rippled down her spine. "They would have done that for you, too, then, right?"

He nodded slowly. "Yeah, especially since they clearly found my car. Two missing cops, who were partners, had to have raised an alarm."

Her stomach twisted painfully. Jackson's body should have been found, in or out of his abandoned car. Even a bloodstain on the ground would normally have alerted someone.

Which meant Noah was right. The police had to be withholding the information from the media. And the likely reason to do that was because Noah himself had to be their prime suspect in the shooting death of his partner.

Chapter Nine

Noah could see by the resigned expression in Maddy's blue eyes that she understood the gravity of his situation. He grieved for the loss of his partner, the murder of a good cop, but that wasn't the only problem.

The more he thought about it, the more he realized this latest turn of events could not only harm his career, but the integrity of Maddy's case against Pietro.

He'd been involved in the bust and subsequent arrest of the narcotic crime boss. If he was being framed and was charged with murdering his partner, his credibility would go swirling down the drain. Why would a jury believe him?

Why would anyone?

A flash of hopelessness swept over him, and for a moment he wanted to rail at God about the unfairness of it all, but on the heels of that thought came a wave of shame.

No, this wasn't God's fault. Or Maddy's. Or his. Pietro was the one facing life in prison for murder and running a massive drug ring. Pietro was the one who hired someone to go after Maddy outside the courthouse. Pietro and his men were the ones behind the murder of Noah's partner and the multiple attempts to take him and Maddy out of the picture, permanently.

He and Maddy needed to figure out who was working for the imprisoned narcotic trafficker and soon. Before things spiraled even further out of control.

If Pietro went after Maddy's family, he was certain she'd hand the case off to another ADA. And really, Noah wouldn't blame her.

As far as the Callahans were concerned, family always came first.

"I think Arvani is the key," Maddy said, drawing his attention back to the immediate issue at hand. "I'm sure he's involved in this somehow."

Working the case in a constructive manner was better than wishing things were different. "Tell me how you know Arvani is a known associate of Pietro's in the first place? What links them together?"

Maddy sat for a moment, her brow furrowed as she picked through her memory. "I need my notes," she said, taking control of the computer keyboard. "I can't remember exactly why I linked them together. I don't believe I was aware of Arvani's background as a cop, and that doesn't make sense. Surely I would have checked him out?"

Noah knew Maddy was extremely thorough, so he remained silent, giving her the time she needed to review her notes. He watched her rather than the screen, thinking once again about how beautiful she was. Not just her physical features, but deep down, where it counted. He remembered the way she'd supported him when he'd explained how Gina had overdosed, by accident or on purpose after he'd broken up with her.

I will if you will.

He'd told her to stop beating herself up over something that wasn't her fault. And she'd told him, "I will if you will." But her memory loss wasn't exactly the same thing as him causing Gina's death. Was it?

No, of course not. Pietro sent someone after Maddy for the sole purpose of scaring her off the case, intentionally causing her harm.

He'd grown weary of Gina's constant neediness, the way she continued to call him incessantly if he didn't return her call right away. The way she always made a big deal out of nothing, imagining that other women were flirting with him, when they really weren't. Or accusing him of cheating on her. It seemed Gina wasn't happy without some sort of drama in her life.

Yet he should have been nicer about the whole thing, letting her down gently. Instead, he'd chosen to interrupt her in the middle of some tirade against a fellow student, abruptly telling her their relationship was over and that he didn't want to see her anymore.

Remembering how Gina had stumbled backward, as if he'd physically hit her, made him wince. She'd covered her mouth with her hand, tears welling in her eyes, before she'd turned and rushed out of his apartment.

And he'd done nothing to stop her.

He'd thought it was best to leave her alone. Wait until she calmed down before trying to talk to her, but that plan had backfired when she'd been found dead the next morning.

"Here," Maddy said, interrupting his internal rehashing of the past. "There was a phone call made from Pietro himself to Arvani's personal cell number. That was the only link I had between them."

That intrigued him. "When, exactly?"

"About a month before the bust. At the time, though, Arvani claimed his phone had been stolen. An allegation that had seemed possible considering he'd purchased a new phone the very next day, with a different number. Not to mention the fact that Arvani was in Chicago at the time but Pietro was here in Milwaukee."

Interesting, since Noah had suspected all along that Pietro was moving his criminal activities from Chicago to Milwaukee. "I'm not sure I believe that. Most phones are password protected," Noah said. "Seems improbable at best that some guy who just happens to be working with Pietro stole Arvani's phone and managed to break the code to use it."

"I agree," Maddy said. "Which is why I listed Arvani as a likely associate. I suspect there was some crisis that came up, causing Arvani to call Pietro directly, then he quickly ditched his phone and reported it stolen."

He liked the way her mind worked. "But you don't have Arvani being employed by the Chicago PD in your file?"

She grimaced and shook her head. "I was focusing on the trial prep. I gave the information I had to the detective working the case but didn't dig into it myself. There wasn't time. Pietro's lawyer was pushing for a quick trial after the judge denied bail."

Noah blew out a breath. "Okay, if we're right about Arvani working with Pietro, then what is our next step? There is a slight problem of jurisdiction, since we can't very well investigate a Chicago cop."

"We could get the FBI involved," Maddy said, her expression thoughtful. "My brother Marc is an agent in the Milwaukee branch of the bureau, and they don't have to worry about jurisdiction."

"We could, but we don't exactly have much evidence, either. A stolen phone and one call isn't much of a connection. But we could check on property owned by Arvani. Maybe he has something here in Wisconsin?"

"Good idea." Maddy went to work, her slender fingers flying over the keys. He couldn't deny he liked sitting next to her like this, working a case together.

Whoa, get a grip, he told himself harshly. Liking Maddy as a friend, someone he cared about, was one thing; imagining some sort of future together was pure crazy talk.

"Noah! You were right!" Maddy turned and grabbed his arm. "Look, Lance Arvani owns a cabin on Willow Lake, just an hour outside of Milwaukee."

He stared at the information on the screen. "We need to check it out, see if we can find evidence that he's been spending time there."

"So what if he was?" Maddy countered logically. "That doesn't mean anything. What we really need is proof that he's working with Pietro."

"We can't legally enter the cabin without a search warrant," he pointed out.

"No, but it's worth driving by and checking the place out. If he's spending time there, I may be able to convince Judge Dugan to issue a search warrant."

"The trial is only five days away. Defense attorneys hate when new evidence is introduced so late in the proceedings."

"Yes, but that's their problem. We have a right to introduce new evidence as we find it." Maddy glanced at the clock on the bedside table. "We should be hearing from Matt shortly."

Noah glanced back at the address of Arvani's lake

cabin, unable to suppress a surge of anticipation. The place might just give them the break they needed to get the local police or even the Feds involved.

It was possible, remotely possible, that proving Arvani's involvement in Pietro's drug dealing would not just solidify Maddy's case.

But salvage his career.

Maddy hated the thought of Noah being a suspect in his partner's murder. Hopefully, a trip out to Arvani's cabin would give them something, anything, to go on.

She scribbled Arvani's address on a scrap piece of paper, then clicked off the site. Where was her brother? He'd assured them he'd be back before eight o'clock, and it was quarter till by now.

"Don't worry, he'll be here soon," Noah said, as if he'd read her mind. "Matt won't leave you here without the ability to escape."

She forced a smile. "I know he wouldn't do that intentionally, but if he was followed or if something happened to my mom…" She couldn't finish.

Dear Lord, please keep Mom and Nan safe in Your care! Please!

"Hey, it's okay." Noah put his arm around her shoulders, giving her a brief hug. "Matt's a good cop. He can hold his own. And he has Duchess with him."

"True." She sighed and leaned against Noah, appreciating his support. "I just don't like feeling helpless."

"None of us do." His breath brushed against the hair near her temple.

She closed her eyes, savoring his embrace. It was odd how comfortable she felt with Noah. After Ratcliff's sneak attack, she had no interest in men. She had barely tolerated being alone in a room with them. Not easy when she'd been stuck preparing witnesses for trial for hours on end.

Back then, she'd been wary of Noah, too. But that fear of being close to a man hadn't been there during the time she'd been alone with him, first at the hospital, then in the squad, or at her condo. Wrapped in his arms on the boat, not once had she felt hemmed in, anxious to escape.

What did it all mean? That she'd subconsciously recognized Noah as someone she could trust? Even though she hadn't felt that way during their trial prep sessions?

She couldn't figure it out, unless this was the first step in the process of healing. Of forgiving Blake Ratcliff for what he'd done. Something she'd been praying about on a regular basis since that fateful night four months ago.

The memory was so fresh in her mind, it seemed to have taken place just yesterday.

"Maddy? You okay?"

Her face had been pressed into Noah's shoulder as the memories wreaked havoc with her mind. So she pulled herself together and pushed upright, subtly swiping at the surprising dampness on her face. "Yes. Excuse me for a moment." She rose to her feet and headed into the privacy of her room.

Matt would surely be there any minute. There was no reason to panic.

As if on cue, twin headlights flashed brightly against the window as a vehicle pulled into a parking spot near her room. She took a step toward her door when Noah rushed forward, intercepting her.

"Stay back," he ordered, flattening himself against

the wall while keeping his gun pointed at the ceiling. "Take cover in the bathroom until I can verify the driver's identity."

She didn't like hiding in the bathroom but did as he asked, closing and locking the bathroom door behind her.

The seconds ticked by with infinite slowness. Even with her ear pressed to the crack of the door, she couldn't hear much of anything. Her chest tightened with fear as she imagined the motel room door being kicked in by an intruder with a gun.

Noah was armed, too, and wore a vest, but that didn't settle her heart rate.

A muffled thud caused her to gasp in alarm. She put her hand on the doorknob, intending to head out to help Noah, when there was a light rapping on the bathroom door.

"Maddy? Matt's here."

The breath whooshed from her lungs and she dropped her chin to her chest in an effort to calm herself. Then she opened the door to find Noah standing there, a grim expression on his face.

"What's wrong?" she demanded, pushing past him to get to her twin. "Mom? Nan?"

Matt held up a hand. "They're fine, Maddy. The intruder didn't get very far before the police nabbed him."

"Intruder?" Her voice rose to a shriek. "Who? When? What happened?"

"They're safe," Matt repeated, gently pushing her down onto the edge of the bed. "But Duchess and I are heading back over there to spend the night. Michael will be here any moment to pick us up. I brought a black truck for you to use."

The room spun dizzily for a moment, then centered. "Good, that's good. You and the rest of the guys should take turns being there, so they're never left alone."

"Miles will pitch in, but he and Marc have their own families to worry about, too."

"Okay, I agree we wouldn't want Miles and Marc to put their children in danger, but that still leaves you, Mitch and Mike to watch over them." She drilled him with a steely glare. "I mean it, Matt, Mom and Nan need twenty-four-seven protection until the trial is over and you know that the MPD doesn't have the manpower to do it, especially since they're not direct witnesses in the case."

"I know." The fact that her twin didn't argue made her realize he'd been shaken by the news of the intruder, too. "The police are questioning the guy who tried to get inside. Thankfully their alarm system went off and there was a squad nearby. The perp's name is Ervin Slotterback, and he's a known drug user. It's possible he randomly chose their house because he needed a fix."

"No way. Surely you don't believe that?"

"I informed the officers that you were assaulted and that our mother and grandmother were threatened, so now they want to interview you, too."

"Not happening," Noah said bluntly. "Not until we know who to trust."

"Not tonight," Matt agreed. "Tomorrow is soon enough. Here's the key to a black 4x4 truck. Figured you may need something decent to navigate the winter roads. And it belongs to the married sister of a friend of mine, so it won't be easily linked to the Callahan name."

Noah took the key. "Thanks."

There was a second knock at the door, and this time,

Maddy stayed where she was, watching as her brother Mike stepped in. The three men spoke for a moment, then Mike came over to crouch beside her. "You hanging in there?"

"Yes, and I'll be even better knowing that you're all watching over Mom and Nan." She gave her brother a quick hug. "Thanks."

Mike nodded, then turned and gestured for Matt to follow him out. She heard the roar of a car engine, then they were gone.

"It's late," Noah said. "We should get some sleep."

Maddy wanted nothing more, but she stubbornly shook her head. "No, we're going to check out Arvani's cabin first."

"Maddy, it's dark and there's no reason to charge over there right this minute—"

"Yes, there is," she interrupted, jumping to her feet. "You don't believe a random drug addict picked my mother's house to break into any more than I do. We're running out of time. We need to do this."

Noah sighed and rubbed his palms over his face. "Okay, but put the vest on beneath your sweatshirt first. Then we'll go."

She hadn't even noticed the bulletproof vest one of her brothers must have brought in for her. Pulling it off the chair, she carried it into the bathroom and managed to get it fastened around her torso. It seemed bulky and awkward, but that couldn't be helped.

Noah was ready to go when she emerged from the bathroom. Wordlessly, she followed him outside to the four-wheel-drive black pickup. He opened the passenger door for her, then had to help her up as the vest made it difficult to maneuver.

The traffic was busy in town, but became sparse as they left the city limits. The headlights aggravated her headache, so she closed her eyes against the glare.

She must have fallen asleep because the next thing she knew, Noah was softly calling her name. "Maddy? Are you okay?"

"Fine," she murmured, wincing and rubbing the crick in her neck. They were parked at the end of a driveway marked with the numbers that matched Arvani's address. "We're here? This is Arvani's place?"

"Yeah, you slept the entire way." Noah's white teeth flashed in a smile through the darkness. "I'm glad you were able to get some rest."

"Me, too." She cleared her throat, embarrassed at the thought of Noah watching her sleep. Hopefully she hadn't drooled all over herself. "Any sign that someone has been here?"

"Yes, within the past few days. See the tire tracks in the snow?" He gestured at the driveway that stretched out in front of them. "Today is Tuesday, well, almost Wednesday now. The last snowfall was Sunday night."

She tried not to get too excited. "Should we go in on foot?"

"Give me a minute to make sure there aren't lights on at the cabin, okay?"

She hesitated, then nodded. "Hurry up, and make sure you come back to get me. I want to go in with you."

"Understood." Noah fiddled with the bulb in the light above their seats before opening his car door. The interior stayed dark. He shut the door and quickly made his way through the wooded area surrounding the driveway.

Her breath fogged up the windows, so she wiped a spot on the glass so she could see. In a flash, Noah disappeared from view, and for a long second she felt horribly alone.

She shook it off, knowing Noah wouldn't leave her, at least not voluntarily. He was scouting out the territory, that was all. And if she couldn't see him, probably no one else could, either.

He returned surprisingly quickly, crossing over to open her door.

"Well?" she asked.

"The windows are dark. He's either asleep or gone. Let's go."

She took Noah's hand, jumping lightly down to the ground. The night air was cold but between the fleece and the vest, she was amazingly warm. Noah led her down the driveway this time, stepping carefully so as not to leave tracks so she did her best to place her feet in the exact same place.

Focused on the ground, she didn't realize Noah had stopped until she bumped into him. "What's wrong?" she whispered.

"Look." Noah pointed at dark spots staining the snow.

"What is it? Oil from a car engine?"

He shook his head and pulled a slender flashlight from his utility belt. Once he aimed the light on the spots, she could see a bit more clearly. No, the spots weren't black like oil.

She swallowed hard, dragging her gaze up to meet his. The spots were a dark rust color.

Like blood.

Chapter Ten

"Is that—blood?" Maddy asked, her eyes wide and bright in the darkness.

He nodded, honestly surprised that they'd found anything useful. "Yeah, I think so. We'll take a sample to be sure."

Maddy opened her mouth, closed it, frowned, then tried again. "Whose blood?"

He pulled a slender tube from his utility belt and twisted it open, then dabbed the cotton-tipped end on the mahogany stain. This was the first break in the case and he could barely contain his relief. Finally, something to go on. "The tire tracks look to be similar to what's on our vehicle, a sixteen-inch truck tire. If the truck had been backed into the driveway, these bloodstains would have come from the passenger-side door."

"Jackson." Her fingers clutched his arm. "You think this is evidence of Arvani shoving Jackson into the passenger seat after the murder."

Noah slipped the vial back in his pocket and turned off the flashlight, hoping, praying this was the clue he needed to prove his innocence. "We'll know more once we get this blood tested in the lab, but yeah. That's exactly what I think. It's the only thing that makes sense. Even if the cops wanted to keep Jackson's murder quiet, they'd still have to notify his next of kin and there's no guarantee that they would keep quiet. But if Arvani got rid of the body and moved the truck, then there would be nothing to report, other than a missing person."

Like the prosecutor she was, Maddy immediately picked up on his train of thought. "And missing adults don't make headlines until they've been gone for an extended period of time. Or unless someone within the family creates a ruckus."

"Exactly. I don't remember Jackson's schedule. Sometimes he took odd days off and if he had, there would be no reason for the police to raise an alarm." He swept his gaze over the area. There was a long stack of chopped wood neatly piled up between two large oak trees off to the right of the cabin. The patches of snow covering the ground were large enough that if they took a direct route up to the cabin, they risked leaving footprints. Yet he really wanted to take a look inside to see if there were additional signs that someone had been inside recently. The tire tracks were good, but they could belong to anyone, even someone driving in by mistake.

Maybe if they went around through the trees, coming in from the side of the house closest to the woods? If Arvani had been here in the past few days, he would have left tracks between the cabin and the woodpile.

"Now what?" Maddy asked, breaking into his thoughts.

"This way." He turned, moving slowly so that he could be sure not to leave footprints. Maddy once again gripped the back of his utility belt, following close, making him smile.

He didn't like knowing Maddy's mother and grand-mother were in danger, yet being with Maddy like this, working the case with her, was no hardship. Noah hadn't experienced this kind of connection since working alongside Matt.

He reminded himself that this was only a temporary arrangement. After Arvani's trial, he and Maddy would go their separate ways.

Depressing thought.

The process was slow, and he hoped that they weren't caught in the act by Lance Arvani's return. The moon was bright in the sky, illuminating the patches of snow. When he finally reached the woodpile, he was disap-pointed to see there were no footprints between the front door of the cabin and the pile of logs.

Was it possible Arvani hadn't been staying here? Or had he given the key to his cabin to someone else? That didn't seem likely without any footprints leading to the woodpile.

The balloon of euphoria he'd experienced at seeing the blood in the driveway instantly deflated. So what if he was able to prove the blood belonged to Jackson? The link to Arvani was slim.

"What's wrong?" Maddy whispered.

"Nothing." He mentally measured the distance from where they were standing to the side of the cabin. There were a few bare patches, but too far apart for Maddy's shorter stride. "Do me a favor and stay here. I'm just going to take a quick peek through the window."

"Okay."

He took long, wide steps, carefully placing his feet

on the parts of the ground not covered in snow. It didn't take long to reach the structure. Cupping his hands around his eyes, he peered through the window.

It wasn't easy to see much at first, but he was able to distinguish shapes. A tall dresser and a wide bed that had obviously been used recently and left unmade. His gaze stumbled across a chair with a duffel bag on it.

Someone staying here might take off for a while, but leaving a duffel bag behind indicated that person would likely return.

Arvani? Or someone else?

Using his penlight, he flashed it in the window, hoping to see through the doorway into the room beyond. He caught a glimpse of a sofa and what looked like a corner of a fireplace. He rationalized that there might be a decent stack of wood already inside the cabin, which could be why no one had come outside yet to get more.

He turned off the light and made his way back to where Maddy was waiting, huddled beside one of the large oak trees. "I believe the cabin is being used. We need to get out of here before he returns."

"Lead the way," she said, shivering in the cold.

Ignoring the sense of urgency wasn't easy, but he forced himself to go slow, unwilling to make any mistakes. After what seemed like an eternity, they reached the road. He opened the passenger-side door and assisted Maddy up into the seat. He was rounding the back of the truck when he spotted headlights on the road, a few miles in the distance.

He leaped into the driver's seat and tapped the brakes long enough to start the engine before letting up and easing on the gas. Racing away would only draw more attention, so he drove slowly at first, gradually picking up speed. He flicked the lights off, but could still see dim running lights. He searched for a way to shut them off, but couldn't find the switch, so he gave up.

Technology didn't help in situations like this.

Maddy leaned forward, turning up the heat. "That was close."

"Yeah, although there's no way to know if that vehicle back there was heading to the cabin or somewhere else." He continued down the highway, trying to keep an eye on the headlights behind them.

The lights vanished from his field of vision as the driver turned off the highway.

Noah quickly slowed down, making a three-point turn to head back.

"What are you doing?" Maddy asked, her voice raised in alarm.

"I want to see if the car pulled into Arvani's driveway," he said. "Help me look as we drive by, okay?"

She nodded and leaned forward so she could see past him. He kept his speed steady but not too fast so they'd miss it.

"There!" Maddy said excitedly. He nodded in agreement as he caught sight of the large shape of a truck parked in front of Arvani's cabin.

He'd only gotten a quick glimpse, but he was certain the vehicle was the same one Jackson had been driving the night of his murder.

Somehow, some way, he needed to prove it.

Maddy couldn't believe they'd gotten away from Arvani's place in the nick of time. If they'd been five or ten minutes later, they would have been caught for sure.

She sent up a quick prayer of thanks to God for watching over them.

Noah slowed the vehicle and turned. The truck bobbed up and down as he went down through the shallow ditch up the embankment and then through a small clearing.

"You're not seriously going back there, are you?" she asked when he threw the gearshift into Park.

"Yeah, just long enough to get the license plate number." He shut down the engine and handed her the keys. "Will you be warm enough for a few minutes?"

"Sure." The word was barely out of her mouth when he pushed open the driver-side door and jumped out, slamming it shut behind him.

Truthfully she didn't like it, but tagging along would only increase the risk of Noah's being seen, so she huddled down in the seat and waited.

Three minutes passed, and she told herself not to worry. Noah wouldn't be rushing down to Arvani's driveway, he'd be moving slowly, taking his time. After five minutes, she twisted around in her seat to look out through the rear window, trying to see if Noah was on his way back.

Seven minutes later, her heart rate sped up with distress. What if something had happened to him? Arvani could have caught Noah sneaking around the edge of his property.

Ten minutes was more than enough. She needed to take action. Scrambling over the middle console, she adjusted the seat for her shorter legs and started the engine. She'd never driven a truck this big, but since there was nothing but trees and brush on either side, she figured she couldn't do much harm.

After putting the truck in Reverse, she drew a deep breath and slowly rolled backward out of the woods. The rear end of the truck tipped downward, scraping along the ground, making her wince.

A loud banging on the side of the truck had her slamming on the brakes, her heart lodged into her throat. Then Noah's face was pressed against her window.

He was all right!

She threw the truck back into Park and unlocked the door. Noah opened it and she made room for him to get inside by scrambling back into her own seat.

"What took you so long?" she demanded. "I was going crazy waiting here for you."

"I know. I hung back, making sure the guy was inside the cabin before creeping close enough to see the license plate."

"And?" she asked, as he maneuvered the truck back out to the highway.

He headed back the way they'd originally come, toward the interstate that would take them to Milwaukee. "The tag number is 555 EVP."

She repeated the series of numbers and letters to herself, committing it to memory. "Does it belong to Jackson?"

"Same make and model, but I don't know his plate number off the top of my head. I'll check with the DMV records when we get back to the motel."

She nodded, knowing cops had access to the DMV database. Even her brother Michael, who worked as a private investigator, had that capability. Several DAs used private investigators to help them find witnesses that might not want to be found, and her brother was just one of the PIs taking on the occasional case for them.

Thinking of her brother reminded her of the intruder who had been caught outside her mom's house. She knew the guy had to have been sent by Pietro's goons, but why would they send someone so low on the criminal totem pole? The guy who'd assaulted her outside the courthouse and rammed them into Lake Michigan hadn't been some low-life drug addict.

What had Matt said the intruder's name was? Slotterback? Yeah, that was it. Ervin Slotterback.

Maybe Pietro had sent him as a scare tactic. To prove he could get to her mom and Nan if he really wanted to. She swallowed hard, reminding herself that Matt and Duchess would take good care of them.

"Are you hungry?" Noah asked, breaking the silence. "I can pick something up on the way back to the motel."

The late lunch they'd eaten prior to meeting up with her twin seemed ages ago. Fast food wasn't her favorite, but it was better than nothing. "Now that you mention it, I could eat. It's pretty late, though, most places won't be open."

"I know. We'll have to settle for a burger."

She wrinkled her nose. "See if there's a salad."

Noah waited until they were closer to the motel before pulling into a fast-food restaurant. They used the drive-through and were back on the road in no time.

She'd given up meat, but the fries still smelled good. Noah pulled into the parking lot of their motel, a place called The American Lodge, and backed into the parking spot so they could drive out in a hurry if needed.

She followed him into his room and waited for him to set up the computer. The vest was heavy beneath her fleece and she toyed with the idea of taking it off, but then decided to wait for a bit.

Noah quickly logged in to the computer. She watched over his shoulder as he brought up the DMV database and punched in his username and password. When he entered the license plate number, the program's icon spun in a circle as it searched for the information.

She began to unpack their food as he stared at the screen. Suddenly a new page bloomed into view.

"I knew it," Noah said with satisfaction. He tapped at the screen. "The license plate belongs to my partner, Jackson S. Dellis." He turned to look up at her. "Arvani is linked to Pietro and to my partner's death. I'm convinced now, and the blood I found at the scene will prove it."

She gave him a hug. "I'm so glad. We'll get to the bottom of this yet. Now, do you mind if we eat? I'm famished."

"Yeah, sure." He pushed the computer off to the side, making room.

Maddy finished unpacking the meal, then took her seat. Noah dropped down beside her. She glanced at him from beneath her lashes, wondering if he'd initiate the prayer.

He did. Clearing his throat, he began, "Dear Lord, bless this food we are about to eat and, um, keep us safe as we seek to bring a murderer to justice. Amen."

"Amen," she echoed. She smiled and reached out to lightly clasp his hand. "That was nice, Noah, thank you."

He ducked his head as if embarrassed. "Thanks, but to be honest I don't know much about praying, other than what I learned at the Callahan family meals."

"Oh, Noah." She ached to throw herself into his arms. "You're always welcome to join us at church services and at brunch. You know very well Mom and Nan make enough food to feed an army."

He took a bite of his burger, then gave her a sideways glance. "I didn't feel welcome, not after Matt's injury."

She grimaced with shame. "I'm sorry. I know that was my fault. I should never have blamed you for Matt's stab wound. I know, better than most, that police officers put their lives on the line every single day."

She thought for a moment about how her father, former police chief Max Callahan, had been shot in the line of duty. In her spare time, which truthfully hadn't been very often since the Pietro case had been dropped in her lap, she pored over the police reports related to her father's shooting, trying to find some clue the homicide detectives had missed. It irked her that his murder still hadn't been solved and deep down she thought part of the reason was that the mayor had refused to let her brother Miles participate in the investigation, claiming he was too close to the victim to be objective.

Now almost two years had passed. The colder the case, the less likely it was they would find the perpetrator responsible.

Not that she planned to give up. Once the Pietro case was finished, she planned on taking some well-deserved vacation time to continue her own investigation. She kept the file related to their dad's murder hidden in her desk.

They ate in silence for several moments, enjoying the meal. When they were almost finished, Noah sat back in his seat with a heavy sigh. "You were right to blame me for Matt's injury," he said in a blunt tone.

"No, I wasn't." She stole one of his french fries and popped it in her mouth, chewing thoughtfully. "I actually saw the case file, you know. I'm the one who brought charges against the woman responsible. A drug addict named Corrine Lobely stabbed Matt, not you. It wasn't fair of me to insinuate otherwise."

Noah pushed the remnants of his meal away. "I hesitated just for a split second, but it was long enough for her to cut him. So just know I've been blaming myself, too."

She hated knowing that he carried that guilt, along with feeling responsible for his college girlfriend's death. "Noah, cops often have to make split-second decisions. Life-and-death decisions. Playing Monday-morning quarterback is easy, but not realistic. I don't blame you at all. In fact, it's hard to blame Corrine."

Noah's gaze snapped up to meet hers. "What do you mean? Of course she's guilty."

She munched another fry. "Yes, she's guilty of a crime, that's true. But I said it's hard to blame her. Do you know her background? She was raised in the foster system, physically abused and shuffled from one house to another. At the time she stabbed Matt, she'd been living out on the street for six months after being aged out of the foster-care system." Corrine's case file had been difficult to read, each word seared into her brain. "Who's to say that couldn't have been me, or one of my brothers, if we hadn't been fortunate enough to have been born into the Callahan family?"

Noah dropped his gaze. "Not all kids from broken homes end up drug addicts, and some kids who have decent families can still get caught up with drugs."

She sensed he was talking about something personal, and wanted to pry, but forced herself to hold back.

"Regardless, Matt blames me, too," Noah continued. "Sure, he claimed that he'd always wanted to be a K-9 cop, but the fact that he went straight into training immediately after the incident tells me that the truth is simply that he didn't trust me anymore. And I can't say that I really blame him."

She turned and took Noah's hand in hers. "That's not true. In fact, Matt was the one who convinced me to forgive you the way Jesus taught us. He held me responsible for you not coming over anymore. Trust me, Matt misses you. The two of you were more than just partners. You were friends."

His brown eyes held a hint of hope. "He really said that?"

"Absolutely. So promise me that once we finish this case, you'll come to church and brunch again."

The corner of his mouth tipped up in a lopsided smile. "How can I turn down an invitation like that?"

"Yes! I'm so happy." Impulsively, she leaned forward and kissed him on the cheek. Noah put his arm around her and held her close for a moment, then he turned his head and their lips met. Clung. Deepened into a toe-curling kiss.

This time, he initiated the embrace and she willingly kissed him back, marveling in the fact that Noah had managed to break through the fear that had held her captive for far too long.

Chapter Eleven

Kissing Maddy hadn't been a part of his plan, but she tasted so sweet he couldn't help himself. How long had it been since he'd kissed a woman? Too long. Years, even.

Maddy broke off from their kiss. But she didn't step away; instead she snuggled against him, her palm spread over his heart.

"I feel so safe with you, Noah," she said in a low voice.

Safe? Gina's pretty face and delicate features flashed in his mind and he felt as if someone had smashed a fist into his gut.

Safe? He didn't do relationships, and even if he wanted to try again, there was no guarantee things would work out for them.

Safe? He'd protect Maddy with his life, but emotionally? Nope, he didn't see how he could accomplish that.

She must have sensed his distress because she pulled away, looking up at him with concern mirrored in her clear blue eyes. "What is it?"

"Dangerous situations often create a false sense of

intimacy," he said, pushing the words past his tight throat. "I'm glad you feel safe with me, Maddy, but we can't read too much into these feelings."

Her frown deepened. "Don't tell me about how I'm feeling, Noah."

The hurt lacing her tone only made him feel worse. His past experiences with his sister and Gina weren't her fault. "I just don't want you to say something you'll regret later, once the danger has passed and your life has returned to normal."

Her laugh was bitter as she abruptly pulled away. "You don't know anything about what I've been through, Noah. Thanks for showing me I can still be near a man without feeling sick to my stomach. I appreciate it."

Her words were like a slap across the face. His hand flailed out, trying to capture hers, but she was already halfway across the room, heading for the connecting door. "What do you mean?" he demanded harshly, moving quickly to catch up with her. "Why would you feel sick? What happened? Did someone hurt you?"

"Good night, Noah." Maddy stepped over the threshold before he could stop her, and she closed her side of the door. There was an audible click as she shot the dead bolt home.

He stared at the door mere inches from his face, his thoughts whirling. Maddy had given him a glimpse at something he'd never imagined. Some guy must have hurt her, but how was that possible? No one would be brave enough to mess with the Callahans, and everyone knew that Maddy was the youngest of six with five older brothers. Any guy daring to hurt her would have to face all of them. Especially her twin.

Wouldn't they?

Unless— He tipped his head down, resting his forehead on the cool, flat surface of the door, his chaotic thoughts torturous now. Unless she hadn't told her brothers, in some weird attempt to protect them from acting crazy on her behalf.

The minute the thought formed in his mind, he knew he'd hit the nail squarely on the head. Her brothers were all involved in some sort of law enforcement, except for Mike, who was a private investigator, one who did some work for the DA's office. Of course she wouldn't want them to risk doing something that might hurt their careers.

So she'd held her silence. Until now.

He let out a low groan, knowing he'd handled that badly. He should have been understanding, gently encouraging her to open up.

Instead he'd chased her away.

And now she'd locked herself in her room.

Idiot. He was a complete and total idiot. But there was nothing more he could do now. Maybe in the morning she'd be more willing to accept his apology.

He turned away from the connecting doorway and stared blindly at Maddy's computer. Showed how upset she was that she'd left it behind. Exhaustion pulled at him, but he thrust it aside and sat down to continue their investigation. Since Jackson's murder hadn't hit the news, and his partner's truck was temporarily parked in Arvani's driveway, maybe Noah wasn't a current murder suspect after all.

It was time to reach out to his boss, Lieutenant Allan O'Grady. For one thing, he had proof that Jackson's murder wasn't his fault. But the bigger issue is that

Maddy would need to go into the police station in the morning to give her statement anyway, so it made sense for him to let his superiors know what was going on, as well. Still, he didn't want to call the precinct again from his disposable phone. He logged in to his work email and sent a brief message.

Sorry I've been AWOL, but my squad car ending up in the lake was no accident. There have also been several attempts on ADA Madison Callahan's life. I've been keeping her safe, but I'd like to meet with you in the morning to discuss next steps.
Thanks, Officer Noah Sinclair.

He reviewed his message before clicking the send button. Because of the late hour, just past midnight, he didn't expect a response, but one popped up almost immediately.

Be in my office at 0900 sharp.

The message didn't sound encouraging. In fact, Noah suspected that if he didn't show up as ordered, he needn't bother coming in at all. He let out a sigh, shut down the computer and forced himself to stretch out on the bed.

Sleep was essential before facing off with his boss in the morning. Oddly enough, his last thought was that he wasn't nearly as worried about maintaining his job as he was about keeping Maddy safe.

Despite her bone-deep weariness, Maddy tossed and turned for the next hour, unable to sleep. She regretted giving Noah even a hint as to what Blake had done. No doubt he'd grill Matt for more information, which wouldn't help as she hadn't said a word about Ratcliff to anyone.

Especially not Matt.

Growing up with five brothers hadn't been easy. They scared off more boyfriends than she could count. They'd also taken a very personal interest in teaching her how to defend herself. She knew how to fight off an attack, but when Blake had pinned her against the desk, she'd somehow missed his true intent until it was too late.

Stupid? Maybe. The fact of the matter was that Blake had been her colleague, another ADA. A lawyer! Why would she suspect he'd stoop so low as to use force against her?

The bite of shame lingered, and she did her best to put it out of her mind. Blake wasn't important; her case against Pietro was.

Noah? Well, it was her own fault for allowing him to become a distraction. He'd been clear from the beginning he wasn't interested in a relationship, so she needed to get over it already.

Two kisses in the grand scheme of things meant nothing. He was a nice guy who'd made it his mission to keep her safe.

But he was also the man who wasn't used to praying. Who'd made it clear everything he'd learned about faith had come from spending time with her family. She couldn't, wouldn't let him flounder on his own. She'd meant it when she'd invited him over for church services and brunch. Maybe even for the Christmas holiday.

So that settled it, then. She and Noah would be friends. Nothing more, nothing less.

She ignored the tiny hollow place in her heart and prayed for sleep to come.

Her internal body clock woke her up at six in the morning. With a moan, she rolled out of bed and padded to the bathroom. A nice hot shower made her feel more human, as did blow-drying her hair. Although looking at the clothes she'd been wearing—for what, two days now?—had her wrinkling her nose in disgust. Ick. No way was she wearing those to the police station, or worse, to her office.

She'd ask Noah to stop at her place for fresh things before going in to give her statement. It would be cheaper than wasting their cash reserves on new clothes.

Thumps and bumps from next door convinced her that Noah was up and about, too. Squaring her shoulders, she crossed over and twisted the dead bolt off. She opened her side an inch or so, then returned to packing her meager belongings together. She set the bulletproof vest aside. She wouldn't wear the fleece sweater to give her statement, and the vest wouldn't fit beneath her business clothes.

"Maddy?" Noah rapped lightly on the door. "You decent?"

She felt her cheeks warm, and inwardly bemoaned her fair skin. "Yes, of course."

Noah pushed open the door and hovered at the threshold, his gaze serious. "I'm sorry for upsetting you last night."

She shrugged and turned away to place the folded fleece sweatshirt he'd purchased for her in the plastic bag. "I'm fine. Let's just forget about that for now. We need a game plan. I thought we could grab something to eat and review how much you want me to tell the police when I provide my statement."

That made him frown. "What are you talking about? You should tell them everything."

She raised her head, looking him directly in the eye. "You want me to tell them we watched your partner die from a gunshot wound before our eyes? But oh, by the way there's no dead body? What if they decide to hold you for further questioning?"

He grimaced and shrugged. "I don't want you to lie for me, Maddy. Besides, I've been ordered in to talk to my lieutenant as well, at nine sharp. The entire truth will come out sooner or later."

Panic squeezed her chest. She stepped closer, her gaze beseeching him to listen. "Please, Noah. Let's talk about this over breakfast. We don't have to lie, but we don't have to tell them everything right away, do we? Can't we give them what we know about Pietro's attempt to get me off the case by threatening my family and leave it at that?"

His gaze was troubled. "I have to explain about how we were followed and rear-ended into Lake Michigan. And how we were shot at while escaping into the boat that was left unattended at the dock. The boat owner deserves a replacement."

"That's reasonable," she agreed. "But what about the blood we found in the driveway of Arvani's cabin? How are we going to get that tested without mentioning Jackson?"

He hesitated, then shrugged. "I don't know. Give me some time to think about it. If you were serious about getting breakfast, we should leave now."

"Okay." She reached for the bag, but Noah beat her to it, taking both the bag and the spare vest. "But I also need to stop at my place for a change of clothes. I can't go into the office looking like this."

"I'd rather you didn't go in at all," Noah muttered. He stood to the side, allowing her to go through first. "Let's hope it's less risky to go in the daylight."

She understood where he was coming from, and truthfully, she didn't want to put Noah in any more danger, either. But appearance was important while preparing witnesses, more so for her as one of the few female ADAs. She needed to look confident, secure in her knowledge and ability to uphold the law.

Fully capable of convincing a jury to put Alexander Pietro away for the rest of his life.

Noah stored their things, including her computer case, in the narrow area behind the front seat of the truck. He drove to a family-style restaurant that served breakfast all day.

Their server poured coffee and brought their meals with record-breaking speed, but this time, Noah simply bowed his head, waiting for Maddy to say the blessing.

"Dear Lord, thank You for providing this food we are about to eat. Please continue to show us the way, following Your chosen path. We ask for Your care and guidance as we seek to bring criminals to justice. Amen."

There was a slight pause before Noah added, "Amen."

"Dig in," she said in a light, playful tone. It was customary for one of the Callahan boys to utter those words after saying grace, making everyone laugh.

Noah's mouth quirked in a smile. "The first time I had dinner at your house and heard Matt say that, I thought your mother was going to yell at him."

"No, she wouldn't do that," Maddy said, taking a bite of her scrambled eggs. "Even my father, who was always the disciplinarian in the household, didn't raise his voice to us very often. Trust me, his disappointment was punishment enough."

Noah nodded but didn't say anything more, focusing instead on his meal.

She couldn't help wondering about his family. She thought back to the few times they'd eaten together. He'd laughed and joked with the rest of them, but hadn't said much about his parents or siblings. She knew he wasn't an only child. Matt had mentioned that Noah had a younger sister and an older brother.

Matt had been born a full three minutes before her, a fact he gloated over incessantly. As if three minutes meant anything. Not hardly.

Despite the overbearing nature of her brothers, Maddy secretly admitted she wouldn't trade them for anything.

"What if we stopped at a department store instead of going to your condo?" Noah asked, breaking into her thoughts.

She shook her head. "Waste of money. We'll be safe enough during the day, won't we? I'm sure we can get in and out before anyone notices."

"Unless Pietro's goons have someone watching the place," Noah countered. "Matt provided plenty of cash and the stores are open early for the Christmas rush."

She didn't like it but sensed there was no point in arguing. "Fine, my favorite department store isn't far from here. We'll stop there, okay?"

"Sounds good," Noah said, with such obvious relief that she instantly felt bad. The night of her attack seemed like a long time ago, but it really wasn't.

And she knew deep down Noah was still worried about her safety.

They finished their meal, then headed to the store. She found a pair of navy blue dress slacks with a matching blazer and paired them up with a crisp white blouse. After purchasing the items, she changed in the restroom.

"You look great, Maddy," Noah said when she emerged. "Ready to give your statement?"

"I am." When they were back out in the truck, she turned to face him. "I've decided to tell the police everything up until Jackson's murder, especially since we know the body has been moved. I don't want to give them a reason to consider you a suspect."

"A lie of omission is still a lie. As an officer of the court, you're sworn to uphold the law."

She winced, knowing he was right. "I understand that, but how can we protect you?"

He reached out to cover her hand with his. "We were both there, Maddy. Two witnesses to a crime. We need to be honest and tell them everything. I'll provide the blood sample we found and request for it to be tested. Getting a positive ID on the blood will add more credibility to our case."

She closed her eyes for a moment, then nodded. "Okay. If you're sure."

"I am. But the one caveat here is that we're both going to speak only to my lieutenant. No one else."

She was relieved to hear it. "I'm on board with that plan."

Noah drove directly to the Fifth District police station parking lot. He led the way inside to Lieutenant O'Grady's office with ten minutes to spare. They were told to wait, and O'Grady opened the door at exactly nine o'clock to let them in.

The lieutenant appeared to be in his early fifties; he had dark hair with a touch of silvery gray at his temples and piercing green eyes. His expression remained neutral as Noah introduced her, and he urged her to start at the beginning.

Maddy explained about leaving the courthouse late on Monday night, being held at knifepoint, the scar on her neck evidence of the blade cutting her skin. She told the entire story, all the way through, without interruption.

When she finished, the lieutenant turned to Noah. "You're sure the person you witnessed being shot was your partner, Jackson Dellis?"

"Yes, sir," Noah answered. "I called him for a ride and distinctly remember seeing his red hair."

O'Grady stroked his chin, his gaze thoughtful. "That's quite a story."

Maddy's face flushed with anger and it wasn't easy to keep her tone level. "It's not a story, it's the truth. I was threatened and shot at. My family was threatened, too. The police caught a guy by the name of Ervin Slotterback trying to get into my mother's house. Pietro is getting desperate, willing to do whatever he deems necessary to derail this trial."

"Okay, I can buy that part," O'Grady said with a drawn-out sigh. "But witnessing a murder when there's no body or other evidence of a crime? That's pushing it."

"Sir, we have reason to believe a Chicago cop by the name of Lance Arvani is involved with Pietro's narcotic trafficking business. He owns a cabin near Willow Lake, Wisconsin, and we took a sample of blood that we found on his driveway." Noah pulled the vial out of his pocket. "I request that this be tested to see if it's a DNA match for Officer Dellis. Jackson's truck was in Arvani's driveway, as well. That and the blood should be more than enough to obtain a search warrant."

O'Grady leaned back in his seat and crossed his arms across his chest. "Okay, fine. Take the blood down to the lab and write up your search warrant. If the blood type matches Dellis, I'm sure we'll find a judge to sign off on the warrant."

Maddy wanted to point out that by then, Arvani could be long gone, but she bit her tongue. She should be used to this sort of delay by now. The wheels of justice never moved as quickly as she and the police would like.

"Thank you, sir." Noah replaced the vial in his pocket and rose to his feet. "With your permission, I'd like to escort ADA Callahan to her office and stand guard as she continues to prepare for trial."

O'Grady's eyebrows levered up, but then he nodded and also stood. He held his hand out to Maddy. "It was nice to meet you, Ms. Callahan. I respected your father's leadership over this department very much."

She shook his hand. "Thank you. I appreciate you freeing up Officer Sinclair from his usual duties in order to provide me assistance."

"Not a problem." The words were polite, but the scowl on his face made her think that the lieutenant didn't relish the thought of telling his boss what he'd just agreed to.

Noah held the door open for her. They walked

through the police station and were almost to the door before she heard Noah's name.

"Sinclair! Wait up!"

Noah made a frustrated sound but turned to look at the officer who'd flagged them down. "What is it?"

"The call just came in about an explosion. The address is a building housing several condos." The officer glanced at her. "ADA Callahan's building."

Maddy gasped, blood draining from her face as the news hit hard. Her building? She gripped Noah's arm tightly. "We need to go over there right away."

"No way, Maddy. It's too dangerous."

She gave his arm a little shake. "I don't care! I need to know that Gretchen is okay."

He reluctantly nodded and escorted her outside toward the truck.

She curled her fingers into fists, hoping and praying that Gretchen was all right. That it hadn't been her roommate returning home from her job as a flight assistant that had somehow triggered the blast.

A bomb potentially meant for Maddy.

Chapter Twelve

The last thing Noah wanted was to take Maddy to her condo, but he didn't know how to talk her out of it. He understood being afraid that her roommate might have been in the building, but going there wouldn't change anything. With the firefighters working the scene, it would be hours before they'd get any specific information.

Days, even.

He helped her into the truck, then slid in behind the wheel. After he pulled into traffic, he handed his disposable phone to Maddy. "Do you know Gretchen's number?"

She thought for a moment, then nodded, punching in the numbers. Her expression was full of hope at first, but as the ringing continued without an answer, it drained from her face.

"Gretchen? It's Maddy. Please call me at this number as soon as possible. It's urgent. You might be in danger." She disconnected from the call but kept the phone clutched in her hand.

"Do you remember her schedule?"

She shook her head, staring grimly out the passenger-side window. "No. It's always changing. At first she used to call me when flights were running late, but not anymore."

He sensed her despair. "This isn't your fault," he reminded her.

"Isn't it? I should have anticipated something like this. I should have tried to get in touch with Gretchen to warn her about the danger!" Maddy's voice was low and full of anguish.

"Then blame me. You didn't even remember you had a roommate after your head injury."

She shook her head, then rested her forehead against the foggy glass. "My memory has been back since late yesterday afternoon."

"And I could have warned her before that," he reiterated.

She turned and reached for his hand. Then she bowed her head. "Dear Lord, please keep Gretchen safe in Your care."

"Amen," Noah added. He continued to hold her hand, hating feeling so helpless. He wished he had thought about calling Gretchen, but his priority had been keeping Maddy safe.

And he'd be lying if he didn't admit it still was.

It was no surprise to find the roads leading to Maddy's building were closed off. He pulled over to the side of the street, then shut off the engine. "We'll have to walk from here."

"I know." Maddy didn't wait for his help but pushed open the door and jumped down. He swept his gaze over the area as he came around to join her. Placing a protective arm around her shoulders, he kept himself positioned between her and the street.

It probably wasn't a trap, but he refused to let his guard down just in case. They'd taken only a few steps before they were approached by two officers.

"I'm sorry, but we can't let you through," the female officer said. Noah didn't know her name, but her name badge identified her last name as Rapine. "This area is a crime scene."

"I'm Officer Sinclair and this is ADA Callahan. She lives here. What can you tell us about what happened?"

The two patrol officers glanced at each other, then Rapine shrugged. "All I know is the call about an explosion came in around zero eight hundred hours. The smoke eaters are working on dousing the blaze now."

"What about the occupants of the building?" Maddy asked. "Did everyone get out safe?"

The two officers exchanged another uneasy glance. "Several people were evacuated. I can't tell you anything more than that."

Maddy made a soft sound of distress so he tightened his grip around her shoulders. "You must have some idea which unit was the source of the blast?"

"Somewhere on the third floor." The male officer, last name of Otto, spoke up for the first time. "But we don't have any information related to possible casualties. The scene is still too hot for that, and besides, you know that it will take time to investigate exactly what happened and to reach everyone living there."

Maddy shivered, and Noah didn't think it was from the freezing cold temperatures. "Thank you," she said to the officers.

"Not a problem," Rapine said. "We'll note for the record that you weren't home when this occurred."

"Will you please continue to try to reach Gretchen Herald? She's my roommate. I own the condo, but she lives there with me."

Otto nodded and took out his notebook. "Sure."

"I'd like to get closer," Maddy added.

Rapine shook her head. "I'm sorry, but we can't allow that. There's really nothing to see other than the firefighters working the blaze."

"Come on, Maddy. There's nothing more we can do here." Noah agreed with the officers that seeing the condo building on fire wasn't going to help her cope.

The only thing that would make her feel better was to hear from Gretchen.

Maddy reluctantly nodded, allowing him to escort her back to the truck he'd accidentally left illegally parked in front of a fire hydrant.

"Please take me to my office," Maddy begged, once they were settled inside the vehicle. "I need to work this case."

He swallowed a sigh. "Okay, but I don't want to take you in the main entrance. Is there another way to get in that's more private? Less risk of being seen?"

"Yes. We can go in the back way. Park in the courthouse parking lot and I'll show you where to go."

Parking for the Milwaukee County courthouse was in an underground structure, not ideal by any means, but there would also be plenty of other cars down there so they could easily blend in. Still, Noah felt as if they were a bit vulnerable as he pulled in and headed down the long concrete driveway, winding down and around until he found open parking spaces.

"Try to find a spot over toward the stairwell in the corner," Maddy instructed.

He did as she requested, getting as close as he could. The stairwell was also lined in concrete walls and had steel railings. Even at ten fifteen in the morning, there were still plenty of people, many of whom were lawyers, heading toward the elevator adjacent to the stairway.

Maddy led the way, which was okay with him since he preferred covering her back. He'd feel better if she was armed or wearing the vest, but as she mentioned before, the courthouse and DA's office building should be safe.

But even though there were sheriff's deputies manning the entrances and exits of the courthouse, there wasn't nearly that level of security for the DA's offices.

When Maddy reached the top of the stairs, she turned right, heading in the opposite direction of the courthouse. The cold air nipped the tips of his ears but he followed Maddy along the narrow walkway to an inconspicuous doorway at the side of the Milwaukee County Government building.

"Isn't it locked?" he asked as Maddy approached.

She nodded. "Good thing this wasn't in my purse, either." She drew her badge from the depths of her coat pocket and pressed it against a black square electronic reader. The door buzzed and he quickly pulled it open.

The offices here were small and cramped, not that the ADA offices were much bigger. He assumed these were lower level government staff members working in this area.

When Maddy turned a corner, the main corridor for the ADA offices came into view. As they walked past, most of the people nodded or greeted Maddy by name.

He was surprised that so far, no one acted as if they knew she hadn't been there in well over twenty-four hours.

Maddy opened a door and entered a large office area, with several smaller offices on the left and the most senior ADA's office, belonging to Jarrod Fine, on the right. His door was open and the minute he caught sight of Maddy, he bellowed, "Callahan! Where have you been?"

"Hi, Jarrod, what's wrong? Did you miss me?" Maddy moved toward her office, but Fine leaped to his feet, nearly displacing his badly fitting toupee.

"In my office, now!"

"Okay." Maddy didn't look at all flustered as she opened her door, took off her coat and draped it over a chair. "Have a seat, Noah. This could take a while."

He stood watching, feeling awkward as she disappeared into Fine's office, the door closing softly behind her.

Dropping into the chair next to her desk, he stared at the closed door, not liking the fact that she was out of his line of sight. In fact, he didn't like being this far away from her, period.

What if Fine was the man who'd tried to hurt her? His stomach knotted, but then he shook his head. Doing something like that didn't seem to be Jarrod Fine's style.

He drew in a deep breath and scrubbed his hands over his face. Frankly, none of this sat well with him. This was going to be a long, tedious day of playing bodyguard.

Especially considering what he really wanted to do was to investigate Jackson's murder, as well as continue digging into the attempts on Maddy's life.

The trial was five days away not counting today. Five days seemed like an eternity when it came to keeping Maddy safe.

Maddy kept her face an emotionless mask as Jarrod glared at her, every muscle in his body quivering, as did the hairpiece he insisted on wearing. "You know how important the Pietro case is, don't you? Disappearing like that without notice, not even a single phone call, was incredibly unprofessional."

"I can provide a doctor's excuse if necessary," Maddy said calmly. "And, oh, by the way, Pietro's men have tried to kill me several times and have threatened my family."

He reared back in his seat, as if shocked by the news. "What? When?"

Maddy filled him in on her attack outside the courthouse and the subsequent attempts on her life and Noah's. For once Jarrod didn't say anything but actually listened intently as she described how they'd managed to escape, not just once, but several times. She finished her story by describing the new lead they'd uncovered about Lance Arvani, the Chicago police officer with property in Wisconsin.

"We need more on Arvani," Jarrod said as if he hadn't taken her to task for being unprofessional. And of course he hadn't bothered to follow up on her offer of a doctor's excuse, either. Jarrod didn't care as much about his employees as he did about their work. She was obligated to fill him in on where she was on the case.

"The blood we found in Arvani's driveway has been sent to the lab. We're hoping to at least get a basic blood type match to Jackson Dellis because DNA will take weeks."

Fine scowled. "I'll call in some favors, see if I can get the DNA fast-tracked. We need those results."

"I'd appreciate that." This was why she put up with Fine's overbearing personality. When he wanted something done, he didn't let anything get in his way. "My plan is to continue with witness preparation, unless you have something else you need."

Her boss waved his hand. "Get to work. But next time, let me know what's going on."

"Of course." She rose to her feet. "I almost forgot to mention that there was an explosion in my condo building earlier this morning." She swallowed hard, the image of Gretchen's face with her shiny blond hair and hazel eyes making her feel sick to her stomach. Still, she forced herself to remain professional. "Number of casualties still unknown."

"Explosion?" For the first time since she'd entered his office, Jarrod actually looked upset. "Related to Pietro?"

She shrugged. "That's the working theory at the moment. The coincidence on the heels of everything that's happened over the past few days is difficult to ignore."

"Be careful, Maddy." Jarrod must have been concerned because he never, ever called her by her first name. "Alexander Pietro may be one of the most dangerous men you've ever faced across the courtroom."

"Yes, I know." She had the concussion and the bullet fragment in Noah's vest, not to mention Jackson's murder, to prove it. "Officer Sinclair is on duty to protect me." When Jarrod opened his mouth to argue, she held up a hand. "I know he's on the witness list and I'll do everything possible to minimize his exposure to the others, but frankly, it's already too late for that. He's been with me since I was first attacked and is a key witness to the attempts to harm us and to his partner's murder. So we'll just need to find a way to deal with that while maintaining the integrity of the case."

Jarrod drummed his fingers on his desk. "Yeah, okay. We'll find a way to make it work."

"Good. I'll keep you posted on how the rest of the trial prep goes." Maddy opened the door and left her boss's office without looking back.

Noah immediately leaped to his feet, his gaze questioning. "Everything okay?"

"Of course. He's more bluster than not." She gave him a rueful smile. "I didn't mention the temporary memory loss. Figured there was no point. But he's up to speed on everything else, including Jackson's murder and our suspicions about Arvani. He's going to use his clout to get a rush on the DNA."

Noah's eyes brightened. "That would be great. I'd like nothing more than to prove the blood belongs to Jackson."

"I know." She brushed past him to reach her desk. His woodsy scent reminded her of their last kiss but she did her best to stay focused on why they were there. To prep her witnesses.

Not to think about how she might find a way to convince him to see her again on a personal level, just the two of them alone, once the trial was over.

"Who's up first?" Noah asked.

His deep voice made her want to smile. "I was supposed to meet with Rachel Graber, Pietro's former girlfriend, but since it's already past ten, it's probably better to focus on Robby Stanford."

"Stanford, Stanford," Noah muttered under his breath. "Why does that name sound familiar?"

She hesitated. "The less you know, the better. Suffice it to say that Robby is currently in jail and is testifying against Pietro in exchange for a reduced sentence."

"Figures," Noah said in a glum voice. "As fast as we get these guys arrested, someone is letting them out on the street again."

Maddy felt her cheeks flush, but bit back a retort. She couldn't deny he was partially right. It wasn't like she enjoyed that part of her job, making deals with low-level criminals to turn against the guys who happened to be higher up in the criminal food chain. But it wasn't as if there was always a better option.

Getting the higher crime bosses off the streets had to be more important. Otherwise it really was all for nothing.

She picked up her phone to call the assistant she shared with the other ADAs. Jarrod Fine was the only one who had his own dedicated assistant.

"Jennifer? I need you to make arrangements for Robby Stanford to be brought to my office at 12:30. I'll call Rachel Graber to schedule her prep for either later this afternoon or first thing in the morning."

"Will do." Thankfully, Jennifer was cool under pressure; nothing seemed to ruffle the woman's feathers.

"Rachel Graber?" Noah raised an eyebrow. "I'm surprised she's willing to testify against her former boyfriend."

Maddy grimaced. "It hasn't been easy. She's definitely skittish about the whole thing." She thought about the last time she'd seen the young woman, barely legal at twenty-two with eyes that were far older than her years. "Rachel is scared to death of Pietro and so far, our offer of protection is the only thing we have working in our favor."

Noah didn't say anything more as she made the call to Rachel's cell number. She frowned as the call went immediately to voice mail.

"Rachel, it's Maddy. Please call me as soon as possible." She rattled off her office number and then added Noah's disposable cell phone number as an afterthought.

"That's strange," she said. "Rachel normally answers right away."

Noah straightened and leaned forward. "Where is she being held? You need to call her protection detail to make sure everything is okay."

She opened a file on her desk and ran her finger down the list of information, seeking the number of the motel, trying to ignore the ripple of unease. "I'm sure they would have called me if there was a problem."

Noah didn't say anything, waiting until she'd found the number of the detective in charge of the case. She dialed Detective Lowenbaum's number, glancing down at the name of the place she knew Rachel was being held, Greenland Motel.

The detective's phone rang several times, then went to voice mail. She left a message, requesting a call back, then quickly dialed the motel number.

"Greenland Motel, may I help you?"

Finally a person! "Yes, this is ADA Madison Callahan, I'm calling to check on the status of Renee Greer in room 104," she said, using the alias they'd given Rachel.

"Greer. Greer..." The woman's voice trailed off.

There was a long silence before she returned to the line. "Would you like me to connect you to the room?"

Relief had her slumping in her seat. "Yes, please."

"One moment." There was a click and then more ringing. Her body tensed as the ringing continued without an answer. After ten rings, the receptionist picked up the call again. "I'm sorry, your party isn't answering the call. Would you like to leave a message?"

"No, thanks, I'll try again later." Maddy dropped the receiver back in the handset and lifted her gaze to Noah's. "Something's wrong. Rachel should have answered. And if she was in the bathroom or something, the officer stationed in her room should have picked up the phone."

Noah's mouth thinned. "Call my lieutenant. Tell him he needs to send a patrol car to check things out."

She reached out to pick up the phone just as it started to ring. The abrupt sound startled her and she fumbled a bit with the receiver before managing to bring it to her ear. "Callahan," she answered in a curt tone.

"Maddy? This is Detective Keith Lowenbaum. I'm sorry to tell you that Rachel Graber is dead."

"Dead? How? When? What happened?" Maddy tightened her grip on the phone, staring at Noah in horror.

"I'm still trying to piece together what happened, but it looks like some sort of drive-by shooting as they were leaving the motel to come see you. One officer was wounded and is currently being treated at Trinity Medical Center, but unfortunately Rachel was declared dead at the scene."

Dead. One of her key witnesses in the case against Pietro had been murdered in cold blood. First the explosion at her condo, not knowing if her friend and room-mate was dead or alive, and now this.

Pietro was getting desperate. She wanted to believe that he'd also be careless enough to make mistakes.

But how many more innocent lives would he take before she could figure out who was lashing out on his behalf?

How long before she found a way to lock Alexander Pietro away for the rest of his life?

Chapter Thirteen

Noah reached across the desk to take Maddy's hand. This case was spiraling way out of control, yet he didn't know how to rein it back in. He hated feeling so helpless.

"I'll be right there," Maddy said. She hung up the receiver, gave his hand a quick squeeze, then pulled away and rose to her feet. "Let's go. I want to see the scene of the crime for myself."

"Maddy, wait." He leaped up and planted his body between her and the office doorway, blocking her ability to leave. "What if this is nothing more than a trap? Pietro's thugs could be lying in wait for you to do just that, head right over to the crime scene."

Her fingers curled into fists. "One of my primary witnesses is dead! How can I just sit here, moving on with my trial prep, knowing that Pietro had her murdered to prevent her from testifying against him? Don't you understand? She died because of me!"

"Because of Pietro," Noah corrected. He stepped forward and gently clasped her shoulders. "You can't blame yourself for everything that's going wrong with this case."

For a moment, tears welled in her eyes, but then she raised her chin and blinked them back. "Logically I know you're right, but it's not easy to let go of the fact that a young woman has died."

His mind flashed to his sister's pale, still features, her body collapsed in a heap on the bathroom floor, the needle hanging out of her arm. Yeah, he understood that kind of guilt only too well. Was he being a hypocrite? Telling Maddy she wasn't to blame for Rachel's death when he still felt responsible for both Rose's and Gina's deaths?

He gave himself a mental shake. The two situations were different. He'd ignored the signs of his sister's addiction and he'd been the one to abruptly break things off with Gina. He was the common link there, but this wasn't the time to get lost in his past mistakes.

"Please don't go to the crime scene," he pleaded in a low voice. "I know it's hard not to, but think about the fact that you've already lost a day of prep. And you have another session scheduled for this afternoon. Robby Stanford's testimony is just as important for your case, isn't it? Especially now?"

A flash of indecision in her eyes caused him to press his point.

"What kind of evidence do you expect to find that the police won't?" Then it hit him. "You don't trust the police, is that it? Do you think someone on the force leaked her location to Pietro's men?"

She briefly closed her eyes, then shook her head. "I'm not sure what to think. They must have some sort of inside help. For one thing, they've been on our heels since Monday, finding us at every turn. And secondly, how else would Pietro's thugs know to look for her at the safe house at the exact moment they were leaving to see me?"

"Good question." He raked his hand over his sandy blond hair. "Could be that someone accidentally told Arvani her location."

"And what if it wasn't an accidental leak? What if someone on the force is working with Arvani?"

He could feel himself wavering, Maddy's blue eyes sucking him in. Steeling his heart, he looked her straight in the eye. "Even if that was the case, there would be a group of officers and detectives working the scene. Don't forget, one of our own was injured by the drive-by. Trust me, MPD will leave no stone unturned as they seek to find those responsible for the shooting."

Her shoulders slumped in defeat beneath his hands and he couldn't stop himself from drawing her close for a warm hug. She didn't resist, tucking her head into the hollow of his shoulder and allowing him to hold her close.

Maddy felt so right in his arms, and he reveled in the way she rested against him. He was humbled by her trust, her faith in him. He wished she'd confide in him about what had happened to her, but he didn't want to push, either. Regardless, he told himself not to get too attached. Their relationship couldn't go beyond friendship.

Why didn't that knowledge make it easier to let her go?

"Okay, you win. I'll stay here." She moved away, raising her head to smile at him. "It's better for me to keep moving forward on this trial."

He reluctantly let her go, missing her the moment she stepped away. "You could ask Judge Dugan for a continuance," he pointed out.

Before the words left his mouth, she was already shaking her head. "No. For one thing, that's exactly what Pietro's lawyer would like. The last thing I want to do is to give them more time to threaten my family and possibly find a way to eliminate more witnesses. No way. The sooner we get into the courtroom, the better."

Deep down, he agreed with her assessment of their precarious situation. He was glad she wasn't heading out to the crime scene, putting herself in danger. Still, the thought of Maddy standing in the courtroom, facing Pietro, made him break out in a cold sweat. Especially since he couldn't sit at her side, offering his protection.

"Well, then." Maddy cleared her throat and went back to take a seat behind her desk. "How about we get a quick sandwich before the deputies at the jail bring Robby over?"

"Sure." He stayed where he was, crossing his arms over his chest. "But send your assistant down for the food, because I'm not leaving you alone."

She sighed and picked up her phone. He listened as she gave Jennifer their orders. She ended the conversation with "I'll have Officer Sinclair give you the cash for our food."

A smile tugged at the corner of his mouth and he dutifully dug a twenty-dollar bill from his pocket. When Jennifer opened the office door, he handed her the money, then resumed his seat across from Maddy.

"What other witnesses are you planning to prep over the next few days?" he asked.

She tipped her head to the side. "I'm not sure I should give you all their names."

He scowled and straightened in the seat. "I thought we'd agreed that I'd be here as your bodyguard."

"Yes, we did agree on that. But I still have to worry about the integrity of the trial." When he opened his mouth to argue, she lifted a hand to stop him. "I have to review my list anyway, so just leave it alone for now, okay?"

He didn't like being in the dark about critical details but gave her a curt nod. She shuffled through the papers on her desk, reviewing her notes and organizing her thoughts.

The knock at the door indicating their food had arrived was a welcome distraction. He bowed his head to pray. "Dear Lord, bless this food and please continue to keep us safe in Your care. Amen."

"Amen," Maddy echoed. She smiled at him but then turned her attention back to her work, setting down her veggie sandwich on occasion to make notes in the margin.

He finished his meal, realizing he had no idea how it had tasted. When Maddy frowned in concentration, he could see a small furrow in her brow, above the bridge of her nose. The fact that he found that dent adorable made him silently admit just how far gone he was.

It was crazy to even consider seeing Maddy again once the trial was over. Their family backgrounds were so different; hers a well-knit cohesive group whereas his was scattered across the globe with barely any contact between them at all. Hers was full of faith, kindness and love; his was filled with guilt, anger and resentment.

The phone on Maddy's desk rang. She picked it up. "Yes? Oh, thanks, please bring him up."

"Robby Stanford?" he asked when she'd replaced the receiver.

"Yes." She took one last bite of her veggie sandwich and then wrapped up what was left and tucked it in her desk drawer. "He's being brought up now."

"Okay." He glanced around her office, thinking it would be a tight fit for the three of them. Tight, but not impossible. "Where do you want me to sit?"

"Outside my office." Maddy barely glanced at him as she gathered her notes in a pile and pulled out a fresh legal pad.

He blinked, then swallowed a burst of anger, fighting to keep his voice even. "I can't protect you from behind a closed door."

"I'm not in danger. Robby won't be armed." She raised her chin in that familiar stubborn way she had. "So yes, you'll need to sit outside."

He didn't like it, not one bit. But before he could continue arguing with her, there was a light rap on the door. He opened it up to see two deputies escorting a skinny kid dressed in prison orange, his wrists cuffed and his ankles chained together. Robby Stanford looked young, barely legal voting age, but there was an aura about him that bespoke of hard living.

"Thanks," Maddy said, bestowing a wide smile on the two deputies. "Appreciate your help. Robby, please take a seat."

Noah didn't like the kid, maybe because he was vying for a reduced sentence for crimes that he should pay for. Considering the cuffs and chains, Noah was forced to admit that the kid was well confined and not likely to be much of a threat. Regardless, leaving the office and closing the door behind him was the hardest thing he'd ever done.

The deputies left and he pulled an uncomfortable-looking hardback chair over to Maddy's closed office door. As he sat down, he could hear the muffled voices inside. Not the specific words but the different cadence to their voices, Maddy's soft melodic voice a stark comparison to Robby's rough, sullen baritone.

Noah let out a heavy sigh and attempted to mentally prepare himself for a long, tedious day. Not easy considering what he really wanted to do was to continue investigating Arvani's potential link to Pietro.

Eliminating the threat to Maddy once and for all.

Maddy took her time with Robby, asking him to repeat what he'd told her during their first meeting. Hopefully his testimony would remain consistent. Certainly something had to go her way in this case, right?

Wrong.

"I don't remember," Robby muttered when she asked him when he first met Alexander Pietro.

Her stomach twisted painfully, and she leveled him with her best no-nonsense glare. "Sure you do. You told me before in great detail how you first met."

Robby avoided her gaze, his shifty eyes moving from his cuffed wrists to the items on her desk to the colorful fall trees in the painting she had hanging on her wall. "Then why are you askin'?"

She strove for patience. "Tell me about the first time you met Alexander Pietro," she repeated.

Robby curled his shoulders in, as if attempting to make himself look smaller. "I told you, I don't remember."

"Fine. Then there's no point in wasting my time."

Maddy picked up her phone and pressed the intercom button to reach Jennifer. "I need you to call the two deputies. Stanford is ready to return to his cell."

"Wait!" Robby leaned forward, his expression panicked. "Just wait, okay? I'll tell you!"

"Hang on for a minute, Jennifer." Maddy put her hand over the speaker. "Last chance, Robby. You either take this seriously or I'll send you back to your cell and your deal for a lighter sentence is off the table. Your choice. I'm finished messing around."

"Fine, yeah, okay. I get it." Robby shifted in his seat. "Relax, will ya? Can't you take a joke?"

"No." Maddy removed her hand. "Never mind, Jennifer, don't call the deputies just yet. I'll let you know when we're finished."

"Sounds good," Jennifer agreed.

Maddy replaced the handset in the cradle, battling a wave of exhaustion. The nagging headache had returned, too, but she did her best to ignore it.

Her witness list was getting smaller, so she couldn't afford to lose Robby's testimony. But she'd learned over the past few years to always keep the upper hand, especially when it came to those criminals who were testifying in exchange for a lighter sentence.

"One more time. When did you first meet Alexander Pietro?"

"We'd just gotten our biggest shipment of high-grade junk delivered to the warehouse when he suddenly showed up, demanding to see it for himself." Robby's lips curled in a sneer. "It was like he didn't trust us or something. I knew Alex was the big boss, but I didn't expect him to show up that day out of the blue."

Finally a statement consistent with what he'd originally told her. "Where was the warehouse?"

"On the south side of Milwaukee. The building is
about half a block down from the intersection of Birch
Street and Carson."

"And what name was on the warehouse?"

"Carson Electronics." Robby smirked. "We kept guns
in there, too, along with the drugs."

"What happened next?" she asked, barely looking at
her notes. She knew this part of the trial well enough
to recite it herself by memory.

She paused for a moment, silently thanking God once
again for restoring her memory.

"Well?" she prodded, when Robby didn't answer.

"He made us count out every bag of heroin, making sure each gram was accounted for. Once that was
done, he looked us over as if he suspected someone of
cheating him."

She raised an eyebrow. "That's different from what
you told me last time, Robby. You claimed you didn't
have time to count the entire shipment."

Robby averted his gaze once again, lifting one
skinny shoulder in a helpless shrug. "So what? Maybe
we counted the entire shipment or maybe we didn't.
What does it matter?"

She jumped to her feet, the sudden movement causing Robby to shrink further into the chair. She turned
her back for a moment, struggling to regain her composure.

What if Robby was lying about that night? What if
he fell apart on the witness stand? The deal she'd made
with him for a lighter sentence would be all for nothing.

And worse, Pietro could walk away from the trial with an innocent verdict rather than being found guilty.

For a moment, she longed for Noah's reassuring presence. Should she break her own rules by asking him to join her? No, that would only hurt her case in the long term.

Masking her expression to one of indifference, she turned to face Robby. "We're done here. I'm calling off our deal," she said in a blunt tone. "You're not a reliable witness."

Robby's expression turned to outrage. "You can't do that. My lawyer says you can't do that!"

"Your lawyer is wrong," Maddy said. "You haven't held up your side of the deal, which makes the entire agreement null and void." At his blank expression, she inwardly sighed. "In other words, since you won't be testifying against Pietro, there is no deal."

Robby glowered at her for a long moment, then shrugged again. "Whatever."

Whatever? She stared at him, wondering what had changed in the week since she'd last met with him. The only explanation she could come up with was that one of Pietro's men must have gotten to him even in jail.

Serving time must look better than whatever they'd threatened him with.

The tightness returned to her belly and for a moment she remembered reading something about Robby's background. What was it again? She leaned over, shuffling through the messy paperwork scattered about her desk.

Robby suddenly lunged to his feet, his cuffed wrists coming up toward her. She saw a flash of silver and let out a screech, jumping backward in order to avoid the blade.

The tip of the letter opener went through her thin blouse, scratching her abdomen. Her office door flew open and she saw Noah grab hold of Robby, yanking him away from her with enough force to make the younger man's head snap backward.

"Are you all right?" Noah asked harshly, leaning heavily on Robby to keep him pinned to the chair. He wrestled the opener away and tossed it far out of the criminal's reach. "Did he hurt you?"

"I—I'm fine," she managed, looking down at the slit the letter opener had made in her blouse. The scratch was barely bleeding, yet the realization of how much worse this could have been made her feel dizzy.

She'd almost been stabbed the same way Matthew had been eighteen months ago.

Worse, this attempt was mostly her fault, for allowing Robby to get his hands on her letter opener. She should have known better than to turn her back on a drug-and-gun dealer.

"What happened?" Noah asked. "How did he get the weapon?"

"My fault. I never should have had it on my desk." She looked at Robby, seeing the frank fear in his eyes for the first time. "Why did you do it, Robby?"

The eighteen-year-old's hazel eyes filled with tears. "Pietro threatened to kill my mother. He told me to kill you." Tears rolled down his cheeks, making him look twelve. "I had to do it, don't you see? He'll kill my mother! She's taking care of my younger brother and sister. What will happen to them if she dies? I had to do it, I had to!"

Maddy closed her eyes and pressed her fingertips

against her forehead. The anguish in Robby's tone was all too real. And she could identify with his fear.

After all, hadn't Pietro's goon said the same thing to her? *Drop the case or everyone you care about will die, including the two old ladies living in the house on the hill.*

Jennifer's voice through the intercom interrupted her thoughts. "I've called the deputies. They're coming back ASAP."

Maddy dropped her hand from her head and nodded. "Thanks, Jennifer." She knew her assistant had noticed Noah leaping into the office to save her life.

Again.

"Robby Stanford, you're under arrest for assault with a deadly weapon," Noah said. "You have the right to remain silent, anything you say can and will be used against you in a court of law…"

"Stop it, Noah," she interrupted. "I'm not pressing charges."

"What?" Noah drilled her with a furious glare. "Why not? He tried to kill you, Maddy."

"Because he's afraid of Pietro. Because someone got to him even while he was in jail." She shifted her gaze to Robby and tried to hide her trembling hands from Noah's eagle gaze. "Didn't they?"

The tears continued rolling down his cheeks. "Y-yes."

She sighed, struggling to remain calm. She was losing her witnesses faster than a dried-out Christmas tree lost its pine needles.

And she had no idea how to stop the destruction surrounding her case.

Chapter Fourteen

❧

"**I** still think you should press charges." Noah's heart thundered in his chest, the impact of Maddy's close call hitting him hard. So close. If she hadn't jumped back in time, if he hadn't busted through her door when he had… He swallowed hard.

Unbelievable that she was nearly stabbed, just like Matthew. There was actually a small tear in her blouse from the letter-opener blade.

Robby squirmed beneath his heavy grasp. He could tell that Maddy was buying Robby's story about his mother being threatened by Pietro's men, so Noah forced himself to relax his hold on the kid's shoulders. But he didn't let go.

Maddy sighed, her expression full of regret. "Robby, will you testify against Pietro if we send your mother and siblings away from here to keep them safe?"

"I think he should testify in exchange for you not pressing charges against him for assault with a deadly weapon," Noah said, his tone harsh. "Just because he's scared doesn't mean he can try to kill you."

Unfortunately she ignored him, her attention riveted on Robby Stanford. "Well?" she pressed. "Will you do it?"

Robby swiped his face against the orange jumpsuit covering his upper arm. "What about me?" he asked. "If I testify, Pietro will kill me, too."

"After the trial, we'll move you to a facility out of state," Maddy said. "You'll remain in isolation, without contact with the other prisoners until then." When Robby started to shake his head—no one liked being left alone, even for their own protection—Maddy's voice hardened. "That's the best I can do, Robby. The trial starts on Monday, and I'll move you up on the schedule so that you're not in the jail here for very long."

Robby's expression was indecisive.

"You better take her offer," Noah warned. "The fact that you failed to take Maddy out means your mother is still in danger. How will you feel if Pietro seeks revenge on her for your failure?"

The logic of Noah's statement must have gotten through to Robby because the kid finally nodded in agreement. As if on cue, the two deputies from the jail arrived.

"What happened?" the deputy named Olson asked.

"Nothing happened. False alarm," Maddy said with a weary smile. "Although I think we're finished for the day. Please instruct the warden to keep my witness protected and isolated from the other prisoners until he testifies. I don't want anything untoward to happen to him before the trial."

The deputies exchanged a questioning glance, then Olson shrugged. "Sure. Anything else?"

"I may need to work with Mr. Stanford again tomorrow. I'll let you know what time."

"Okay," Deputy Olson said. He and his partner each

grabbed one of Robby Stanford's arms and hauled him to his feet. The kid didn't resist and for a brief moment, the resigned expression in the boy's eyes gave Noah a sense of hope that the kid would actually follow through with his promise to testify against Pietro.

Thanks to Maddy.

Watching her in action was something. Noah couldn't deny that Maddy had been able to turn a potentially catastrophic situation into something that worked out in her favor. And he didn't doubt for one moment that she'd attempt to make good on her part of their bargain.

Although, ensuring Robby's and his family's safety from the long reach of Pietro wouldn't be easy, but he knew she'd do everything possible to make that happen.

If only he could be as certain of her safety. First Pietro's girlfriend, Rachel, then this.

What next? He wished he knew.

Noah and Maddy remained silent until Robby and the deputies had disappeared from the office suite. He regarded her warily, trying to gauge her mood. "Are you ready to call it quits for the day?" he asked.

She grimaced. "I shouldn't. There's still so much to do. And it's bothering me that we haven't heard anything from Gretchen, either."

He hated to admit that the lack of news related to her roommate didn't bode well. "We need to head back to the safety of our motel. Gather up what you'll need to keep working from there and I'll check with my boss about what we know so far about the explosion in your building."

She didn't look thrilled with the plan, but didn't argue. While she gathered up her things, he used her desk phone to call Lieutenant O'Grady, placing the call on speaker.

"What?" O'Grady snarled in lieu of a greeting.

"This is Sinclair," Noah identified himself. "I'm looking for an update on the explosion at ADA Callahan's condo."

"The smoke eaters have the fire under control," his boss said. "That's as much as I know."

"Has there been any mention of casualties?" Noah pressed. "They must have some idea by now if anyone was near the blast."

"Hey, you want answers? Call the ADA's brother. Mitch Callahan is the arson specialist assigned to investigate the fire."

"Thanks." Noah disconnected and looked at Maddy. "Do you know Mitch's number off the top of your head?"

"Yes. Here, I'll dial." She punched in the numbers and then hit the speaker button on her phone so they could both talk.

"Callahan."

"Mitch? It's Maddy. I need to know if anyone has gotten in touch with Gretchen."

"Maddy, I'm so glad you're all right." The relief in Mitch's tone was evident. "So far we haven't identified any casualties from the blast, although the source appears to be on the third floor, near the elevator."

Her gaze clashed with Noah's. Noah remembered the door to her condo wasn't far from the elevator. "I haven't heard from Gretchen and I'm worried about her," Maddy confessed. "I'm fairly certain that bomb was meant for me."

"Yeah, that's the primary theory at the moment," Mitch said in a flat tone. "I assume this is related to your upcoming trial, same as the threat against Mom and Nan?"

"I'm afraid so." Maddy's expression was full of contrition, a fact that made Noah angry. Maddy and her family shouldn't have to live in fear just because she was doing her job.

"It's not Maddy's fault," Noah spoke up defensively. "Pietro is getting desperate. Once the trial is over, things will get back to normal."

"Who's that with you?" Mitch demanded.

"Noah Sinclair," Maddy answered. "He's my self-proclaimed bodyguard."

"Hrmph." Mitch didn't seem impressed. There were voices in the background, then Mitch said, "Listen, I have to go. I'll let you know if I find out anything about Gretchen, okay?"

"Thanks, Mitch, take care." Maddy hung up. "I'm going to call Gretchen's cell phone one more time."

Noah nodded, understanding her concern. As the phone rang and rang, she finished shoving her paperwork into a large accordion file. She left her roommate another message, her expression grim. "Let's go."

He nodded, more than ready to return to the relative anonymity of the motel. He guarded Maddy closely, keeping himself between her and any potential threat as they made their way back down through the back entrance to the parking garage.

Robby's attempt on Maddy replayed itself over and over in his mind as they wove between stationary vehicles, taking a circuitous route to the borrowed truck. Even after he'd helped Maddy inside, Noah couldn't relax, not until they'd reached the street level without incident, leaving the courthouse and her office behind.

Daylight was beginning to fade thanks to the clouds gathering overhead and the upcoming winter solstice. Noah hoped they weren't in for a snowstorm. He and Maddy hadn't had time to listen to the news; for all he knew, a blizzard could be on the way.

Although he couldn't deny the idea of being snowed in with Maddy held a certain appeal. At least as far as keeping her safe.

"I forgot to thank you," Maddy said, breaking into his thoughts. "For rushing to my rescue."

He shrugged. "Not necessary. That's my job."

She wrinkled her nose. "No, it's not. I still can't believe he grabbed my letter opener. It all happened so fast…" Her voice trailed off.

"I know." And he did. Hadn't his split-second hesitation caused her twin brother to be stabbed eighteen months ago?

Her small cold fingers closed over his in an unexpected gesture of comfort. "I'm sorry, Noah. I know I mentioned this before, but Robby's attempt to hurt me made me realize even more just how unfair it was of me to blame you for Matt's injury."

She was being far too kind. "I hesitated that night," he said abruptly. "The second I waited to act was enough for that girl to stab your brother."

"Don't, Noah. Stop taking the blame, all right?" Her tone was testy now. "I understand why Matt told me to forgive you, so you need to do the same."

"Did Matt mention my younger sister, Rose, who died of a heroin overdose?"

She sucked in a harsh breath. "What? No! Oh, Noah, I'm so sorry. What happened?"

He kept one eye on the road, the other watching his

rearview mirror to make sure they weren't being followed. "I was in my first year of college and had come home for spring break. Rose was a senior in high school. I knew that she'd been looking bad recently, and I was determined to confront her about it. But I never got the chance. The following morning, I found her lying on the bathroom floor, a needle stuck in her arm. The syringe contained remnants of heroin."

Her fingers tightened on his. "How terrible for you."

For a moment, he glanced at their clasped hands, wishing things could be different. "That girl who stabbed Matt... I saw Rose in her eyes. The desperate need for drugs. That's why I was so determined to bring Pietro to justice. I only wish I'd have confronted Rose much sooner."

"Oh, Noah," Maddy said with a sigh. "Do you know how many times I played the what-if game? What if my dad hadn't gone to the crime scene that day? What if he'd retired the year before when he'd been offered the chance? Don't you see? This is all part of God's plan. We have to put our faith and our trust in Him."

God's plan? Taking Rose at eighteen? Taking Maddy's father? Gina? Those were hard pills to swallow, yet maybe she was right. Maybe each of those events had brought him and Maddy together now.

God was trusting Noah to keep her safe. And that was one mission in which he was determined to succeed.

No matter what.

Maddy wasn't sure if she'd gotten through to Noah or not. She was touched that he'd told her about his past, and she could understand why he was so determined to do whatever was necessary to keep Pietro behind bars. Alexander Pietro wasn't the only source of heroin in the city, but he was one of the largest suppliers. Getting him off the streets had put a nice dent in the illegal drug business.

Thinking about all the adversity Noah had faced, his sister's overdose, then his girlfriend's death in college, humbled her. In retrospect, she'd been extremely fortunate to have her family and her faith to lean on in times of stress and adversity. Her family had come together after her father's murder, supporting one another and keeping on with the family traditions.

Who had helped and supported Noah?

She debated telling him about what had happened with Blake, the secret shame she hadn't shared with anyone else, but then the moment was gone. Noah pulled into the parking lot of the motel, driving around the building to park out of sight from the road.

A few minutes later, they were safe inside their connecting rooms. She set her file folder on the small table next to her computer and wondered where to start.

"Will you allow me to help?" Noah asked, his deep baritone voice causing her to flush with awareness. "Please?"

How could she deny him after what he'd told her about his sister's death? Very simply, she couldn't. There had to be something she could give him that wouldn't compromise her case.

She rifled through her notes and found the description of the warehouse where Noah and his fellow officers had taken down Pietro.

"Will you look at this and see if you can find any other spots where Pietro's men could have a secret stash of either drugs or weapons? The stuff you found that day of his arrest was impressive, but I heard from you and several others that you always suspected there was more than one spot Pietro used."

"Absolutely." Noah took the paperwork from her hand. "It's good for me to review this again, now that we know Arvani is a suspect."

"Great. I'm going to review my trial notes, see if anything else jumps out at me."

"Shall I make a small pot of coffee?" Noah asked.

She smiled. "I'd like that."

The table was cramped with both of them seated there, but she didn't mind. In fact, being here with Noah, working toward the same goal, was nice.

Better than nice. Amazing. She'd never experienced this level of camaraderie before. Not with a man.

Especially not since the incident with Blake.

Enough, she inwardly chided. This wasn't the time to think about her personal life. She had the biggest trial of her career to prepare for. Witnesses to prep.

Yet all she could think about was Noah's strength. His kindness. His kiss.

"What?" He raised his gaze to meet hers.

She blushed, belatedly realizing she'd been staring at him. "Um, nothing. I was just thinking." *About throwing myself into your arms.*

His smile lit up his entire face. "I like working with you, too."

For a moment, she wondered if she'd spoken her wistful thoughts out loud, but then he went back to reviewing the paperwork in front of him.

She took a deep breath and followed suit. Thankfully,

her notes were extensive. She'd been smart enough to complete a lot of work before the night of her attack.

There were still three officers on her list that she hadn't spoken to in several weeks, so she made a note of their names, determined to complete those prep meetings tomorrow. She took her time going through the list of accomplices Noah's team had arrested that night, wondering if she could lean on any of them to turn on Pietro. According to her notes, they'd all refused to talk, but that had been almost three weeks ago.

Maybe now they'd reconsider. Although truly, it wasn't likely. Still, she needed to ask, so she began to make a list of everyone she needed to talk to before Monday.

There were a lot of things to do before Monday. What if she couldn't get them all completed? A wave of helplessness hit, but she shoved it back.

Failure was not an option.

"Maddy?" Noah's voice was a welcome distraction.

"Did you find something?" She leaned forward, eager for good news.

"I think so." His tone was thoughtful. He tugged his chair closer and showed her the map of the city he'd brought up on her computer. "There are two buildings, one here and here." He pointed to the spots on the screen. "They're both owned by Chicago businessmen."

"Chicago." Her eyes widened. "You think they may be linked to Arvani?"

"It's possible. They're both within ten miles of the arrest site." He shrugged good-naturedly. "Or it could be nothing."

"You don't really believe that, or you wouldn't have pointed them out." She stared at the places he'd identified. "Those are both located in sketchy parts of the city. I'm not sure we should head over yet tonight, maybe it's better to wait until morning?"

Before Noah had a chance to answer, his disposable phone rang. He lifted it to his ear. "Sinclair."

Maddy watched his face, trying to gauge his reaction.

"Gretchen? Okay, hang on, she's right here." He handed her the phone. "It's for you."

Maddy took the phone, her heart in her throat. "Gretchen? Are you okay?"

"Maddy? What's going on? What happened to our building?" Her roommate's voice was full of fear.

"I'm so glad you're safe!" Tears of relief welled in her eyes. "I've been so worried about you. I'm glad you weren't in the condo when the bomb went off."

"Me, too," Gretchen agreed. "Your brother Mitch is here. He's claiming you were the intended victim. Is that true? Was the explosion meant for you?"

"It's likely, but hasn't been proved yet one way or the other."

"I can't believe it," Gretchen murmured. "What if you and I had been home? We would have been killed!"

Maddy had a bad feeling her friend was about to lose it. "I'm sorry, Gretchen. I know this is difficult, but the trial will be over soon and everything will return to normal."

"Oh, yeah? You mean until your next trial, don't you?" Her roommate's tone was bitter. "No, thanks, Maddy. If you don't mind, I think I'll look for a new place to live. Your condo is beyond destroyed now anyway."

"Gretchen, wait…" *Click.* Maddy pulled the phone from her ear, staring at the blank screen.

"That didn't sound good," Noah said, taking the phone from her fingers. "I'm sorry."

"Me, too." Maddy couldn't blame Gretchen for wanting to distance herself from the criminals Maddy worked to put behind bars.

Losing Gretchen's friendship was just one more casualty in her battle against Pietro. She dropped her head in her hand, trying to hold it together.

"Come here." Noah pulled her upright and into his arms, holding her close. "It's okay. Give her some time. She might come around."

"I don't think so," she whispered.

Noah stroked his hand over her hair, pressing her cheek against his chest. "I'm sorry, Maddy. You've been through a lot over these past few days."

"Yes, and so have you." She wanted so badly to kiss him, but the last time she'd done that he'd pulled away. If he rejected her again, she wasn't sure how she'd handle it.

If only she could find a way to show him how much she liked being with him. Not just working together, but being close to him.

Noah must have read her mind, because he pressed his mouth against her temple in a soft kiss. Then he moved to her cheek, the sweetness of his kiss making her heart race.

She waited, practically holding her breath until he placed his finger beneath her chin, tipping her face up so he could cover her mouth with his.

Clinging to his shoulders, she lost herself in his kiss. Noah's embrace felt like coming home.

Chapter Fifteen

Noah knew he should have resisted the temptation to kiss her, but she'd looked so lost, so forlorn, he hadn't been able to help himself.

And now that he'd tasted her sweetness again, he didn't want to stop.

In some tiny corner of his mind, he reveled in the fact that beautiful, smart Maddy Callahan was holding on to him, kissing him back. He had no idea what he'd done to deserve such a precious gift, and he didn't want to let her go.

But the need to breathe eventually had him raising his head, burying his face against her hair, inhaling her cinnamon scent. His heart pounded erratically in his chest and it took a significant amount of effort to gather his scattered brain cells together long enough to form a coherent thought.

He wondered again what had happened to her in the past, who had tried to hurt her, but before he could ask, his phone rang. The loudness had the same effect as having a bucket of ice water dumped on his head.

"It may be related to the case," Maddy said.

"I know." He didn't completely let her go, but reached into his pocket to pull out his phone. "Sinclair," he said, his voice rougher than normal.

"We have ballistics back on the slugs recovered at the Racine Marina," O'Grady said bluntly. "They came from a Smith & Wesson M&P 15 tactical rifle."

Instantly Noah's brain cleared. "The same weapon the Milwaukee police department transitioned to last year."

"Yeah," his boss agreed. "Anyone can buy one, but it's interesting that it's a known cop weapon. And many police departments have been using them."

Like Chicago? Noah intended to find out. "What about the blood sample I gave you? What's taking so long to get a simple blood type?"

Lieutenant O'Grady grunted. "I'll see what I can do. Any new information from your end?"

Noah quickly filled him in on the drive-by shooting death of Maddy's witness Rachel Graber. "She was Pietro's girlfriend," he finished. "If we keep losing witnesses, there won't be a trial."

"I need your expertise in following up on all these loose ends," his boss said. "Can't Callahan's brothers keep an eye on her?"

"She's still in danger. One of her witnesses, Robby Stanford, attempted to stab her earlier today. There have been threats against her family, too, so two of her brothers, Matthew and Mike, are taking turns staying at her mother's house. Mitch is investigating the fire at her condo."

"Miles and Marc are keeping an eye on their own families," she added in a soft voice. "It wouldn't be fair to put the children at risk." Maddy gently pushed away from him. He reluctantly let her go.

He gave those details to O'Grady. "Look, I'd like your permission to stay close to Maddy for now. I'll check in as often as I can, okay?"

"Fine." His boss wasn't happy, but stopped arguing. "See that you do."

Maddy frowned. "I don't like interfering with your ability to do your job," she said when he hung up the phone. "I can talk to my brothers, maybe there's a way to make it all work out."

"No," Noah said with more force than he intended, every cell in his body rejecting that idea. "I'm not leaving you, Maddy. Besides, it won't be much longer, the trial is just a few days away."

"As of tomorrow morning it will be four days away, that's longer than a few," she countered, but her tone lacked conviction. She stayed close and he couldn't deny liking the fact that she liked being with him.

Was he crazy to think there was something more than friendship growing between them? The kisses they'd shared couldn't be ignored. But what if her feelings toward him changed once the danger was over?

Wait a minute. Maybe Maddy had come to depend on him for protection, but he was still the same man who'd let down his sister and his former girlfriend.

Besides, if things didn't work out between him and Maddy, her brothers would come after him and rightly so. Hurting her would be far worse than hurting himself.

He took a slight step backward, forcing himself to think about the case. What had he been working on? Oh, yeah, the two warehouses owned by people who lived in Chicago.

"I think we should take a drive past those two warehouses," he said.

Maddy wrinkled her nose. "It's dark and both of them happen to be in a rough part of town. We should wait until morning."

He didn't want to wait until morning, but driving by once wasn't really going to help. He suddenly snapped his fingers. "Cameras," he said. "That's what we need, small trail cameras pointed at the warehouse entrances. That way we can run video and see who's going in and out."

She hesitated. "We wouldn't be able to use a secret surveillance video in court."

"We could if the camera is posted on public property," he argued. "There is no expectation of privacy on a public street."

"That's true," she agreed, although her expression held skepticism. "If we can find some public property to use. Other buildings in the area or across the street are likely private property."

He wasn't about to give up the idea. "There's bound to be a lamppost or telephone pole nearby. But we need to buy the cameras before the stores close. Ready?"

She glanced down at her notes for a moment, then shrugged. "Why not?"

It didn't take them long to drag on their winter coats to head back outside. The snow was falling now in soft gentle flakes, pretty yet covering the road enough to cause hazardous driving conditions.

Remembering how his squad car had been rammed into Lake Michigan made him grateful that Matt had provided them with a four-wheel-drive truck. Not that he had any intention of getting too close to the lake-shore.

The sporting-goods store was busy with Christmas

shoppers. He and Maddy blended in, edging through the crowd to find the trail cameras. They were pricey, especially the ones with motion sensors that turned on the video streaming when there was activity nearby.

Reading a box, he frowned when he realized that there were only thirty-six hours of video available. Good for hunters in the woods, but not so good when using them in the city when there would be a lot more people and traffic. But it was better than nothing, so he purchased four devices, hoping to install two of them at each warehouse. They needed to be mounted, so he added black electrical tape and zip ties, as well.

He didn't want to drag Maddy along with him to get these installed, yet he didn't want to leave her alone, either. He inwardly debated the pros and cons as they stood in a long line of customers for almost twenty minutes. Finally he paid the bill and carried the supplies out to the truck.

"I guess we should wait until later to install these, right?" Maddy asked once they were back on the road.

"Yeah, that's what I was thinking." He didn't add the part where once Maddy fell asleep, he'd call her brother to come stay at the motel for a bit while he mounted the cameras.

She swiveled toward him. "Don't even think of going without me."

How had she known what he was thinking? Was his face really that transparent?

"I know how you think," Maddy went on as if he'd spoken out loud. "But it's best if there are two of us— one to do the work and one to keep watch."

Since she had a point, he grudgingly nodded. "Okay. In the meantime, let's get something to eat."

"I could eat. However, we should also find these warehouses, see what we're up against. We may need additional supplies."

He'd tried to plan ahead with the zip ties and electrical tape, but she was right. They might need something more. The first warehouse was located south of the area where they'd taken down Pietro, so he drove there first.

Houses grew more and more dilapidated until they disappeared altogether, leaving nothing but old structures, many with broken windows and bars across the doors. The warehouse he was looking for, owned by George Lamb from Chicago, was the last building on a dead-end street.

Noah felt a bit as if their truck had a bull's-eye painted on it as he quickly turned around. Maddy kept her gaze focused on her passenger-side window, looking for anything out of place. And for spots where they could legally mount their cameras.

"I saw an old, abandoned telephone pole," Maddy said once they'd left the area. "But the fact that it's on a dead end adds a new element. We'll have to park a few blocks away and go in on foot."

"I'll manage, not a problem," he assured her. "Let's check out the other site."

Maddy nodded, settling back in her seat. The second location was owned by Moving and Storage, Inc. No name was listed, just a Chicago address.

Moving and Storage, Inc. happened to be in even a worse part of the area. As Noah turned onto 3rd Street, a large truck was backing away from the warehouse in question.

"Get down, but help me get the license plate number," he said, making a quick turn into the driveway of a two-story home that looked as if a strong wind could blow it over. Dousing the lights and turning off the engine, he slid down in the seat, hoping the driver of the truck wouldn't notice them sitting there.

Maddy slouched down, too, her eyes wide in the darkness. When the truck lumbered past, she quickly turned and stared at the license plate.

"55-TFRU," she said. "Although the F could be an E. I can't say for sure."

He repeated the number and letter sequence until he had it memorized, then quickly dialed the MPD dispatch in his district. "This is Officer Sinclair. I need the name registered to 55-TFRU."

The clacking of keys could be heard in the background, then the dispatcher said, "Peter Durango is listed as the owner."

The name meant nothing. Maddy touched his arm. "Try 55-TERU."

He repeated his request with the new license plate number and this time the dispatcher responded quicker. "Owner is listed as a corporation, Moving and Storage, Inc."

"Thanks." Noah hung up and turned to Maddy. "We need your computer. I want to know who exactly owns the company."

"Let's grab a pizza on the way back," Maddy agreed.

He liked the way she thought, and restarted the truck. "First I need to see the layout around the warehouse." He twisted the key, bringing the engine to life, then slowly backed out of the driveway. A light pole was located a good block away from the building, yet well within line of sight of the warehouse.

Perfect.

Satisfied they had a good plan, he drove around the block, then headed for the interstate. They picked up a pizza from a place not far from their motel, half veggie for her, the works for him.

Inside, he set the pizza down, then went straight to the computer. He searched again for the owner of Moving and Storage, Inc., digging deeper this time, wishing he'd done that before getting the cameras.

The enticing aroma of pizza caused his stomach to growl, nearly derailing him from his mission. Then he found it, the name on the screen hitting him hard.

"What is it?" Maddy asked, coming to lean over his shoulder. She sucked in a harsh breath and he nodded, knowing this was exactly the link they needed.

"Lance Arvani." He turned to look up at her. "Do you think this is enough to get a search warrant?"

She grimaced. "Not yet. What do we have other than seeing your partner's truck outside his cabin?"

He knew she was right. He didn't like it, but the law was there to protect the rights of the innocent.

"Once we get the blood test results back, we may have enough for a warrant," she added.

Noah nodded. The results should be back by tomorrow. One more day couldn't hurt. Especially since he still planned on mounting the cameras.

He'd find the proof he needed to put Arvani and anyone else working for Pietro away for good.

Maddy dropped into the seat beside Noah, her thoughts tumbling around in her brain. Should she try to get a search warrant? There wasn't any hard evidence, but maybe it was worth a shot.

Then again, disturbing a judge this late in the evening would likely get her head bitten off. No, they needed something more. The truck belonging to a dead cop wasn't enough.

Noah surprised her by clasping her hand in his and bowing his head. "Dear Lord, we thank You for this food we are about to eat and we ask for Your help in keeping us safe in Your care. Amen."

She smiled and gently squeezed his hand. "Amen."

"Dig in," Noah said lightly. For a moment she flashed back to when her father was alive, sitting at the head of the table. It bothered her that the police had never been able to find the person who'd shot him. Or even a true motive as to why he'd been murdered. She knew both Miles and Matt had tried to get answers, but to no avail. She'd dug a bit into the mystery, too, going through some of the court cases in which her father had played a role in the indictment.

But she hadn't found anything yet. Mostly because her real job had taken over her life, especially this particular case. But maybe once the Pietro trial was over, she could go back to spending her free time digging into her father's case. Especially since she didn't have much of a personal life.

She glanced at Noah beneath her lashes, remembering every second of their last kiss. She liked Noah, more than she should.

He was the first man in months whose touch hadn't made her jerk away in fear. Odd how her amnesia had actually helped her get over that fear of men. Since that night, she'd been with Noah nonstop.

Her cheeks heated as she recalled just how much she'd enjoyed Noah's touch. His kiss. Being held in his arms.

Stop it! This wasn't the time to be thinking about romance. She was being terrorized by a murderer who was not just threatening her family but trying to systematically kill off her key witnesses.

Focus, she told herself. They had important things to do. Kissing Noah again wasn't one of them.

"Maddy? Are you all right?"

She snapped her head up, meeting his concerned gaze. He was already on his second slice of pizza, whereas she hadn't touched her first. "Yes, of course." She lifted a slice and took a healthy bite. "It's great."

"I think we should mount the cameras at the warehouse owned by Moving and Storage, Inc., first. That's our more likely target."

"Agreed. Although we shouldn't ignore the other warehouse, either. We might get something from that one, as well." The idea of shutting down more of the heroin and gun trade gave her a sense of satisfaction.

"I think we should wait until about midnight, then head out," Noah said thoughtfully.

That seemed a bit too early, but she was afraid that if she went to bed to get some sleep, Noah might sneak out to go alone. Unacceptable. She wanted to be there, at least as a lookout and helper.

"Fine with me," she said, finishing one slice and reaching for another. "Can you think of any other supplies we may need?"

He shook his head. "No, besides, it's too late to pick up anything else. The cameras don't have to be mounted super high, just enough to record the activity at the doorway."

They finished the rest of their meal in silence. When she finished, she began cleaning up the mess. Noah pulled out the spare bulletproof vest and handed it to her. "Put this on just in case, okay?"

"Sure." She took the vest along with the sweatshirt Noah had purchased for her and disappeared into the bathroom to change. The vest was as bulky as she remembered, but there was no point in complaining. She knew Noah was wearing his, as well.

Hopefully, they wouldn't need them.

Noah went through the equipment, checking each device to be sure they were working. Then he replaced everything in the bag and opened the door for her.

Once again they walked back out in the cold December night. The snow flurries had stopped, but the clouds overhead still obscured any light from the moon.

A strange sense of foreboding hit hard as Noah drove toward the warehouse. She told herself the darkness was their friend; it would help hide them and the cameras.

So why the strange sense of dread?

The trip down to the warehouse didn't take long. They arrived twenty minutes before their designated midnight time frame. Noah parked a block away, then turned in his seat. "Do you have your disposable phone?"

She nodded, pulling it out of her pocket. It rang in her hand, startling her. She pressed the talk button and immediately realized the caller was Noah.

"Let's keep the connection open—that way if either of us needs something, all we have to do is to say so. Okay?"

"I like it," she agreed. Knowing she could hear Noah if something bad happened made her feel better.

He leaned forward and gave her a quick, unexpected

kiss before sliding out from behind the wheel. He closed the driver-side door behind him with a loud click.

She sat for a minute, a bemused expression on her face. Once Pietro was permanently behind bars, she was absolutely going to find a way to convince Noah to give them a chance.

He was wrong about not doing relationships. She suspected he'd do just fine with the right woman.

With her.

A muffled grunt reached her ears, drawing her attention to the issue at hand. She heard more sounds of movement, then Noah's voice suddenly spoke in her ear. "Maddy?"

"What's wrong?"

"There's a guy walking toward the warehouse," he said, speaking in a low whisper. "I think I'm going crazy, because the guy looks an awful lot like Jackson."

She frowned, thinking she must have heard wrong. "Your partner? That can't be right. We watched him die!"

"I know, but I'm telling you, it's either Jackson or his identical twin. Either way, I'm following him."

Maddy straightened in her seat, fumbling with her seat belt. "Noah, wait!"

But he didn't respond and in her heart, she knew he wasn't about to stop.

Filled with a steely determination, she pushed open her door and jumped down to the ground. If Noah was going into the warehouse, then so was she.

They were in this together.

Chapter Sixteen

The man making his way down the street toward the warehouse wore a heavy winter coat and a black knit hat, but there was just enough bright red hair peeking out beneath the fabric to draw Noah's attention.

He was short, rather stocky and had red hair. Just like his partner Jackson Dellis. But that wasn't possible. Jackson was dead.

Wasn't he?

Yes. He and Maddy had watched him get shot in the chest, watched him crumple to the ground in a heap. So this guy couldn't be Jackson. Unless his partner had a brother? Someone who looked just like him?

The fact that the man was walking up toward the warehouse they'd already linked to Lance Arvani was enough to escalate Noah's suspicions to frank alarm. Was Jackson's brother working for Arvani? Had his partner been shot by his own flesh and blood?

Noah didn't know, but he intended to find out.

He finished mounting the camera, making sure it was pointed toward the doorway across the street. He spoke softly as he moved away so that Maddy could hear him through his phone. If she knew what was going on, maybe she wouldn't worry.

The alarm in her tone when he'd left the truck bothered him, but not enough to make him hesitate. He pulled his weapon and darted across the street. He sidled up to the side of the warehouse, staying in the shadows, then peeked around the corner.

The guy who looked like Jackson's double glanced over his shoulder, as if sensing Noah's gaze, then went up to the side door next to the loading dock. He opened the door without using a key and walked inside.

Well, that was interesting. There didn't seem to be anyone positioned outside the door to stand guard, so maybe the warehouse didn't contain drugs or guns. Usually valuable items like that warranted some sort of patrol.

Then again, the armed guards could be stationed inside.

A sudden movement off to the left had Noah bracing himself for a possible attack. He turned to glance over and nearly choked when he saw Maddy heading toward him. He scowled and tried to wave her back, but she ignored him. She was talking on her phone, although he didn't know who she was talking to, since their call had ended. She appeared to finish up the conversation, tucking the device back into her pocket. She lightly jogged toward him, her expression full of determination.

Noah didn't like it, but hung back waiting for her to catch up to him. He grasped her arm and drew her close to the building so they were both out of sight.

"What are you doing here?" he asked in a harsh whisper.

She glared at him. "Did you really think I was going

to sit in the truck doing nothing? I called for backup. Matt is on his way."

Having backup wasn't a bad thing, especially his former partner who he missed working with more than he'd thought possible. But at the same time, he didn't want Maddy anywhere near the danger. "Good job calling Matt for help. But I need you to wait out here, okay? You're not armed."

Her frown deepened. "Oh, yeah? Well, I don't want you going in alone, either. Let's wait for Matt. Are you sure that the guy you saw was Jackson?"

"No, I'm not sure of anything right now. He sure looked like Jackson Dellis, but I only caught a glimpse of his face in the dark. Dellis never mentioned having a brother, but it's possible that's who I saw heading inside. I'd really like to check for myself to be sure."

"Do we have probable cause?" Maddy asked.

He raised his brow. "A man who was shot in front of our eyes went inside the building owned by the man we suspected of shooting him. I think that's enough for probable cause." At least, he hoped so.

She didn't look convinced. "So what's the crime in progress?"

There were times when being teamed up with a lawyer wasn't much fun. Like now. He thought fast. "Aiding and abetting a murderer."

Maddy rolled her eyes and shook her head. "We need to come up with something better than that."

He hunched his shoulders against the wind and glanced around the area along the side of the warehouse. He firmly believed there were illegal activities going on inside, headed up by none other than Chicago police officer Lance Arvani, but Maddy was correct in that the law required proof. Then again, claiming to see his dead partner would only make him look crazy, rather than working in his favor. If the front door was open and not locked, he wouldn't be forced to break in. One minor point in his favor.

If only they had something more. He looked around; at first he saw a whole lot of nothing. Then a sliver of brass caught his eye. Noah moved forward and squatted on his haunches, peering down at the ground.

"What is it?" Maddy whispered.

He carefully picked up the bullet with his gloved fingers, attempting to preserve any potential prints, and showed it to Maddy. "This is the same ammo that's used in the Smith & Wesson M&P 15 tactical rifle. Matches the slugs found at the crime scene at the Racine Marina." He rose to his feet. "I think that's enough of a link to establish probable cause, don't you?"

She reluctantly nodded. "Yeah, that works."

His phone vibrated and he pulled out the device. His boss. Stifling a sigh, he answered. "Sinclair."

"We have some interesting results on the blood you found on the ground in Arvani's driveway," O'Grady said bluntly.

Noah's pulse spiked with anticipation. "Yeah? What?"

"It's not human. Belongs to the bovine family."

His gaze crashed with Maddy's as he grappled with the news. "Cow's blood? I don't understand."

"Me, either. Can you explain how else the blood got there? You thought it belonged to your partner, but that's obviously not the case."

O'Grady was right about that. He and Maddy had been there when the shot was fired. They had watched

Jackson go down. But what if that was nothing but a big show?

He sagged against the side of the building. Why would Jackson do something like that? Noah didn't understand what his partner and his accomplice had hoped to gain from the charade.

Other than maybe setting a trap to kill him and Maddy?

And if that didn't work, framing Noah for his murder?

The more he considered that option, the more it grew on him. Especially since he'd almost rushed forward with Maddy to meet Jackson when he'd stepped out of his truck at the marina. Only Maddy had held back.

"Sinclair? Did you hear me?" O'Grady demanded.

"Yeah, boss. I don't know why cow's blood was in the driveway, but that doesn't matter right now. I just saw Jackson heading into a warehouse owned by Arvani." Noah knew now the man he'd seen was actually his partner. "I'm heading in."

"I'll send backup."

"Good idea. Matt Callahan just arrived," Noah said, noticing the dark vehicle without lights that pulled up to the curb. He could see the familiar face of Duchess, Matt's German shepherd, in the back. "We're going in. Make sure the other squads that respond come in without lights or sirens."

O'Grady snorted, then hung up. Noah slid the phone back into his pocket and glanced at Maddy. "I need you to go back to the truck to wait for us."

"Not happening." Her tone was firm.

He hoped Matt would be able to talk some sense into her. Matt and Duchess quickly joined them.

Noah quickly filled him in on the bullet he'd found and the owner of the warehouse. He finished with how he'd witnessed his partner heading inside.

Matt scowled. "What's the plan?"

"I'm going in. I'd like you and Duchess to back me up, and Maddy to wait in the car."

"His lieutenant is sending additional backup," Maddy interjected. "We can always wait for them to arrive."

The sounds of loud voices wafted from inside the warehouse. Then the sharp retort of a gunshot ripped through the air.

Noah knew there wasn't time to wait. He turned and ran toward the doorway. It wasn't locked, so he drew it open and flattened himself against the inside wall, raking his gaze over the area.

The inside of the warehouse wasn't a wide-open space the way he'd expected. It was partitioned off into separate rooms. The entryway where he stood was clear, but he could still hear the raised voices arguing heatedly. He slid along the edge of the wall, trying to pinpoint exactly where the argument was coming from.

Noah could tell by the slight click of toenails on the concrete that Matt and Duchess had come inside to join him. He hoped and prayed Maddy had returned to the truck.

Since thinking about Maddy being in danger was nothing but a distraction, he pushed it from his mind and slipped farther into the warehouse.

Matt tapped him on the shoulder and pointed to a room off to the right, indicating that was where the shouting was coming from. Noah nodded and turned in that direction.

A few steps brought him within arm's reach of the

door. The arguing continued, only now he could distinguish what was being said.

"You failed to get rid of the ADA," someone said. "Why should we pay you?"

"Because I need the cash to complete the task," the other one shouted. The voice sounded an awful lot like Jackson's. "There's still time. I'm doing my best considering she has cops all over her."

"You should have taken care of her and your partner on that first night, before they left town."

Noah wondered if the latter voice belonged to Arvani. His memory of the guy who'd trained with him at the academy was faint at best. They hadn't been friends, and Noah had been focused on learning everything he needed to be the best cop he could be.

Only that hadn't worked out very well, had it? His inability to keep a partner didn't bode well for his future as a cop. At least now he understood why Jackson hadn't given him any grief about trusting Noah to have his back.

The guy himself had probably been involved with Pietro's business dealings all along. Nothing else made any sense.

Focus, he told himself harshly. He glanced at Matt, struck by a horrible sense of uncertainty. Should they wait for the rest of their backup to arrive? Or barge in?

Matt steadily held his gaze, giving the impression he had confidence in Noah's decision. Too bad he wasn't so sure he deserved it.

Noah was about to give the signal to move in when the door behind them barged open. A man entered, pulling Maddy along with him, a gun pointed at her head.

Lance Arvani. The bitter taste of failure stuck in

Noah's throat, knowing that he and Matt were now out-numbered.

If Maddy was injured or worse, he knew it would be his fault.

He'd failed her once again.

Maddy hated seeing the sick expression on Noah's and Matt's faces. Her stubborn insistence on sticking around until their backup arrived had not only placed herself in danger, but Noah and Matt, as well.

She wasn't sure who had her, but the gravelly voice had been all too familiar. It was the same guy who'd assaulted her outside the courthouse the night she'd lost her memory.

"Okay, let's stay calm," Noah said, raising his hands up in the universal gesture of surrender. "You really don't want to shoot a couple of cops and an ADA, do you?"

"Release Pietro and we'll see what we can work out," the gravelly voice said.

It took every ounce of effort she had not to react to that ridiculous demand. Even if she believed the gun-man would let them all go, which she didn't, there was no way she'd allow Pietro to walk away from his crimes.

Never.

There had to be a way out of this. There just had to be!

Noah's gaze met hers for a long moment before shift-ing to the man holding a gun on her. In that second, she knew that Noah planned to do whatever he deemed nec-essary in order to save her life.

That he'd sacrifice himself to avoid having another death on his conscience.

But this mess was her fault for not obeying his directive to return to the truck, not his. And really, all she needed to do was to stall until the rest of their backup arrived. In fact, she was a bit surprised they hadn't shown up already.

Tension shimmered in the air as the gunman faced off with her brother and the man she'd grown to care about.

To love.

Maddy didn't let herself dwell on that thought; she needed to stay focused on finding a way out of the situation she'd gotten them into. The gunman held her tightly, but not so much that she couldn't move.

She'd grown up with five older brothers, each of them making it their mission to make sure she knew how to protect herself. There had to be a way to escape. Even if none of the scenarios her brothers had taught involved a man actually holding a gun to her head.

Maybe she could improvise.

"Come on, Arvani," Noah said. "Let's find a way to end this in a way that we're both happy."

The man, obviously Lance Arvani, snickered. "I don't care what you want. I'm the one holding a gun to the pretty ADA's head. You'll both do exactly what I tell you. Drop your weapons and kick them toward me, nice and easy now. Any wrong move and I'll shoot the woman."

She doubted he'd do that since they still outnumbered Arvani, at least for the moment. But she was sure the men arguing inside the room off the hall would be coming out soon. Their voices were still raised in anger, or they might have heard the commotion already.

Maddy nearly missed the hand signal Matt gave Duchess, but suddenly the dog let out a series of ferocious barks. Arvani instinctively recoiled, moving backward a step, and she took advantage of the gunman's momentary distraction to twist out of his grasp, pushing his gun up and out of the way.

"Get down," Noah roared seconds before shots filled the air.

This time she listened without question, dropping to the ground and rolling away from Arvani. Noah's aim was true; his shot hit the Chicago cop in the chest, sending him staggering backward. She wondered if he was wearing a vest, too, since he didn't go down and there was no evidence of blood. Arvani sagged against the wall, struggling to breathe.

Unfortunately the sound of Noah's gunfire brought the others running from the adjacent room. Matt stood with his legs wide and his weapon raised. "Stop! Police! Put your hands up where I can see them!"

Arvani's upper lip curled with derision and he brought his gun up, aiming at Noah. *No!* Maddy surged to her feet, intending to rush forward, hoping to disarm him when he turned and shot at her instead of Noah.

The slug hit her in the chest dead center over her heart. Despite being protected in part by the bulletproof vest, she heard a distinct crack of a broken bone. The force of the blast knocked her off her feet. She fell to the ground, pain spreading through her chest as she fought to fill her lungs with oxygen.

A red haze of pain clouded her vision and she felt completely, utterly helpless. Being shot even while wearing a vest hurt! More than she'd thought possible.

Her head jerked up as Noah fired again, this time hitting Lance Arvani in the head. The Chicago cop fell straight back like a tree hitting the forest floor.

She put a hand to her chest, still fighting the pain. Every breath was painful, a sharp stabbing sensation. Was it possible that a shot to the chest could cause a heart attack? Because that was how it felt.

Noah turned to help Matt apprehend the others. Duchess did her part, chasing after one guy who'd taken off toward the rear of the warehouse. It didn't take long for the dog to catch him, taking him down with a flying leap and then standing on top of him, her jaws open across his throat.

Matt glanced at Maddy, and she gave him a reassuring nod. He went after his partner, throwing cuffs on the wrists of the man Duchess had apprehended.

Noah was securing a short guy with bright red hair. "Jackson Dellis, you're under arrest for attempting to shoot a police officer."

The door to the warehouse burst open and more cops swarmed in, their weapons held ready. Maddy scooted over to the side of the hallway, trying to stay out of their way. Her chest ached so bad she didn't think she could stand under her own power.

"Are you all right?" Noah asked, coming over to kneel beside her, his brown eyes dark with concern.

She tried to nod, grimaced. "Hurts," she managed. Thinking about the way Noah had run after being shot in the back of his vest filled her with admiration. She couldn't do anything but lie there, struggling to breathe.

"We need paramedics," Noah said in a sharp tone.

An unexpected gunshot echoed through the room. Noah's reaction was to throw himself over her body as an added protection.

Her head hit the concrete with a loud crack.

And then there was nothing but darkness.

Chapter Seventeen

What was going on? Who'd discharged their weapon? One of the cops who'd responded to the call?

Noah lifted his head in time to see Matt take out the perp who'd taken that last shot. The gunman was dressed head to toe in black, his face hidden behind a scruffy beard. The guy howled and dropped to the ground, holding his hands over his belly. He must have been hiding, because Noah had been certain they'd secured the area.

His heart thundered in his chest. That had been far too close.

The rest of the police officers who'd arrived on the scene spread out in an effort to make sure they hadn't missed anyone else.

Noah lifted himself off Maddy. "Sorry about that. Are you okay?"

Maddy didn't move and a sharp stab of fear lanced his heart.

"Maddy?" he called, trying again. Her face was pale, her eyes were closed and it was difficult for him to tell if she was breathing. Panic hit hard. "We need that ambulance! Now!"

"What's wrong?" Matt finished cuffing the perp Duchess had chased down, then came over to kneel beside him.

"I'm not sure," Noah confessed. "She was awake and talking, but now she's out cold." He placed his fingers along the side of her neck searching for a pulse, only slightly reassured when he found the weak, rapid beat.

"The ambulance just pulled up." The officer who spoke wore a nametag that identified him as Jennings.

"Tell them ADA Callahan needs attention." Noah glanced down again at Maddy's motionless face. "Maddy? Can you hear me?"

Still nothing. He took a deep breath, lowered his head and prayed.

Dear Lord, please heal Maddy's injuries and keep her safe in Your care!

"Was she shot?" Matt asked, pushing her sweatshirt out of the way and running his fingertips over the material of the vest. His hand stopped when he found the slug. "She took one right over the center of her chest. Let's get this thing off, make sure she's not bleeding."

Noah assisted in removing the Velcro straps to remove the vest. Thankfully Maddy wore a T-shirt underneath. There was no sign of blood, but he knew only too well how being hit in the vest at close range could still cause serious harm. What if somehow the bullet had managed to damage her heart or her lungs?

Two paramedics pushed their way through the crowd of cops, heading toward them. Matt rose to his feet, gesturing for them to come closer. Noah didn't let go of Maddy's hand, afraid that if he did she'd slip away.

"Hang in there, Maddy. I'm here and so is Matt. Hang in there, understand?"

She didn't respond to his running commentary, and that only worried him more. She had to be okay. She just had to!

The thought of living his life without her made his eyes grow damp. He didn't do relationships, hadn't wanted to hurt anyone the way he'd hurt Gina, but his heart hadn't listened to his head.

He'd fallen in love with Maddy Callahan.

"There's a small lump on the back of her head," one of the paramedics said. "She may have a brain injury."

"She was hit on the head a few days ago, but that was along her right temple," Noah said with a frown.

"This one is dead center on the back of her head. She may have hit her head against the concrete."

Noah's stomach knotted and he forced himself to look at Matt. "I did this," he said in a hoarse tone. "I threw myself on top of her and must have knocked her head against the floor by accident!"

"Hey, it's okay," Matt said reassuringly. "You were only trying to help. Besides, Maddy has a pretty hard head. I'm sure she'll be fine."

Noah wanted to believe him. Guilt rose in the back of his throat, threatening to choke him, but he pushed it back and focused on the power of prayer.

He desperately needed to believe Maddy would wake up. And God was the one who could make that happen.

Muffled voices pierced the darkness. While it was tempting to shut them out, melting back into the soft velvet blackness, she couldn't shake off the sense of urgency.

With a low moan, Maddy pushed past the pain in her head and her chest and tried to open her eyes.

"Maddy?" The familiar scent of spicy aftershave

helped bring the image of Noah's concerned face into focus. "You're awake!"

She winced at the volume of his tone. "Yes," she managed. "Water?"

"Right here." Noah's voice was soft and gentle now. He slid his arm beneath her shoulder blades and held a cup to her lips. The cool water tasted amazing and she took several long sips. "Thanks."

"I'm so glad you're awake," Noah said, concern etched in his features. His appearance was ragged, dark stubble covered his cheeks and chin and his eyes were bloodshot. He looked as if he'd been awake for days. "I'll get the doctor."

"Wait," she said as understanding dawned. "I'm in the hospital? For how long?"

"It's almost noon on Thursday," Noah informed her. "You've been in since late last night."

Good to know she hadn't lost too much prep time. Well, other than what she'd already lost since Monday night when she'd left the courthouse and been assaulted. By Lance Arvani, she remembered now.

"Arvani was the one who accosted me and threatened my mother and grandmother," she said. "I recognized his voice."

"He's dead, so you don't have to worry about him any longer," Noah said. "And we've arrested Jackson Dellis, too. He's not talking yet, but I'm sure he'll break down eventually. I'd really like to know why he faked his death."

Images from the scene at the warehouse fluttered through her mind. "Maybe he tried to set you up."

Noah shrugged. "Anything's possible. I'd better get the doctor. Your family should be here soon. They took a quick break for lunch."

"You stayed," Maddy said, looking down at their joined hands. "Thank you, Noah."

"I'm sorry I caused you to hit your head again," he said, averting his gaze. "I never wanted to hurt you."

He tried to pull away, but she tightened her grip, keeping him there. "You protected me from the very beginning," she reminded him. "I owe you my life, Noah. Thank you."

"I almost killed you," he corrected.

She glared at him, even though it made her headache worse. "I'm pretty sure it was my own fault that Lance Arvani caught me and held me at gunpoint in the first place." She lifted her hand to her chest, wondering how badly she was bruised. "Just accept my gratitude, would you? Please?"

He slowly nodded. "Okay. Now can I get the doctor?"

Her fingers reflexively tightened around his. She didn't want to let him go.

Not now. Not ever. But how to explain that she felt safe only when she was with him? That he was the only man she could tolerate being close to?

The only man she wanted with her whole heart?

There was a knock at her door, then it opened, revealing a tall, thin bald man wearing a lab coat. "Good morning, Ms. Callahan. I'm Dr. Eduardo and I'm glad to see you're awake. How are you feeling?"

"Fine," she lied. The pounding behind her eyes was reminiscent of the first time she'd hit her head. But she knew the headache would fade in time. "How soon can I be discharged?"

Dr. Eduardo's eyebrows levered up. "Discharged? We'll see how you're feeling by tomorrow morning. I have a repeat CT scan scheduled for this afternoon. I want to be sure you don't have any internal bleeding in your brain. And you may be interested to know you have a cracked rib."

The cracked rib wasn't much of a surprise, but a repeat CT scan? Weird that she couldn't remember the first one. "Okay, that's fine, but if the scan is clear I'm leaving. I have a case going to trial on Monday."

Dr. Eduardo's scowl deepened. "You need to rest and relax."

"And I will," Maddy said. "After the trial."

He made a disgusted sound, then proceeded to examine her. By the time he'd finished, her family had returned from lunch. All of them.

"Oh, Maddy." Her mother's eyes were suspiciously bright as Margaret Callahan rushed over to hug her. "I'm so glad you're awake."

Her mother always smelled like chocolate-chip cookies, maybe because she was always making a new batch. Maddy kissed her cheek, then smiled at her mother and her grandmother, who came up to the other side of her bed. Nan, who loved to knit, held Marc and Kari's seven-month-old son, Max, on her hip. The boy stuck his fist in his mouth, revealing several new teeth.

"I'm glad you're both safe," Maddy said in a low tone. "The man who threatened you is dead, so there's no need to worry."

"Worry? Me?" Her mother patted her arm. "I've never worried about myself, just my children. Especially since each one of you seems to be constantly in harm's way. No more injuries, you hear me?"

"At least I don't have a bullet wound," Maddy pointed out, trying to lighten things up.

"Only because you were smart enough to be wearing a vest," Matt said drily.

Her twin, along with the rest of her brothers, crowded around. Paige and her daughter, Abby, stood next to Margaret. The baby, Max, wasn't Marc's biological son, but the way the Callahans fawned over him, you'd never know it. Both kids, Max and Abby, were well loved and welcomed with open arms.

Her mother had found a way to speed up the process of getting the grandchildren she'd always wanted. Although Maddy knew she was literally counting the days until either Kari or Paige announced they were pregnant.

"I'm fine, really," she assured them. She looked for Noah, disappointed to see he'd stepped back, remaining near the doorway as if he didn't belong. "Thanks to Noah. He saved my life more times than I can count."

Several Callahan heads swiveled in his direction and even from here she could see him blush from the intense attention.

"Thanks, Sinclair," Matt and Mike said at the same time. They glanced at each other and snickered.

Maddy kept her gaze on Noah, silently asking him to come closer. He didn't.

Max squirmed and kicked so Nan handed him over to Marc. His wails grew louder.

"Oh, dear, we'd better get Max home for a nap," Kari said, taking her son into her arms.

"Yes, we'll need to head home, too," Paige said.

"I wouldn't mind some rest," Maddy said.

"We'll all go," her mother agreed. "We'll check back later, okay?"

"Thanks, Mom." It took several minutes for her family to file out of the room, and she couldn't help but be thankful for the silence they left behind. She loved every one of them more than anything, but the ache in her head appreciated the quiet. When she saw Noah move toward the door, she called, "Wait."

He stopped, then turned toward her. "What is it?"

"Please stay." When she raised her hand, he stepped forward to take it. "I feel safer when you're with me."

"Of course," he said without hesitation.

"Remember when you asked me if someone—a man—hurt me?" she asked.

Noah went tense instantly knowing what she meant. "Yes."

"Thankfully I escaped, but it was a close call," she admitted. "I've avoided men since the incident, except for you, Noah."

His expression softened and he bent down, gently pressing a kiss to her forehead. "I'm glad. Even though I want to break his face."

She smiled, filling her head with his woodsy scent. "He's not worth the effort. But I do have a favor to ask."

"Anything."

His quick response warmed her heart. "Will you keep me company as I continue prepping for the trial?"

"Absolutely. Although I want you to remain in the hospital overnight. No more taking chances with your health."

Tomorrow was Friday, which would leave only three days to get ready for the trial. She should continue preparing witnesses. There were several officers yet that she hadn't worked with.

The pain in her head intensified, making her realize that maybe she was about as ready as she needed to be.

"I will if you stay with me," she acquiesced.

A smile tugged at the corner of his mouth. "You have a deal."

Maddy closed her eyes and felt every ounce of tension leave her body. With Noah at her side, she could face just about anything.

The three days before the trial passed in a blur. Maddy couldn't work nonstop the way she normally did, and that only added to her frustration.

Noah displayed infinite patience, and she knew she was fortunate to have him staying close to her side while she either slept or prepared for the trial. Since Maddy's condo was still fire damaged, she and Noah moved to a motel not far from the courthouse, paid for by her boss, Jarrod Fine.

Early Monday morning, Maddy woke up feeling better than she had since the warehouse shooting. Her rib still screamed at her if she moved too quickly, or coughed or sneezed, but the pain in her head had finally receded to a tolerable level.

She dressed carefully in a red power suit and a black blouse, refusing to let Pietro know how close he'd come to achieving his goal of getting rid of her.

"Wow," Noah said as he emerged from his connecting room. His gaze held frank admiration. "You look amazing."

"So do you." Noah wore a navy blue suit, white shirt and red tie. She'd rearranged her witness list so that Noah would be first to testify. It was good for her case, plus, she thought selfishly, he'd be free to sit in the courtroom once he'd finished testifying.

For a moment she just stared at him. In the past few days she'd avoided personal conversations, forcing herself to focus on the trial. But at the moment, she couldn't think of anything but how much Noah meant to her.

She walked over to him, reaching up to straighten his tie, even though it wasn't at all crooked. "Noah, once this trial is over, I'd like to see you again."

He seemed flabbergasted by her statement. "Um, you would?"

His less than enthusiastic response wasn't reassuring; still, she soldiered on. "I'd love for you to join me for church services followed by Sunday brunch with my family."

The tension eased from his body. "Oh, sure. That sounds great. In fact, you should know that I've been praying a lot recently."

"You have?" She was touched by the return of his faith. "I'm happy to hear that."

He reached up and brushed a stray hair off her cheek. "Mostly about you, Maddy. You keep saying I've saved your life, but in reality, you've saved mine, too. More than you realize."

"Oh, Noah." She reached up and kissed him. For a moment he held her close, then he quickly let her go. She missed having his arms around her but stepped back, anxious to get to the courthouse. "We'll talk further after the trial, okay?"

"You and your deals," he lightly teased.

They pulled on their winter gear and walked outside. There was a hint of sunlight on the horizon, but the air was crisp and cold.

They were the first ones in line at the courthouse doorway. She showed her badge so the sheriff's deputy waved her through without making her go through the metal detector. Noah had to go through the process of emptying his pockets and being scanned through, but since he was a witness, he couldn't carry his weapon.

Up in Judge Dugan's courtroom, Maddy took her seat at the prosecutor's table and pulled out her notes.

This was it.

The moment she'd been waiting for. Despite losing a few of her witnesses, she still had what she believed was a solid case. In fact, the news of Lance Arvani's death had rippled through what was left of Pietro's organization and Jackson Dellis was among others who were now willing to talk in exchange for a lighter sentence.

Dellis had admitted that setting up his own murder had been an attempt to discredit Noah Sinclair and his subsequent testimony against Pietro. A plan that had, unfortunately, backfired. Maddy was sure that putting Dellis on the stand would be the final nail in Pietro's case.

Over the next ninety minutes, the courtroom filled up. Two deputies brought in Alexander Pietro, dressed in a suave pin-striped suit that was supposed to make him look professional but only reminded her of old gangster movies.

A woman dressed in a tight gold sweater dress and spiked heels entered the gallery, choosing to sit almost directly behind Pietro. Maddy frowned, wondering who she was. Pietro didn't have any family that they'd been able to find, and his former girlfriend, Rachel Graber, had been gunned down outside her safe house.

Maddy leaned toward her brother Matt. "I need to know who that woman is," she whispered.

Matt nodded, rose to his feet and subtly snapped a picture with his phone before leaving the courtroom.

Judge Dugan called the proceedings to order and once they finished with their jury selection, Maddy was allowed to call her first witness, Milwaukee police officer Noah Sinclair.

Noah did an amazing job on the stand, the way she knew he would. The jury listened intently to his testimony and one of the younger female jurors kept staring at Noah with obvious interest.

Maddy swallowed the ridiculous surge of jealousy and continued asking questions related to Alexander Pietro's arrest. By the time she finished and Pietro's lawyer had a chance to cross-examine Noah, it was clear that Pietro's defense was in trouble.

When Noah was finished, Judge Dugan excused him from the stand. Maddy looked at her notes for a minute. "The People would like to call Officer Charles Wynn to the stand," she said, turning toward the back of the courtroom.

Without warning, the woman in gold lunged at Maddy, her long fingernails aimed directly at her face. Before Maddy could do more than take a stumbling step backward, Noah grabbed the woman around the waist and swung her away from Maddy. The woman's talon-like fingernails raked down Noah's neck, drawing blood before he managed to get her under control.

"Order," Judge Dugan shouted, banging his gavel. "Order in the courtroom!"

The bailiff and another deputy ran over to help subdue the woman, slapping cuffs on her and hauling her away. Maddy rushed toward Noah. The scratches were long but not deep. "Are you all right?"

"I'll live," Noah grunted.

Matt came in and headed toward them. "I guess I'm too late to tell you that the woman is Aleshia Tanner and she's Pietro's newest girlfriend."

Maddy let out a sigh. "I figured something like that."

"I want this courtroom cleared immediately," Judge Dugan said. "Counsel will report to my chambers in five minutes."

Maddy didn't want to leave Noah, but she didn't want to be held in contempt, either. "Matt, stay with Noah, okay? I'd like you both to wait for me. This shouldn't take long."

Judge Dugan was not at all happy with the defense and quickly made his feelings known. "The courtroom will be closed to the public moving forward," he said in a stern voice. "And I strongly suggest Mr. Pietro consider accepting a plea bargain. After that fiasco in there, the State will give him a better deal than the jury will."

"I'll see what I can do," Pietro's attorney muttered.

"Twenty-five years with the chance at parole after twenty instead of life in prison without a chance of parole," Maddy said. "The offer is only good until tomorrow morning. Trust me, the jury won't hesitate to sentence him to life without a chance at parole."

Pietro's attorney nodded again and quickly made his escape.

As she left Judge Dugan's chambers, she stopped short when she saw ADA Blake Ratcliff standing just outside the doorway, obviously coming from some other trial. Instantly nausea swirled in her stomach. "What do you want?" she asked harshly.

"Hi, Maddy." He smiled without humor. "I've been waiting for a chance to talk to you."

"Too bad. I'm not interested in talking to you." She was glad that her voice sounded strong, hoping he wouldn't notice the way her hands trembled. How was it possible that she once thought he was handsome? His fancy suit and slicked-back hair seemed ridiculous compared to Noah's rugged attractiveness.

Blake took another step toward her. She froze, then raised her chin as if daring him to come closer. Her brothers had taught her to fend for herself, and right now she couldn't think of a better person to lash out at than the man who'd tried forcing her against his desk.

Suddenly Noah came around the corner, his gaze zeroing in on Blake the way an eagle spied a fish. "Didn't you hear the lady? She said she's not interested in talking to you."

Blake scowled and turned toward Noah. She took advantage of Noah's interruption and quickly walked past, holding her head high. Once she reached Noah's side, she glanced back over her shoulder.

"Don't come near me again, Blake," she warned. "Next time, I'll press charges."

Blake's face turned beet red with anger, but when Noah wrapped his arm around Maddy's shoulders, he shrugged, turned and walked away.

"He's the one who tried to hurt you, isn't he?" Noah asked in a low voice.

Maddy raised her gaze to his. "Yes."

Noah's brown eyes darkened with anger. "You really should press charges."

"Maybe I will." She slipped her arm around his waist and rested her head against his shoulder. "Blake isn't important, Noah, but you are."

"Me?" He sounded confused.

She shifted so that she could see his face. "I care about you, Noah. I know you said you didn't do relationships, but I hope you'll make an exception for me."

"Maddy, I—don't know what to say."

The flame of hope in her heart flickered. "Say you'll give us a chance."

Noah's answer was to pull her close and to kiss her. She clung to him, reveling in his embrace. This was what had been missing from her life. A man, a partner to share things with.

To love.

"I'll be honored to give us a chance, because I love you, Maddy," Noah whispered in her ear.

The flame brightened, filling her heart with warmth. "I love you, too."

"Oh, yippee skippy," Matt said in a sarcastic voice intended to be overheard. "Another Callahan bites the dust."

Noah let out a choked laugh but didn't loosen his grip. "I don't think being in love qualifies for biting the dust."

"Go away, Matt," Maddy said, waving a hand at him. "We don't need you after all."

"Good thing she loves you, Noah, since I distinctly remember telling you to stay away from her," Matt said.

"Knock it off already!" Maddy threw the words over her shoulder. "Three's a crowd, Matt."

"Okay, but you need to answer your phone, sis," Matt said. "Your boss is on the line. Apparently Pietro accepted your offer. The trial is officially over."

"That's great news," Noah agreed.

"Yes." Maddy rose up on her tiptoes to kiss him again. The trial was over.

But her life with Noah was just beginning.

Epilogue

Christmas Eve

Maddy opened the door, smiling brightly in greeting. Noah stepped over the threshold into the Callahan family home, struck anew by the plethora of Christmas decorations. The place looked amazing, and he was glad Maddy was living there while her condo was being rebuilt. Although she'd already mentioned that living downtown had lost its appeal.

He hoped that meant she'd be willing to consider living somewhere more modest, like the small home he'd purchased last summer. It wasn't nearly as grand as her mother's home, but it was a start.

"Noah!" Maddy greeted him with an exuberant hug and kiss. He held her for an extra minute, savoring the cinnamon scent that clung to her skin. "You're late," she accused softly.

He wasn't about to explain why he'd run late, at least not yet. "Everyone else is here?" He swallowed hard. "Your entire family?"

"Yep. Come on. Dinner won't be ready for a while

yet, so everyone is gathered in the family room." She took his hand and tugged him toward the sound of voices intermixed with laughter.

The idea of giving Maddy his gift tonight had seemed like a good idea at the time, but now he was having second thoughts. The family room was chock-full of Callahans. He knew them all by name, of course, and in birth order, too. Marc was the eldest, married to Kari, then came Miles, who was married to Paige. Then there was Mitch, Michael, Matthew and finally Maddy.

The woman he loved with his whole heart.

Maddy took a seat on the corner of the sofa and indicated he should sit beside her.

Instead he walked around until he was directly in front of her and dropped to one knee.

The room instantly went silent; even the kids didn't make a sound. He wasn't sure if that was a good thing or not, but he'd come this far. It was too late to turn back now.

"Maddy? Will you please marry me?" He took the ring box out of his pocket, opened the lid and held it out to her. Picking up the diamond ring had been the reason he'd run a little late.

"Oh, Noah! Yes! Of course I'll marry you!" She didn't bother looking at the ring but launched herself into his arms.

"Yay!"

"It's about time!"

"Wow, that was quick!"

"Aw, isn't that sweet?"

The comments from her family were like white noise in the background. Nothing mattered at that moment except Maddy.

She'd said yes!

"Is there gonna be a baby in her tummy, too?" a young voice asked. "Like Auntie Kari?"

The adults laughed at Abby's innocent question. Noah hoped his face wasn't too red.

"Wait, what?" Maddy pulled out of his arms, turning to look at her eldest brother. "You're having a baby?"

"We are," Marc confirmed. "In about four and a half months, so please plan to have your wedding before Kari delivers."

"Yeah, because, um, so are we," Paige spoke up, blushing as Miles placed his hand over her still flat belly. "Having a baby, I mean. About the same time as Marc and Kari."

The room broke out into laughter and applause with a few low male groans from the brothers who were still single. Noah didn't mind fitting in his wedding to Maddy before or after babies. This was the family he'd dreamed of.

With Maddy at his side, he was exactly where he belonged.

* * * * *

IDENTITY UNKNOWN

Terri Reed

To my family for always believing in me
and to Leah for friendship and laughter.

Have I not commanded you?
Be strong and courageous. Do not be afraid;
do not be discouraged, for the Lord your God
will be with you wherever you go.
—*Joshua* 1:9

Chapter One

"Two guards at the south entrance." Canada Border Services Agency officer Nathanial Longhorn spoke into the microphone attached to his flak vest.

On the cold December morning, Nathanial stared through the scope on his C7 assault sniper rifle from his perch on the southeast corner of a warehouse overlooking the commercial shipping port of Saint John Harbour, New Brunswick. The overcast sky shadowed the world in a gray haze.

His breath condensed into a white cloud, obscuring his vision in the threatening chill of an impending snowstorm. A whiteout was the last thing his team needed. He prayed the bad weather held off for a few more hours.

"Copy that." Through Nathanial's earpiece came the reply from his friend and fellow Integrated Border Enforcement Taskforce team member, US Immigration and Customs Enforcement agent Blake Fallon.

Blake motioned and two members of the team below split off to subdue the guards.

Nathanial kept an alert eye for anything that would

impede or jeopardize the IBETs members on the ground as they stealthily made their way down the street to another warehouse a block away.

They were determined to bring down an arms dealer and his network of smugglers who illegally brought small and large weapons across the border between the two countries. The latest intelligence reported a shipment of handguns would be brought into Canada tonight.

The men who made up the IBETs team were from various law enforcement agencies on both sides of the international boundary line between Canada and the United States. Nathanial was proud to be a part of the team and would give his life for each and every one of the other team members regardless of their nationality.

The successful completion of this mission would be a welcome Christmas present, indeed.

He intended to head home to Saskatchewan for a much-needed respite with his family. Though he doubted the visit would be very relaxing. His mother and grandmother would be on him about fulfilling his destiny and settling down to provide grandchildren.

An old sorrow stirred, but he quickly tamped it down.

Despite his grandmother's certainty that there was a soul mate out there for him, Nathanial was skeptical about love and marriage. He'd come close once with his high school sweetheart, but that relationship had ended in tragedy and heartbreak. He'd decided then going it alone was better than opening himself up to that kind of pain again.

Besides, he liked his bachelor life too much to tie the knot like some of his friends and coworkers. Though

Nathanial never lacked for female company, the thought of hearth and home made him want to run screaming into the night.

Being domesticated wasn't on his agenda. He was over thirty and set in his ways. He liked the freedom of taking off on an assignment at a moment's notice. He enjoyed the variety of dating different women, always careful to make sure any woman he spent time with knew he wasn't interested in anything serious or long-term.

Some ladies took that as a challenge to change his mind, and others walked away before they became too attached.

He tolerated the former until he couldn't and appreciated the latter.

He'd yet to meet a woman who made him want to change his mind. And frankly, he doubted he ever would.

A chill skated over the nape of his neck, drawing his attention to the current assignment. Once the two guards were out of commission, Nathanial did another visual sweep. All appeared clear. Good. He was cold and ready to wrap this up so he could have a cup of hot coffee and warm himself by a roaring fire.

He was about to give the go-ahead to the team when his attention snagged on a gold luxury sedan turning onto the street a few blocks away.

The arms dealer? Or someone in the wrong place at the wrong time? "Hold up."

He prayed the car kept driving, because if it didn't, this op was going to become more complicated.

Behind him, the scuff of a shoe on the concrete roof sent his heart hammering. He rolled onto his back, bringing the rifle up, his finger hovering over the trigger. A man loomed over him. Confusion and panic vied for dominance. Then the butt of an automatic submachine gun rammed into his skull.

And the world went dark.

Deputy Sheriff Audrey Martin sang along with the Christmas carol playing on the patrol car radio. The first fingers of dawn rose over the horizon. From her spot parked on a rise overlooking the small fishing village she'd been born in, she surveyed the streets and buildings of the township of Calico Bay, Maine, dusted in white.

This early-morning patrol was her favorite time, especially in winter. Gone were the summer windjammers and tour boats from the harbor. Now only the commercial fishing vessels and tugboats remained, most of which were already out to sea, while everyone else stayed snug in their beds. The population of the town receded to those whose lives began and ended here. Fishermen who made their living off the ocean, always hunting for a good day's catch, and those who supported the fishing industry.

She'd been on the job for less than a year and already she wanted to run for sheriff when the office's current occupant retired. There would be those who would cry nepotism, because Sheriff David Crump was her mother's aunt's husband. And there would be those who would oppose her for the simple fact she was female. Two strikes against her.

But she'd win them over with her capabilities. She had to. Failure wasn't an option. Too many people expected her to fail. She wanted to disappoint them. She wanted to make her family proud. Especially her mother and father, rest his soul.

He'd been gone since she was a child, but she still wanted to honor his memory by doing well and serving her community.

Having grown up with a doctor for a mother and a fisherman for a father, she knew hard work and commitment were the keys to succeeding. Not that she needed much beyond her studio apartment and the respect of the town.

Though her mother constantly warned her if she didn't take another chance on love, she'd end up old and alone.

Better that than having her heart trampled on all over again. Those were three years of her life she'd never get back. Three years wasted on a man who had cheated on her and then called her a fool for believing in love.

Well, she wouldn't be making that mistake again.

She warmed her hands in front of the car's heater vents and sang beneath her breath, not really in tune but enjoying singing anyway. Outside the confines of the patrol car, snow flurries swirled in the gray morning light and danced on the waves of the Atlantic Ocean crashing on the shores of Calico Bay, a sweeping inlet that formed a perfect half-moon with a picturesque view of their friends across the waterway in New Brunswick.

The radio attached to her uniform jacket crackled and buzzed before the sheriff's department dispatcher, Ophelia Leighton, came on the line. "Unit one, do you copy?"

Thumbing the answer button, Audrey replied, "Yes, dispatch, I copy."

"Uh, there's a reported sighting of a—"

The radio crackled and popped. In the background, Audrey heard Ophelia talking, then the deep timbre of the sheriff's voice. "Uh, sorry about that." Ophelia came back on the line. "We're getting mixed reports, but bottom line there's something washed up on the shore of the Pine Street beach."

"Something?" Audrey buckled her seat belt, shifted the car into Drive and took off toward the north side of town. "What kind of something?"

"Well, one report said a beached whale," Ophelia came back with. "Another said dead shark. But a couple people called in to say a drowned fisherman."

Audrey's gut clenched. All sorts of things found their way into the inlet from the ocean's current. None of those scenarios sounded good. Especially the last one. The town didn't need the heartache of losing one of their own so close to Christmas. Not that any time was a good time.

Her heart cramped with sorrow for the father she'd lost so many years ago to the sea.

She prayed that whoever was on the beach wasn't someone she knew. It would be sad enough for a stranger to die on their shore.

Pine Street ended at a public beach, which in the summer would be teeming with tourists and locals alike. She brought her vehicle to a halt in the cul-de-sac next to an early-model pickup truck where a small group of gawkers stood on the road side of the concrete barrier. Obviously the ones who'd called the sheriff's department.

Bracing herself for the biting cold, she climbed out and plopped her brimmed hat on her head to prevent her body heat from escaping through her scalp. With shoulders squared and head up, she approached the break in the seawall.

"Audrey." Clem Previs rushed forward to grip her sleeve, his veined hand nearly blue from the cold. The retired fisherman ran the bait shop on the pier with his two sons. "Shouldn't you wait for the sheriff?"

Others crowded around her. Mary Fleischer from the dime store. Pat Garvey from the hardware store and the librarian, Lucy Concord. All stared at her with expectant and skeptical gazes. These men and women had watched her grow up from a wee babe to the woman she was today. She held affection for each one, and their lack of confidence in her hurt.

Pressing her lips together, she covered Clem's hand with hers. He felt like a Popsicle. "Clem, I can handle this," she assured him and the others.

Her breath came out in little puffs. The ground beneath their feet crunched with a top layer of ice. "You all need to get inside somewhere warm. I can't deal with more than one crisis at a time, and I sure don't want to be having to give you mouth to mouth out here in the cold."

Clem clucked. "Don't get lippy with me, young lady."

She smiled and patted his hand. "I wouldn't dream of it. Now I've got to do my job."

"Seems someone is already taking care of it," Lucy said, pointing.

About ten yards down the beach, a man dressed from head to toe in black and wearing a mask that obscured his face struggled to drag something toward the water's edge.

Audrey narrowed her gaze. Her pulse raced. Amid a tangle of seaweed and debris, she could make out the dark outline of a large body. She shivered with dread. That certainly wasn't a fish, whale or shark. Definitely human. And from the size, she judged the body to be male.

And someone was intent on returning the man to the ocean.

Heart thrumming and adrenaline flooding her body, she took off at a fast clip, but the thirty-two pounds of gear she carried on her person, plus her bulky boots, made maneuvering in the sand difficult. Careful to keep from tripping over clumps of kelp and driftwood that had settled on the beach from the wind and ocean tide, she narrowed the gap.

"Hey!" she shouted. "Stop where you are! Sheriff's department."

The suspect froze, then dropped the prone man's feet in the surf. The perpetrator whipped toward her with a large-caliber gun aimed in her direction.

Her breath caught. She faced her worst fear as an officer.

He fired. And missed.

The sound of the gun blast echoed through the morning air, scattering a flock of seagulls from the water's edge. Fragments of sand pelted her uniform.

Stunned, Audrey dropped to her belly, knocking the wind momentarily out of her. Sand clung to her, getting in her mouth, her nose, as she drew in a breath. She fought through the panic and called on her training. She drew her sidearm. "Halt!"

He ignored her and ran across the sand, heading for the berm separating the road from the beach. She shot at him, the sound exploding in her brain and muffling the world.

He hunkered inward, protecting his head, but kept running. With her ears ringing, she jumped to her feet, torn between giving chase and checking on the man in the sand and making sure Clem and the others weren't hit by the assault.

But the man with the gun posed a threat she needed to neutralize. Now, before he hurt anyone else.

She sprinted after him, kicking up sand with each step while radioing for help. "Shots fired! Officer needs backup."

"Sheriff's on his way!" came Ophelia's barely audible reply through the fuzzy haze inside Audrey's ears.

"Suspect heading toward Prescott Road," Audrey relayed to the dispatcher, praying Ophelia could hear her, since she couldn't be sure how loud or soft she was yelling because her hearing was muffled from the gunfire.

The deep drifts of sand hindered her progress but also the perpetrator's.

Audrey gained on him while trying to aim her weapon. "Stop or I'll shoot!"

Before she could pull the trigger, the suspect reached the berm and disappeared over the top. Tall sea grass obscured him from view. Deep grooves in the sand from his boots were the only sign he'd even been there.

Breathing heavily, Audrey reached the berm and crawled up the sandy embankment in a crouch. She crested the top in time to see a black Suburban peel away from the edge of the road and speed down the street. Before she could get off a shot, the vehicle careened around the corner and disappeared from view.

Frustrated, Audrey pounded the hard-packed sand with a fist. She thumbed her mic while sliding down the sandy berm. "I lost the suspect on Prescott. Black Sub-urban with missing plates and tinted windows."

She didn't wait to hear Ophelia's answer as she scrambled to the sandy shore and hurried back toward the seawall. "Clem! Mary!"

The four popped up from behind the concrete barrier. "Here!"

Relief nearly made Audrey's knees buckle. "Anyone hit?"

"No, Audrey," Pat yelled back. "You?"

"You okay, Deputy Martin?" Lucy called out.

"I'm good." She did an about-face and ran back to the man lying motionless on the shore. The water lapped at his feet. If she'd arrived any later, the man would be fish bait once again. How had the masked man known where he'd washed ashore?

Keeping her gaze alert, in case the assailant returned, she knelt down next to the supine body, noting with a frown that he was dressed in what could only be categorized as tactical attire, minus the hardware.

Definitely not a fisherman.

And definitely not from around here.

She pressed her fingers against the side of the man's neck, fully expecting to find no pulse, as no one could survive for long in the frigid Atlantic Ocean, not to mention being exposed to the elements onshore. The skin on his neck was like ice, but beneath her cold fingers a pulse beat. Slow, but there!

With a renewed spike of adrenaline, she grabbed the mic on her shoulder. "Send the ambulance to the beach. We have a live one here. Hurry, though!"

"Copy that." Ophelia's surprise matched Audrey's.

Audrey slipped her arms under the man's torso and

dragged him to the dry sand. Then she unzipped her jacket, thankful she'd worn her thick, cable-knit sweater over her thermals today, and shrugged out of the outerwear. She laid it over the man on the beach.

Turning to the group of town elders still gawking like she were the main act at the circus, she called out, "Clem, is that your truck parked out there?"

"Sure is," he yelled back.

"Do you have any blankets or jackets? I need them!"

Clem and Pat hustled away, leaving the two older ladies huddled together, staring in her direction. Audrey turned her attention back to the man lying on the sand. Dark hair hung in chunks covering his face. Dried blood matted some of the hair near his temple. He had on black jackboots, similar to the ones she wore, black cargo pants, a black turtleneck and gloves.

She made a quick check for identification. None. She placed a hand on his shoulder. "Lord, I don't know why this man has washed ashore here or what purpose You have, but I pray that he lives. Have mercy and grace on this man. And let us find the masked man without any lives lost. Amen."

The man stirred and moaned as he thrashed on the sand, giving Audrey her first real glimpse of his face as his hair dropped away. Dark lashes splayed over high cheekbones. A well-formed mouth with lips nearly blue from the cold. He had handsome features. Curiosity bubbled inside her. Who was he and what was his story? Why was someone trying to kill him?

"Sir." Audrey gave his shoulder a gentle shake.

A word slipped out of his mouth.

"What?" Audrey bent closer, turning her ear toward his mouth.

"Betrayed…" He stilled and slipped back into un-consciousness.

A sense of urgency trembled through her. What did he mean? Had he betrayed someone? Or had someone betrayed him?

She still didn't hear the siren. Where was the ambulance? It wasn't like the medical center where Sean James kept the bus parked was that far away. Calico Bay was barely the length of a football field. Keeping her gun ready, she stayed alert for any signs of the masked man returning.

Clem and Pat picked their way to her side, their arms loaded with a plethora of blankets and jackets. She quickly packed them around her charge. Whatever this man's story, whether good or bad, she had a sworn duty to serve and protect the community of Calico Bay, and for now that included this man.

The shrill siren filled the air. Good. About time. Within minutes Sean, his intern and the sheriff were hustling across the beach with a stretcher. Sean ambled toward her on an unsteady gait. He carried his medical bag in one gloved hand. A yellow beanie was pulled low over his auburn hair and covered his ears.

His intense brown gaze swept the area as if looking for insurgents. He'd been a medic in the military before losing a leg at the knee when an IUD exploded. The town had been heartbroken at his loss but thankful their star high school quarterback had returned to Calico Bay alive.

Though Sean had slipped into a depression when he'd first come home, the town's people wouldn't let that continue and had pooled their resources to buy the ambulance and make him the town's official EMT.

Audrey moved out of the way to allow Sean and his intern, a kid named Wes, to work on the unconscious man.

"I've got all deputies out looking for the SUV. What do we have here?" Sheriff David Crump asked. He was a big, brawny man with a shock of white hair that had once been as dark as night and a ready grin that had captured her great-aunt's heart back when they were in high school. Now if only Audrey could capture his respect as easily.

She related what she knew.

Sean and Wes rolled the man onto the stretcher. She reached for the edge of the litter along with the sheriff and helped Sean and Wes carry the man to the waiting ambulance. The older folks, still congregating near Clem's truck, watched with avid expressions.

Once the bay doors were closed, the ambulance drove away. The sheriff climbed into his car and took off with his lights flashing. This was going to be big news in town. Audrey moved toward her vehicle, intent on following the ambulance to the medical center. For some reason she felt an urge to stick close to the unconscious man. Probably because he was helpless and at their mercy.

There was something about him that made her think he wasn't going to like being in that state long once he came to. Maybe it was the strength in his chin or the boldness of his cheeks or the width of his shoulders. Or possibly woman's intuition mingled with her cop sense.

"Do you know who he is?" Mary asked, trying to waylay her.

"No, ma'am," Audrey replied and popped open the driver's side door. "You all go home now before you catch a chill. We still have an armed man loose in the township. Be careful and call the station if you see anyone or anything suspicious."

Without waiting for their reactions, she drove through the center of town toward the medical center that served as the town's hospital without turning on her lights. Up ahead the ambulance stopped for a red light at one of only two traffic lights in the town. She stacked up behind the sheriff's car.

When the light turned green, Sean stepped on the gas. The ambulance was in the middle of the intersection when the same dark SUV with a huge brush guard on the front end ran the red light and plowed into the back of the ambulance.

Audrey's mind scrambled to make sense of what she was seeing even as she rammed the gearshift into Park, unbuckled her seat belt and jumped out of her car while once again palming her sidearm. Twice in one day was a new record.

The SUV's tires screeched as it backed up, spun in a half circle and sped off in the direction it had come from. The sheriff's car jolted forward, jumped the curb and took off after the hit-and-run vehicle. Audrey radioed for more backup, then raced to the front of the ambulance. Smoke billowed from the engine block. "Sean! Wes!"

The world tipped and jostled. Pain exploded everywhere. He tried to force his eyelids open, but nothing cooperated. His arms were strapped down. So were his legs.

Where was he? Why was he trapped in some sort of roller coaster? His head pounded. He tried to recall what had led him to this place in time, but a dark void sucked him in. The last thing he heard before the blackness took him back was a woman's panicked voice. He wished he could help her, but he couldn't even help himself.

Audrey reached the ambulance driver's door just as Sean swung it open. She helped him to the curb. A gash on his forehead bled. Then she ran back for Wes. Thankfully the passenger side door opened easily. The kid was slumped sideways, the white air bag in his lap.

"Let me get the door," a male voice said from behind her.

She nodded gratefully at a local man who'd been passing by on the sidewalk. Once the passenger door was open, Audrey and the Good Samaritan, Jordon, got Wes out. He came with a groan, too, as they sat him beside Sean.

"Jordon, help me with the guy in back," Audrey instructed. The brunt of the impact had been aimed at the back bay. The double doors were crumpled. She let out a growl of frustration and ran to her car's trunk, where she kept a set of Jaws of Life. She'd never needed the equipment before and had hoped never to use it, but she hefted them into her hands, feeling their unfamiliar weight.

The sound of the Calico Bay fire engine rent the air. Momentary relief renewed her energy. Help was on the way. But she had to get inside the bay and make sure the man she'd rescued from the beach hadn't died in the crash, which was no doubt the guy in the SUV's intent.

Before she and Jordon could get into the back bay, the fire truck pulled up. Three men and two women hustled over. Audrey let two of the biggest fire crew members take over with the door.

As soon as the doors on the bay allowed access, she climbed inside. The stretcher had tipped but was wedged between the two benches, providing some protection for the man strapped to the gurney. Thankfully the impact of the SUV crashing into the ambulance didn't seem to have caused the patient any more damage. She checked his pulse and let out a relieved breath.

But someone was determined to kill this man.

And it was her job to keep him alive.

Chapter Two

Audrey finished her after-action report on the shooting and put it on the sheriff's desk—he liked things old-school—but she also sent him an electronic version. Her heart still hammered too fast from this morning's activities. Focusing on the paperwork helped to calm her nerves. But now a bout of anxiety kicked back in. Danger had come to her small part of the world. And she didn't like it one bit.

She stopped by Deputy Harrison's desk. His light brown hair was shorn short, which emphasized the hard lines of his jaw. "Hey, Mike, any idea where the sheriff is?"

"Home, I'd imagine," the thirtysomething deputy replied without glancing up.

She corralled her irritation. He was one of those who weren't comfortable having a female on duty. Earning his respect would be nearly as difficult as that of her great-uncle. Infusing goodwill into her voice—it was Christmastime, after all—she said, "If you see him, would you mind letting him know I'm heading to the medical center to check on our John Doe?"

Mike lifted his gray eyes to her. "Why? The guy's still unconscious. And Gregson's there."

She couldn't explain her driving need to go to the medical center or the need to make sure the man from the beach was safe. So she settled for something the other deputy would understand. "It's my case."

She hurried from the sheriff's station, acknowledging to herself she easily could have called her mom, the primary doctor who was tending to the man they'd rescued on the beach, for an update. But she wanted to see for herself.

Night had fallen several hours ago, and now the world was bathed in the soft glow from the moon and the streetlamps decorated with twinkling lights. A large Christmas tree in the middle of the town park rose high in the air and shimmered with a thousand tiny lights and a brightly lit star.

Normally she enjoyed seeing the tree and the town in the throes of the holiday season, but tonight edginess had her hands gripping the steering wheel in nervous anticipation as she drove.

The news media had picked up the story, reporting an unconscious John Doe found on the beach. The sheriff hadn't released the man's photo. Yet. If the man didn't regain consciousness soon, they'd have to reach out to the public in hopes of identifying the stranger.

No doubt reporters from the bigger towns would descend on Calico Bay and the medical center, making the sheriff's department's job harder. With more strangers in town, finding the masked man would be more difficult. She'd already made calls to all the gas stations, restaurants and grocery stores, asking everyone to keep an eye out for an outsider. In winter, visitors were an oddity in the close-knit community.

Audrey's gaze searched the streets for any sign of trouble, namely in the form of a masked man in black with a large gun. It bugged her no end that the bandit in the SUV had disappeared. The sheriff had chased the offending vehicle for several miles before the creep threw out a handful of spikes that had punctured the sheriff's tires, allowing the suspect to escape. That wasn't an amateur move. Given how the victim and the assailant were dressed, Audrey had a suspicion there was some paramilitary-type thing going on here. Not a comforting thought.

She parked at the side entrance next to her mom's sedan and went inside the brick building, pausing at the nurses' station to ask for her mom.

"Dr. Martin is with a patient at the moment," Katie, the nurse on duty, informed her. Katie shoved her red hair off her shoulder and leaned close. "So was there really a shootout this morning on the beach?"

Resting her hands on the utility belt at her waist, Audrey towered over the other woman. "Yes. No one was hit, thankfully. Where's the man who was brought in this morning?"

"Second floor. Deputy Gregson's on duty."

"Thanks." Audrey bypassed the elevator and took the stairs, preferring to move at her own rapid pace rather than waiting. When she emerged from the stairwell, she halted. Deputy Gregson wasn't at his post.

A bad feeling tightened the muscles of her neck. He should've been sitting outside one of the rooms, but the chair at the other end of the hall was empty. A magazine lay on the floor nearby. She unlatched the strap on her holster and gripped the butt of the Glock as she moved with caution toward the last room.

She passed the nurses' desk. The older woman manning the station glanced up from the report she was studying. "Evening, Deputy."

"Where's Deputy Gregson?"

The nurse popped up from her chair and frowned. "Well, he was sitting right over there last I checked, but I've been busy so I haven't paid much attention." She sat back down with a shrug. "Maybe he's using the restroom."

"Maybe." Though the itch at the back of Audrey's neck was saying no. Something was wrong. She paused outside John Doe's door, withdrew her weapon, took a calming breath and then pushed the door open.

Lying in the hospital bed, the man blinked at the dark figure towering over him.

The stranger grabbed a pillow, his intent clear as he held the white fluff in both hands and brought it toward the man's face, clearly meaning to smother him. Why would he choose that method of elimination? The answer came with lightning speed. Suffocating him was soundless, providing the goon more opportunity to get away cleanly.

Fear, stark and vivid, flooded his system, short-circuiting his brain in a shower of pain. The patient in the bed lifted his arms to ward off the attack, but his limbs felt heavy. His body responded sluggishly, as if he were fighting to move through mud.

There was no way he could defend himself.

He was about to die. He didn't know why.

His mind reeled. The world receded. His limbs flopped back to the bed at his sides, and darkness claimed him once again.

* * *

Several things registered at once for Audrey as she stepped into John Doe's room. Deputy Gregson's prone body just inside the doorway. Blood from a gash on his head.

The same tall, muscular man dressed in dark clothing, with sand still clinging to his boots, stood holding a pillow in his hands, about to suffocate the unconscious man lying in the bed, hooked to a heart monitor and an IV.

"Stop, police!" she shouted.

The intruder spun to face her. The fury in his dark brown eyes, the only thing visible between his black beanie and the black neoprene half mask, was unmistakable when his gaze locked with hers. "You! Not again!" His voice was deep, gruff, muffled by the mask. "Stop interfering."

"Drop the pillow. Put your hands in the air," she commanded, bracing her feet apart in case she had to fire.

He threw the pillow, hitting her in the face and blocking her view for a split second, just enough for the man to use his shoulder to slam into her like a battering ram and knock her off her feet.

"Hey!" She landed on her backside with a jarring thud, her weapon hitting the tile floor and skidding away. The man jumped over her. She grabbed his ankle and hung on, tripping him. He went down, landing on his knees and hands with a grunt. He kicked her with his free foot, his heel smashing into her shoulder.

She ignored the blast of pain and scrambled for a better hold, but he twisted and jerked out of her grasp to race out of the room. She jumped to her feet, grabbed her gun from the floor and dashed after him. He disappeared down the stairwell.

"Call nine-one-one," Audrey shouted to the startled nurse as she raced passed the desk. "Check on Gregson and the patient."

Using caution, Audrey opened the stairwell door and peered inside. She heard the man's pounding footfalls going downstairs. She chased after him, leaping down the last few steps and careening out of the stairwell onto the first floor. Up ahead, the man slammed into an orderly, knocking him sideways, then the assailant hit the exit. Audrey ran outside but lost sight of him.

Not far away an engine turned over, and then tires screeched on the pavement.

Heart pumping with adrenaline, she rushed back inside and up to the second floor. She checked on Gregson, who now was sitting up. A nurse tended to the wound on his head.

"What happened?" Audrey asked the dazed officer.

"I was reading a magazine when someone came out of the room across the hall and attacked me," Gregson replied. "It was a blur. The guy had on a mask, and he hit me in the head with something hard. I didn't see what it was."

With her hand on her gun, Audrey stepped out of the room and pushed open the door to the unoccupied room across the hall. The window was open. She stuck her head out.

Footprints in the dusting of snow on the ledge gave Audrey a pretty good idea of how the perpetrator had gained access—he'd climbed the fire escape and shuffled along the ledge to the window. The lock had been broken. She slammed the window closed and made a mental note to have someone fix the latch as soon as possible.

Audrey returned to John Doe's room and addressed the nurse helping Gregson. "Is he going to be okay?"

"Yes," the woman said. "He'll need a couple of sutures. Dr. Martin will want to examine him to be sure he doesn't have a mild concussion."

"Okay, see that he's taken care of," Audrey said. She put her hand on Gregson's shoulder. "I'll take over the watch tonight. The sheriff should be here any moment. He'll want a full account."

Gregson nodded and looked a bit green around the edges as the nurse helped him to stand and led him out of the room.

Once alone with the unconscious man in the bed, Audrey checked the window, making sure the lock was intact and secure. She took several deep, calming breaths and let the adrenaline ebb away. She'd had more excitement in the past twenty-four hours than since graduating from the academy. She positioned the chair so she had a clear view of the door and the window in case the masked attacker decided to return.

"You're beautiful."

Startled, Audrey whipped around to find herself staring into the dark eyes of John Doe. His lopsided grin sucked the breath from her lungs. She'd never understood the term *roguishly handsome* until this moment. Even groggy and on pain meds, he affected her on an elemental level. Which made her extremely uneasy. What would he be like fully conscious?

Heart pounding, she stepped closer to the bed. "Who are you? What's your name?"

His eyelids fluttered, and he said something unintelligible.

She reached for the button to call the nurse when his fingers closed over her wrist, pressing against her skin where the sleeve of her uniform rode up. His touch was firm but gentle. Strong hands, and calloused, she noted in a bemused way that made her twitchy. She tugged on her arm, hoping he'd get a clue and release his hold. He didn't.

"You look like a Christmas ornament." His words were slurred. "Shiny. Pretty."

His hand dropped away as if he could no longer hold on. His head lolled to the side, and his eyes closed.

"Hey," Audrey said, giving him a slight shake. "Mister, I need you to wake up."

But he'd gone out again.

Okay, that was weird. He'd likened her to a Christmas ornament. Shiny—that was a new one. If she hadn't known he'd been conked on the head and was on mild painkillers, she'd have thought he was on some sort of hallucinogenic. Maybe he was on something stronger than the medical grade medicine. She'd have to ask her mother.

She sat but was too antsy to stay still. She paced at the foot of the bed, every few seconds checking to see if the man had regained consciousness again.

The door opened suddenly, sending her pulse skyrocketing and her hand reaching for her sidearm.

"Whoa, there," her great-uncle's deep voice intoned as he stepped into the room. "Just me."

She relaxed her stance. "Did you see Gregson?"

"Yep. He'll be fine." David moved to the end of the bed and set a fingerprint kit on the chair. "You've saved this man's life thrice now."

Her mouth twitched at her uncle's words. He'd once been a scholar of Old English before giving up academia and carving out a path in law enforcement. "I have a feeling the masked villain isn't going to give up."

He tipped his chin toward the man lying on the bed. "Has he come to?"

"Briefly."

"Did he say anything?"

She hesitated, unwilling to reveal the words that were still echoing inside her head. "Nothing useful. Gibberish. Do you know if a tox screen was done?"

David arched an eyebrow. "You know your mother. Of course that was one of the first things she did."

"Right." Her mother couldn't abide drugs. She'd lost her younger brother to the poison years ago. "And?"

"Clean blood. No track marks."

"Good." For some reason knowing John Doe wasn't a junkie pleased her. But just what and who he was remained a mystery, as did why someone was so ardently trying to kill him. What did John know? "The man who shot at me wasn't some garden-variety bad guy. Whatever John Doe is, he's into something bad."

"Yeah, I have that feeling, too. The road tacks the perp used to stop my car when I chased after him can be bought online easy enough. But there was skill involved."

In the melee of the crash and aftermath, she'd forgotten what John Doe had said on the beach. "He'd muttered a word when I first reached him—*betrayed*."

"That's interesting. And concerning. The masked man may have been his attacker from the get-go and is very determined to finish the job. I don't like it. I want you to go home," the sheriff said. "I'll stick around until Harrison and Paulson can get here."

She straightened. Did he think she wasn't doing a good job? "I'll stay."

"You've been on duty since five a.m."

"I'm not tired."

He sighed. "Let's get his prints and a photo. Then I'm ordering you to go home. In the morning you can search the criminal and missing-persons databases. Hopefully you'll come up with a name and a reason why someone wants him dead."

Audrey arrived at the station at 6 a.m. and uploaded the fingerprints she'd taken from their mysterious John Doe and his photo off her phone into the FBI's national criminal information center as well as the violent criminal apprehension program for missing persons.

Nothing turned up.

The man could be a Canadian, since the border between the two countries was only a few miles across the ocean. She sent his prints and his photo to the criminal investigation division of the Royal Canadian Mounted Police, Canada's federal policing agency. She provided her cell phone number so they could contact her directly.

Then she headed back to the medical center to relieve the sheriff. She met Deputy Paulson outside John Doe's room. "How did it go?"

"All quiet," he replied. "Sheriff's inside."

She entered, half hoping John Doe had awakened. He still slept. His face looked relaxed. His dark hair fell over his forehead, covering one eye. Beside him sat the sheriff with his arms folded over his massive chest, his chin tipped down and his eyes closed. Audrey hesitated, debating stepping back out.

"You're here early," the sheriff said softly, lifting his head.

She straightened and came fully into the room. "No hits on NCIC or ViCAP. I sent his info to the RCMP."

"Good thinking." He stood and stretched. "I'm going to grab some coffee. You want some?"

"No, thank you," she replied. His praise eased the worry from the night before that she wasn't doing a good job. Her spine straightened as she moved aside to let him pass.

She went to the window. Frost laced the edges of the glass. She stared at the tree line flanking the west side of the building. The green pine trees were sprinkled with a soft layer of new snow that had fallen during the night. Today, the sun peeked out from behind gray clouds. With 80 percent of the state of Maine forested, there were many hiding places for the masked man to lose himself in. Was he out in the woods now, waiting for another opportunity to strike?

A noise behind her sent a jolt of adrenaline straight to her heart. She spun to find John Doe springing from the bed and landing on the balls of his feet to face her. He ripped out his IV line. It fell to the floor, and the heart monitor sounded an alarm.

Audrey quickly shut off the shrill noise.

The hospital gown they'd put on him stretched across his wide shoulders as his hands went up in a defensive position. Words flowed from his mouth, but she had no idea what he was saying.

She held her hands palms up. Adrenaline flooded her veins. She didn't want to have to take the guy down, but if he didn't calm himself, she'd do it. "Hey, take it easy. You're in the hospital."

More words in a language she didn't understand came at her.

"I don't know what you're saying," she said. "Please speak English."

His panicked dark eyes swept over her and the room. Looking for an escape?

The door behind him opened. A young nurse rushed in, followed by the sheriff, carrying his coffee in one hand. John Doe whirled to confront a new threat.

"Don't!" Audrey shouted, afraid either man would attack the other. "He's okay. It's okay. Everyone's okay."

The sheriff held up his free hand. "Whoa, there, son. No one is here to hurt you. My name is Sheriff Crump. You're safe now." To the nurse, the sheriff said, "We've got this."

She clearly wasn't reassured, as her scared gaze zinged from the sheriff to the patient and back again. "He shouldn't be up. He's bleeding where his IV line was. I should check on his wounds."

Audrey glanced at the smear of blood on the unknown man's arm. The amount wasn't life threatening, just messy.

"You can come back in a bit," David said in a tone that left no room for argument. "I need to question the man."

With a frown, the nurse retreated, leaving them alone with the mysterious man. John Doe let out a string of words that made no sense to Audrey. Worry churned in her gut. What was going on? Obviously he was a foreigner, but from where? She couldn't place the language.

The sheriff cocked his head, his gaze going to Audrey. She shrugged, at a loss for how to communicate with the patient. The sharp sense of helplessness was too familiar. She hated the feeling. She'd felt this way the night her father hadn't returned from the sea. Only then it had been more intense. Now it was enough to make her jittery.

"I can understand a few words," the sheriff said. "I think he's speaking in Cree. One of the professors I worked with at the university taught a class in Native American studies and had a segment on languages. Cree has a very distinct dialect." He turned his attention back to John Doe. "Does that sound right?"

Confusion played over the man's face. He took a shuddering breath and then spoke in English. "I don't know. I can hear the words in my head, but they mean nothing to me. Where am I?"

"You're in Calico Bay," Audrey supplied. "Were you on a boat?"

John Doe backed up so he could see both Audrey and the sheriff. "I don't know. I don't remember. Calico Bay?"

"Downeast Maine," the sheriff supplied. "The northern tip of the state."

The man kept his gaze on Audrey. "I've seen you before. Where?"

"You woke up for a moment on the beach and again last night while I was here."

John ran a hand through his dark hair. He stilled when his fingers touched the bandage near his left temple. "What happened?"

"We were hoping you could tell us," the sheriff said. "There've been three attempts on your life since you washed ashore on our beach. Why is someone trying to kill you?"

The man frowned and paced a few steps. "I don't know."

Audrey fought the urge to tell him it would be all right. She didn't know if it would, and she wasn't sure he'd appreciate the platitude.

He staggered to the bed and sat, dropping his head into his hands. "I can't remember anything. Every time I try to recall, my head feels like it's going to explode."

Her heart ached to see his distress. The need to comfort prodded her to take a step closer. The sheriff arched a disapproving eyebrow at her. She halted. Her great-uncle had warned her often enough not to become emotionally involved in cases. She needed a clear, objective head. And if she wanted to be sheriff one day, she had to remain detached and professional at all times.

The patient rolled his shoulders then lifted his gaze to Audrey. "Only your face seems familiar. Nothing else."

The defenselessness on his handsome face tugged at her. She swallowed. Her heart beat erratically. No way was she going to repeat his delirious proclamation that she reminded him of a Christmas ornament. "On the beach you muttered the word *betrayed*. Ring any bells?"

His mouth gaped and he shook his head.

She tapped her fingers against her utility belt. "You can't remember your name?"

He stared at her, the panic returning to his eyes. "No. I can't remember my name. Or who I am. Or where I'm from. I don't know what I meant by *betrayed*." He let out a shuddering breath. "Or why someone wants me dead."

Chapter Three

He couldn't remember his name.

Sitting on the hospital bed under the scrutiny of the deputy and the sheriff made him feel vulnerable. An antsy sort of energy buzzed through him. He might not know his name, but he knew in his gut he didn't do vulnerable.

His body ached everywhere. His head pounded like a jackhammer going to town inside his skull. His mouth felt like cotton. An encompassing terror gripped him. A shiver racked his body. Cold. So very cold. How could he not know who he was? Or recall his past?

Why did someone want him dead?

His heart slammed against his ribs. A looming sense of dread and foreboding threatened to pull him back into darkness. He hung on to the edge of the bed and fought the tug. He needed to stay awake. Some innate knowledge told him he needed to keep a clear head if he were to survive. He grabbed the water pitcher on the bedside tray and poured a glass. He drank it down and then another.

"Then we'll call you John."

"What?" He stared at the blonde, blue-eyed deputy. Her hair was pulled back away from her face and secured behind her head in a knot. She wore little makeup. She didn't need any. She was absolutely stunning with her high cheekbones, delicately carved beneath smooth, unblemished skin and full lips. He forced himself to concentrate on what she'd just stated. "Is my name John?"

It didn't ring any bells. And every time he tried to concentrate, to conjure up a memory, his head felt like someone was taking a pickax to his skull, bringing on a blinding pain that was nearly incapacitating. Only keeping his focus on the beautiful woman's face kept him from keeling over.

She smiled and her eyes filled with compassion. "John as in John Doe. I don't know your name. You weren't carrying identification."

That explained why they didn't know his name. "Where did you find me?"

"The tide deposited you on the public beach early yesterday morning," the man who wore the gold sheriff's badge replied. Sheriff Crump, he'd said. He sipped from his coffee and eyed John with a mix of wary suspicion and empathy.

He'd washed up on the beach like driftwood, which accounted for the bone-deep chill he felt even though the room was heated. Had he been on a boat and fallen overboard? Something else the sheriff said finally registered like a punch to the gut. "You said someone tried to kill me *after* you found me?"

"Yes." The woman told him of the attempts made on his life.

Pressure built in his chest, and his head throbbed.

He scrubbed a hand over the back of his neck, hoping to ease the tension that was taking root in the muscles. "I'm sorry about the ambulance. And your patrol car. I'd offer to reimburse you for both, but I've no idea if I have the means to do so." The enormity of the situation weighed him down. "This is all so surreal, like I've walked into a bad horror flick. Has the doctor said how long my mind will be blank?"

"I haven't talked to her yet. We should let her know you've regained consciousness." The deputy reached for the call button.

The deputy smelled like sunshine on a spring day. He breathed in deep, letting an image of a grassy meadow form. Was it a memory or just a generic thought made up of a lifetime of images that had no emotional attachment?

As she moved away, he asked, "What's your name?"

"Deputy Martin," she replied in a brisk tone. She was tall and he'd guess shapely beneath the bulk of her uniform. He'd like to see her with her hair down and wearing a dress that showed off her long legs.

Whoa. Where had that thought come from?

Better to keep his mind on staying alive and not on some errant attraction to the woman who had rescued him from certain death. Pushing the attraction aside, he went with gratefulness. "Thank you, Deputy Martin, for saving my life."

He wished he could do something more for her, but he had no idea what. He had no clothes, no identification and no money. He was trapped in this hospital room until he either remembered who he was or someone claimed him.

Or the man who wanted him dead got to him first.

Anger at the unknown man and dread that he might succeed heated his blood but did nothing to chase away the chill that had settled in his core. Was he married? His heart contracted in his chest. Did he have a family worried about him somewhere? He glanced at his left hand. No wedding band. A sign that he was single or just that he didn't wear a ring? His pulse thrummed in his veins. Frustration drilled into his skull. What kind of man was he?

Why couldn't he remember?

The door opened, and an attractive female doctor wearing a white lab coat walked in. John gauged her age around fifty. Her blond hair was pulled back in a low bun, and she viewed him with bright blue eyes. His gaze darted from the doctor to the deputy. The similarities between the two left little doubt they were related. Mother and daughter?

"Good morning," the doctor said as she hustled forward. "I see you ripped out your IV. Are you in pain?"

He was, but he didn't want meds. "I'm fine. I can handle it."

Her mouth twisted. "Right. You gave us all quite a scare, on many levels. I'm Dr. Martin. What is your name?"

John grimaced. "I don't know. I've lost my mind."

Dr. Martin's eyes widened for a fraction of a second. "You sustained a rather dramatic blow to the head as well as some hypothermia. You have a linear skull fracture that will heal with time. I saw no evidence of a brain bleed. You certainly have a concussion, so you'll need to be monitored for the next twenty-four to forty-eight hours. Most likely the severity of the inciting event coupled with the force of the hit to your temple region caused your memory loss. Retrograde amnesia isn't uncommon. What can you remember?"

"Nothing before waking up here." John darted a glance at the deputy. She'd said he'd awakened last night and that was why she seemed familiar. But he had a feeling she was holding back, not telling him everything. Why would she do that?

The doctor listened to his heart and his lungs, then checked his pupils. "You seem to be in good order. I have no doubt your memories will return. Just be aware that they may come in spits and spurts and be disjointed. Like putting together a jigsaw puzzle. Eventually your memories will slide into place, and you'll be back to your old self."

Foreboding prickled his flesh. Whoever he'd been was someone worth killing. What had he been mixed up in? Something illegal? Was he a criminal? "I shouldn't stay here. Whoever broke in last night might return. I don't want to put anyone at risk."

Deputy Martin's gaze zeroed on the sheriff. "The captain's place. I could take him there."

The sheriff shook his head. "No. The safest place for him, and our town, is a jail cell."

"What!" The deputy shook her head. "No way. We can't lock him up without any evidence of wrongdoing. That would be setting us up for a lawsuit."

The sheriff arched an eyebrow. "Not if putting him in a cell is for his own safety. I know the law, Audrey."

Ah, so that was the pretty deputy's name. John liked the sound of it. He rolled the name around his brain and tried to remember if he'd known her before his memories had been wiped clean, but his mind remained empty, like a void in space. At least thinking about Audrey didn't induce any pain in his head.

Audrey's shoulders dropped slightly, and her mouth pressed into a straight line. "You don't think I can handle this situation?"

The distress in her voice had John tensing. He wasn't sure what was at play between these people, but clearly she had a chip on her shoulder. A strange protective urge surfaced. His hand clenched a fistful of sheet. He didn't know why he wanted to defend this woman. He wasn't sure if she deserved to be defended or not. Maybe she couldn't handle his situation. Maybe she could. But the one thing he did know was he didn't want to cause her harm.

"I didn't say that." The sheriff's tone suggested they'd discussed this conversational land mine before. "But you have to admit, this isn't something we deal with often here in our little corner of the world."

Audrey opened her mouth to reply, but the doctor held up a hand. "David, Audrey, take your discussion outside, please. This is upsetting to the patient."

"No, wait," John was quick to say. "The sheriff's right. The best place for me is somewhere I won't pose a threat to innocent bystanders." Or a pretty deputy sheriff.

Audrey's eyebrows pinched together as she turned her baby blues on him. "You won't be comfortable there. You're recovering from a nearly fatal head wound, not to mention nearly drowning and freezing to death in the ocean."

"Better I'm uncomfortable than anyone getting hurt."

Her gaze narrowed. "That's very self-sacrificing."

"Or very self-serving," John countered. "I have no

desire to die. If being locked up keeps me alive until my memory returns, then so be it."

"That's settled," the sheriff intoned. "Carol, when you're ready to release Mr. Doe, I'll take him to the sheriff's station."

Carol's gaze darkened with concern. "If you're sure."

"I am," the sheriff confirmed. "It's best for everyone this way."

Audrey made a distinct harrumph noise but didn't comment.

"I'll have the nurse bring our patient's clothing while I process his discharge papers," the doctor told them. "He'll need careful monitoring to make sure his concussion doesn't worsen. If he loses consciousness again or throws up or complains of dizziness, call me right away."

"We will." The sheriff held the door open for the doctor. "I'll be outside," he said to Audrey before he followed the doctor out of the room.

"That went well," Audrey said on a huff. She offered him a stiff smile. "Sorry you had to witness that little drama."

"What was that about?" he asked. "Are you new to the job?" That had to play into the dynamics between the deputy and sheriff.

She lifted her chin. "Sort of. I did a year on patrol in Bangor before returning home to Calico Bay."

"And how long ago did you return?"

"Less than a year."

Okay. She was inexperienced. The sheriff was being cautious on many levels. John could appreciate that. He'd be the same if he had a fairly new recruit under him.

The thought stopped him. Recruit? What did that

mean? Was he in law enforcement? Or was the thought just a random scenario that had nothing to do with his life prior to waking up in the hospital?

The throbbing in his head intensified. His stomach cramped.

"Hey, you better lie down," Audrey said, moving quickly to his side. "You're not looking so good."

"Headache," he said as he scooted back to rest his head on the pillow. "I don't remember the last time I had food."

"You don't want the hospital's grub," Audrey warned. She withdrew a protein bar from the side pocket of her pants. "This will tide you over until we can get you some real food."

Grateful for the snack, he took the bar, ripped open the top and consumed it in three bites and washed it down with another glass of water. The bar hit his stomach with a thud, but it stopped the cramping. "Thanks."

"You're welcome," she said. She rested her hands on her utility belt. "What kind of seafood do you like? It's the season for crab and monkfish now. But mussels are available, as are scallops."

His mouth watered at the thought of some good seafood, but no memory surfaced to support the visceral reaction. "Any of that sounds delicious. You're related to the doctor."

A wry smile curved her lips. "Caught that, did you? She's my mom, and the sheriff's my great-uncle."

"Good to know."

She shrugged. "You were bound to find out eventually."

"I'm not judging. You get flack for being related?"

"Some. But mostly there are those in town who don't

think a woman should be on duty. The world is slow to change here in Calico Bay."

He could imagine that was hard for her. She struck him as independent and capable with a soft side that she kept close to the vest. "You said you returned here?"

"Born and raised until I went to college and the police academy."

He admired her commitment to her roots. Did he have roots? He searched his brain until the pain made him back off.

A brunette dressed in scrubs entered the room carrying two bags. "Your clothes." She set the bags on the end of the bed. "Hello, Audrey."

"Morning, Sarah. How's Rich?"

Sarah's face softened. "He's good. He'll be four next week."

"Wow. I hadn't realized." A curious sadness entered Audrey's eyes. "I'll stop by to wish him happy birthday."

"He'd like that. Thank you." Sarah turned to John, her green eyes sharpening with attentiveness. "Do you need help dressing?"

"No. I can manage on my own."

Disappointment shot through Sarah's gaze. "Call me if you need anything."

"Thanks." He was glad when she exited. He met the deputy's gaze. She didn't look pleased. "What's Sarah's story?"

"She's a widow, if that's what you're asking," Audrey replied in a tense voice.

"Okay, it wasn't. I'm more interested in why you looked so sad when you were talking about Rich, who I assume is her son."

Surprise flashed in Audrey's eyes. "Oh. Yes, Rich is her little boy. He's such a sweetie." That sadness was back. "Ben, Sarah's husband, worked on a fishing boat. About two years ago there was an accident, and he was killed."

Sympathy twisted in his gut. "That's too bad. I've watched those fishing reality shows, and that life seems brutal."

Audrey's eyebrows hiked up and anticipation blossomed in her gaze, no doubt hoping his memories were returning. "You remember the show?"

He cocked his head, groping his mind for information. "Yes, sort of. I know I've seen it, but I can't recall where or when." And it was so maddening. He wanted to howl with frustration.

"Give it time," she said as the light in her eyes turned slightly to disappointment. "You heard my mom. Bits and pieces."

"Right." He had a feeling patience wasn't a strong suit of his, but he really didn't know. He opened one of the bags and glanced inside. A pile of dark material pooled in the bottom. Then he looked at the pretty deputy and arched an eyebrow.

"I'll wait outside." Audrey's cheeks pinkened as she walked out.

Audrey hesitated outside John Doe's hospital room door and tried to calm the flutter in her stomach. So many thoughts and feelings were swirling through her at the moment. Empathy for John Doe. She couldn't imagine losing her memories of her father, her childhood, her life. She could only imagine how bleak and desperate the man must be feeling. Not to mention the pain that seemed to hit him every time he tried to remember.

Then there was the embarrassment of having her mother and John witness the acrimony between her and her great-uncle. She usually did a better job of refraining from showing her emotions in public.

She could only attribute her lack of control to the strange and forceful reactions that flared within her the moment John awoke. Beyond empathy, she felt an intense protectiveness, which had manifested in her strong defense of him. A part of her knew it was logical for the sheriff to take the man into custody, but putting him behind bars without any proof of wrongdoing didn't sit well with her sense of justice.

Hopefully John would soon regain his memories and they could figure out the truth behind what, who and why someone was trying to kill him.

Left alone, John withdrew his clothes and boots from the bags and stared at them for a long moment. He didn't remember putting these on. Why was he dressed all in black? For nefarious purposes?

He was thankful the garments were dry as he quickly donned the cargo pants, turtleneck and socks but struggled with the boots. Finally, giving up, he padded to the door and stuck his head out. Audrey and her great-uncle stood near the nurses' station. The brunette noticed him first and hurried toward him. He tried not to grimace as he held up his hand. "Can you ask Deputy Martin to come here?"

Nurse Sarah pursed her lips, clearly miffed by his request for someone other than her. "Sure." She walked back to the desk and spoke to Audrey, who nodded and headed his way.

"You need me?"

He did. For reasons he couldn't explain she grounded him, anchored him to the moment. When he looked at her, thought about her, he only felt peace, comfort. Strange, considering she'd said they'd only just met. Again that niggling feeing she was keeping a secret from him itched, demanding to be scratched. He let it go, confident he'd get her to open up and tell him. Where that confidence came from, he didn't know. "I need help with the boots. Bending over to undo the laces is more than I can take right now."

One honey-blond eyebrow arched. "All right."

She crouched and undid the laces on the right boot and held it out for him to slip his foot into. He watched as her slender and capable hands quickly cinched up the laces and tied the boot snugly.

After the left boot was on, he stood. The world tilted. He swayed. Audrey wrapped an arm around his waist and drew him close to her side. If he weren't feeling a bit woozy, he'd have leaned in for a kiss.

He frowned at the thought. Okay, he found Audrey attractive and had some strange connection to her that he didn't understand, but he'd better keep his emotions in check. He could be married. And he doubted the deputy would appreciate him taking advantage of the situation.

Was he a man that took advantage? He prayed not. Which led to another question—was he a man that prayed?

He hated not knowing who he was.

Some part of his brain said to let go of the past and

become who he wanted to be for the future. But that wasn't really a possibility. Not when there was someone out there willing to hurt other people to end his life.

He knew deep inside, with a certainty he couldn't deny, he had a responsibility to uncover the truth and to protect those around him.

But he dreaded what the cost would be. He hoped and prayed it wouldn't be the life of the deputy at his side.

Chapter Four

$\sim$

Sitting in the passenger seat of Deputy Martin's car, John stared at the passing scenery, taking in the quaint and rustic town. The overcast sky washed the world in a gray light. Signs of recent snow collected on awnings and sidewalk gutters. Colorfully painted buildings added cheeriness. Had he seen this village before? If so, had he liked it the way he did now?

There were the usual businesses one would find in any town—a bank, a law firm and a real estate office—but the picturesque storefronts didn't boast any recognizable brand names. Instead, there were places like Melinda's Bakery, the Java Bean, Ted's Fill and Eat.

They passed an Irish pub, numerous fish houses and an art gallery with the name Maine Inspired displaying blown-glass art and paintings in the window. His gaze snagged on the exercise studio advertising dance and fitness classes. He wondered if they had a treadmill and free weights. The need to pump some iron sent nervous energy rippling through him.

"This is a nice place," he commented. Despite the

threat stalking him, he felt comfortable in this town. Why was that?

"It's quiet at this time of year," Audrey said. "In spring the tourists start showing up and don't fully vacate until after Oktoberfest. We have tons of festivals throughout the tourist months. Anything to drive up business to sustain us through the lean season. After Christmas most of the shops and restaurants close for vacations. Some people head to a warmer climate. Others hunker down and wait out the weather."

"What do you do?"

"My job." She lifted a shoulder in a careless shrug. "Though the sheriff insists we all take some vacation, so we rotate through, each taking a week off. Sometimes I stick around to catch up on reading or binge watch movies."

That sounded good to him. "And other times?"

"A warm beach with warm water."

Sun and sand. That sounded good to him. "I could go for a hot day in the Caribbean about now."

She slanted him a glance. "You've been?"

He could picture crystal clear waters, beaches that stretched for miles and sea turtles swimming just below the surface. Memories? Or data stored in his brain from flipping through a travel magazine?

Frustration beat a steady rhythm behind his forehead. "Don't know."

There weren't many pedestrians out on the main street running through the holiday-decorated town. He wondered where he'd be spending Christmas if he hadn't nearly been fish bait. "It's peaceful today."

"Yes. Yesterday's events were very dramatic for our town. Most people are staying off the streets."

A rush of guilt swamped him. "I'm sorry about that. Sorry I washed up on your shore and brought danger to your community."

Audrey brought her patrol car to a halt outside a restaurant called Franny O'Flannery's. She looked him in the eye. "I'm not. The alternative would mean you were dead."

Her words poked at him, reminding him how close he had come to death. And thanks to this woman, he was still here. He unbuckled and put his hand on the door handle.

"Nope," Audrey said. "Stay put. Fran will bring our order to us."

"Curbside service?" he remarked, studying her. Normal or had the deputy asked Fran for the courtesy?

"Perks of a small town. Here we go," she said just as a knock on the window jarred his attention away from her face.

An older woman bent down to peer inside the cruiser. Her lined face was a wreath of smiles and her dark blue eyes regarded him with curiosity. He hit the button on the door panel, and the window slid silently down. A rush of cold air hit him in the face, along with the briny smells of the ocean. But he also caught the aroma of fried food, and his hunger returned with a vengeance.

"Morning, Fran." Audrey leaned over him to talk to the woman at the window, bringing with her a whiff of apple shampoo.

His stomach muscles contracted. His hand tightened around the door handle to keep from reaching up to touch her golden hair.

"Good morning, Audrey," Fran returned. "I see you have a guest."

"Indeed I do," Audrey replied. "This is John. John, Fran O'Flannery. She makes the best crab cakes in the whole state."

Fran grinned. "I don't know about that, but they are popular. Welcome to Calico Bay, John. Are you here on business—" the woman slanted an assessing glance at Audrey "—or pleasure?"

For some odd reason, heat infused his cheeks. Clearly Fran wondered if there was something going on between him and the pretty deputy. "I'm not sure." What business would he have had been doing dressed as a commando wannabe?

"How much do I owe you?" Audrey said before straightening.

Fran handed him the large bag of food. The delicious smells made his insides cramp and his mouth salivate.

"I'll put it on your tab. You can swing by later to settle up."

"Much obliged, Fran," Audrey said. "Give Don my regards."

"Will do. Stay safe." Fran walked back into the restaurant.

"That was nice of her to let you pay later," John commented.

"Yeah, well, she knows where I live." Audrey started up the car and continued to the sheriff's station, a square white building with the fire department on one side and a large steepled church on the other. Audrey parked in front and led him inside, through a lobby where a woman sat behind a Plexiglas window. She waved at Audrey and eyed him with wariness.

John didn't blame the woman. None of them knew what he was capable of, including him. Was he a criminal? He certainly had an element of danger dogging him.

They walked down a hallway with walls decorated with photos of the town. Summer scenes depicted smiling children at a fair. There were pictures of fishing boats with proud fishermen mugging for the camera. The gallery of photos filled him with a strange longing. Was there some place where he belonged? Did he have a community where people knew him? Loved him?

At the end of the hall, Audrey opened a door to a large squad room. A dozen desks, separated by short partition walls, formed a mazelike pattern stretching all the way to the back wall, ending at the closed office door with the sheriff's nameplate. Only four people sat at their desks. They stopped what they were doing to stare at him. He studied each face for a moment but felt no sense of recognition.

Audrey stopped at her desk. He knew it was hers by the collage of photos on her partition. Pictures of her mother and a man he assumed was her father. A family photo with a preteen Audrey, her hair plaited in braids, standing in front of a fishing boat named *Audrey*. A younger adult version of Audrey in a cap and gown. College? Then her in full uniform at her academy graduation.

She pulled a vacant chair over. "Here. Have a seat."

He'd expected her to take him straight to a cell. "Thanks."

She laid out their lunch of crab cakes, tater tots and coleslaw on her desk then took her seat. She bowed her head for a moment, her lips moving silently. Something inside his chest loosened. He followed her example and bowed his head. Lifted up a silent plea. *Lord, bless this food to my body. Heal me. Heal my mind. Amen.*

The crab cakes were as delicious as advertised. "I can't imagine having anything taste better than this."

Audrey wiped her mouth with a napkin before replying. "Right. I'm telling you, Fran's is the best. Her recipe has won awards."

"Tell me about you." He picked up a bottle of water that Fran had also supplied.

"Me?" She shook her head. "Not much to tell."

"Are you married? Kids?" He didn't think so, since there were no photos of her with a man or child, but it felt normal to ask, like something he'd do in his life prior to waking up in the hospital.

Her gaze collided with his. "No to both. What about you?"

His mouth twisted in a rueful grimace. "I wish I knew. You'd think if I were married, if I had a family waiting for me that would be something I'd remember."

"Unless you wanted to forget."

He considered her words. His pulse ticked up a notch. "Maybe that's why I can't remember my past. There's something I want to forget."

"Being hit over the head and thrown in the ocean are traumatic events. Your brain may be protecting you."

"I don't want to be protected. I want to remember." He picked up a tater tot. But his appetite fled.

He hated this not knowing. He had a horrible feeling that something bad was happening, or was going to happen, and he needed to stop whatever it was as soon as possible. Considering there was an assassin trying to kill him, his sense of doom was understandable. But there was something else dancing at the periphery of his mind. Yet when he tried to lock on to the thought, a sharp pain was his reward.

Fatigue dragged at him. He could barely keep his eyes open. "Thank you for lunch, Deputy Martin."

"You're welcome." She canted her head. "You look wrung out. The cell has a cot that I've heard is pretty comfortable."

That comment elicited a smile. "Critiques from past residents?"

She returned his smile. "Something like that."

He liked her smile. It made her blue eyes light up. His gaze drifted down her straight nose to her lush, full lips. He noticed the slight cleft in her chin that gave her face character.

She rose and held out her hand. "Come on, I'll show where you'll be spending the next few hours."

He stared at her smooth skin and long, slender fingers before grasping her hand. Her fingers closed around his, and she tugged him to his feet. She was surprisingly strong, yet her hand felt almost delicate within his clasp. The dichotomy left him unnerved. He braced his feet apart. The room momentarily swerved then righted itself. Expecting her to let go, he loosened his hold, but for a fraction of a second she held on, her gaze fixated on their joined hands. Then she yanked her hand back and rested it on her utility belt. "This way." She turned and walked briskly away.

He rolled the tension from his shoulders and followed her.

The cell wasn't big by any means, but it was roomy enough and thankfully empty. He didn't relish the idea of sharing the space.

Audrey opened the door. "Sorry about this."

"Don't be." He stepped inside. "This is the safest place for me. No one can get hurt with me in here, and I'll be able to rest without worry."

"I guess." But she didn't sound convinced. That was sweet. He liked that she was upset on his behalf. He wondered if anyone else had ever been upset on his behalf and if so, who?

Needing to reassure her, he moved closer and reached out to tuck a stray strand of blond hair behind her ear. "Are you always so accommodating with your guests?"

"No. But these circumstances are a bit out of the ordinary."

His finger skimmed over her jaw before he dropped his hand. "I appreciate all you're doing for me. You're a very caring person, Deputy Martin."

He liked the way her cheeks took on a rosy color. "Audrey."

A grin tugged at his mouth. "Okay. Audrey. Such a pretty name for a pretty woman."

Her eyes widened a fraction, then something cold flashed in her gaze and she stepped back. "And you're charming. A flirt."

Wary that he'd offended her, he said, "You say that like it's a bad thing."

"It's been my experience that charming men aren't to be trusted."

Had the man who hurt her been a boyfriend? "Don't paint every man with the same brush as whoever hurt you."

She made a wry sound in her throat. "Easy for you to say. I don't know you. I don't know if I should trust you."

"But you want to," he observed, realizing how badly he wanted her to trust him. "Otherwise you wouldn't have shared your lunch with me. You wouldn't feel so bad for locking me up."

She frowned and pressed her lips into a straight line. He much preferred when she smiled.

"It's okay," he told her. "You shouldn't trust me. I wouldn't trust me."

"I want to release your photo to the media. See if someone comes forward to identify you."

"You should. I'm guessing you already ran my prints and face through your databases."

"Yes, with no results."

He wasn't sure if that was reassuring or more alarming. The thumping in his head intensified. His energy waned. He needed to sit before he fell down. But he didn't want her to leave, which was exactly why he said, "I'm sure you have work to do. And I really need to rest."

She nodded. "I do. I'll be checking on you every two hours."

"I look forward to it."

Without a word, she closed the cell door with a deafening click that echoed in his ears long after she walked away.

Night came faster than Audrey would have imagined, despite the fact that December in Maine the sun set around four in the afternoon. She switched on her desk lamp because the dim overhead lights weren't bright enough for her. The station was quiet. Only a few deputies were at their desks. The sheriff had come and gone, promising he'd be back to relieve her of guard duty for

John Doe. She was surprised the sheriff didn't squawk at the overtime she was accruing.

She'd spent the day doing paperwork that had stacked up over the past few weeks. Though she had trouble concentrating on vandalism of the local middle school or Mrs. Keel's runaway cat.

Audrey kept replaying John's words.

Such a pretty name for a pretty woman.

She wasn't sure why his compliment had affected her. Maybe because the first time he saw her he'd thought she was beautiful, like a Christmas ornament. She'd chalked his flirting up to his injury. But earlier he'd been lucid. She didn't trust his flattering words. He was one of those types of men who used their good looks and charisma to their advantage. He might not be able remember his name and his past, but he certainly remembered how to use his charm.

She'd have to be careful around him, because for some unfathomable reason she wanted him to find her attractive.

She gave herself a mental shake. When had her ego hit bottom?

She didn't need a man or anyone else to make her feel good about herself. She was capable, smart and knew what she wanted in life. And it wasn't a charming stranger, no matter how attractive, or what yearnings he stirred.

The radio attached to her shirt came on. Ophelia's disembodied voice came through clear. "Sean is here to see you."

Audrey sighed. She pressed the talk button. "Send him back." She liked Sean, but she wasn't interested in dating him, though he'd asked on numerous occasions.

It wasn't that the EMT wasn't handsome or kind or that they didn't get along. They did. As friends. There was no spark between them. She thought of him more as a brother. She and his older sister had been friends forever.

A few moments later, Sean leaned against the partition wall next to her desk. Today he wore jeans and a plaid shirt beneath a puffy dark blue jacket. The stubble on his face matched his dark auburn hair. The only sign he'd been in a car crash yesterday was the purple bruise on his forehead. His searching gaze was trained on her face. "How's it going?"

"So far it's been an uneventful night," she replied. "How are you doing?"

"I've a tough noggin, or so your mother tells me," he said.

"And Wes?"

"Good. Scared. He'd never been in an accident before."

"I'm glad you both walked away with only minor injuries. It could have been so much worse."

"True." He made a face. "The ambulance was totaled. Ted said there was no fixing it."

Audrey trusted Ted's judgment. He'd been a friend of her father's and had been the town mechanic for as long as Audrey had been alive. "It was insured, right?"

Sean nodded. "Yup. Mayor Grantree was adamant about full coverage when the town bought the ambo. We've already ordered a new one, and the insurance company isn't happy to be paying for it."

Audrey almost felt sorry for the insurance adjustor working the case. Mayor Ginger Grantree was someone Audrey wouldn't want to be on the bad side of. The woman was formidable, and when she wanted something, everybody had better stand back because she was relentless. "I'm glad to hear we'll have a replacement soon."

"How's the guy you found on the beach?"

"He's faring well."

The lights above them winked out. Adrenaline flashed through Audrey. She rose and stared out the large window that showed the lights of the town were on. The outage was isolated to the sheriff's station. The generator would kick in any moment now.

"That's weird," Sean said.

A bad feeling prickled the skin at her nape. "Yes. Too weird."

Just as the generator brought up the emergency lights, Harrison stepped out of the men's restroom. Audrey could make out his silhouette.

"What's happening?" Harrison's voice reverberated with unease.

"Don't know," she replied. "Sean, stay with Harrison. Get Ophelia and get to safety."

She hurried toward the back where John Doe was locked in a cell. In the time she'd worked for the sheriff's department, the electricity had never failed without cause. She could only assume the man after John Doe was behind the outage. She reached the cell door. She couldn't make out John in the dark. She reached for the keys attached to her utility belt.

A loud explosion rocked the building.

Chapter Five

John jerked awake to a cacophony of noise. Emergency sirens bounced off the cell walls. He heard shouted voices. Heart pumping with a jolt of adrenaline, he rolled from the cot, landing soundlessly onto the balls of his feet in a crouch. Every muscle tensed in anticipation. Fight or flight? Not flight. He was trapped in a cell. He scanned the darkness, momentarily disoriented. He'd been lying with his feet facing the cell door. Staying low, with his hand stretched out before him, he moved toward where he thought the door was located.

"John?" Audrey's call rang in his ears.

Relief tempered the adrenaline racing through his veins. "Here."

A beam of light swept over the cell and landed on him.

He wrapped his hands around the cold steel of the bars. Though he couldn't see her behind the glare of the flashlight, the rapid pace of her breathing pinpointed her location. "What happened?"

"Someone killed the lights. The explosion was likely the generator." The flashlight bobbed. The rattle of keys echoed in the cell, then he heard the faint squeak of a hinge as the door opened.

Warm, strong hands grasped his and pulled him toward the back exit. "Come on. We're getting out of here."

He tugged her to a halt. "They'll be expecting us to go out the door. It'd be too easy to pick us off." He wasn't about to let her put herself in the line of fire. She might be a deputy sheriff, but it was his head they wanted, not hers.

"So we wait for them to come blazing in? I don't think so."

He didn't like that option any better. "Are we the only ones in the station?"

"No. We have to get everyone out alive."

"Are there only two exits?"

"The break room window. It drops onto a strip of grass between this building and the community church." She tightened her hold on his hand. They ran back to the squad room, where another deputy held a flashlight illuminating a male civilian and the woman John had seen behind the glass in the lobby.

"I've called the sheriff," the deputy announced to the people next to him. "He's on his way. We're safe here. The fire department has the fire under control in the back parking lot."

The deputy turned suddenly, his hand going for his sidearm as John and Audrey approached.

Audrey dropped John's hand. "Whoa, Harrison. It's me."

"Audrey, what's happening?" the woman said, her voice shaky with panic.

"I don't have answers yet, Ophelia," Audrey told her.

"But we need to get out of here. But not through the doors. We'll go out the break room window and hide inside the church."

"You think the explosion was deliberate?" the younger guy asked.

"Unfortunately, Sean, I do," she replied. "It's the same person or persons who crashed into the ambulance."

John didn't like the way Sean moved to Audrey's side in a clearly possessive way. She'd said she wasn't married and had no kids but hadn't mentioned if she was involved with someone. Though why John was upset didn't make sense. He could very well be married or engaged or involved with someone he couldn't remember. Until he knew his past, he couldn't contemplate a present or future that included anyone else.

Needing to act and not let his mind play games with him, he said, "We should hustle before the perps decide to storm in."

"This way." Audrey grabbed the sleeve of his shirt and tugged him closer. "Stay behind me."

Though he appreciated her protectiveness, it felt wrong. He should be the one going first, blazing a trail for her to follow. His empty hand flexed with the need to feel the weight of steel pressed against his palm. He tucked the thought away to examine later as he did as the very determined female deputy directed. Sean, Ophelia and the other deputy fell in line behind them, with the deputy taking up the rear position.

Inside the break room, Audrey released her hold on his sleeve and went to work on prying out the window screen. He helped her and took it from her hands to set aside.

"I'll go first to make sure it's clear," Audrey said. "John, you follow me. Then the rest of you."

"I'll go first," the other deputy blurted before John could.

"Harrison, I need you to protect our flank. You're a much better shot than I am." Audrey's voice had lowered to a measured beat.

John arched an eyebrow at her placating tone, meant to both defuse a potential issue and bolster the deputy's confidence at the same time.

Deputy Harrison ate up her words and totally missed the subtle undertone. "You're right. I'll make sure you all get to safety."

Audrey didn't waste any more words but slipped quickly and soundlessly out the window. John had to give her major credit for getting her way without causing a rift. He wondered if it were true that Harrison was a better shot or if she was downplaying herself for the deputy's benefit.

He leaned into the open window. Moonlight from the full winter moon revealed that there indeed was a wide strip of grass separating the sheriff's station from the side of the church. The white-painted wood building gleamed in the moon's glow. He could smell the acrid smoke of the burning generator.

He spotted Audrey right away—her darker form outlined against bushes growing along the church's side yard as she motioned for him to follow her out the window. He climbed over and dropped to the ground. The grass beneath his boots was crusted in ice and crunched beneath his weight.

He turned to help the dispatcher, Ophelia, out of the window. She hopped out of his hands as soon as her feet touched down. When Sean swung one leg over the side of the windowsill, his pant leg rode up, revealing a metal prosthetic above the tennis shoe.

John's heart twisted with empathy. He reached out a hand to help the man. After a moment of hesitation, Sean grasped John's hand and slipped out the window. John steadied the guy then let go.

"Thanks, dude," Sean whispered.

Deputy Harrison came through the window less gracefully. He grunted when he hit the ground. John grabbed him by the arm to keep him from going down on his rear.

"Hurry." Audrey's voice carried on the slight breeze coming off the ocean.

John ushered Ophelia and Sean to her side. She led them to a wood door in the side of the church.

Harrison reached past her to try the handle. "It's locked."

"Give me a second," Audrey shot back. She shuffled through the keys on her key ring. "Pastor Wilson gave me a key."

"Why?" Harrison demanded to know. "I didn't get a key."

Seeing that Harrison wasn't watching their six, John took a position with his back facing the church so he could see both entrances of the side yard. His hands flexed again, and the urge to hold cold metal against his palm was strong. Sean moved to stand beside him. Curiosity about the man burned in John, but now wasn't the time.

A movement to the right caught John's attention. His muscles tensed. The shape of a tall man carrying an automatic weapon was clear for a moment before a shadow swallowed him up.

"Combatant at three o'clock," Sean whispered.

"I see him." John had to deal with this. He couldn't let these people get hurt. "Make sure they all get inside," he said at a level barely considered a whisper.

Keeping to the shadow of the building, John made his way toward the armed man. Moving on instinct and some buried muscle memory, John prepared for hand-to-hand combat.

His first priority would be to disarm then disable. He mentally pictured the tactics for neutralizing his opponent. As he closed in on the man, John heard the faint, telltale sound of boots on the ground behind him.

He flattened himself against the wall just as Audrey bumped into him. He knew it was her by the fresh apple scent of her hair. He ground his teeth together. She needed to be inside, where she was safe.

A foot away the masked man stopped, as if sensing he wasn't alone.

John held his breath. He didn't know what Audrey planned. He didn't like being out of sync with his partner. They needed to be of one mind for an assault to work. That he considered her as a partner was something he'd deal with later.

He touched Audrey's hand. Using his index finger, he tapped her palm twice, though what he was trying to convey to her lurked beyond his mental reach. Frustration crimped the muscles in his shoulders. They were going to get themselves killed.

Audrey's fingers curled over his and pulled him toward her, obviously wanting him to go with her to the safety of the church. He resisted. This could be their only chance to catch this guy. She elbowed him lightly before she squeezed his hand and then stretched her arm to the left in a semicircle. Then she moved their joined hands to his chest and thumped. He squeezed her hand, not comprehending her message.

She thumped him again and then stretched her arm past him to the right. It dawned on him that she wanted him to go behind the man while she confronted from the front. He didn't like it. He brought her hand to his face and shook his head no.

She released her hold on him and broke away. She was going to take this guy on herself.

Gritting his teeth, he made a wide sweep so that he ended up behind the perp.

A bright spotlight beamed on the man. "Halt, sheriff's department. Drop your weapon."

The man brought his rifle barrel up. John slammed into him from behind, wrapping his arms around his torso and trapping his arms at his side, making it impossible for the man to fire at Audrey, as they went to the ground with John landing on top of the intruder.

John swiftly sprang up enough to dig his knee into the man's back, keeping him glued to the ground while he wrestled the guy's hands behind his back.

Audrey was there in a flash with a set of handcuffs. John slapped them over the man's wrists and secured him in a tight hold. He patted him down by rote, vaguely aware that some part of his brain had given the command.

He found a money clip holding some cash and a blank key card. No other weapons and no identification. A shudder worked over John. He'd washed ashore dressed nearly the same, also without ID. Had John and this man worked together? If so, why was this guy trying to kill him?

He yanked the man to his feet. Audrey grabbed the man's rifle from the ground. The sheriff and several other deputies rounded the corner of the building with their flashlights aimed at them.

"Audrey!" The deep timbre of the sheriff's concerned voice rang out. "You okay?"

"Yes, sir." She stepped close to John. "Good job."

"Thanks." He relinquished custody of the criminal to Audrey. To the sheriff, John said, "There might be more of them."

The sheriff instructed the half dozen officers to spread out and search the area. The door to the church opened. Deputy Harrison came out, followed by Ophelia and Sean.

"All right, everyone," the sheriff said. "Let's take this back inside the station."

"They blew the generator," Harrison said. "The station's dark and the fire department's on the same electrical circuit, so it's dark, too."

"Paulson," the sheriff called.

A deputy hustled over. "Yes, boss."

"Get someone out here to fix the generator and the electricity," Sheriff Crump commanded. Turning to the group huddled around him, he said, "Let's take this inside the church. Harrison, call Pastor Wilson, let him know what's up."

"On it." Harrison moved away to use his cell phone while the sheriff ushered them all inside the church.

Someone flipped a switch and wall sconces lit up, dispelling the inky shadows and revealing a small wood-paneled room with several doors. The sheriff pushed open a set of doors to the left and led their suspect into an office. He pushed him into a chair and took the black beanie from his head, revealing cropped sandy-blond hair.

John moved so that he could face the man. He was a stranger to him. Or at least John assumed, since he felt no recognition at all. The man had wide-set eyes, broad features with a nose that had been broken in the past and a jutting chin. "Who are you? Why are you trying to kill me?"

The man stared through him. "I'm not talking to you," he said in a softly accented voice.

Eastern European. John didn't question how he knew. John stalked to the window, careful to keep the majority of his body out of the line of sight in case the suspect had a cohort who might want to take a potshot at him. He stared out at the parking lot shared by both the church and the sheriff's station. The glowing embers of the burned-out generator and the dozen or so firefighters in turnout gear were visible.

"What do we do now?" Ophelia asked. "Ed will be wondering where I am."

"Deputy Harrison will take you home," Sheriff Crump said. "Sean, you need to go on home, too."

John turned from the window, his gaze on the man in the chair. "Is it safe for them to leave?"

The man shrugged but held his gaze. "They're not the target."

A fist of dread hit John in the solar plexus. "Right. I am."

Sean's gaze bounced to Audrey. "Are you sure you'll be okay?"

"I'm fine, Sean," Audrey assured him. "Tell Jessie hello for me."

John heard the faint thread of annoyance in her tone

and again wondered what exactly her relationship with the younger man was.

Sean nodded, but there was no mistaking the frustration on his face as he left with Ophelia and the deputy.

Sheriff Crump sat on the edge of the large desk dominating the office. "It would be helpful if you told us your name since we're all going to be here for a while."

"Sasha," the man said with a shrug. "My name is Sasha."

Audrey stepped closer. "Thank you, Sasha, for telling us your name. Do you know his name?"

Sasha's lip curled. "No."

"Are you hungry?" she asked, fishing around in her cargo pants pockets and producing a protein bar.

Sasha shook his head.

"Thirsty?" She walked to a small refrigerator in the corner. "Pastor Wilson keeps water here." She pulled out bottles of water. "Sheriff? John?"

"I'm good," replied Sheriff Crump.

Seeing the sharp way Sasha stared at him, John nodded. "Sure. I'll take one." What John really wanted was to shake the man and force him to talk, but he knew torture in any form wouldn't give the desired results, so he followed Audrey's lead to build a rapport with their suspect. "What about you, Sasha? A cold bottle of water?"

Sasha looked away and shook his head.

Audrey walked back with two bottles of water and handed one to John. "You know, Sasha, at the moment all we have you on is assault with intent to do bodily harm by pointing a loaded weapon at an officer. We can't prove you blew up the generator. If you help us by telling us who and why someone wants this man dead—" she pointed to John "—we can help you."

Sasha snorted. "You can't help me. I'm dead. Just like he's dead."

His pronouncement shuddered through John.

"We can protect you," she insisted.

The door to the office opened, and Paulson stuck his head inside. "The electricity's back on."

Sheriff Crump straightened and took Sasha by the arm. "Come on, I've got a jail cell waiting for you."

The sheriff led Sasha out the door.

Audrey met John's gaze. The anxiety in her eyes had him stopping in his tracks.

"He's not the man from the hospital."

John's heart slammed to a halt. "What?"

"The man at the hospital didn't have an accent and was leaner." Her grim tone constricted his lungs. His stomach dropped. There were more bad guys out there determined to kill him.

A shout from outside drew their attention. They ran to the door. The sheriff and Paulson had their guns drawn and their flashlights lighting up the dark as they stood back to back. Sasha lay on the grass.

Immediately John grabbed Audrey, dragging her farther into the shelter of the windowless vestibule. "Kill the lights."

Audrey hurried to the wall panel and flipped the lights off, shrouding the church in darkness.

"Where'd the shot come from?" Crump demanded.

"I don't know," Paulson responded in a high-pitched tone full of panic.

John crouched in the doorway. "Sheriff, you two need to find cover."

The sheriff knelt on one knee and checked Sasha's neck. John already knew the sheriff wouldn't find a pulse. Sasha had been dealt a catastrophic head shot directly to the brain stem. He was dead before he hit the ground. Just as John would have been if he'd stepped outside the church.

Chapter Six

"I have to leave," John said, barely able to discern Audrey's outline in the darkened vestibule. They stood inside the door, careful to stay in the shadows and out of the ambient light coming from the moon outside the church. His gut clenched. Leaving was the only answer. "I can't stay here. I'm putting you and your town in danger."

"I know. I've got to move you to a more secure location." The hard determination in her tone came at him through the shadows.

He frowned in the dark and shook his head. She didn't get his meaning. "Not *with* you. I have to go on my own. I can disappear."

"No." Her voice was adamant. "That's not happening."

Her stubbornness could get her killed. "It will be safer for you."

"Don't make this about me." She stalked forward until she was standing in front of him. He could feel the heat of her annoyance buffeting him. He could imagine her blue eyes sparking and wished he could see her face.

"I'm a professional and I have a job to do," she insisted. "Part of that job is protecting you. I'm not letting you take off alone. You don't have any money or ID. And unless you plan to become a criminal, you're not getting either one."

He hated to admit it, but what she said was true. Frustration banded across his chest. "How do you know I'm not already a criminal? I'm dressed exactly like Sasha."

She let out a little noise of irritation. "Black clothes don't make you a criminal."

He had to make her see his point. "But I could be. You said I'd muttered a word when you found me on the beach." He reached out, and though it was too dark to see her, his aim was true. His hand gripped her shoulders. "Do you remember what I said?"

"Of course. *Betrayed.*"

The word hung between them, sending a shudder down his spine.

"Then doesn't it stand to reason that whomever I betrayed is after me?" He released her to pace into the inky corner. "And if I betrayed someone who has the means and the mind-set to hire guns to kill me, I'd say that there's no doubt a criminal element is at play here and I'm smack-dab in the middle."

"I agree there is a criminal element at work." Her voice took on that soothing, you'll-do-as-I-want tone he'd heard her use on others.

A smile tugged at the corners of his mouth despite himself. She really was something, this beautiful and determined deputy.

"But until you're proven to be a criminal, I have to consider you a witness and a victim." Her words were a punch to the gut.

He let out a scoff. "I'm a victim, all right. A victim of a defective mind."

"Can you hold off on the pity party until we get out of here?"

He barked out a laugh. The woman never gave an inch. He liked that about her.

Audrey drew in a breath. "John, you also have to consider the fact that someone might have betrayed you."

The darkness pressed in on him. Had someone betrayed him? Was that what this was all about? The reason someone wanted him dead? His fingers curled into a tight fist.

Audrey's cell phone lit up as she dialed the sheriff. She covered the screen with her hand to mute the light. The ringing of the sheriff's phone placed him still in the side yard. Audrey put the phone on speaker when the sheriff answered.

"I'm taking John out of here through the tunnels," she informed him. "Then I'm driving him to the captain's."

Where exactly was this captain located? And what tunnels? John kept his curiosity in check. He'd ask later.

There was a moment of silence before the sheriff responded. "That's probably the safest place. I'll send Paulson with you and then I'll relieve him tomorrow."

"Fine. Tell Dan to go home and pack a bag. Ask him if he has anything that might fit John," Audrey said. "John and I will swing by and pick him up in an hour after I've stopped by my place."

"Copy." The sheriff hesitated before adding, "Audrey, be careful."

"Of course." She hung up and grabbed John's arm and slid her hand down until she clasped his hand. "Come on. We're leaving."

He allowed her to pull him from the vestibule to one of the double doors. "Uh, how exactly are we getting out of here?"

"Have you ever heard of the Embargo Act of 1807?" She led him into the sanctuary.

"Couldn't tell you one way or another."

"Right. Okay, fair enough." Moonlight streamed through the high stained glass windows, allowing enough multicolored shards of light for them to weave their way through the pews toward the front of the church. "Construction on this church began in 1805 and was finished in 1810. In the year 1807, President Jefferson imposed an embargo on foreign trade that lasted for two years. Needless to say the whole Down East was hit hard. The small settlement at Calico Bay was in jeopardy of disappearing. Being that people still needed to export and import goods, the craftsmen working on the church devised a plan. They proceeded to build a tunnel under the church that extends all the way to the cliffs."

She knelt in front of the altar and patted the floor. He squatted next to her. "Lose something?"

"I'm looking for the handle. It's inlaid into the wood."

"Handle?"

"Smuggling goods to and from ships anchored off the coast was how people survived. Then the War of 1812 happened, and the tunnels were used by the militia to defend the bay. Aha. Found it."

"How do you even know the tunnels are still there?"

"I grew up in this town, remember? I've explored every inch of the tunnels, the cliffs and the forest on the west side of the town." She planted her feet and grasped the handle to lift a two-by-two hatch carved into the floor. "Grab the edge."

He did as she asked, easily lifting the lid all the way. He peered into darkness below. He thought he heard a rustling sound. Were there snakes in Maine? An image from a movie slammed into his mind. The hero of the action flick fell into a pit of snakes. A shudder of revulsion vibrated outward from John's core. Why could he remember a movie and not something important like his name or his life?

"There's a ladder" she said. "We'll have to go by feel until we close the hatch. I don't want to use my light until we're safely below ground."

She sat on the ledge and felt around with the toe of her boot until she found the ladder rung. "Got it." She held out her hand. "Sit next to me."

John slipped his palm flat against hers. Warmth shot up his arm from the point of contact. Her fingers entwined with his as he settled on the edge.

"Can you balance the hatch while you go down the ladder?" she asked, her voice oddly breathless.

"I can manage that."

She slipped off the ledge and disappeared into the pit below. After a few moments, she called out, "Okay, start down."

John used the toe of his boot to find the rung of the ladder, then he climbed down, slowly allowing the hatch to close behind him, blocking the moonlight until only darkness remained. His hands tightened on the rung as his foot touched the ground. Audrey flipped on her flashlight, illuminating a long tunnel carved through the earth and bolstered by thick wooden beams.

Damp, earthy scents filled his nose, making him itch. An uneasy shiver worked its way through him. He decided he wasn't fond of enclosed places. "Are you sure this won't collapse on us?"

She laughed. "Yes, I'm sure. This way."

They traveled through the dark, dank tunnel for several yards. A rodent scurried along the ground beside him.

They finally came to a wooden door with large black hinges and a lever latch that let out a loud squeak as Audrey lifted it. Then she pushed the door wide enough for them to slip through.

They were at the base of a cliff just north of the beach where John had washed ashore. He breathed in deep of the salt-tinged air, liking the refreshing way it cleared off the itch to his senses and made his chest expand. Definitely more comfortable in open spaces.

Audrey walked away from the water to a berm separating the beach from the street. John followed, the sand making his gait unbalanced. He paused to turn back to the sea, his gaze on the churning ocean. Moonlight danced on the white-crested waves that undulated with the rough current. The lights of Canada twinkled in the distance like little beacons.

Audrey retraced her steps to his side. "John?"

Could he have washed ashore from the country across the bay? "Have you heard from the Canadian government?"

"Not yet. You have to be patient."

"I wonder if patience is one of my virtues."

She tucked her arm through his and steered him toward the road. "Patience takes discipline. There may be people who are born with an extra dose, but it's been my experience that patience takes effort. We've become too much of an instant-gratification world."

Staying to the shadows, they walked at a steady pace

down the quiet residential street to the main street. Audrey led him to a steep staircase behind the mercantile. "My apartment's up here."

He followed her up the staircase, curious to see how this woman lived. "You don't live with your mom?"

"No. She lives in a cottage near the medical center." She unlocked the door and stepped inside.

He entered the studio, taking in the very feminine decor. Bright color spots popped against earth-toned furnishings. She'd carved out very distinct sections in the open studio space.

Just inside the entrance was the kitchen and eating area. Whitewashed cabinets and stainless steel appliances took up one wall, while a small antique-looking table with folding sides and two wooden lattice-back chairs sat across from the stove and sink.

For the living space, a well-loved sofa with plush throw pillows butted up against the exterior wall, and a glass coffee table sporting a stack of books sat on a round area rug covering hardwood floors.

On the opposite wall above a six-drawer dresser, a television had been mounted on a swinging arm so that she could watch from the sofa or from the full-size bed decked out in shades of purple and pink bedding.

A small vanity table laden with jewelry and makeup paired with a curved-back chair sat next to a door that he assumed led to the bath. The whole effect was impressive. She'd made the most of the tight space.

"This is nice," he commented out loud. "Homey." He couldn't help but wonder what his accommodations were like. Did he live in a studio apartment or a house? Did he share his living space with someone? A wife? A roommate? Or did he live alone? He rubbed at the biting sting at his temple.

"Thank you," Audrey replied. "I like it."

She pulled a duffel bag from beneath the bed then proceeded to throw some clothes from the dresser into it. She grabbed a few items from the bathroom. After zipping up the bag, she lifted the strap and dropped it over her shoulder. "All set."

"Let me take that," he said, reaching for the strap.

She stepped back. "I'm capable of carrying my bag."

He held up his hands. "Whoa. I didn't think you weren't. Just trying to be a gentleman."

Embarrassment charged across her face. "Sorry. I don't mean to be testy. I'm always having to prove myself, and sometimes I forget that I can allow someone else to do things for me."

"You don't have to prove anything to me," he assured her. "I've been impressed with you from the moment I awoke in the hospital."

Her gaze narrowed slightly as if she weren't quite sure she should believe him. He remembered her disdain of charming men. He wanted to smash in the face of the man who'd hurt her.

"We should get moving," she said briskly. "My car's parked on the street."

He nodded and followed her out of the apartment. Her car was a beautiful early-model Mustang GTO in a metallic blue. The charcoal-gray interior looked brand-new. The passenger seat was comfortable. She started the engine, and the beast of a car growled. "Sweet ride."

She pulled away from the curb and headed away from the main drag. "I love this baby. I saved up for years before finally finding the right one. It has a V8 engine and had very low mileage when I bought it."

"Not very stealthy," he commented at the rumbling beneath the floorboards.

"Yeah, well, I hadn't expected I'd need stealth. But it will pretty much outrun any other car on the road."

"You sound sure. What about in the snow?"

"Snow tires." She turned down a residential street.

"Doesn't seem like a practical car."

"I manage in the winter. I keep the trunk weighted." She grinned at him. "I take this baby to the racetrack in Bangor during the summer."

For some reason he wasn't surprised. She struck him as a woman who liked adventure. "That sounds fun."

"It is." She brought the car to a halt in front of a box of a house trimmed in twinkling blue and white lights. An inflatable snowman stood sentry on the front lawn, and behind the front window curtains was the outline of a Christmas tree.

Deputy Dan Paulson hustled out of the house with a bag slung over his shoulder and carrying a thick jacket, which he thrust into John's hand when John jumped out to push the backrest forward so Paulson could climb into the small backseat. It was a good thing it would only be the three of them, because no way could another person fit back there.

"Sheriff said we're going out to Quoddy Head," Paulson remarked as she gunned the engine and they took off.

"Yep. I know a safe place." She turned onto the highway heading away from the ocean.

"Is this where the captain lives?" John asked.

She chuckled. "Not anymore. But fair warning, it's rustic."

John studied her profile, liking the curves and angles of her face. "How rustic? As in no restrooms? No heat?"

"Not that uncivilized. No internet, no cell service."

No biggie for him. He didn't have a cell phone or a computer.

Paulson nearly sputtered. "But what if we need help? How do we contact the sheriff?"

"Satellite phone," she replied. "Don't worry, Paulson. There's no way anyone will be able to find us out there."

"Yeah, from your mouth to God's ears," the other deputy groused and sat back.

"Amen to that," John said. He sent up a quick prayer that whoever was after him didn't know about this place. Audrey exited the highway onto a two-lane road that stretched out before them with dense woods on either side. Snow covered the forest floor. Occasionally John checked the side-view mirror to make sure there were no other cars traveling in the same direction. The longer they drove, the denser the foliage became.

Suddenly beams of light appeared behind them.

Adrenaline pumped through John's veins. What were the chances that someone else would be out on this road at this time of night? How had they found them? "We've got company."

The lights gained on them. The hairs on the back of his neck jumped to attention. This was no casual driver out for an evening drive.

"Hang on," Audrey warned. She cranked the wheel and sent the car into a spin. She straightened the wheel when they were facing the oncoming car.

"What are you doing?" Paulson shouted. "Are you crazy? This isn't a time to play chicken."

"I'm not," she replied in a tight tone. "Normally we'd

be dealing with a couple feet of snow at this time of year, but it's late in coming. We have only a dusting to make things slick."

Facing the oncoming vehicle allowed John to determine the rapidly approaching car was an SUV. A monster of a thing with a large brush guard, looking a bit beat-up.

"It's them," Audrey said. "The men who are trying to kill you."

Grabbing onto the dash, John asked, "What are you doing?"

"I told you this can outrun anything," she said. "That beast of a machine won't be able to turn around quickly enough to follow us. We'll be taking a more scenic route."

The distance between them and the oncoming SUV lessened. John gritted his teeth. He had to trust Audrey. Trust that she knew what she was doing, because he and Paulson were at her mercy.

Blinded by the SUV's headlights, he braced himself for impact, but at the last second, Audrey swerved, roaring past the SUV. She floored the gas, and the Mustang raced away, the studded tires thumping on the snow-crusted road. She shut off the headlights and the interior dash lights, plunging them into darkness.

"Hold on, because there's a turn up here and I'm going to make it without braking," she said.

From the backseat Paulson groaned. "You're going to kill us."

"Have a little faith, Paulson," Audrey shot back. Her heart pumped a frantic rhythm beneath her breastbone. Her hands gripped the steering wheel. She eased her foot off the gas. The car incrementally slowed. How had they found them? Her mind grappled with possibilities. Something that had been bugging her roared to the center of her mind.

How had the bad guys known where to find John when he'd washed ashore? And then when exactly to hit the ambulance?

She downshifted and cranked the wheel, smoothly taking the turn into a break between two copses of trees, and brought the car to an abrupt halt.

"John, check your clothes and your boots for a tracker."

"Tracker?" His voice held a glint of surprise. "Of course."

John searched his clothes and gritted his teeth through the pain as he finally yanked off his boots, inspecting them. "Found it." He rolled down the window, allowing the frigid air to swirl through the interior of the car while he chucked the tracking device out into the woods. "It was embedded in the heel of my boot."

Gratified and yet mad at herself for not thinking of it sooner, she pressed on the gas and they bounced along on a rough road with only the moonlight as their guide. A layer of snow that had crusted into ice crunched beneath their tires and twinkled in the moonbeams. She kept the car at a moderate speed, compared to how she'd been driving.

"Do you know where you're going?" Paulson asked in a shaky voice.

"Of course. I know every inch of these woods," she said. "Besides, there's no way for them to know where we're heading now."

After ten minutes and no sign of being followed, she

flipped on the headlights, illuminating the trees and the snow covering the ground.

The dirt road ended at a T. She slowed and took the turn to the right. They headed down another road, barely wide enough for the car. A pristine layer of white covered the swath of road, which ended at a large circle.

She parked and popped open her door. The crashing of waves on the rocky shore could be heard even though she couldn't see the ocean from where they were. "Okay, boys, we're hiking from here."

"Hiking to where?" Paulson asked from the backseat.

She twisted around to look at him. "The lighthouse."

Paulson scoffed. "I thought you said you knew a safe place out here. I thought you meant a nice warm vacation home."

She held back a smile. "The lighthouse is safe."

Paulson shook his head. "And if they decide to look for us at the lighthouse, then what?"

"We'll see them long before they reach us," she told him. "And if we need it, there's a dory we can use."

"A dory?" John opened his door.

"A small flat-bottomed boat," she answered. "There's one docked at the lighthouse."

"Great," Paulson groused. "We can be ducks in a boat. And if the bad guys don't do us in, the ocean will."

"Relax, Dan. The dory has a motor." She climbed out of the car and shut the door. She flipped up the collar of her uniform jacket and regretted they couldn't have driven right up to the lighthouse.

John climbed out, slipped on the borrowed jacket and then hustled to the back of the car to pick up Audrey's bag from the back hatch. "You lead the way," he told her.

She hesitated, fighting her need to be independent. "Thank you." She flipped on her flashlight. "We're going to be forging our own trail until we meet up with the official one."

They hiked for an hour through dense trees and bushes before they came to an actual trail carved through the forest. Then they followed that trail until they reached an area with darkened outbuildings surrounding the lighthouse that stood sentinel at the easternmost edge of the state park.

"Is the lighthouse manned?" John asked.

Audrey shook her head. "No. The lighthouse became automated in the late 1980s—"

"And the park closed in mid-October for the winter," Paulson interjected. "So basically, were alone out here without internet or cell service."

"There's a satellite phone in the watch room," Audrey assured him through gritted teeth. His whining was getting on her nerves. "The mayor insisted on putting one in several years ago when the automated system failed during a storm. That way if it ever fails again or needs to be serviced and the lighthouse has to be manned, there's a way to communicate with the outside world."

Inside the lighthouse, they made their way to the watch room. The glow from the lantern beam reflected off the oblong windows encasing the watch room. Audrey stared out at the dark night beyond and thanked God they'd made it safely.

Paulson dropped his duffel in the middle of the room. "The sheriff said to bring you a change of clothes." He tugged open the drawstring top and pulled out several things. "I grabbed some of my brother's things he'd left in our spare room when he last visited. You're about his size." Paulson then made a beeline for the satellite phone set up in the corner. "I'm going to let the sheriff know what's happened."

John snatched up the clothes Paulson had provided before moving to stand beside Audrey. "You okay?"

Turning to stare into his dark eyes, she felt the need to share her thoughts. "Just thanking God we made it here in one piece. I'll admit I was a bit nervous out there."

One side of his mouth lifted in a lopsided grin. "Only a bit? I was downright petrified."

She cocked one eyebrow, and a smile tugged at the corner of her mouth. Her hair had come loose from the clip in the back during their hike. Long tendrils curled over the collar of her uniform and tickled her neck. She pushed a strand back. "Oh? So you doubted me? But I got us here safely."

He reached up to lay claim to a lock of blond hair, rubbing the silky strands between his fingers. "Yes, you did. And very expertly, at that."

His praise softened something inside her. She mentally scrambled to reclaim her professional detachment, but apparently it was hiding behind tender affection.

John glanced at Paulson, who had his back to them. Then he tugged her close and leaned toward her but stilled with just a few inches between them, allowing her the opportunity to step away, to put a stop to what was about to happen.

Appreciation and attraction heated her skin. She knew the right thing to do would to be step back, create space between them, both physically and emotionally, but her feet stayed rooted to the ground. Longing welled from deep inside her, and she found she wanted, needed his kiss.

"Hey, guys." Paulson's voice broke through the moment. "The sheriff has some news you might want to hear."

Irritated by the interruption, and without breaking eye contact with John, Audrey asked, "What is it?"

"Sheriff knows John's real name."

The words dispersed the intimacy of the moment.

John sucked in a breath. Audrey felt his anticipation and his dread in her gut. Finally they would find out who he was and hopefully why someone wanted to kill him.

Chapter Seven

"Yes, sir," Paulson said into the phone. "I'll let them know." He hung up.

Audrey's gaze jerked away from John, and her jaw dropped. She couldn't believe Paulson had dropped the bomb that the sheriff knew John's identity and then disconnected without letting her or John talk to the sheriff. "Wait! Why did you hang up?" She rushed across the room to grab the phone from Paulson. "What did the sheriff say?"

John stalked closer, his jaw set in a tight line. His dark eyes bored holes into Paulson. So different from the man who moments ago had nearly kissed her. She swallowed back the disappointment at being interrupted, even though she knew kissing John would have been a huge, colossal mistake. She couldn't let herself be taken in by his charm and good looks, even though there was more to him than that.

He'd trusted her when he had no reason to. He'd shown her respect and consideration. He was struggling in a difficult situation yet had shown concern for others. She admitted to herself she liked him.

However, she had to keep an emotional distance. Once he discovered who he was and where he belonged, he'd leave Calico Bay behind, while her life was rooted here. Letting herself become attached would only set her up for heartbreak, both personally and professionally. She had to keep her eye on the future, on her goal of one day being sheriff. The town deserved a leader that could keep her emotions in check.

"Hey, don't get mad at me." Paulson held up his hands, palms out. "Sheriff said he received a call from someone in the Canadian government." He glanced at John. "They're sending people here."

"What kind of people?" Officers to take John into custody? The thought made her blood run cold.

"Did he give you my name?" John asked in a razor-sharp tone that sent a shiver down Audrey's spine. His fingers flexed around the bundle of clothes in his hands.

Paulson nodded eagerly. "Nathanial Longhorn. Ring any bells?"

Audrey held her breath. John's blank expression didn't bode well.

Slowly he shook his head. "No. Did he tell you anything else? Do I have a family?"

Paulson shook his head. "Sheriff said no wife, no kids."

That was good, wasn't it? He turned on his heel and paced back to the window overlooking the ocean.

Directly above them, up a ten-rung metal ladder, was the lantern room, where the electrical, nonrotating lighthouse signal was housed. It blinked every two seconds, throwing a beam of light fifteen nautical miles over the water, warning of the rocky jut of land they stood on.

Empathy engulfed her. She couldn't imagine the frustration of not knowing who he was or his past. She wanted to go to him, wrap her arms around him and tell him it would be all right. But she doubted he'd believe her. Not to mention that would be so inappropriate.

Something bad had happened to this man. Someone was still trying to kill him. And despite others' misgivings, she felt deep inside that he was a good man. A man who deserved her protection.

She couldn't be wrong about him. Could she? She sent up a silent prayer asking God to make the truth known. If she were proven wrong, then so be it, but until then she would continue to believe in him and hope for the best.

"Sheriff requested we head to the station first thing in the morning and he'll give you all the details," Paulson continued. "He's also got Harrison and Dietrich out patrolling, looking for the SUV."

Audrey cradled the phone, tempted to call the sheriff back, but she knew her great-uncle liked to do things in person. If he'd wanted to discuss John—er, Nathanial—over the phone, he would have. She set the phone aside. "I guess we have to exercise some patience. Morning will come soon enough."

She walked to Nathanial's side and stared at his proud profile. His jaw worked. Most likely gnashing his teeth with irritation at having to wait to learn more about himself. "I'm sorry you don't recognize your name."

His lips twisted. "Not your fault. It's strange, you know. When I apply the name *Nathanial* to myself, it feels tight in my brain." He grimaced. "I'm not sure how to explain."

"Maybe it's part of whatever your mind is protecting you from. You know—" she dropped her voice an octave "—the betrayal."

He blew out a breath. "Yeah. I guess." He turned to face her. His dark, troubled eyes searched her face. "Thank you."

Surprise bloomed in her chest. "For what?"

"Saving my life. Keeping me safe. I have the strangest feeling that I should be the one protecting you."

She smiled and put her hand on his arm. His muscles bunched beneath her palm. "I'm not the one in danger."

"Except that when you're with me, you are," he countered.

She squeezed his arm. "Part of the job." She removed her hand. "Come with me to the visitors' center. There's a restroom where you can change your clothes. And I'll see if I can find us some food, since we skipped dinner."

He extended his hand, indicating she go first. "Lead the way."

She took him down an interior spiral staircase and opened the door to an attached portion of the building with a key on her key ring. "This once was the lighthouse keeper's quarters but was renovated into a visitors' center and museum. The US Coast Guard had a station here back in the day. When they abandoned the property, the Yeaton family took it over and made the old station into rental property, which is where we would have been staying had our enemies in the black SUV not followed us." She pointed to the left. "Restrooms are there."

"Why do you have keys to the lighthouse?" he asked.

"My great-great-great-grandmother was related to Hopley Yeaton, a naval captain in the late 1700s. He was considered to be the father of the US Coast Guard.

The lighthouse association wanted me on the board because of the relation, and they gave me a set of keys."

"Not only are you beautiful, you're American royalty," he commented with a gleam of interest in his eyes.

A heated flush rose up her neck and settled in her cheeks. He was so smooth with his compliments. If she weren't careful, she'd find herself following through on the promise of a kiss. "I'm going to go look for some food."

His soft laugh followed her into the store part of the visitors' center. She gathered bags of trail mix, beef jerky and bottles of water. She wrote out an IOU and set it on the counter. In the spring when the center reopened, she'd settle up. It wasn't like anyone wouldn't know where to find her.

"Any chance there's a razor around?" Nathanial stepped into the store wearing the change of clothes provided by Paulson.

He looked so different in well-worn jeans that looked like they were tailor-made for his long, lean legs and trim waist. A plaid flannel shirt in Christmas colors stretched across his broad shoulders. He'd rolled the sleeves up to reveal muscled forearms. He'd dampened his hair and slicked it back with his fingers. He rubbed a hand over his stubbled jaw, and her own fingers curled with the yearning to do the same.

"Sorry, no." Normally she didn't go in for the scruffy look, but on him it worked well. "Tomorrow when we go back into town, we can hit the mercantile."

He eyed her bounty. "You found a feast." She handed him a couple bags of trail mix and a bottle of water.

"It's not fancy but will have to do." They took the stairs to the watchtower.

Paulson was on the outside catwalk. When he saw them he came inside. He rubbed his arms and shivered. "It's definitely going to snow again soon. I hope we don't get stuck here."

"See anything out there?" Audrey asked. There was no way the men in the SUV would just give up. She figured they were waiting for daylight before resuming their hunt for Nathanial. At least she hoped that was the case.

If they found the gravel road to the trailhead, they could hike in and stage an assault. But that could happen anywhere. At least here in the lighthouse, they had the advantage of a high viewpoint and could see them coming.

"No. It's dark and quiet out there," Paulson replied as he accepted the bottle of water she offered him. "I found a pile of blankets in the closet. I'll grab a couple and head downstairs to watch the door."

She handed him a stick of beef jerky and a bag of trail mix. "I can take the first watch."

"Not necessary," Paulson said, taking the offered treats, and grabbed two blankets from the pile on the floor. "We can trade off in a few hours."

There was something in his tone that grated on her nerves and led her to think he wouldn't make the trade out of some chivalrous need to protect the female. For half a second she contemplated arguing with him and demanding she take the first watch, but then she decided it wasn't worth the aggravation. She'd set her watch alarm and relieve him from guard duty whether he wanted her to or not.

Nathanial found a chair and dragged it to the center of the room. "Do you have cuffs on you?"

She turned to face him. "Excuse me?"

"Your boss was right to put me in a cell," he stated. He sat and placed his hands on the armrests of the chair. "We don't know my story. The people coming to claim me could very well be taking me to prison."

"No." She wouldn't accept that despite the validity in his words. "If the sheriff thought you were a threat to me and Paulson, he wouldn't have called—he'd have shown up and taken you into his custody."

"Why do you believe in me?" He tilted his head and stared at her with curiosity gleaming in his dark eyes.

She stepped closer. "My grandmother always told me I had a good sense of people. The sheriff says it's what makes me good at my job." Her mouth twisted wryly. "It just seems to be in my love life that my judgment fails." Oh, brother. Had she just said that out loud? Embarrassment sent a heated flush through her. Maybe he'd let the admission slip by without comment.

He reached out and took her hand. "Tell me."

She tried to disengage from his grasp, but he held firm. His thumb made little circles on her palm, igniting a maelstrom of tingles to career through her. Totally distracting her. "What?"

He rose, pulling her closer, trapping her hand against his chest. Warmth infused her, chasing away the chill of the lighthouse. "Tell me about the man who made you so shy of relationships."

She had to tilt her head back to meet his gaze. She wasn't used to having to do that. More often than not, she was taller than the men in her life. The look in his eyes enthralled her. Her breath caught in her chest and held. She didn't want to think about Kyle, much less talk about him. She licked her lips. Nathanial's gaze tracked the movement. Her insides quivered. "What makes you think there was someone?"

His mouth curved. "I may not remember my name or my past, but I can read you. You're uncomfortable with compliments, which suggests you don't trust flattering words. You have a chip on your shoulder about being regarded as an equal by your peers and your boss that tells me you've had to prove yourself over and over again. And you keep an emotional barrier up." He grinned. "Plus, my innate charm seems to offend you."

His words dug into wounds she'd thought she'd kept hidden. She lifted her chin. "I'm sure everything you just said could apply to most women in my position. And it isn't so much offense I feel at your charm. I just distrust it."

He conceded her point by inclining his head. "Probably. And you're wise to distrust charm until you're certain it's genuine." A wry expression spread over his handsome face. "It takes a strong and intelligent woman to enter a field that has traditionally been dominated by men. And you, Deputy Audrey Martin, are a strong and intelligent woman."

If he only knew. Shame and guilt rushed in to kick her in the gut. She dropped her gaze and once again tried to put distance between them. He lifted her hand to kiss her knuckles, effectively stopping her in her tracks.

She swallowed and watched his nicely formed lips place feather-like touches against her skin. He was torturing her without inflicting pain. Instead, he stirred yearnings deep in her heart.

Yearnings for someone to make her feel special. Someone whom she could be herself with, not always have to be brave and tough. Someone who would be true, genuine.

She'd be foolish to look for that with this man. There was too much unknown about him. And she needed to remember what she really wanted in life—to be sheriff. Not some lovesick, wimpy woman trailing after a man with no memory.

"I would never purposely hurt you," he said softly, as if he could read her mind. "That's why I think you need to cuff me to the chair and stay far away from me."

Probably good advice. But every instinct rebelled at the thought. "Not happening. If you want to talk, we can talk. But I'm not chaining you to a chair without a reason."

This time when she tugged on her hand, he released her. She moved to the pile of blankets. She wrapped one around her shoulders and then handed him one. He did the same. They sat on the floor with their backs propped up against the wall. They munched on trail mix and beef jerky.

"So," he finally said. "Spill."

Her jaw clenched. Her teeth sank into an almond. Her mouth went dry. She took a swig of water, debating how and what to say. "It's not a big deal," she said, hoping to play nonchalant. "I fell in a love with a jerk. We broke up. I've been gun-shy of romance ever since. End of story."

"I doubt that. What made him a jerk?"

"He was a player. Had me on a string along with several other women. He'd led me to believe I was special, that he cared about me." She let out a mirthless laugh. "I should have known better. I did know better, but I was blinded by his charm. He'd talked me into setting aside my values and faith with empty promises of forever."

"Ouch. How did it end?"

She grimaced, remembering the scene she'd made. "I broke it off. In the quad. Very loudly."

Nathanial chuckled. "Good for you. You don't strike me as the type to quietly slip away. You're a woman of action."

That made her smile. "I haven't seen him since that day I told him we were through, but I heard he went on to Georgetown and became a lawyer."

"I'd make a crack about lawyers, but I don't believe in generalizations," he said. "Not all lawyers, just like not all men, are made from the same cloth."

What cloth was he made from, she wondered.

"And you haven't dated since the jerk?"

She shrugged. "A few dates. Nothing serious." No one had made her heart beat faster. But Nathanial did. She didn't understand her attraction to him. Was it the allure of mystery surrounding his loss of memory? Or was he the one her mother had always said would come along and make her rethink her life? She frowned at that thought. She had no intention of rethinking her path.

"What's Sean's story?"

She tucked in her chin at the sudden change in topic. Did he know about Sean's crush on her? "What do you mean?"

"I saw his prosthetic."

Her heart thumped with sadness and pride for the young man she thought of as a brother. "Afghanistan. Four years ago. His unit was ambushed by Taliban insurgents."

"That's rough."

"Yeah. He was a combat medic." She couldn't keep the bitter taste of anger out of her tone. "He was there to help others."

"He was also a soldier," Nathanial stated quietly.

"Yes. He earned his Combat Medical Badge for providing care under fire. From what I've heard, he helped others while he was injured himself." She swallowed past the lump in her throat. "He's a hero."

"It must have been hard for him to return to this quiet community after the chaos of war."

"He had a hard time adjusting at first," she admitted. "Watching him come to terms with his loss was difficult for everyone. The town pulled together, sent him back to school to become a civilian paramedic and bought the ambulance."

Nathanial winced. "Which was destroyed because of me."

"No, it was destroyed because criminals tried to kill you. The insurance will get Sean another ambulance."

"He has a crush on you."

Biting back a groan, she popped a handful of trail mix into her mouth and chewed, giving herself time to formulate an answer to a complicated situation. After she took another drink of water, she said, "He's the younger brother of one of my childhood best friends. I couldn't... I mean, he's like the little brother I never had."

"Ah. Good."

She arched an eyebrow. "Good?" She turned to face him fully. Though shadows played over his features, there was no mistaking the intensity in his expression.

"I wasn't sure if you and he..." Nathanial's mouth lifted at the corner. "I was hoping you weren't involved with him."

Her pulse kicked up. "Why?"

"Because then I'd feel guilty for kissing you."

"But you haven't kissed me."

"You're right, we were interrupted."

He touched her cheek, his fingers trailing across her skin. She sucked in a quick breath. Her heart hammered. She was torn between wanting him to kiss her and wanting, needing, to keep a distance. He lowered his head, once again pausing, letting her make the final decision.

So many conflicting thoughts swirled in her head. She was setting herself up for hurt. She was curious, wanting to know what it would feel like to kiss this man. She was supposed to be protecting him, not forming some romantic attachment. But would one kiss qualify as an attachment? One kiss couldn't hurt anything, could it?

Her mind flashed to Kyle. To the seduction he'd laid on her, beguiling her into believing that taking one step wouldn't lead to another and another, until he'd led her down a path that had left her filled with guilt and shame. And anger when he'd shown his true colors.

She put her fingers against Nathanial's lips. The warmth of his mouth flowed through her, making her hesitate. But she forged ahead, knowing she was making the right choice. "I can't. This isn't going to happen."

Disappointment shone in the dark depths of his eyes, but he nodded, retreating from her both physically and emotionally. It was like an invisible barrier had gone up between them. She didn't like it but had no idea what to do about it, either.

He settled his head against the wall. "We should get some rest. Tomorrow you won't have to worry about me anymore. I'll become someone else's problem."

You're not a problem, she wanted to tell him. But she held her tongue. And he was wrong. She'd continue to worry about him as long as someone was out to kill him.

Chapter Eight

The next morning, after dropping Paulson off at his house, Nathanial and Audrey headed to the sheriff's station and parked at the curb outside. Nathanial gripped the interior door handle of Audrey's bright blue muscle car. A muscle car. Go figure. The woman was full of surprises.

Last night when they'd climbed into the Mustang, he'd thought the sweet ride too much car for the beautiful deputy, but the way she'd outmaneuvered their pursuers had made it clear that the woman knew how to drive. And was skilled. He'd been impressed and attracted. He had a strong feeling he'd never met anyone like Audrey. But then again, how would he know? His brain wasn't cooperating.

Learning his name was Nathanial Longhorn had been surreal. The name fit like a too-small glove, making his mind and heart anxious. He'd tried to explain the sensation to Audrey, but how did he explain something he didn't understand?

Like his attraction to the pretty blonde. Well, okay, that he could understand. What man in his right mind—

or not right, as the case might be with him—wouldn't be attracted to a tall, curvy, beautiful woman?

But it was more than her looks. She was special on the inside, too. Resourceful. Calm in the face of danger. Protective but not overbearing. And that chip she carried on her shoulder was so obvious, yet she tried not to let it rule her.

He'd noticed that she hadn't liked it when Paulson had taken the first watch last night. She'd wanted to prove she was up to the task. There was no question in Nathanial's mind that she was capable, and he was thankful she'd chosen to swallow her need to take action. He'd been able to spend more time with her, and she'd opened up to him, trusting him with the story of her past romantic relationship. Though he had a feeling there was more to the story, he hadn't pushed. Instead…

His hand flexed on the door handle.

He'd made a fool of himself. He'd allowed his attraction and a deep-seated yearning for connection to overtake his common sense. He'd made a pass at her and been rebuffed.

As he should have been. He had no business starting something with the lovely Audrey when he had no idea why someone was trying to kill him.

Once they stepped inside the sheriff's station, she would no longer be in danger because of him.

He would accept whatever awaited him inside the brick building, despite the constriction in his lungs and the pounding in his head. By the grace of God above he would leave Audrey and Calico Bay behind, taking with him the danger that lurked in the shadows.

From the driver's seat, Audrey asked, "Are you nervous?"

Nathanial slanted her a glance. No doubt she was wondering why he was hesitating. Maybe he was a coward at heart. Something inside rebelled at the thought, but he couldn't shake the dread crimping his shoulder muscles and making his breathing labored. Forcing air into his lungs, he gave her a rueful twist of his lips and admitted, "Yeah, I am."

She reached across the center console and touched his arm, her hand warm against his skin exposed by the rolled-up sleeve of the plaid flannel shirt he wore. "It's understandable. But I'm here, and I'm not going to let anything bad happen to you."

The tightness around his mind and heart eased a fraction. He covered her hand with his. He was amazed by her dedication to him. She had no reason to believe in him. For all they knew, he would be taken into custody by the Canadian government and hauled away for crimes he couldn't remember.

His throat closed. He blinked back the emotions choking him and managed to say, "I appreciate your support. Whatever happens, I hope you know that you have been a bright spot in an otherwise bleak existence."

The corners of her mouth lifted slightly. "Melodrama much?"

He chuckled. "I guess so."

She gave his arm a squeeze before withdrawing her hand and opening her door. "Come on. Better to get this over with quickly rather than drawing it out."

He liked her pragmatic outlook. He rolled his shoulders, took a deep breath and popped the door open. He stepped out into the brisk morning air. He glanced up and down the street, studying the vehicles, looking for the SUV and the men inside.

Reflexively his gaze lifted. He wasn't sure what instinct made him search the rooftops of the buildings stretching along the main road of town.

Something glinted in the morning sunlight.

A jolt of adrenaline kick-started his pulse. He grabbed Audrey and yanked her to the sidewalk. A fraction of a second later, a *crack* split the air. He dived over her, covering her with his body. A bullet slammed into the cement inches from his head. Bits of concrete stung his flesh. The noise stunned his ears.

"Get off me!" Audrey yelled.

He rolled toward the cover of the car, taking her with him as a barrage of gunfire followed in their wake. They landed with a thud against the back passenger door. He scooted them over to use the tire for extra cover.

Audrey scrambled to a squat and drew her sidearm. "Where's the shooter?"

"Two blocks up. Southeast corner." His hand flexed with the need to return fire.

The sheriff and four other men rushed out of the station, each with a gun in hand. Nathanial glimpsed gold badges on belts beneath various types of jackets. He didn't have time to study the men as Audrey waved them back.

"Shooter," she called out. "Southeast corner of the bank."

Sheriff Crump nodded and disappeared inside. The four strangers spread out in a tactical pattern with weapons drawn. They took cover behind bushes and poles. Clearly these were the men sent to retrieve him. One man, tall and well-dressed in a long wool coat over slacks and a dress shirt and tie, motioned for him and

Audrey to come to the safety of the station. He had dark
hair swept back from a hard-edged face.

"We'll cover you," he called out.

Nathanial shared a quick glance with Audrey.

"You go," he told her. "You're not the target."

Her gaze narrowed, and her jaw firmed. "I'm not
leaving you. We go together."

The stubborn resolve in her blue eyes let him know
arguing with her was futile. He gave one sharp nod. She
scrambled to his other side—the side that put her in the
direct line of the shooter. Tension vibrated through his
body. A siren rent the air. Obviously the sheriff had
called for reinforcements.

She put her hand on his shoulder. "Move with me."

Hating the vulnerable feeling stealing over him, he
had no choice but to let her do her job. "Let's go."

They hurried across the expanse of sidewalk. The
men closed ranks behind them, covering their flank.
Nathanial braced himself for another round of gunfire
that never came. They made it inside the building, and
the sheriff hustled them out of the lobby and into the
bull pen where the deputies had their desks.

"Get down," the sheriff instructed.

Nathanial crouched beside Audrey behind a thick
metal desk.

The men spread out, covering windows, while the
one who'd taken the lead stayed near the doorway. The
sheriff's radio crackled.

"Sheriff." Deputy Harrison's voice echoed in the station. "Shooter escaped. Found spent shell casings, but
nothing else."

"Copy," the sheriff said. "Stay put. Keep alert. I'll
send Lindsey and her team over."

"Lindsey? Team?" Nathanial asked Audrey.

She rose and holstered her weapon. "The county's forensic specialists."

He stood and faced the congregated men. The leader leveled Nathanial with an intense, searching stare. Not that the other three men's gazes weren't equal in intensity, but for some reason this man's eyes provoked an odd sensation of alertness within Nathanial.

Disconcerted by the response, Nathanial studied the other men. They ranged in age from roughly twenties to somewhere in their thirties. He mentally shrugged. It was hard to tell with intense men like these. They held themselves with an air of authority that no one could miss. They were dressed in civilian clothes, so Nathanial hadn't a clue which branch of the Canadian government they worked for.

Audrey stepped to his side, silently offering her support, drawing the men's attention. He didn't like the way they assessed her with both curiosity and wariness. He had the strangest urge to slip an arm around her in a show of possession. He wanted to stake his claim on Audrey and make it clear she was off-limits.

He clenched his jaw. That was so out of left field and not going to happen. She'd been very direct that she wasn't interested. And he shouldn't be, either.

He cleared his throat, drawing the men's focus back to him. "You may have heard my memories before waking on the beach here in Calico Bay are gone."

The man nearest him nodded. "We've heard. The doctor says retrograde amnesia. Your memory could return at any time."

Surprise flickered through Nathanial. They'd discussed his condition with Dr. Martin. "I've been told my name is Nathanial Longhorn. But that doesn't tell me who I am or why someone wants me dead."

The bigger of the four men stepped forward. "We can fill in some of the first part but not the latter." There was sympathy and wariness in his hazel eyes.

Frustration mingled with relief. "Then tell me what you can. Starting with who you are."

The big man's mouth twitched. He stuck out his hand. "Inspector Drew Kelley with the Royal Canadian Mounted Police."

Nathanial grasped his hand. "Nice to meet you."

"I'm Luke Wellborn," the youngest of the group said as he moved forward with his hand out. He was slighter in frame than the others, with intelligent gray eyes and a firm grip. "US Border Patrol."

The other man hung back. There was no mistaking the anger in the man's blue gaze as he tipped his chin. "Chase Smith, ATF."

The acronym for the United States Bureau of Alcohol, Tobacco, Firearms and Explosives slammed into Nathanial. American and Canadian law enforcement. What did that mean?

"You really don't remember anything?" Chase asked.

Studying the other man, Nathanial tried to find some spark of recognition and failed. He shook his head. "No. Nothing."

By the derisive curl of Chase's lip, Nathanial had no problem discerning the guy didn't believe him. What were RCMP, USBP and ATF doing here? Nathanial turned his focus on the last man in the group. The one he'd pegged as the leader. There was something in the man's expression that tugged at Nathanial, making him want to remember, but the more he probed his mind, the more his head throbbed.

"Blake Fallon, ICE."

"Immigration and Customs Enforcement," Nathanial said beneath his breath.

Blake moved closer, his dark eyes going to the place on Nathanial's head that still bore the mark of the blow he'd sustained prior to washing ashore on the beach. "What is the last thing you *do* remember?"

"I told you," Nathanial said. "Nothing of my life before waking up in the hospital. I didn't know my name until you gave it to the sheriff." He looked at Drew. "You said you could fill me in on who I am. How do I know my name really is Nathanial?"

Blake withdrew a black wallet from the inside pocket of his long wool coat. "Here. This belongs to you."

Mouth turning to cotton, Nathanial accepted the offered item. The soft leather felt strange in his hand. He flipped it open. On one side was a gold badge with the Canada Border Services Agency emblem, and the other held a driver's license issued in Saskatchewan, Canada, with his photo, name and stats. So many questions ran through his head. He was Canadian? Why did an ICE agent have his wallet? What waited for him at the address on the driver's license? The pounding in his head intensified, making him wince. He passed the wallet over to Audrey.

"I knew it," she said beneath her breath. "I knew you were one of the good guys."

He wanted to believe she was right. Was she? "I'm a border officer?"

"For several years," Drew said. "A good one, too."

Pressure built behind his eyes. "Why does it take four federal agencies from two countries to come for me?"

"You're one of us," Blake said. "We are all part of a cross-border task force. We've been working together for four years."

"Task force." The words reverberated through his brain, setting off a pinging of pain that made him clutch his head for fear his skull would crack open. The room dimmed. He could feel his legs weaken. Blindly he reached for Audrey. He grasped the sleeve of her jacket.

Her strong hand gripped his shoulders. "Nathanial." His name sounded foreign on her lips. "What is it? What can I do to help?"

Audrey's soothing voice brought him back from the edge. He fought the pain, found strength in her touch, her presence. He focused his gaze on her concerned face, letting the sight of her ground him, calm him. It didn't make sense that this woman, whom he barely knew, should be the one to anchor him, rather than these men he apparently worked closely with.

"Here, sit." Blake dragged a chair to him. "The doctor said you'd been having headaches."

Bracing his feet apart, Nathanial remained standing. He gave Audrey a nod to let her know it was okay for her to let go of him. She removed her hands from his shoulders but stayed glued to his side. To Blake, Nathanial said, "What happened? How did I end up on a beach in Maine?"

Blake ran his fingers through his brown hair. "We don't know."

"We were in the middle of a mission when you went rogue," Chase said, his voice hard.

"We don't know that he went rogue," Drew interjected with a tone of warning.

Chase's mouth set in a firm line, and he spun away to stare out the station window.

A shudder of dread rippled through Nathanial. "What was the mission?"

"To take down a known gunrunner operating out of Saint John Harbour, New Brunswick," Blake supplied. "We had good intel that a shipment had been smuggled over from the States."

"You were on overwatch," Drew told him.

Nathanial winced as a fresh sliver of pain pierced through his brain. "I don't know what that is."

Chase made a disgruntled sound. Nathanial wondered if they'd been enemies before, or was his animosity due to his belief that Nathanial had gone rogue? The thought that he'd abandoned his post willingly left him feeling hollow inside.

"You're an expert marksman," Blake said.

"And you're lethal with a knife," Luke, the USBP agent, chimed in.

Nathanial absorbed their pronouncements, but the words held no relevance for him. Yet…hadn't he longed to feel the weight of a weapon in his hand? Now at least he knew why. But he couldn't visualize himself with a gun or a blade.

"What happened on that day?" Audrey asked. "I take it from your comments Nathanial disappeared."

"Yes." Blake's dark gaze focused on Audrey for a moment. Nathanial recognized the gleam of speculation there before Blake turned his gaze on him. Nathanial wasn't prepared for the bleak sadness flooding the man's expression. "You were on the roof with an assault rifle. Your job was to scout the area and to keep those on the ground informed of any potential threats."

Nathanial's stomach dropped. He had a horrible feeling that he'd failed. Purposely? "I left my post?"

A tense moment of silence met his question. Finally Blake gave a short nod. "Yes. One moment you were on the com device in my ear telling me to hold on. Then static."

"We sent men to the roof to see what happened," Drew said. "They found your rifle, com devices and your Becker Necker lying abandoned."

Nathanial wasn't sure what a Becker Necker was, so he glanced at Audrey to see if she did.

"A combat knife made by the US company Ka-Bar," she answered his unspoken question. Then she turned her sharp-eyed gaze on Blake. "What's a Canada Border Services officer doing carrying a US-made military knife?"

"It was a gift," Blake replied. A muscle jumped in his jaw, as if he were struggling to contain some emotion.

Had the knife been a present from a woman? Nathanial hadn't yet asked if there was someone in his life waiting for him. His chest ached thinking about it.

"I have one, too," Drew interjected. "Which is why I know you didn't leave that roof of your own free will. You wouldn't have left that behind."

Nathanial's gaze bounced between the two men. "Who was the gift from?"

Drew looked at Blake.

Blake swallowed. "From me. It was a groomsman gift."

"I was in your wedding." Nathanial's voice sounded strangled to his own ears. Obviously they'd been good friends. His heart ached. *Why, Lord, can't I remember these men?*

"You were my best man," Blake added in a rough voice.

Best friends.

He heard Audrey's sharp intake of breath. A wave of frustration hit him, making his stomach roil and his heart feel crushed. He tried to remember, to call up memories of a happy period in his life. But there was nothing but a black abyss that threatened to swallow him whole.

As if sensing the turmoil going on inside him, Audrey slipped her hand into his. He took comfort from her touch, her steady presence.

"Enough with the bro-fest." Chase whirled from the window and stalked toward him.

Nathanial tensed. Drew made a move to intercept Chase, but the ATF agent held up his hand and shook his head before he returned his attention to Nathanial. The barely suppressed fury wasn't as surprising as the pain underlining the more volatile emotion.

"We came here to uncover the truth." Chase's tone was ragged, haunted. "My men deserve that."

Everything inside Nathanial froze. "What aren't you telling me?"

Nathanial looked to Blake. The grimness in his eyes didn't bode well. A lump of dread lodged in Nathanial's throat. A heavy, oppressive weight bore down on him. He focused back on Chase. The world narrowed to where he could see only the other man's blue eyes.

"Two of my men died because you left your post."

Chapter Nine

The air rushed out of Audrey's lungs. Warmth from the sheriff's station's heater had sweat breaking out on her skin beneath the heavy weight of her uniform vest. The declaration by the man named Chase echoed in her head. Men had died because Nathanial hadn't been there to warn them of an attack.

Her gaze swept over the other men, hoping for some sign of denial, but the anguish in each man's eyes told the truth. Her heart twisted with empathy. Losing a comrade in arms was never easy. That these men blamed Nathanial sent a shiver across her nape. She wanted to defend him, tell them he would never do what they were accusing him of, yet did she really know what he would or wouldn't do?

Was she letting her heart rule over her head?

She knew next to nothing about this man, yet she couldn't shake the deep, instinctive reaction that kept her glued to his side. She wouldn't condemn him without proof. But she'd better keep her heart in check. Letting herself become attached to this man wasn't wise, because if her gut was wrong, she'd not only be embarrassed and in potential danger but she risked having her heart bruised again. A fate she wanted to avoid at all costs.

Standing beside her, Nathanial swayed. For a moment she thought he was going down. She reached out to steady him as he sank onto the chair the ICE agent, Blake, had previously offered him.

Nathanial put his head into his hands. "I wish I could remember what happened."

The tortured tone of his voice tugged at her heart. She met Blake's gaze. "He was hit over the head and thrown into the sea. We found a tracking device embedded in his boot heel. That has to mean he wasn't involved, right?"

Blake's eyes widened, and he shared a glance with the Mountie. "Someone took him out of commission."

"But the question is who," Drew stated.

Luke Wellborn, the US Border Patrol agent, had been hanging back but now stepped forward, his boyish face pale. "One of Kosloff's men."

The AFT agent, Chase, rubbed his jaw. "Or one of ours," he stated grimly. "There's no way Kosloff knew we were there unless a mole told him. But whether Officer Longhorn was involved or not is still up for debate. We don't know that he was attacked. He could have easily slipped, hit his head and fallen into the ocean. After giving up my men's location."

"Then how do you explain someone trying to kill him? Repeatedly," Audrey shot back.

"There's no honor among bad guys." Chase shrugged. "He may have outlived his usefulness."

"I don't believe that," Blake said. "I know Nathanial. He would never betray his country or the team."

Did they forget he was sitting there? She didn't like that they talked about John, er, Nathanial—it was weird to be calling him by a different name now— so callously. Yet he couldn't defend himself, because he didn't know the truth. His mind refused to cooperate. It was maddening and frightful at the same time.

"I agree," Drew said. "I trust Nathanial."

"We'll let the director make the determination of his guilt or not," Chase said. He fixed his gaze on Nathanial. "We're taking you to the IBETs headquarters."

Nathanial lifted his head. "Which is where?"

"Washington, DC." Blake moved closer and put a hand on Nathanial's shoulder. "Don't worry, we'll keep you safe." Blake glanced at her. "Thank you, Deputy. We'll take it from here."

For some reason his assurance didn't alleviate the worry in Audrey's gut. She couldn't just let go of the case, not to mention she didn't quite trust these men. It was her job to protect her community, to protect this man and to do her job she needed to uncover the truth.

And the only way she would be able to discover what was really going on was if she stuck close to Nathanial. She was about to tell the ICE man that when Nathanial jerked to his feet.

"No. I'm not going with you," he said. The panic in his dark eyes wrenched at her heart. "I don't know you. You say I do, but I don't remember you, and I'm supposed to just trust you?"

She couldn't stop herself from putting her hand on his arm, offering him some comfort.

His gaze jerked to her and held for a long moment, and then he took a shuddering breath. His expression clearing, his jaw hardened. "I have to go with them."

Narrowing her gaze, she protested, "No, you don't. You're in my custody. I'm not ready to release you."

His eyes softened before shuttering, closing off his emotions. "It's time. I've put you in enough danger."

Her back teeth slammed together as she curbed the jolt of disbelief and anger that reared up. If he thought he was going to sacrifice his safety by going with these men that he'd already admitted he didn't know or trust because of some misguided sense of chivalry, he had another thing coming. She didn't need anyone protecting her. She was capable of protecting herself and him. "If you go, I go."

He blinked and tucked his chin. "I can't ask that of you."

She arched an eyebrow. "You're not. And hear me clearly, I'm not asking for your permission, either."

A small smile curved his lips. "You're a force to be reckoned with, Deputy Martin."

Heat crept up her neck, but she held his gaze. "Yes. And don't forget it."

He laughed at that. "I wouldn't dream of it."

"Then that's settled," Sheriff Crump said, stepping into the conversation. "Deputy Martin will escort Officer Longhorn to Washington, DC, for his debriefing with Director Moore."

All four federal agents stared at the sheriff.

Blake canted his head. "How did…"

The sheriff's smile wasn't exactly smug, but Audrey had seen that look on her great-uncle's face before. He'd already checked out these men. She wasn't surprised. Great-uncle David wasn't a pushover. And he was thorough. She hoped to be just like him when she became sheriff.

"The minute you contacted me, Agent Fallon, I was on the phone with Homeland Security," the sheriff said, confirming Audrey's thoughts. "I'm sure Director Moore will appreciate the extra security for your team."

The looks on the men's faces said they sure didn't appreciate it, but she didn't care. She was going to stick close to Nathanial. She couldn't deny the prospect pleased her more than it should. Though she had a feeling keeping her heart safe from unexpected emotions stirred by Nathanial might prove to be a harder proposition than finding the truth about what had happened to him.

When they touched down in Washington, DC, they were whisked away from Reagan National Airport in black SUVs. Nathanial and Audrey were in the second vehicle with ICE agent Blake Fallon driving and RCMP inspector Drew Kelley in the front passenger seat. Up ahead in another identical Suburban, the ATF agent Chase Smith and US Border Patrol agent Luke Wellborn led the way through the late-afternoon metro-area traffic.

Snow covered the ground and piled at the curbs, where snowplows had pushed back the white powder and sprinkled salt on the asphalt to make the roads passable. Strings of white lights clung to the streetlamps and trees lining the avenues. Pedestrians, bundled beneath heavy coats and scarves, made their way along the sidewalks.

From the back passenger seat of the second SUV, Nathanial stared out the side window at the many passing monuments and statues memorializing the United States of America. He could name the monolithic Washington Monument bathed in white lights, but he didn't know how he knew its name or whether he'd seen it before. He recognized the Lincoln Memorial and the White House. But putting labels to the structures was as far as his memory allowed.

His gaze moved to the brightly lit, large evergreen Christmas tree located south of the White House as a headache born of frustration and tension pounded at his temples and tightened the muscles of his neck and shoulders. *Merry Christmas*. He rolled his shoulders and glanced at his seatmate.

Audrey peered through the windows with an avid expression of awe.

"You've never been to the nation's capital before?" he asked.

She smiled at him, and his heart thumped in his chest. She had a great smile, and it eased some of his anxiety. There was something about this woman that calmed his nerves. He figured there was some psychological mumbo jumbo that could explain his reaction to her.

She shook her head, and he caught a whiff of her vanilla-scented perfume. "I've always wanted to come here for vacation. There's so much to see."

Before leaving Calico Bay, she'd changed into civilian clothes when she'd hurried to her apartment to pack a bag. And she'd let her hair down. Literally.

Her blond hair hung down in a silky sheet just past her shoulders. His fingers itched to touch the strands. Had he always had this fascination with hair? Or was it just hers?

She wore a kelly green turtleneck beneath a black leather jacket and jeans tucked into calf-high black boots with low heels. Her gold shield and sidearm were at her waist, as a reminder that she was working and not on vacation.

"You'll have to come back when you can," he stated softly. "The Smithsonian museums are world-class."

Excitement lit up her eyes. "You remember them?"

He gave her a wry grin. "Not really. It's more of a vague recollection than an actual memory. I don't know if what I see in my mind is from experience or pictures. But I feel certain that you'd like the various aspects of the museums."

"I'm sure I would. I'm especially interested in the American first ladies collection."

He grinned. "Do you have aspirations of being a first lady?"

She returned his grin. "No, if I wanted to live in the White House it would be as president."

He chuckled at her declaration. He admired her pluck and confidence. It would take a special man to contend with this woman.

"I like seeing strong women prevail," she continued. "And you have to admit, it would take a certain amount of courage to be married to the president of the United States."

"True." What kind of courage would it take to marry a man with no memory?

Wow, that was a leap. He wasn't even sure how he felt about this pretty, capable and determined deputy. Letting his mind and heart venture down the perilous road of romance wasn't smart. The last thing he wanted was to hurt Audrey or anyone else.

Did he have someone waiting for his return? Not a wife, he knew, but a girlfriend? Where did he even reside? Canada was a big place.

His gaze strayed to the man at the wheel. Blake Fallon would have the answers Nathanial sought.

But did he want to ask? Would the answers bring pain or trigger his memories?

Didn't he owe it to Audrey, for saving his sorry hide, and to himself to dig into his past and uncover who he was?

Fear that he'd not like the answers bubbled inside him, adding to his headache. When he could get Blake alone, he'd seek the answers despite his trepidations. Better to hear who he was without worrying about Audrey's reaction. He hated the thought of her thinking less of him. He leaned back against the headrest and closed his eyes against the pain throbbing in his head. Soon enough he'd find the courage to confront his past.

The vehicle rolled to a stop in the underground garage of a nondescript building, and they were hustled inside to a conference room on a high floor with a direct view of the Washington Monument. Nathanial went to the window. Was this why the monolith seemed so familiar? Had he stood in this room before, this exact spot, even?

"It's beautiful," Audrey commented as she halted at his side.

He turned to look at her. She was beautiful. And sweet and had a core of steel that he respected and admired. "Yes. Very beautiful."

She slanted him a quick glance as if she somehow suspected he wasn't referring to the tall stone pillar.

"Welcome back from the dead, Officer Longhorn," a deep voice intoned from behind them.

Nathanial and Audrey turned toward the room. Nathanial's gaze landed on the man standing at the head

of the conference table. He was tall and distinguished
looking in a well-tailored dark suit, white button-down
shirt and burgundy tie. His salt-and-pepper hair was
swept back from his angular face and sharp deep blue
eyes assessed them. Nathanial assumed this must be
Director Moore of Homeland Security.

"And welcome, Deputy Martin," Moore continued
as he skirted around the table toward Audrey. "We owe
you a huge thank-you."

She met him with her hand outstretched. "Not a problem, sir." They shook hands. "Doing my job."

"And doing it well, from what I've heard," he replied.
Then he shifted his focus to Nathanial. "You look well,
but I understand you have no memory of your work
with IBETs."

"No, sir, I don't," Nathanial replied, accepting the
man's offer of a handshake. He had a strong and firm
grip but didn't squeeze his hand in a show of power,
which Nathanial appreciated. "I hope you'll forgive me
my ignorance. IBETs?"

"Integrated Border Enforcement Taskforce, a joint
effort by the Canadians and the United States to keep
our mutual boundary line secure." Moore gestured to
the chairs. "Have a seat, Nathanial, Deputy."

Nathanial pulled out a chair for Audrey. She arched
an eyebrow, and her mouth curved into a slight smile,
but she made no comment as she took her seat. He
claimed the chair next to her, bumping his knees against
hers. Awareness of how close she was raced over him,
making him ruefully shake his head. What was he, a
junior higher with his first crush?

No, but he was a man without a memory, crushing
on the woman who'd saved his life. *Better snap out of*

it, he told himself. He really needed to have a discussion with Blake. He forced his attention to the director.

"We'd like you to meet with our doctors here," the director was saying as he leaned a hip against the table. "Not that we don't trust Dr. Martin's assessment, but we do have the most advanced therapies and practices in the country, if not the world, at our disposal."

"Yes, sir." Nathanial didn't have a problem meeting with anyone who could potentially help him regain his faculties. He shushed the nervous voice inside his head that questioned if he really wanted to know. Instead, he sent up a silent prayer that he'd be strong enough to withstand whatever he discovered.

"Deputy Martin, I'll have someone escort you to your hotel while Officer Longhorn meets with the docs."

"With all due respect, sir, where Nathanial goes, I go," Audrey said in a tone that was courteous but firm, leaving no doubt her words weren't a request but a fact.

The director matched her level gaze with one of his own. Nathanial waited to see if the director would try to match her resolve, but then the man smiled and he spared Nathanial an amused look.

"Well, it seems you have your very own bodyguard, Nathanial." Moore straightened. "I have an escort ready to take you and your guest to Walter Reed medical center."

"Thank you, Director Moore," Audrey said and rose from her chair.

Nathanial stood and shook the man's hand again. For some reason Director Moore inspired a sense of trust.

"If you'll follow me." Moore moved to the conference room door.

Audrey hesitated, obviously waiting for Nathanial to take a step, but his gaze once again went to the lone obelisk standing like a sentry over the city, the white lights highlighting the gray stone. A sense of loneliness swamped Nathanial. A forgotten memory surfaced, sharp and desolate. Him as a child of maybe seven, standing in front of a Christmas tree only half-decorated, while voices shouted and shrieked from another room. Fear and anger roiled in his gut, his small fists clenched at his sides. Who did the voices belong to? Why was he so upset?

Nathanial tried to hold on to the recollection, to expand it, to make the memory clear, but it slipped away, leaving him feeling strangely hollow.

"Nathanial?"

Audrey's voice brought him back to the present. Aware of the director's gaze, he kept the snippet of recall to himself. "Sorry, I was distracted by the view."

He followed the director out of the room with Audrey's hand gently folded in his.

Audrey paced outside the closed office door of one of the country's top psychiatrists. Or so she and Nathanial had been informed. Nathanial had stepped inside the office over an hour ago and hadn't emerged. Audrey was growing antsy.

The ding of the elevator brought her gaze from the waxed linoleum floor in time to see Blake Fallon step out of the car. His handsome features were dark with worry as he strode toward her, stopping a couple feet away as if afraid to get too close. But why? What made the man wary of her?

"Is he still in with Dr. Pembley?" Blake asked, his voice deep and cutting.

Audrey straightened her shoulders, unwilling to let this man's sheer size and commanding presence intimidate her. "Yes."

"So what's the story?" Blake asked, his gaze narrowing. "What is it you want from Nathanial?"

Audrey tilted her head. "Want?"

"I've never seen him so dependent, especially on a woman," he said.

Interesting. Not sure how to address the complicated levels that tidbit opened up, she went for the obvious and honest answer. "He's in a vulnerable state right now. I'm only here to discover the truth and to protect him."

"I can do that."

"He isn't ready to trust you."

Hurt flashed across Blake's face. "He was—is my best friend. He's a good guy. Someone I trusted my life with, someone I trusted to have my back."

"But now you're not so sure."

A frown marred Blake's brow. "I am sure. The man I know wouldn't have willingly put his team in danger. Something bad happened." His fingers curled into fists. "He needs to remember."

Empathy unfurled inside her chest. "He will. And he'll be that man again. He just needs some time." She sent up a quick prayer that Nathanial's memories would return sooner rather than later. Or worse yet, not at all. "Tell me about him. About who he was before I found him on the beach."

Blake raked a hand through his dark hair, making the already tousled strands even more unruly. A gold wedding band on his ring finger glinted beneath the overhead lights. "We would joke that Nathanial was *ka peyakot mahihkan*—a lone wolf.*"

Surprise washed over her. "You speak Cree?"

"Just a few words that Nathanial taught me."

She digested the statement. *Lone wolf.* "What do you mean by *lone wolf*? He doesn't play well with others?"

One corner of Blake's mouth lifted. "He does. It's not that. He prefers recon missions and to be on watch."

She remembered he'd said that had been Nathanial's job on the assignment. "And in his personal life?" She hated the heat creeping up her neck, but she was curious. For his sake, not hers. *Right. And pigs fly.*

Wariness flared in Blake's eyes. "He's unattached, if that's what you're wondering."

She shrugged. "Just asking."

"The last thing he needs right now is his heart being tethered to you," Blake said with warning in his tone.

Though she appreciated Blake watching out for his friend, she didn't need the counsel. She wasn't looking to tether her heart to anyone, least of all Nathanial. She might like him, care for him, even, but that was a long way from tethering. From loving.

The door to the office opened. Audrey's heart leaped as Nathanial walked out and reached for her hand.

"I remembered something."

Chapter Ten

"That's good, right?" Audrey gripped his hands.

A rush of warmth traveled up Nathanial's arms at the contact. He should have told her about the memory back at the IBETs headquarters, but the sudden flood of images and sensations he'd experienced had made him feel too raw, too vulnerable. Still did. But it was a step in the right direction toward regaining his past.

Blake lurched forward. "You remember what happened to you on that rooftop?" Blake's urgent, hopeful tone twisted bitter regret within Nathanial.

Nathanial flicked a glance at the agent. "No, unfortunately."

Blake blew out a frustrated breath. Nathanial didn't blame Blake for his frustration. Men had died, and the key to bringing those men's killers to justice lay locked within Nathanial's skull. If only they could hook him up to some sort of machine that could pull out the memories.

Nathanial focused on Audrey. "I remembered something from my childhood. An image of a Christmas tree."

He didn't know what had triggered the memory, but Dr. Pembley had been able to draw out more of the details of the tree, with dangling homemade ornaments and the house filled with the scents of wood smoke and gingerbread. They agreed this was probably his childhood home. As for the yelling voices, the doctor speculated it could be from that time or another memory that was trying to come through. Hopefully the memory of what had happened to him on that rooftop. "The doc suggests I travel to my childhood home, since that seems to be where my mind wants to go."

Audrey tilted her head. "In Saskatchewan?"

He shrugged and turned his attention on Blake. "You said that is where I'm from. Do you have an address for my family?" His heart bumped. Were his parents still alive? Did he have brothers or sisters? A wife? He slipped his hands from Audrey's and stuffed them into the pockets of his jacket. Why couldn't he keep a distance from this woman?

"I do. I'll take you there," Blake offered.

Anxiety knotted his chest. He didn't want to go with Blake, even though it would be the wisest decision. A decision he had to make, because he needed to release Audrey. Though from the way her lush lips pressed together, he had a feeling she wouldn't cooperate. She'd made it clear that she would see this, whatever this was, through to the end.

"I appreciate the offer," Nathanial finally said. "No offense intended, but Audrey and I can make it there on our own."

"Not happening." Blake stepped closer. There was no mistaking the hurt beneath the man's hard exterior. "If you don't want me to accompany you, fine. But you need a team with you. I'm sure the Kelleys wouldn't mind the trip and would provide more protection."

"The Kelleys?" Nathanial felt as if he should know who they were, but the knowledge was just out of his mind's reach.

Blake huffed out a breath rife with exasperation. "Drew and his wife, Sami."

"The Mountie?" Audrey asked.

Barely sparing her a glance, Blake nodded. "Yes. His wife is FBI and works for the US legal attaché to Canada. They would make the perfect escort for you both."

Nathanial sensed an undercurrent of strain between Blake and Audrey. He wondered what had happened between them while he was in with the doctor. He looked to Audrey to see what she thought of the backup plan.

She shrugged. "Couldn't hurt to have more protection."

He nodded. "All right, then."

Having the couple along would provide a barrier between him and Audrey, too. He needed a buffer, something to keep him from giving in to the temptation to kiss the pretty sheriff's deputy. Because the need to do so hovered close to the surface any time she was near. He inwardly sighed as he followed the others to the parking garage. He had to get a grip.

Blake drove Nathanial and Audrey to a popular hotel chain a few blocks away from the IBETs headquarters. The lobby was quiet as they waited near a warm gas fireplace while Blake checked them in at the registration desk. Overhead, chandeliers gleamed with multiple lights. Marble floors covered with intricately woven area rugs provided texture and comfy seating invited lingering. A thirty-foot Douglas fir tree adorned in gold ornaments and shiny gold ribbon took center stage in the lobby.

Nathanial's curiosity prompted him to ask Audrey as he sat on a dark cherry-colored chair. "What's going on between you and Blake?"

As she took the seat across from him, she seemed to consider her words before speaking. "Nothing, really. He's concerned about you and wants to make sure you don't end up hurt."

Something in her tone made him think she and Blake weren't only referring to his physical well-being. Had Blake warned her off for some reason? Pain lanced through his head. He winced.

Audrey leaned forward to touch his knee. "You okay?"

The concern in her voice touched him. She cared. The knowledge filled him with pleasure that he quickly tamped down. So much for getting a grip. Her care and concern were born of her job, not from any heartfelt affection. They barely knew each other. The irony that he knew more about her than he did about himself nearly made him laugh, but the mirth died a fast death as helpless anger clawed through him. He wanted his memories, his life, back. Whoever had robbed him of both would pay a high price.

Blake's approach drew Nathanial's attention. There was something familiar about the man that seemed to knock at Nathanial's consciousness. Knowledge of their shared past taunted him, just out of reach, ratcheting up his frustration several notches.

"Your rooms are next to each other," the ICE agent said as he handed over the key cards.

Taking the card holder from him, Nathanial decided

he needed answers. "Audrey, you go on up. I would like a moment with Blake." He held up his hand as storm clouds gathered in her eyes. "Please."

Her gaze bounced between him and Blake before she said to Blake, "You'll see that he gets safely to his room?"

"Of course." Blake's affronted tone made her scowl.

Though Nathanial appreciated their concern, he didn't like being talked about as if he were a child. "I can get myself to the room, thank you very much."

A smile slid across Audrey's face. "I didn't mean to imply you couldn't."

He narrowed his gaze at her placating tone, but instead of offending him, her words touched him. "You're worried about me. I get it. But apparently I can handle myself."

The concern didn't leave her gaze. "But you don't have a weapon with you."

Her statement stirred hesitation within him. Could he handle himself in a hand-to-hand situation? Was using a sniper rifle or a knife the only means he had to defend himself? Doubts swirled. But his need for answers outweighed his need for self-preservation. "Go on. I'll be up shortly, and I'll even knock on your door to let you know I arrived in one piece."

Though it was clear from the worry in her pretty eyes that she didn't like leaving him, she inclined her head and walked to the elevator. As soon as she stepped inside and the doors closed, Nathanial spoke to Blake. "What did you say to Audrey? She seemed upset."

Blake snorted. "I told her what I'm going to tell you. Don't go getting all goofy over the deputy. She's not your type."

"I have a type?" Nathanial would have thought leggy blondes with attitude would be right up his alley. At least this particular one was.

"Yes, you do. Ones that aren't looking for forever," Blake stated and moved to sit on one end of the couch in the lobby.

The heat from the gas fireplace buffeted Nathanial as he followed Blake, sat in the chair and leaned in so his voice wouldn't carry despite the fact they were alone in the lounge area. "So I don't have any *one* special lady pining away for me?" He needed to confirm what Blake was saying. Not having a girlfriend waiting for him was good news and eased some of the guilt at his attraction to Audrey constricting his chest. He still wasn't sure he was good enough for the pretty deputy.

"Oh, I'm sure there are women across both borders who'd be more than willing to be your special someone," Blake replied dryly. "But no." He let out a wry chuckle. "You date. A lot. But you don't get serious."

That didn't sound so good. "Why not?"

Blake shrugged. "How should I know? You always boast you like your freedom. I don't want to see you making a decision that affects your future out of some misguided sense of gratitude for Audrey saving your life."

Digesting that statement left a cold spot in Nathanial's heart. He was a serial dater? Afraid of commitment? But why? What had happened in his past to make him want to be free of relationships?

Blake's lips twisted in ironic amusement. "But you were more than happy to push me toward my wife, Liz. Let's see, you told me I was afraid of feeling." He let out a chuckle. "You were right, as you usually are. I was afraid."

Hearing the other man talk about something Nathanial had said in the past sent a fresh sliver of pain slicing through Nathanial's brain. He wanted to remember the conversation. To remember what it had been like to see this man fall in love. Nathanial assumed Liz was now Blake's wife. "You married her."

"I did. Best decision I ever made." Love for his bride shone in his dark eyes. "We live on Hilton Head Island." His happiness dimmed. "You've been to the house several times."

Nathanial's chest caved slightly. "You said I was your best man at your wedding. So I take it you and I know— knew—each other well."

Blake splayed his hands on his knees. "Yes." He reached inside the breast pocket of his overcoat for his wallet. He flipped it open to reveal two photographs. One of his bride, an attractive honey blonde that Nathanial didn't recognize.

The other image was a group shot of at least eight men dressed in tuxedos. Nathanial recognized the members of the IBETs team he'd recently reconnected with. Nathanial had his arm slung around Blake's shoulders while mugging for the camera. Staring at the photo, Nathanial fought his faulty mind, desperate to recall this day when he'd appeared to be happy. A splitting headache was his compensation.

Rubbing at his temple, he said, "Tell me about the mission."

Blake put the wallet away. "We'd been tracking the movements of Sergei Kosloff, a Russian immigrant to the US. Over the past few years he's been slowly building his empire, dealing in arms, drugs, human trafficking…you name it.

"An informant within his organization flipped for a reduced sentence. Naming dates and times of illegal weapons crossing the US–Canada border. Our task was to seize this latest shipment and turn as many of his men as we could in hopes of finding Kosloff's base of operation.

"We know it's somewhere on the East Coast and that he has connections in several states where firearms are bought, then transported to other states before they're finally smuggled into Canada. From there many of the weapons are dispersed within Canada, but some are also transported to Europe."

Nathanial scrubbed a hand over his jaw. "The man we captured at the Calico Bay sheriff's department had had an Eastern European accent."

"That's what Sheriff Crump said. He, no doubt, worked for Kosloff but he didn't come up in any database. He must have been new to the organization."

"And Kosloff had him killed," Nathanial pointed out. Clearly the master criminal didn't like loose ends. Was Nathanial one of Kosloff's loose ends? Had he been working for Kosloff as Chase suggested? The thought tied his insides into knots. "Have you checked all the team members for any unexplainable payouts?" He held his breath, waiting for the answer and hoping nothing showed in his own bank account.

"I did. Came up empty."

A small measure of relief filled Nathanial. But they were no closer to solving the mystery of who and why. He hated to think he'd been involved with Kosloff. But the possibility lingered like a bad odor.

Going home might be the only way to regain his

memory, the only way to clear his own name and find the guilty party.

Anxiety kicked up in his gut. A part of him was afraid to remember, but he had to know—good guy or bad?

Audrey freshened up in her hotel room. The view from the bedroom window overlooked the Capitol Building. The sun had set while she waited for Nathanial to reach his room. The world had been cast into inky shadows broken by the glow of a million lights—streetlamps, inside the many buildings and monuments, and the cars crawling along the avenues.

Despite the cheer of Christmas decorations everywhere, there was franticness about the city that made her antsy. Or it could be she was worried that something would happen to Nathanial and she wouldn't be there to protect him.

The slight knock on the door connecting her room to the next had her heart jumping. She hurried to the door and yanked it open.

Backlit by the glow of the lamp on the dresser, Nathanial grinned. "Miss me?"

She had, but she wasn't going to admit it. "Glad to see you made it alive."

She brushed past him to enter his room, which was laid out exactly like her own. A new suitcase sat on the bed, the tag still hanging from the handle. Inside the bag were some fresh clothes.

"I stopped in the gift shop before coming up."

"Good idea." Though she didn't like the idea of him wandering around unprotected. She went to the window and studied the line of sight from the buildings across the street. Not detecting anything untoward, she closed the room-darkening curtains. "Stay away from the window. If anyone knocks on your door, don't answer. Come knock on my door."

He didn't acknowledge her comment, but instead asked, "Are you hungry?"

She hadn't thought about food. But she knew they both needed to eat to keep up their energy. "I'll order room service."

"We could head downstairs to the restaurant."

"Better to stay out of sight," she said. "We don't know if your pursuers have found out where we are. We need to keep an extra-low profile so we can make it safely to your home."

Seeming to accept her pronouncement, he picked up the room service menu. "Then we'll dine in. I think the blue cheese hamburger, fries and a side garden salad sound good." He handed her the menu.

"I'll take care of it." She headed toward the connecting door, but he stepped into her path.

"I don't think I'm the kind of man who lets others take care of him."

She arched an eyebrow as her heart rate ticked upward. "You know this how?"

His wide shoulders lifted and fell. "Just a feeling. I get all twitchy when you get bossy and mothering." He softened his teasing words with a smile.

She pressed her lips together to keep from grimacing. She'd heard similar statements before. The jerk from college, Kyle, had claimed that was one of the reasons he'd cheated on her—he couldn't take her controlling nature. She couldn't help it if taking charge came naturally. Not only did her job require her to be in command of every situation, but she also came by her bossiness honestly. Her mother had the same trait, which made her good at her job of running the Calico Bay Medical Center.

Nathanial narrowed his gaze. "I've upset you. I'm sorry."

She shoved her shoulders back and lifted her chin. "I'm doing my job, Nathanial. Putting your safety first is my priority." She stepped around him, needing to put some space between them. She didn't want him digging into her psyche. It was bad enough she'd told him about Kyle—she didn't want to humiliate herself further with the details. "I'll make the order."

"You do that."

His amused toned chased her back to her room. She put in the order for two hamburgers, fries and side salads, and a pot of coffee. She would need to stay alert in case the men trying to kill Nathanial took the opportunity of striking in the middle of the night.

Fifteen minutes later there was a knock on her hotel door. With a hand on her weapon, she checked the peephole. A man dressed in the hotel's green, black and gold livery stood on the other side of the door with a cart bearing two silver domes presumably covering their dinner.

She signed for the food and wheeled the cart in, tipped the man and sent him on his way. A second later another knock sounded at the door. Nathanial. She opened the door and stepped back.

Nathanial poked his head inside the room. "Dinner?" He entered, closing the door behind him.

"Yes." She lifted the lids, and the most delicious smells wafted up, making her stomach cramp with hunger.

They each took a plate and sat. Nathanial took the desk chair while she took the cushy chair in the corner.

For a moment both were content to eat in silence.

"Blake told me about the mission I was on," Nathanial said as he set his half-eaten burger back on the plate.

She listened, riveted, as he spoke about the criminal Kosloff. She wiped her hands on a napkin. "Did Blake say whether he'd checked the team's financials?"

"I asked and he had. Nothing to report there."

Reaching for her tablet, she did a quick search in the national criminal database for Sergei Kosloff and found a photo. She held it up for Nathanial to view. Sergei Kosloff had a round face, with wide-set eyes and dark hair. "Now we not only have a name but a face for the man who's trying to kill you."

She watched Nathanial closely for any flare of recognition, but none came as he studied the image.

His mouth twisted. "But the question is, why does he want me dead? What threat do I pose?"

Questions she prayed would be answered soon.

The next morning Nathanial and Audrey stood in the lobby of the hotel waiting to meet their escort to Saskatchewan. Nathanial couldn't take his eyes off Audrey. He was struck once again by her beauty. Not just the outward package. Though that was certainly pleasing. She wore loose wool trousers and a lightweight sweater and had a coat folded over her arm. Her blond hair was loose again, falling about her shoulder with one side tucked behind her ear.

He also found her intellect and determination appealing. Her alert gaze swept the lobby and the street outside the window. To the world she most likely appeared at ease, with her legs braced slightly apart and her right foot marginally forward in a stance that looked natural but also afforded her an anchor and a push-off point.

She was nervous. Her fingers drummed on her hipbone, much like he'd seen her do on her utility belt when she was in uniform.

Blake had called them first thing in the morning saying they were booked on an 8 a.m. flight to Saskatoon with a short layover in Minneapolis, and from there they would drive three hours to Nathanial's hometown of Pierceland. Anticipation revved in his veins. Remembering was paramount to solving this case and to taking back control of his life.

The knowledge had promptly given him a rip-roaring headache.

A black Suburban pulled to the curb outside the hotel door. Blake climbed from behind the wheel while Luke Wellborn jumped out of the passenger seat.

"Here's our ride," Nathanial said to Audrey. He grabbed her bag and the small one he'd purchased for himself in the hotel's gift shop. Grateful that she didn't put up a fuss, they headed outside. The frosty air bit at him. He pulled the corners of the wool-and-shearling coat closer, thankful Deputy Paulson had let him borrow it.

Luke took the bags and stowed them in the far back while Blake opened the back passenger door for them to slide onto the bench seat. Once everyone was secured inside the vehicle, Blake took off, expertly weaving through the early-morning traffic.

"Drew and Sami will meet you at the airport in Saskatoon," Blake informed them.

Snow began falling, gently coating the world in a blanket of white, reminding Nathanial Christmas was only days away. He sent up a silent prayer that he'd have his memory, his life, back by then.

When they landed in Saskatoon, they were met by Drew Kelley and his wife, Sami Bennett-Kelley. Both were dressed in what Nathanial would call work attire—Drew wore black slacks, jackboots and a warm-looking midlength wool peacoat. There was the slight bulge at his side where he no doubt carried a firearm.

Nathanial nodded a greeting to Drew before studying Sami. She was petite, with a wild head of curls and alert blue eyes, and was also dressed in dark slacks and a red button-down top beneath a short, thick leather jacket. She yanked a black glove off her right hand and thrust her hand out to Audrey.

"Deputy Martin," Sami said in a clipped voice. "Thank you for all you're doing for this one." She tipped her chin in Nathanial's direction.

"You're welcome." Audrey matched the FBI agent's formal tone.

Sami turned her vivid gaze to him, and there was no mistaking the affection in her eyes. "No memory, huh?"

He grimaced and shook his head, already liking the direct way the woman took on life. "Sorry."

She shrugged. "Unless you've gone dirty, no apology needed." She reached out and took his hand. Her fingers were strong as they curled over his. "We're glad you're alive. We were worried you weren't."

Nathanial accepted her welcome and her concern. These people had cared about him. And still did. Warmth spread through his chest, taking the edge off his headache.

They hustled from the smaller airport to an American-made super-duty dual-cab truck marked with the RCMP initials and logo.

Sami climbed in front with Drew taking the wheel while Audrey and Nathanial took the back passenger seats. Sami kept up a running dialogue, asking questions and commenting on the passing scenery. Seemed this was her first time in this part of Canada.

Nathanial had hoped seeing the landscape of his birthplace would jog something loose inside his brain, but the flat, snowy countryside was unfamiliar. Groves of trees dusted with white powder dotted large stretches of undeveloped pastures.

"Hey, look." Sami's excited tone made Nathanial smile. "What is that?"

A large, dark-colored animal stood off in the distance. Its compact body was covered with thick fur, and the beast's snout was long and rounded at the end. Flat antlers rose off its head.

Môswa. The word floated through Nathanial's brain. Was this more of the Cree language that apparently he'd been speaking when he first awoke in the hospital? Was the word the name for the creature in the pasture?

"Prairie moose," Drew said with a grin. "Sami grew up in the Pacific Northwest."

Moose. Nathanial was pretty sure he'd just named the animal in Cree.

"They don't have moose on the West Coast?" Audrey asked.

"Oh, they do somewhere, I'm sure," Sami explained. "But I grew up on the coast of Oregon then moved to Portland. I've never seen anything that big."

"What's this?" Drew asked, drawing Nathanial's

focus to a car pulled to the side of the road about fifty yards ahead.

Drew took his foot off the gas.

"Probably someone stopping to take a picture of the moose," Sami said, but there was a thread of tension in her tone.

"Or someone with car trouble," Audrey ventured, but she didn't sound convinced. She put her hand on his shoulder. "Slide down, just in case."

Nathanial wanted to argue. No way could anyone be gunning for him out here. Could they?

As the gap between the truck and the car closed, all the doors on the sedan popped open. Four gunmen jumped out and aimed semiautomatic weapons at the truck.

Chapter Eleven

Λs bullets riddled the heavy-duty truck and shattered the back window, raining pebbles of safety glass onto them, Audrey's heart slammed against her rib cage, and she screamed, "Get down!"

She yanked Nathanial's arm at the exact moment he pushed her to the truck's back passenger floorboard, toppling onto her. His weight forced the air from her lungs.

"Hang on!" Drew shouted. The truck engine roared, tires dug into the layer of snow and the vehicle fishtailed before finding traction and shooting forward, passing the car and the men. A barrage of gunfire hit the truck, the pinging of bullets echoing in Audrey's head as she did her best to protect Nathanial. But he wasn't cooperating. He kept trying to shield her.

"Hey! I'm supposed to be protecting you," she grumbled, her voice muffled into his chest. The scent of the hotel soap mingled with his masculine scent, and if she weren't so mad and admittedly scared, she'd have snuggled closer.

He braced his elbows on either side of her head to

keep from crushing her. "You can be the bullet stopper next time," he muttered huskily, close to her ear.

Their faces were close, so close she could see herself reflected in his dark eyes. His promise of a kiss screamed through her mind, and she had the wildest urge to lift her head off the floor and press her lips to his.

Frustration whipped at her back, and embarrassment heated her skin. She would not give in to her attraction to this man, despite the affection embedding itself in her heart. She pushed at him as best she could, since her arms were trapped. He might not remember being a law officer, but his reflexes were in working order. The instinct to duck and cover and protect was strong in him, strong enough that he'd overpowered her by sheer muscle strength.

The truck continued to career down the road. The onslaught of bullets lessened until the only noises were the tires against the snowy road, the icy wind whistling through the cab and Sami calling in the attack, her voice clipped and concise. Nathanial dropped his forehead next to Audrey's, and he relaxed as if his body had deflated. Pressure built in Audrey's chest. Her breath lay entombed in her lungs. Panic clawed at her. Had he been hit?

"Nathanial?" Audrey's heart faltered. "Nathanial? Are you okay?" She couldn't keep alarm from creeping into her tone.

He stirred and eased off her, allowing her to breathe. He blinked and shook his head. "I blacked out for a second." His dark eyes searched her face. "Are you hurt?"

Her relief that he was not injured was immediately chased away by her need to take back control of the situation. "No, I'm not hurt, but you will be if you don't get off me," she ground out between clenched teeth.

The corner of his mouth lifted in challenge. He had her pinned to the truck floor. There was no way to bring her knee up or room for her hands to reach her weapon. He glanced up toward the top of the bench seat, where Drew and Sami sat. "Is it safe?"

"Yes" came Drew's terse reply.

The truck hadn't slowed down. Were they being chased? "You heard the man—it's safe. Get. Off. Me."

"Right." He crawled onto the backseat, but kept his head down. He brushed glass off his shoulders and off the seat for her.

She sat up and stifled a groan at the aches and pains shooting through her back and hips. She accepted his offered hand of help and scooted onto the seat. The road stretched out in front of them as the truck barreled onward. Audrey glanced out the busted-out back window. The car full of armed men chased after them. The little sedan didn't have the weight or the studded tires of the truck and began to fall back. Audrey sent up a quick prayer that the gunmen didn't have more men waiting up ahead to box them in.

The sound of sirens drew closer. Up ahead three identical small SUVs with flashing lights and the RCMP logo rushed toward them. Audrey whipped her attention behind them and watched the sedan slow, whip a U-turn and race away in the opposite direction. Drew brought the truck to a halt. One of the SUVs halted beside them while the other two zipped past in hot pursuit of the armed men in the sedan.

Drew rolled down his window, and the driver of the SUV did the same.

"Inspector Cavendish," the man introduced himself.

"Inspector Kelley," Drew replied and quickly explained the situation.

"I'll let my men know to be careful," Cavendish assured him. "Follow me to the station. We'll need statements."

Drew waited for the other Mountie to turn his vehicle around, then they followed him for several minutes on the lonely stretch of road cutting through the prairie until they came to civilization. They rolled through the small town of Meadow Lake. The low-roofed buildings lining the main street held a certain charm that made Audrey think of Calico Bay, though here the terrain was flat and trees in planters provided a little greenery.

Audrey noticed Nathanial's clenched jaw and his hands gripping his thighs.

"You okay?"

He met her gaze. She sucked in a breath at the torment in his dark eyes.

"I don't know."

"You said you blacked out." She covered one of his hands with her own. "What happened?"

"I had a flash of memory." He turned his hand over and laced his fingers with hers. For a moment the sight of their entwined hands distracted her. "I think it was from the rooftop."

Her gaze jerked up to meet his. "Tell me."

He closed his eyes. "I was lying on the roof, looking through the scope on my rifle." His brow furrowed. "A noise." With his free hand, he rubbed at his temple. "I rolled to my back." He shook his head with a grimace. "That's it." He opened his eyes. "Something hovers right at the edge of my mind, but every time I try to hang on to it…" He gave a shrug.

She squeezed his hand. "You'll remember."

He looked away, as if not ready to acknowledge her encouragement. "We're here."

The vehicle halted outside a one-story brick building. The Canadian flag flew from a twelve-foot flagpole next to the sidewalk near the front door, and a blue sign with the RCMP logo was planted in the middle of what Audrey guessed would be a lawn in the warmer seasons but now was covered in snow. Drew turned off the engine. "We have to assume we're being tracked."

"We found one tracker in Nathanial's boot, but he tossed it out the window a long time ago," Audrey stated.

"Doesn't mean there couldn't be more tracking devices. We all need to check our clothing," Drew stated grimly. "I'll check the vehicle as well."

They piled out of the truck. The temperature outside had dropped below zero. Shivering from the onslaught of frigid air, Audrey made quick work of checking her clothing and found nothing then shoved her hands into her coat pockets.

"Found it!" Drew held up a small wireless GPS tracker. "It was tucked inside my to-go bag." He threw it on the ground and smashed it with his heel.

The unspoken concern that someone close to them had planted the device had them all on edge.

They followed Inspector Cavendish inside, where they gave him their statements. By the time they were done, the two Mounties who'd given pursuit of the gunmen returned empty-handed.

One of the men, a big burly guy with shorn blond

hair and green eyes, stopped and stared at Nathanial. "Hey, I know you."

Beside her, Nathanial tensed. "Do you?"

"Yes. You grew up near here, eh?"

"Apparently so." Nathanial held out his hand. "Nathanial Longhorn."

"Kurt Siebol." The man grasped Nathanial's hand. "You played point guard for Pierceland Center High. I remember playing against you my senior year. You were good."

"Thanks." Nathanial turned to Audrey. "I played basketball."

She smiled at the wonder in his voice. She'd have liked to have seen him on the court. She was sure he'd have moved with the same easy agility he displayed as an adult.

Inspector Cavendish offered them the use of one of their official vehicles. After saying goodbye, they headed to Pierceland with Kurt providing an escort. Once they hit the town, Kurt waved farewell and headed back to Meadow Lake.

They stopped at a small hotel and secured rooms before venturing to the heart of the town. To say Pierceland was small was an understatement. Stand-alone buildings dotted the snow-covered main drive. A gas station, credit union and village post office lined one side of the road. Across the street stood a grocery store and a restaurant called Bartlett's Family Dining.

"Stop here," Nathanial said. "Let's go into the restaurant."

Audrey eyed the welcome sign in the front window— Family Owned and Operated for Fifty Years.

"Do you recognize this place?" Sami asked before Audrey could.

"I don't know. It seems familiar," Nathanial said. "I want to stop."

Drew and Sami exchanged concerned looks. "We still need to be careful."

"I'll only be a moment." Nathanial leaned forward. "Pull in around the back, out of sight."

Drew circled the building and brought the borrowed Mountie vehicle to a halt near the back door.

"I'm going in," Nathanial said with a determination that let them all know there was no way they'd be able to stop him unless they knocked him out.

Audrey hurried to his side. She'd at least do her best to keep him safe.

"Make it quick," Drew instructed Nathanial as they rounded the building for the entrance. He and Sami took up positions where they had a clear view of the road out front.

Audrey was thankful for the restaurant's warmth seeping into her bones. A string of bells attached to the door jingled when the door shut behind them.

The restaurant wasn't crowded; only a few tables were occupied. And those that were there turned to stare at the newcomers. Cheery Christmas decorations hung from the rafters. A line of stocking cutouts danced across the front desk, where a woman stood behind the counter. She wore an oxford cotton shirt with the restaurant's logo on the right breast pocket. Her dark hair hung in a tight braid over her left shoulder.

"Good afternoon," the woman said with a smile. Then her gaze landed on Nathanial, and she paled and her smile fell away. "What are you doing here?"

Audrey stepped next to Nathanial as a strange sensation of protectiveness and possessiveness surged through her. Drew and Sami took positions behind them as if ready to jump in.

He cocked his head and stared at the woman. "I'm sorry," he said. "I don't remember your name."

The woman took a step back as if shock gave way to anger. "Really? You're going with that?" Her gaze flicked to Audrey and then back to Nathanial. "Is this your wife?"

"No, this—" His words cut off as he slanted Audrey a glance.

Clearly he was at a loss how to explain what he was going through. Audrey decided to borrow a page from her great-uncle's playbook—*when in doubt, stick to the facts.* She flashed the badge fastened to her belt at her waist. "Deputy Audrey Martin with the Calico Bay, Maine, sheriff's department. Officer Longhorn suffered a blow to the head and is suffering retrograde amnesia. We're hopeful he'll regain his memories here where he grew up."

The woman's brown eyes widened. Her rose-colored lips formed an O. "I didn't think things like that really happened."

"They do," Nathanial said softly. "I take it we knew each other."

Confusion stole over face. "Yes. I'm Laurie. Laurie Bartlett. You really don't remember me?"

What was the story between Nathanial and Laurie? "We're you two close?" Audrey asked Laurie.

Laurie's mouth twisted in a half grimace. "High school. We were high school sweethearts."

Over a decade ago. And yet Audrey had the feeling

Laurie still carried a torch for Nathanial. The knowledge burned in Audrey's chest. She didn't like the jealousy stirring to life. She had no claim on Nathanial.

Whatever the outcome and wherever this journey took him, Audrey would be returning to her own life in Calico Bay. Alone. Becoming upset over Nathanial's old flame was wrong on so many levels.

She needed to shore up the walls around her heart and keep perspective. Even though she liked Nathanial and was attracted to him, she had to find a way to keep an emotional distance.

"Your family owns this restaurant," Nathanial stated. "That's why it seemed familiar."

Laurie nodded. "Yes. You used to work here. We worked here together."

"Can you tell me how to get to my parents' home?"

"Sure. I can do that." Laurie grabbed a piece of paper and scribbled down the directions. "They'll be glad to see you."

Taking the piece of paper she offered, Nathanial said, "Thank you, Laurie. I appreciate your help." He hesitated. "And I'm sorry I don't remember you."

Laurie shrugged and walked away, leaving them standing in the entryway.

Audrey didn't buy Laurie's nonchalance. She was upset and trying hard not to let it show.

"That was interesting," Sami said beneath her breath. "I guess we're not eating here."

"We've worn out our welcome," Drew's deep voice intoned.

They left the restaurant. Audrey glanced back to see Laurie watching them through the window. She climbed into the truck next to Nathanial. He handed Drew the directions.

On the drive along the country road leading to his family home, Nathanial leaned forward to ask Drew, "Did you know about Laurie? Had I ever mentioned her?"

Audrey's pulse ticked up. She watched Drew meet Nathanial's gaze in the rearview mirror, his expression stoic. "No."

Nathanial's nod was terse as he sat back and stared out the side window at the sparse landscape.

Audrey let out a silent huff. *Men.*

They arrived at a single dwelling with a detached garage on an acre lot. A large Christmas tree twinkled in the front window, and strands of colored lights hung from the eaves. As they parked in the driveway, the front door opened. A tall man with the same dark hair as Nathanial—only this man's was sprinkled with gray—stepped out of the house. He wore jeans and a thick sweater over wide shoulders. He squinted at them, no doubt wondering what the RCMP was doing at his house.

Audrey glanced from him to Nathanial and noted the striking resemblance between the two men. This had to be Nathanial's father.

"You ready for this?" she asked Nathanial.

He rolled his own wide shoulders. "I have to be." He caught her hand. "Would you mind saying a prayer?"

Surprised yet pleased by the request, she sought words. "Dear Lord, we come before You with humble hearts asking for clarity. We pray that Nathanial's mind will open up and remember his past. In Your name, amen."

"Amen," Nathanial murmured then gave her hand a squeeze. "Thank you. I can't express how glad I am that you're here. I don't think I could do this without you." He slipped his hand away and then stepped out of the truck.

Audrey swallowed back the pleasure of his words and fought for the emotional distance she knew she needed but was proving elusive.

Nathanial's heart pounded with trepidation. After the chaos of being chased and shot at, then coming face-to-face with a woman from his past, he was surprised by the depth of anxiety flooding his system.

Please, Lord, let me remember my father.

As he approached the man standing on the stoop, a glimmer of recognition ignited inside Nathanial's chest. There was no question in his mind that this man was his father. God was listening.

But Nathanial didn't know how to greet his dad. Were they the kind of people who hugged, or did they regulate their physical contact to a handshake?

"Son," the man boomed, his voice working its way through Nathanial to soothe away the worry. "What a nice surprise." He pulled Nathanial into his embrace. Nathanial breathed in the scent of pipe tobacco and pine. For a moment an image flashed of this man, his father, smoking a curled pipe near the fireplace, and a sense of security wrapped around Nathanial, much like the strong arms holding him close.

"Your mother will be giddy with joy." He released Nathanial and beamed at him. "She's at Coralie's having her hair done. I'll give her a call."

"Thanks, Dad," Nathanial said, though the word felt

strange on his tongue. "But first I need to tell you something." He quickly explained about his memory loss, leaving out the attempts on his life. The last thing he needed to do was upset his parents any more than he had to.

A frown deepened the lines around his father's light brown eyes. "You don't know what happened to you?"

"No, but I'm hoping that being here will trigger my memories." Feeling awkward, he gestured to his companions. "This is RCMP inspector Drew Kelley and his wife, US FBI agent Sami Bennett-Kelley."

Dad shook hands with Drew. "I've heard about you, Drew. I'm glad to meet you."

"Good stuff I hope, sir," Drew replied.

"Of course. And please, call me Leo."

Dad smiled at Sami and engulfed her hand in his large one. "Welcome, Sami."

"Thank you, Leo," Sami replied.

"And this is Deputy Sheriff Audrey Martin." Nathanial drew Audrey forward.

"A deputy." Curiosity radiated off Dad as he shook Audrey's offered hand. "It's nice to meet you."

"Likewise," Audrey said with a smile.

"Come in out of the cold." Dad led the way inside the house and immediately went to the landline on the kitchen counter to call his wife.

Nathanial remembered arguing with Dad about making sure he and Mom kept the landline despite the expense when everyone they knew had converted to cell phones. In case of an emergency at the house, the emergency response dispatcher would immediately have their address to send help, whereas a cell phone didn't provide the same sort of specific location, only a general area, which could take up precious time in getting rescue personnel to the scene.

Nathanial stepped inside, and a gush of emotion choked him. Sharp pain streaked through his head. He fought past it. "I do remember this place."

"That's good," Audrey said. "Just let your mind work at its own pace."

He nodded, knowing that every time he tried to force the memories to come, he only succeeded in causing himself pain. "Right."

He moved to the tree and touched the ornaments as more images rushed over him. The years of his childhood flooded in. Not all of them were happy memories. He closed his eyes, recalling the fights, the yelling between his parents and the scared little boy he'd once been, who'd hidden in the closet or under the covers of his bed to escape their furious voices.

An involuntary shudder rippled over him. Audrey touched his shoulder, her hand gentle but firm.

"Tell me what you remember," she said softly.

Sending a quick glance toward where his father spoke on the phone, Nathanial dropped his voice. "I don't think my parents' marriage is a happy one. They fought a lot."

Audrey's eyebrows rose. "But they're still together, so it couldn't be that bad."

She had a point. Something for him to ponder. Or ask his parents about. Later.

Dad hung up and joined them. "Your mom is on her way home. Can I offer you something to eat or drink?"

"Food would be great, Dad," Nathanial said, his mouth suddenly watering for a homemade meal.

Dad rubbed his hands together. "Perfect. I'll warm up your mother's split-pea soup and crusty bread."

"Thanks, Dad." Nathanial liked saying the word. It helped him to feel somewhat normal.

"Can we help?" Drew said, drawing Sami into the kitchen with Dad.

"Why don't you take a walk through the house, see what else you remember?" Audrey advised.

Nathanial headed down the narrow hallway with Audrey behind him. He stopped at the closed door of a room that had his name etched on a wooden plaque. His room. He pushed the door open, not sure what to expect.

Apparently his mother had turned his childhood space into her sewing area. A table with a large sewing machine was positioned beneath the overhead light. Knitting supplies spilled from woven baskets. Bolts of cloth and other paraphernalia were scattered around the floor.

A photo hung on the wall, drawing Nathanial's gaze. It was a family picture of his parents and him when he was around twelve. He held up a fish he'd apparently caught in the lake that provided a scenic backdrop. He touched the image of his mother. She was a beautiful woman with long straight black hair, black eyes that sparkled and a kind smile. They looked happy in this photo.

"You were a cute kid," Audrey commented as she moved to stand beside him.

"Thanks." The tantalizing scent of her vanilla shampoo teased his nose. He faced her. "What if that cute boy turned out to be a not-so-great guy?"

She tucked in her chin. "I don't believe that."

Needing an anchor, he fingered the silky strands of her hair.

It hurt his soul to think he'd been that guy.

Audrey placed a hand on his chest, over his heart. "We don't know all the details. You were both young. Don't condemn yourself without all the facts."

She always looked for the best in people and in situations. He was glad her time in law enforcement hadn't jaded her. "I admire how you keep giving me the benefit of the doubt," he said. "I don't think I deserve it."

"Everyone deserves the benefit of the doubt."

"Even a man who can't remember his past?"

"Especially a man who can't remember his past."

Attraction flared bright, like the North Star, guiding him toward her. She leaned closer as if she, too, were struck with the same powerful magnetic pull. His mouth hovered over hers, giving her a chance to back away. Her direct gaze welcomed him. He drew in a breath, prepared to follow through on the promised kiss.

"Nathanial!"

Audrey jerked back, disengaging from him in a split second. He closed his eyes for a moment as awareness and the most elemental memories washed over him. He recognized his mother's voice. He turned toward the woman who'd given birth to him with emotion choking the breath from his lungs.

Mom stood in the doorway, her face lit up with joy. She was about Audrey's height but slighter. Her long black hair was streaked with silver strands. Her blue pants were tucked into faux-fur winter boots. She wore a knitted sweater with a Christmas motif. She rushed forward to hug him.

"You've been gone too long," she breathed out.

"I'm here now." He held her tight as love swamped him.

She pulled back to look at him. "Your friends told

your father you'd sustained an injury that put you in the hospital. You have amnesia?"

He told her of waking up on the beach in Calico Bay, not knowing how he had ended up there. "Audrey saved my life." His throat nearly closed on the words. His mom didn't seem to notice, but the quick look Audrey shot him made it clear she had. He quickly looked away before revealing how much she'd come to mean to him.

Mom captured Audrey's hands in hers. "Thank you."

"You're welcome." Audrey extracted her hands, her self-consciousness obvious only to him. "Is there a washroom available?"

"Across the hall," Mom said.

Left alone with his mom, Nathanial broached the subject of Laurie Bartlett. "What can you tell me about my relationship with her?"

Mom arched a black eyebrow. "What do you remember?"

"Nothing." He tried not to let frustration color his words. "We crossed paths with Laurie earlier today. She told me we were together for a while." And he'd seen the hurt in her eyes when she'd realized he didn't remember her. Had he broken her heart at one time?

Mom let out a long-suffering sigh. "She's a nice enough young lady. However, I never thought she was right for you. But what does a mother know?"

"Mom."

She patted his arm. "You two dated for most of high school and planned to get married the summer after you graduated."

"We didn't get married, though." Had he been commitment shy even then?

"No, you didn't."

Though he had no recollection of that time, something inside him reacted with a deep welling of sorrow that seared him in the heart. "Why didn't I marry her?"

"That's between you and Laurie."

Disappointed at the lack of information, he ran a hand through his hair. The sensation of guilt stole over him. Had he callously ditched Laurie? Had he ever loved her? He needed to talk to her again. To know the truth, to make amends. "Have I been engaged to anyone else?"

"Not that I know of." Mom cupped his cheek. "I'm so proud of the man you've become."

He wished he could remember that man.

She linked her arm through his. "So tell me about Audrey."

"There's nothing to tell, Mom. She's helping me find my past." Because it was her job. But he wished it was so much more.

She patted his arm. "You keep telling yourself that."

Chapter Twelve

❧

Audrey closed the bathroom door behind her and pressed her hands to her hot cheeks, mortified that Nathanial's mother had nearly caught them in a kiss. Great, just the impression she wanted his family to have of her. Not. How totally unprofessional!

But she'd been unable to stop herself from offering Nathanial comfort. He was understandably upset over learning about his past relationship. Most likely Laurie had been his first love. But what had happened between them? "Lord, I'm not even sure what to pray. Healing, comfort? Forgiveness? You know what's needed."

Taking a breath to gain control of her emotions, she went in search of Nathanial and found him, his parents and the Kelleys seated at a round dining table. A hot bowl of soup and warm bread waited at the empty space next to Nathanial. She sat and ate the delicious food.

Mr. and Mrs. Longhorn regaled them with stories of Nathanial's childhood and teen years. Audrey liked the couple. They were so in sync with each other, often finishing each other's sentences and then laughing companionably. She wasn't sure what made Nathanial think his parents' marriage was less than happy. From her viewpoint they appeared to love each other deeply.

Audrey remembered what it had been like in her home before her father's death. Her mom and dad had been like the Longhorns, their love and affection evident in all they did. That wasn't to say Mom and Dad hadn't fought. They had. Mostly about Dad taking the boat out in too-rough water or during a storm. He'd always counter her arguments with the brief statement that he had to make a living and the fish didn't care what was going on above the water. Audrey knew her mother's objections stemmed from fear.

A fear that had come true when his boat had capsized during a raging storm. His body had never been recovered.

Nathanial nudged her with his knee, drawing her attention. "You okay?" he asked beneath his breath.

She sat up straighter. Letting melancholy drag her down and distract her focus wouldn't do. "Yes. I'm fine." To Mrs. Longhorn, she said, "This is the best soup I've tasted in a long time. Thank you."

"I'm so glad you're enjoying it," she replied.

When they were finished and had cleared the table, Sami drew Audrey aside.

"I think we should let Nathanial have some time with his parents alone," the FBI agent said. "He might remember more if we're not looking over his shoulder."

"I'm not comfortable leaving him here alone."

"We'll wait in the car."

Realizing Sami was right, Audrey grabbed her coat. She was prepared, after all, to do whatever necessary to help Nathanial fully regain his memory. Even if it was like pulling a fishhook from beneath her fingernail to let him out of her sight.

Nathanial watched the trio walk out the front door, leaving him with his mom and dad. As his parents had told stories of his past, he'd had flashes of memories that corresponded to their words. He sent up a silent prayer that his brain was healing and soon he'd regain all of his past, including the fateful day he'd disappeared from the rooftop in New Brunswick.

His mother hooked her arm through his and drew him to the couch. "I like your friends."

"Me, too. They're good people."

"Your grandmother will want to see you," Dad said as he took his seat in a leather chair facing the couch.

His grandmother. The word conjured up an image of an older version of his mother, with silver hair and a wreath of wrinkles around kind, laughing eyes. The ache of missing her clogged his throat. "I'll talk to the others about a visit."

"How long can you stay?" Mom asked.

"The night. The others have to get back to work, and I still have—" He stopped himself from revealing that someone was trying to kill him. He didn't want to worry them. "We're staying at the hotel on the edge of town."

"The Renners' place?" Dad asked.

"That's it."

"Nice people," Mom commented. "Do you remember Skip Renner? He was in your grade?"

He didn't. But he encouraged his parents to talk, to tell him more about his life. Though most of their stories weren't familiar, every once in a while he'd lock on a memory. Bits and pieces of his life took shape in his mind. There were still holes, and later that night after promising to swing by his parents' again in the morning before leaving, he lay in bed fitting the fragments together like a puzzle.

"Dear God, please help me to remember," he prayed in the dark hotel room. With Audrey next door and the Kelleys across the hall, Nathanial let his faith rise, hoping God would help him fill in the blanks.

But no matter how hard he concentrated on the one image connected to the mission that had gone so horribly wrong, his mind wouldn't move past that point of when he'd rolled over on that rooftop. He'd heard a noise from behind him. Something out of place. He was supposed to be alone. His heart hammered. He'd turned to face the threat...

Then nothing.

Always nothing.

He fell into a fitful sleep full of sinister figures that haunted his nightmares. And then there was Audrey banishing the shadows, offering him her hand, telling him it would be okay.

But would it? Would he ever remember? Or would he die first?

The next morning arrived with a swirl of fresh snow. Nathanial stepped out of the motel into the cold, tense with frustration and something else. A pending sense of doom that he'd awakened with and couldn't shake. As he waited for the others, he turned his face toward the sky and tiny flakes landed on his skin like kisses. He purposely relaxed his shoulders, but the unease clinging to him wouldn't release.

"You going to stick your tongue out and catch a snowflake?" Audrey asked with mirth lacing her tone.

Thankful for the distraction, he grinned at her and did just that.

She laughed, the sound cascading over him like sweet water, unaccountably smoothing away the frayed edges of his tension. An intense longing gripped him, making him want to whisk Audrey away, to go someplace where it was only the two of them. Somewhere the past didn't matter and no one was trying to kill him.

But he couldn't. The past did matter. He had to find the truth about it all.

And Audrey would never agree to shirk her responsibilities. He couldn't shirk his responsibilities. Nor could he ignore the guilt camping out in his chest. He had to know what he'd done to Laurie and apologize, though he doubted an apology would make up for whatever heartache he'd caused.

"I'd like to stop by Bartlett restaurant on the way to my grandmother's. I have to talk to Laurie again," Nathanial stated. "Apparently we were engaged once. I need to know what happened."

Audrey's blue eyes widened and then darkened with understanding. He could always count on her to comprehend doing the hard thing.

"I'll let the Kelleys know," she said, glancing at the motel entrance.

It wasn't long before the Kelleys walked out. Drew had his arm around Sami's shoulders. She smiled up at him with a heartfelt love shining on her pretty face. A twinge of something unfamiliar panged within Nathanial's heart. As they approached, he examined the feeling and realized with a start that it was envy.

He envied this couple their love, their togetherness. He wanted what they had with every fiber of his being. He almost let loose a laugh. Everything he'd heard about the man he'd been said he wasn't the type to settle down. Blake had made it clear he dated a lot but never got serious. Because of what happened with Laurie?

"I checked in with Director Moore," Drew said as he and Sami joined them near the SUV. "They received another tip that Kosloff is moving another shipment of arms north through the States. Blake and a team are going to intercept."

Nervous energy bounded through Nathanial. He wanted to join in the mission, to bring in Kosloff and make him tell them what had happened to Nathanial. But since that wasn't possible, he focused on clearing one aspect of his past at a time. He prayed Blake and the other IBETs team took Kosloff into custody.

"We'd like to stop by the Bartlett diner and grab breakfast," Audrey said.

Sami's eyebrows shot upward, and she pushed back a blond curl. "Okay. I could eat. And coffee would be welcome. But let's make it to go. I don't think we should linger."

Drew met Nathanial's gaze. "You sure?"

Nathanial nodded. "Very."

"All right. Load up." Drew climbed behind the wheel with Sami taking shotgun once again.

Audrey and Nathanial climbed into the borrowed RCMP SUV's back passenger seat. Heaviness pressed down on him. Was he doing the right thing by stopping there and wanting to talk to Laurie?

When they arrived at the restaurant, he hesitated.

While Sami and Drew left the vehicle and headed inside, Audrey remained seated next to Nathanial.

"What do you hope to accomplish?" she asked. There was no judgment in her tone, only curiosity.

He told her what he'd learned last night from his mother. "I need to know why we broke up."

"Why?"

"I need to understand. To know what kind of man I am."

Audrey reached for his hand. "I don't think it matters who you were then as much as who you are now." She lowered her voice, and it seemed as if she struggled to say her next words. "I like the man you are now."

He curled his fingers around hers. "How is it that you always know the right things to say?"

"It's a gift." She extracted her hand and climbed out of the vehicle.

He followed her inside the eatery, the bells hanging on the door jangling. The place had just opened so they were the first customers of the day. And Sami and Drew had a booth by the front window, where they could keep watch in case a threat appeared. They joined them. An older woman came to take their orders. Her short dark hair framed an oval face that reminded Nathanial of Laurie. Her mother?

She eyed him with surprise. "Laurie mentioned you were home," she said with a smile. Her name tag read Martha.

"Is she here?" he asked. "I'd like to talk to her."

Creases appeared between Martha's eyebrows. "She's in the back. When I put your ticket in, I'll let her know you want to say hello."

"Thank you."

They each ordered breakfast to go, and then Martha headed to the kitchen. A few minutes later, Laurie walked out. She had an apron on over jeans and a long-sleeved T-shirt. Her dark hair was clipped back. Nathanial watched her approach and felt nothing. No stirring of attraction, no remembered intimacy. Nothing. She was a stranger to him.

She stopped beside their table. "Mom said you were asking for me."

"I'd like a moment of your time," he said and slid out of the booth. He gestured to the table a few feet away. "Can we sit?"

Her gaze settled on Audrey, who stared back at her with an implacable expression. Laurie finally nodded and moved to the table and sat. She folded her hands on the tabletop. "What is there to talk about? Are you still claiming amnesia?"

"Not claiming," he replied. Suddenly he wasn't sure if he wanted or needed to do this. What good would it accomplish? Knowing that he'd done this woman wrong would only eat at him. But he'd come this far; he had to see it through. He went for the heart of the matter. "We were going to get married. We didn't. Why?"

A pained expression marched across her face. His heart rate tripled.

"You don't remember the baby, either?"

He nearly choked. "I have a child?"

She shook her head. "No. I miscarried in the first trimester."

He tried to absorb her words. For a short time he'd been a father. He wasn't sure how to feel about that.

"You wanted to get married. You assumed because

of the baby that was what we had to do," she continued softly.

Confusion reared up. "I don't understand," he said. "You didn't want to marry me?"

She lifted her chin. "Because of the baby I would have. But after...there was no point. I didn't love you. Not enough to spend the rest of my life with you."

He sat back as if someone had doused him with cold water, waking him up. Energy buzzed through his system. He wasn't sure how to process her words. "We must have had some feelings for each other if we made a baby."

She gave a dry chuckle. "Of course we did. We were seventeen and thought we were in love. But the reality of the baby and—" she waved a hand "—everything. It was too much for me. I couldn't handle it."

The guilt that had been slowly suffocating him let go. And he could breathe again.

"I know I hurt you." Guilt flashed across Laurie's face. "I'm sorry."

He felt almost giddy with relief. He hadn't dumped her. "I survived."

Though he couldn't remember the hurt, it didn't take a degree in psychology for him to comprehend the wound of her rejection had kept him from seeking love again. He'd used the rejection as an excuse to keep from committing. Because some part of him had understood that he didn't want to go through that kind of heartache again.

But was he willing to now? His gaze strayed to Audrey. She lifted her mug of coffee and met his gaze over the rim. He saw questions and concern in her pretty eyes.

She worried about him. He knew she didn't have

to—he was in no danger at the moment—but still she cared. Warmth spread through his chest.

And he searched his own heart and found the answer to the question. Yes. He was willing to risk everything for his beautiful deputy. But would he? Did he have the guts? This trip home might not have accomplished the desired effect of regaining his memories, but he'd gained something else. His heart back.

Movement outside the window behind Audrey snagged his focus. A gold-colored luxury sedan pulled up near the front entrance. He recognized the car. And the three men exiting the vehicle, all dressed in dark clothes and hefting heavy artillery in their hands. Their faces and heads were uncovered, which didn't bode well.

Heart smashing against his breastbone, Nathanial jerked to his feet. "Kosloff's men."

Without hesitation Sami, Drew and Audrey scrambled out of the booth.

"Get the civilians out of here," Drew instructed as he drew his sidearm from the holster at his waist. He moved to a partition near the cash register where he'd have the tactical advantage when the men breached the front door.

The men outside let loose an onslaught of gunfire from automatic assault rifles that riddled the front of the restaurant with bullets.

"Hurry!" Sami waved the few waitstaff toward the kitchen. "Stay low." She hustled them out of harm's way while dialing for backup. Sami's voice sounded muffled in Nathanial's ringing ears.

"Go," he urged Laurie to follow Sami. Eyes wide with panic, Laurie jumped from her seat, toppling the chair in her haste to run to the back of the restaurant. The gunfire stopped.

Audrey rushed to Nathanial's side. "Let's get you somewhere safe."

"No." Nathanial resisted her prompting. He flipped the table over and they crouched down out of the line of sight behind it. "Do you have a backup piece on you?"

She hesitated for a fraction of a second before reaching for the small-caliber handgun holstered to her inner calf. She handed over the weapon. "We'll never win a shoot-out against their automatic weapons. We need to get out of here."

"We can't run," he said. He needed to end this. If they could capture one of the men and make him talk, then this nightmare could end. But it was a big *if*.

He put his hand on Audrey's shoulder. "Cover me."

Panic flared in her eyes. She opened her mouth to protest, but he was already moving toward the front door. He pressed his back on the opposite side from Drew. A busing cart rattled as Nathanial shoved it aside.

With jaw set, Audrey knelt behind the table, gripping her sidearm with two hands and keeping at the ready with the barrel aimed down but close to her chest. Her disapproving gaze burned through him.

Through the stuffy echo in his ears, Nathanial heard shouted commands.

"Send out Longhorn and no one else has to get hurt!" A heavily accented voice seeped beneath the front door. "We have the place surrounded. If we have to kill everyone, we will."

Nathanial met Audrey's gaze. She gave a vehement shake of her head.

He had no intention of dying today, but he also knew

he couldn't let anything happen to his team or the innocent people in the kitchen. Slanting a glance at Drew,
Nathanial wondered what he'd have done before losing
his memories. Would he have given himself over for
others, or would he have found a way to escape?

Leaving, saving his own hide, didn't sit well. In fact,
the very thought was abhorrent to him. No way did he
want to put others in unnecessary danger. "I'll come
out, but you have to promise you'll let everyone else go."

"Dude," Drew barked at him. "We've seen their
faces. They're not going to let any of us live."

"Sami is calling for backup. We have to stall for
time," he insisted.

Audrey scrambled closer. "No way. As long as they
stay outside, we can fend them off or pick them off if
they enter. The RCMPs in Meadow Lake will arrive
soon. I have to believe that. God won't let us die like
this."

Her faith was strong and inspired him to hope she
was right. He sent up a silent plea for help, for wisdom.

Screams from the kitchen jolted through him. Adrenaline spiked, making his blood freeze in his veins while
his heart struggled to pump. What was happening?

"Sami!" Drew was across the diner before Nathanial
could take a step.

The kitchen doors were kicked open. A man with a
shaved head and dressed in camouflage clothes stepped
into the dining room with an arm around Sami and a
gun to her head. Drew halted abruptly. His shoulders
heaved, and his fists clenched.

Audrey hissed in a shocked breath and aimed her
weapon at the man.

"Put your weapons on the floor," the man said, his light eyes cold, devoid of emotion.

Nathanial held up his hands, showing the gun. "I'll go with you. Don't hurt anyone." As he slowly bent to place the gun on the floor, he bumped the busing cart. The rattle of utensils inside a plastic tub on the bottom shelf set off something inside him, but he didn't stop to think, he reacted. His hand reached into the tub and wrapped around the sharp blade of a steak knife. He met Sami's gaze, saw her fury but also saw the slight nod she gave him.

"Let me see your hands," the gunman barked.

Nathanial yelled, "Down."

Without hesitation, Sami went limp in her captor's arms, slipping from his grasp to the floor. As soon as she was clear, Nathanial, acting on some buried training, flung the steak knife. The blade hit its mark, embedding deep into the sinews and tendons of the bald thug's forearm. He screamed with pain and dropped his weapon.

Sami jumped to her feet and kicked the discarded rifle away as Drew lunged forward, seized the man and wrestled him to the ground, where he flipped the assailant onto his stomach and jammed a knee into his back. He took out a set of metal handcuffs and slapped them onto the thug's wrists.

Sami grabbed her weapon from the thug's waistband. "That's mine."

The bells over the door jingled as it opened. Drew and Sami took defensive positions.

Audrey swiveled toward the door. Two more gunmen stepped into the diner.

Terror smacked through Nathanial. No! Audrey was right in the line of fire.

Audrey squeezed the trigger of her sidearm, hitting the thug in front, who was shorter and broader than his cohort, in the leg. He went down, clutching his thigh.

The man's companion swung the barrel of his assault rifle toward Audrey.

Before the thug could pull the trigger, Nathanial tackled him, ramming the goon into the cash register counter. The guy was strong and wily. He pushed back from the counter, flinging his head back.

Agony vibrated down Nathanial's arm from the point of contact where the attacker's skull connected with his collarbone, but he fought through the glaring spots of pain to grasp the rifle, intent on gaining control of the weapon. They fell to the ground in a heap as they grappled for dominance.

Nathanial gritted his teeth with determination as he infused every ounce of power he had to wrest the rifle from the man's hands. The assailant's finger was on the trigger.

Boom.

Chapter Thirteen

The thunderous crack of several rounds exiting the assault rifle lodged between Nathanial and the assailant reverberated through Audrey, making her heart stall out with sudden fear.

Lord, please, no! I can't lose him.

The silent prayer screamed through her consciousness as plaster from the ceiling fell in bits and pieces. Her breath expanded in her chest as agonizing seconds ticked by. Was Nathanial hit? Was he alive? She refused to look too closely at the emotions welling up inside her.

Then Nathanial rolled away from the attacker, taking the rifle with him, and jumped to his feet in a defensive stance, ready to continue the fight. "Don't move!" he commanded the man on the ground. "Hands up where I can see them."

The man's sharp features reminded Audrey of a hawk—a beak of a nose, beady eyes and thin lips that twisted with rage—but he complied, slowly lifting his hands in the air.

Relief weakened Audrey's knees, but now wasn't the time to let down her guard. She quickly nudged both assailants' rifles to the side. Then, needing the action of cuffing the shorter man she'd shot as a way to distract herself from the rush of feelings flooding her heart, Audrey pulled the man's hands behind his back and encircled his wrists with a set of heavy-duty zip ties she'd pulled from her pants pocket. The smaller type of plastic ties could be easily broken, but these newer ones were more difficult for suspects to break. She handed Nathanial a second set.

"You've been carrying these around?" he asked as he took them and expertly secured hawk guy's hands behind his back.

"Of course," she said. "I may not be in uniform, but I'm always prepared."

"I like that about you," he said, his dark eyes holding hers with an intensity that had heat creeping up her neck.

Discomfited by his stare, she grabbed a cloth napkin and tied it around the wounded man's injury, then helped him to a sitting position next to the bald thug with his back resting against the booth bench.

"The civilians?" Drew asked Sami as he pulled her into his arms for a quick hug.

Seeing the couple together made Audrey's heart squeeze tight. She'd seen the panic and fear in Drew's eyes when Sami had been held captive, but he'd maintained his composure. She wasn't sure how. The man had a core of steel.

Her own heart had cramped when she realized Nathanial's intent. When he'd launched the steak knife, Audrey's mouth had dropped open in shock that had turned to awe when he'd disarmed Sami's assailant. How had Sami known Nathanial's aim would be true?

"They're safe," Sami replied to Drew's question about the restaurant's patrons and employees. "I had them squeeze into the pantry. I was coming back to help you when that one got the drop on me." There was no mistaking the bitter anger in her tone.

"My heart literally stopped beating," Drew said softly.

Sami leaned up to look into her husband's face. "Mine, too."

Seeing their obvious love for one another made Audrey's throat tighten. Longing for someone in her life with whom she could share that type of love and affection scraped along her nerves. Her glance slid to Nathanial. He watched her, his dark eyes unreadable.

Audrey dropped her gaze, her mind whirling. Earlier she'd feared for his life, and in that moment she'd realized she'd allowed herself to get too attached, too emotionally invested in Nathanial. Keeping him safe had become personal. Her feelings for him had become personal.

How could she let this happen? To cover her dismay, she busied herself by holstering her weapon. She had to stay focused on the job and keep her heart under better control.

Sami headed into the back to assure the civilians all was clear.

Drew hunched down in front of the two injured men. "Who sent you? How did you find us?"

Both men stared at him and remained mute.

Nathanial hauled the third attacker to his feet and pushed him to sit by his friends. "Why are you trying to kill me?"

The man sneered. He had deep-set eyes beneath thick

brows. "You think you're safe. But you're not. None of us are."

Remembering what happened to the last thug they'd caught and questioned, Audrey said, "These men are in danger."

Nathanial glanced at her sharply. His eyes narrowed then widened with realization. "Right." He gave her an approving nod. "Their boss, Kosloff, will kill them for failing to do their job just like he did Sasha."

That got their attention. All three men reacted as if someone had poked them in the back with a sharp stick.

"That's right. We know who you work for," Nathanial said. "Tell me why Kosloff sent you and how you found us."

The bald thug laughed. "You think we know?" He had no discernible accent. Audrey figured the guy had to be American. "We do as we're told."

"You were told I'd be *here*?" Nathanial asked.

"We were told to watch for a RCMP vehicle and we'd find you," Baldy shrugged.

The answer only made Nathanial more convinced one of their own was working with Kosloff—how else would anyone know they'd changed vehicles? He discounted the Mounties they'd borrowed the SUV from because they'd had no clue Nathanial was headed here.

"Shut up," hawk guy barked in a heavily accented voice.

"You shut up!" Baldy shot back.

The screech of tires outside jolted an alert through Audrey. Doors slammed. Nathanial looked out the window. "The cavalry has arrived."

A moment later Inspector Cavendish stepped through the entrance, followed by two more Mounties with guns drawn.

"Well, seems you have everything under control here," Cavendish stated as he surveyed the scene.

"These two will need medical care," Audrey told him, pointing to the man she'd shot and the guy holding his arm where the steak knife had struck him, which was now wrapped with a blood-soaked cloth napkin. "The third guy is unharmed."

Cavendish nodded. "Thank you, Deputy Martin." He turned his attention to the three intruders. "I'm obligated to inform you of your right to counsel."

"We want to make a deal," hawk guy stated. "We'll tell you what we know for immunity."

"Which, apparently, isn't much, according to your friend," Audrey interjected.

Through the side window, Audrey observed the customers and employees leaving. She had no doubt Sami had taken their names and contact info for Inspector Cavendish to contact them later for statements.

"Not true," the man with the bullet in his leg said. He, too, had a thick Eastern European accent. "We have intel to trade."

The bald man smacked his accomplice. "No, we don't. Don't let them play you."

"No one is playing here," Drew stated in a deadly calm voice. "Tell us what we want to know. Make it easier on yourselves."

"Not without assurances," hawk guy said. "If we give you Kosloff's location, you let us walk."

Like that would happen. Audrey didn't blame the guy for trying, but he wouldn't be skating on attempted murder. The best he and his associates could hope for were reduced sentences.

Bald guy groaned. "We're dead. Kosloff's spies are everywhere."

"We can talk to the minister of justice," Inspector Cavendish said. "But it's up to the minister's judgment." He nodded to his sergeants. "Take them into custody. We'll hold them at the station until the crown attorney can be dispatched from Regina."

After they were gone, Nathanial slammed a fist on the table. "We have to find Kosloff. I can't keep living like this. I have to know what happened."

Wincing at his pain, Audrey wished there was a way she could help him. But she had no idea how. Returning to his hometown and seeing his parents hadn't dislodged the crucial memory of what happened to him. "We should go where you were last before losing your memory." She prayed that would be the catalyst to bring back the events of that day.

"Good idea," Drew said. "Maybe on that rooftop you'll remember."

Nathanial ran a hand through his dark hair. "It certainly couldn't hurt."

"I'll call Blake and let him know where we're going," Drew said, taking out his cell phone.

Sami followed her husband outside to the borrowed RCMP vehicle.

The desolate expression on Nathanial's face made Audrey's heart twist. She went to his side and put a hand on his shoulder. "You okay?"

"Not really." He took her hand in his. "Everywhere I go, death and destruction seem to follow me." He let out a mirthless laugh. "Merry Christmas."

His sarcasm echoed through the empty restaurant. Audrey moved to stand in front of him, forcing him to meet her gaze. "Look. This isn't your fault. We'll get the man responsible. You have to believe that."

He frowned. "I do. I know eventually the IBETs team will take down Kosloff and whoever is working for him."

"And you'll be with your team."

"Maybe."

A noise near the kitchen door sent alarm exploding inside Audrey. She spun toward the sound while reaching for her weapon. Nathanial stepped in front of her as a shield. Even as it registered what he was doing, Audrey's heart melted a little. Strangely she wasn't irritated by his move, as she normally would be if any other man had thought she needed to be protected.

With Nathanial, she knew it wasn't a power play but his natural instinct to guard, to protect. To show he cared.

Laurie stood in the doorway, frozen. Her brown eyes were large and scared. A visible tremor ran through her. "Sorry. Didn't mean to startle you."

Taking a calming breath, Audrey relaxed her stance and dropped her empty hands to her sides.

"Laurie, I thought you left with your mother," Nathanial said but didn't move toward her.

"I came back to see if you were still here," Laurie replied. She took a deep breath and squared her shoulders as if bracing for battle.

Audrey pressed her lips together. Did the woman hope to reclaim him? Why did that thought make Audrey's blood pressure rise? It wasn't as if she and Nathanial were a couple. They worked together for now, but that was all.

Yet she couldn't help the thrum of possessiveness

that ran a ragged course through her. She purposely stepped back as if somehow putting distance between herself and Nathanial could control her feelings. Feelings that were simmering below the surface and threatening to boil over. Feelings she didn't want to name or look at too closely. Her pulse ticked up.

Nathanial slanted a curious glance at Audrey, and she was careful to keep her expression neutral so he wouldn't see what was bubbling inside her.

"We were just heading out," Nathanial replied to Laurie. "I'm sorry for what happened today. I shouldn't have come here."

Laurie stepped closer. "I wanted to make sure you were okay. That you don't...still hate me."

Audrey cocked her head and stared at the pair. Hate her? What had happened between them? Curiosity burned beneath her breastbone, and she absently rubbed at the spot. It didn't matter. It wasn't her concern. She had no right to wonder, let alone ask. But knowing that didn't squelch her interest.

"I'm good," he said. "I don't hate you." He grimaced. "The past is gone for me. I may never remember." He took a shuddering breath. "I'm glad you told me, though. It helps to know." He took her hand. "I hope that you find happiness."

A tentative smile spread over her face. "Thank you." Her gaze jumped to Audrey then back to him. "I hope you do as well." He dropped her hand, and she turned to leave the way she'd come in. "Goodbye."

"Goodbye, Laurie." Nathanial put his hand to the small of Audrey's back and ushered her out the restaurant's front entrance.

Giving in to the curiosity itching at her, she peered at him. "What was that about?"

"Putting the past to rest," he murmured as he led her to the vehicle, keeping her from asking any more questions.

Drew hung up from his call. "Blake and the team will meet us in New Brunswick."

"Great." Nathanial opened the back passenger door for Audrey. "Let's pray I can recall something that will put an end to this nightmare."

The trip from Saskatoon to Saint John, New Brunswick, took three plane changes. On the first leg Nathanial was too keyed up to rest, but Audrey slept. When her head bobbed for the third time, he'd gently positioned her so that she pressed against his arm and her head rested on his shoulder. The fragrance of the hotel shampoo clinging to her hair teased his nose, but the subtle scent that was completely hers, and hers alone, filled his senses.

Tender affection invaded his chest, clutching his heart in a fierce grip. He didn't know why God had allowed this amazing woman to be the one to find him on the beach, but he was grateful nonetheless. There was something about her that called to something deep inside him. He couldn't say if he'd ever felt this way before, and the feeling was strange and wonderful all at once.

He called himself all kinds of a fool for letting himself become attached to the lovely Audrey, but how could he not? She was a treasure. And the fact that some jerk had abused her trust and love made Nathanial's blood boil and his heart hurt.

When they landed in Winnipeg, Audrey awoke. She jerked upright as if stunned to find she'd been leaning on him. "Ugh. Did I drool?"

He chuckled. "Not that I noticed."

She busied herself gathering her belongings, but there was no hiding the blush raging on her fair cheeks.

They disembarked and met Drew and Sami for a quick bite to eat before boarding the next plane. On the second leg of the trip, he finally succumbed to exhaustion. He awoke as the captain was announcing their descent into Toronto. He lifted his head from Audrey's shoulder and grinned. "Did I drool?"

She laughed, her blue eyes sparkling despite the dim lights of the plane's interior. "Like a hound dog."

He wiped his mouth and flushed with embarrassment. "Sorry."

"I'm joking," she said.

"Good. I'd hate to have you think I'm a Neanderthal."

She scrunched up her nose. "Never."

This time when they disembarked, they had to hustle to their next gate to make the last leg of the trip to Saint John. Audrey and Nathanial sat together again with Sami and Drew in the row behind them. Night had fallen long ago. Outside the airplane's small oval windows lay a vast darkness.

Since they both had slept, they were both wide-awake. Nathanial could tell Audrey had something on her mind because she kept sending him sideways glances, and her bottom teeth tugged on her lower lip. He'd seen her nervous, irritated and determined, but not uncertain. And it made him nervous. When she started picking at a hangnail, he finally reached over and covered her hands.

"What is it?" he asked.

Her eyebrows rose. "What do you mean?"

"You're fidgeting. Something has you twisted up inside. Maybe I can help?" He'd like to do whatever he could to repay her for all she'd done for him.

She made a face. "I didn't realize I was that transparent. I keep telling myself it's none of my business, but…"

"But?"

"What happened between you and Laurie? What did she say when you two talked?"

Ah. He should have known she'd wonder. Who wouldn't? He thought about how best to answer. Straightforward was the best and only approach. "Apparently whatever we had was one-sided." He told her the gist of his past with Laurie. "She only agreed to marry me because of the baby. Afterward, she rejected me."

Audrey's mouth formed an O. "I see. The decisions we make when we're young can haunt us the rest of our lives."

He let out a dry laugh. "If one can remember them."

Audrey's steady gaze held. A man could happily drown in those blue pools. "You can't give up hope that you'll remember."

Her optimism was endearing. "From what I've gleaned from Blake and Drew, I haven't let myself fall in love again."

"Understandable. She broke your heart."

He shrugged. He couldn't remember, but if Laurie had thought he was mad at her because she'd turned down his offer of marriage, then maybe she *had* broken his heart. Or at least made him wary of relationships.

He surely never wanted to compromise his faith again. "All I know for sure is that the future looks so much brighter than it did."

A shadow crossed her face. "That's good."

She hadn't healed from the wound inflicted by her college love. "Do you trust me?"

She tucked in her chin and eyed him warily. "Yes."

He gave her his most dazzling smile. "Even if I'm charming?"

With a roll of her eyes, she shook her head. "Don't let it go to your head."

He chuckled then sobered. "I'm serious. I hope you won't let your past hurtful relationship keep *you* from finding love."

"It's not just Kyle that has held me back," she admitted softly. "I have dated since Kyle. Most men are either intimidated by me or want to change me into something I'm not."

"So you mentioned." It pained him to think she'd been treated poorly and made to feel bad about herself. "I like you, Audrey. A lot. Just as you are."

For a brief second, pleasure flared in her eyes, then she dropped her gaze to their entwined hands. Slowly she extracted her hand from his grasp. "Thank you for saying that. I like you, too, Nathanial. You're a good man."

He could feel her withdrawing from him emotionally as well as physically. It stung more than it should. "I hear a *but* in there."

She sat up straighter. "No *but*."

Hmm. Okay. Then why did he feel disappointed—let down, even?

They sat in silence the rest of the flight. It was nearly

three in the morning when they touched down in Saint John. Blake was waiting for them at the curb outside the airport. The temperature was below freezing. Ice crusted on the walkway and road. Nathanial was thankful he'd grabbed a down jacket, wool cap and gloves from his parents' house. They piled into a warm minivan.

Blake drove them to a hotel and handed out key cards. "We'll meet back in the lobby in four hours."

Nathanial was grateful for the opportunity to shower and change clothes. He tried relaxing by stretching out on top of the bed but was too restless. He watched the minutes tick by on the clock. Finally it was time to leave his room. He opened the door to find Audrey about to knock.

"Couldn't sleep, either?" he asked as he closed the door behind him.

She gave him a wry smile. "No."

They met the others in the lobby, and Blake drove them to the warehouse district where their mission had gone wrong. A dozen men waited for them at the entrance to a redbrick building.

Nathanial scanned the faces of the men, hoping for some hint of recognition, and found none.

"Where's Chase?" Blake asked one of the men.

"Not sure. I would have thought he'd beat us here, since he was nearby following up on a lead," the man said, his badge identifying him as Agent Phillips of the Immigration and Customs Enforcement agency, like Blake.

"And Luke?" Drew asked.

"No sign of the border patrol guy, either," ICE agent Phillips stated.

A man came running up. His jacket had the RCMP logo on the breast pocket. "Inspector Kelley!"

"What is it, Sergeant?" Drew peered at the younger Mountie.

The sergeant pointed down the block. "I was doing a perimeter sweep as Agent Phillips asked when I came across an abandoned SUV. There's signs of a struggle. And blood."

Chapter Fourteen

"That doesn't sound good," Audrey said beneath her breath to Nathanial. She had a bad feeling about this. Two agents were missing. And there was blood at the scene of one agent's abandoned vehicle. She shivered at the implications. If someone in their ranks was working for Kosloff, they could all be walking into a trap. "We need to leave."

Nathanial shook his head. "We've come this far—we can't give up yet. I have to try."

She understood his need to recall what had transpired on the roof of this building. She glanced around, seeing the swarm of agents and officers from both sides of the international boundary line. There was tension etched on each person's face. They, too, felt exposed, vulnerable. She moved closer to Nathanial with her hand on her weapon. He was a target, and a kill shot could come from any of the rooftops or cars parked along the street. She met Sami's gaze and saw the worry in her eyes. Audrey turned back to Nathanial. "The risk is too great."

"Not your call, Deputy Martin," he said in a firm,

impersonal tone that bit into her. To Blake he said, "I'm going up while you search for Luke and Chase."

"We're coming with you," Drew stated. Sami nodded her agreement.

Audrey thrummed with frustration. However, she had no choice but to go with Nathanial as he headed inside the large four-story brick building. Aggravated by his bullheadedness, she sent up a quick prayer for protection and hustled after him.

At one time the large building had housed the offices of a shipping conglomerate, but it had long been abandoned, like so many older buildings in the area. The place smelled musty with disuse. Office windows were missing; doors hung on broken hinges. Chunks of plaster had fallen from the ceiling where water damage had seeped into the structure. She hurried by Nathanial to take the lead. She didn't miss the wry twist of his lips. Thankfully he didn't argue. Drew and Sami took the rear position.

Audrey held her sidearm in a two-handed grip as they stepped into a rickety elevator, which took them to the top floor. From there they had to take a steep flight of stairs to the roof. At the door to the rooftop, she paused, putting her hand out for Nathanial to wait as she eased the door open and peered out, bracing herself in case they came upon a hostile.

The roof appeared clear. She pushed the door wider and stepped out into the overcast morning. Wind whipped across the roof, stirring up debris. There was no one on the roof.

Nathanial nudged her aside. "I would have been positioned there." He pointed to the southeast corner that faced the warehouse where the raid on Kosloff had been scheduled to take place.

"That's right," Drew confirmed. "That's where we found your discarded hardware."

"Were there signs of a struggle?" Audrey asked.

"The crime scene techs found one drop of blood," Drew told them. "We had it DNA tested, and it was a match to you."

"The blow to his head happened here, then," she said, trying to envision the scene. "He was lying there, facing the street. He'd have been vulnerable to an attack from behind."

"I was struck on the left side of my head," Nathanial said, his dark eyes taking on a faraway look. He rubbed his forehead; no doubt another headache was taking hold of him.

She hated that he had to go through this pain. "The perp struck him, then stripped him of his accoutrements, leaving them behind for his team to find. Why not take them?"

"Good question. If it was one of Kosloff's goons, one would think they would want the flak vest and the weapons," Drew stated.

"Or they didn't want to risk being seen with my equipment. Too identifiable." Nathanial moved toward the edge of the roof.

"Which takes us back to the idea it was an insider. Someone who needed his cover to stay intact." She stuck to Nathanial's side, her gaze alert for any sign of danger. Drew followed while Sami monitored the door in case someone tried to come through and catch them from behind.

Nathanial lay down and mimed the action of looking

through a rifle scope. "I had a clear view of the warehouse," he said. "And of the neighborhood."

"A car turned on the street a few blocks down to the right," Drew said.

Nathanial shifted his attention to where Drew indicated.

"Tell us about the car," Audrey said.

"A black sedan with tinted windows," Drew supplied. "It rolled down the street slowly. Nathanial must have seen it, because he said to hold. We all held our positions, waiting for more info. None came. Two ATF agents approached the car and were fired upon."

"And killed." There was no mistaking the note of self-incrimination in Nathanial's tone.

Audrey hurt for him. "By then you were already out of commission. It's not your fault."

He glanced over his shoulder. Frowned, then rolled onto his back. Shielding his eyes from the overcast sun's glare with his hand, he said, "Step closer."

She did as he asked, casting a shadow over him. "What is it?"

Without answering, he moved onto his stomach and sighted the warehouse with his hands. He closed his eyes, then suddenly turned over onto his back to stare up at her. He blinked and then sat up abruptly. "I never saw my attacker's face."

Surprise washed through Audrey. "You can't identify him?" That was good news, wasn't it? Then why did Nathanial seem upset?

Nathanial shook his head with frustration. He'd so wanted to be able to proclaim the name of the man who'd assaulted him and thrown him into the ocean in the hopes he'd die. And was still trying to do him in. "No. He'd have been standing where you are with the sun at his back. All I would have seen was the dark outline of his body."

"The person trying to kill you doesn't know that. He fears you'll be able to identify him if you regain your memory," Audrey said with excitement in her voice. "We have to get this news out there so he'll stop coming after you."

"No." Nathanial rose to his feet. His head pounded, but he ignored the throbbing ache. "We have to catch the perpetrator. Whoever attacked me is working for Kosloff. If we can draw the suspect out into the open, then maybe we can capture him and use him to get Kosloff."

"That sounds risky," Audrey said.

"No more risky than letting him off the hook so he can continue to put other lives in jeopardy," he countered.

She pressed her lips together. As an officer of the law, he knew she couldn't refute his logic. But she wanted to. He could see it in the worry darkening her blue eyes.

"Maybe we need to start looking at how you ended up in the ocean," she said. "You were knocked unconscious here. The guy would have had to carry you out of the building and put you in a vehicle."

"We need to know where every agent and officer was at the time," Nathanial said. "Someone had to have seen something."

"Let's go confer with Blake," Drew instructed. "He'll have the schematics of the operation."

"It would also be helpful to learn if you were dropped into the ocean from shore or a boat," Audrey said as they walked toward Sami, where she stood waiting by the stairwell door. "If you were taken out on a boat, which seems most likely, we could look at all the harbors to see if we can find video-surveillance cameras."

"Good idea. Director Moore has been in contact with the New Brunswick authorities, requesting security videos in a ten-block radius from here," Sami said. "We're still waiting for them. I'll add the harbors to the request." Her curious gaze shifted to Nathanial. "Did you remember something?"

His gut churned with failure. "Unfortunately, no. This trip was a bust."

Audrey arched an eyebrow at Nathanial. "That's not really correct. You may not have remembered what happened, but we know what you didn't see."

He shrugged. She tended to see the bright side of things. To him, they were no better off than before coming to the roof. He wished he were more like Audrey. "True, but that doesn't get us any closer to taking down Kosloff and finding out who tipped him off to the raid. Besides, there may still be some memory of seeing my attacker locked in my brain."

"What happened?" Sami asked.

Drew quickly explained as they entered the stairwell. Their footsteps echoed off the concrete walls.

"Ah, I can see how that would be frustrating," Sami said.

They stepped into the elevator, and the doors slid shut. Drew pushed the button for the first floor. The car moved with a groan. A few seconds later, it jolted to an abrupt stop.

Nathanial jabbed a finger at the elevator car panel. Nothing worked. The doors remained closed. They moved neither up nor down. He wasn't sure if they were between floors or not.

Drew opened the call box. At one time it held a receiver connected to a security office in the building. But both were gone now.

Audrey checked her phone. "No bars."

"Me, either," said Drew as he looked at his cell phone.

A thud sounded on the ceiling.

Audrey reached for her weapon and gripped Nathanial's arm. His heart beat in his ears. Was someone up there? Had someone dropped something on the top of the elevator? If so, what?

A scraping noise echoed inside the elevator car, tightening his nerves. The emergency panel in the ceiling shifted slightly to allow a small tube to dangle into the car. Someone was up there!

"What is that?" Sami asked.

"It looks like a hose," Audrey replied.

"That's exactly what it is," Nathanial said. A wave of apprehension crashed over him as a hissing sound came from the hose. "Cover your mouths and noses!"

The compartment filled with a toxic gas that stung his eyes. Panic revved through his blood. Audrey jumped and batted at the hose with her free hand while her other hand covered her mouth and nose, trying unsuccessfully to push the hose out of the opening.

Nathanial took shallow breaths and attacked the elevator door. His muscles strained as he dug his fingers into the crevice where the doors met. Drew crowded in to help.

With their combined strength, they managed to inch the two sides apart, enough to let in some fresher air.

They were between the floors. Nathanial could see the cables and stone wall outside the elevator.

"Sami!" Audrey's cry jerked Nathanial's attention to the FBI agent. She was slumped on the floor, having succumbed to the gas.

Drew shoved the two sides of the door farther apart. "We have to get out of here."

Nathanial reached out and grabbed a set of cables. Hand over hand he shimmied up the cables until he could see the top of the elevator car. A black hose connected to a canister sat on top. The doors to the building were open. A black shadow appeared. Not a shadow—a man dressed all in black. He aimed an assault rifle at Nathanial.

His heart stalled. He had nowhere to hide.

The emergency panel in the elevator car ceiling flipped up, knocking the canister over. Audrey crawled out of the opening, quickly pushing the offending hose aside.

"Watch out!" Nathanial warned. "Shooter in the doorway."

Audrey reached up with her sidearm and fired at the man. The man dived out of the way, and the bullet hit the metal side of the door.

Audrey's panic-filled gaze jerked to Nathanial. "You okay?"

"Yes." He swung his feet to the top of the elevator car. Inside the car, Drew held Sami in his arms.

"You help them up," Audrey instructed. Before he could protest, she rose and in one graceful move, reached for the doorsill and muscled her way to the floor. She rolled out of sight with her gun at the ready.

Terrified something would happen to her, Nathanial

had to force himself not to follow her. Sami and Drew needed his help. He sent up a silent plea for God to keep her safe. To protect her, to bring her back to him.

He reached into the elevator car as Drew hefted Sami's petite, unconscious frame up. Nathanial caught her under the arms and dragged her as gently as he could out of the elevator. Then Drew jumped up, catching the lip of the opening, and pulled himself out of the car. Nathanial gripped the doorsill, much like Audrey had, and climbed out of the elevator shaft. He pressed his back to the side panel and peered around the edge. The hallway was empty. He quickly helped Drew with Sami. Once they were all out, Drew lifted Sami in his arms. "We have to find the stairs. She needs a medic."

Nathanial looked at Drew. "Let me have your weapon."

Drew didn't hesitate. "Take it."

Withdrawing Drew's sidearm from his holster, Nathanial led the way into the darkened interior in search of the stairwell. "Audrey?" he called out.

Nothing.

Where could she be? He prayed for her safety. They came to a corner in the hallway. He held up his hand to indicate to Drew to halt. He peered around the corner. A door opened at the far end of the hall. He lifted Drew's Glock. A figure stepped out of the stairwell. A shaft of gray light shone on blond hair. Audrey. He lowered his weapon with an exhale of relief. He called out her name.

She hustled toward him. "Suspect got away. I chased him down the stairs that lead to the back alley. By the time I reached the bottom, he was nowhere to be seen."

Drew rounded the corner with Sami held close to his chest. They hurried down the stairs and out the building's back exit. They moved swiftly down the alley and around to the front where the IBETs team waited. Blake paced with his cell phone pressed to his ear. When he saw them, his eyes widened and he hung up. Nathanial tucked Drew's gun into the waistband of his jeans.

"What happened?" Blake's concern shone on his face.

"We need an ambulance." Audrey explained what had transpired.

Blake's eyes darkened with anger. "How could this happen?" He barked out orders for other agents to secure the building and call in the crime-scene technicians.

Drew sat on the tailgate of an SUV with Sami secure in his arms. She'd awakened but still appeared weak from the gas.

Nathanial cupped Audrey's elbow and tugged her out of earshot of the others. "You shouldn't have taken off like that."

"Excuse me?" She drew back from him. "One of us had to go after the perp."

She was right and he knew it, yet he couldn't shake the dread that had taken up residence in the middle of his chest. If something had happened to her...

He couldn't bear the thought. Wow. He had it bad. And she wasn't the one who wanted or needed protection, but he couldn't help feeling protective. He was letting his feelings for her affect his judgment. He needed to put some distance between them, to give himself some space to figure out exactly what he felt for her.

And then he'd have to decide what to do about it.

Audrey tamped down the irritation crawling up her neck as she watched Nathanial striding away. He stopped to check on the Kelleys. She knew Nathanial well enough to know he wanted to protect her. He was that kind of guy. Protecting others was second nature to him. But she was a deputy sheriff, and running toward danger was a part of her.

For as long as she could remember, she'd been the one to step in to break up fights on the school yard, the first one to defuse volatile situations. Going into law enforcement had fit perfectly with her personality. She was good at her job. And if Nathanial couldn't see or accept that, then there was no future for them.

Her stomach knotted. Future? With Nathanial?

Did she want one? Her heart rate ticked up, and she took an involuntary step back. Maybe. She didn't know. There was still so much unresolved in his life. And there were issues she needed to face. Like did she trust him not to break her heart?

That was a no-brainer. Of course she did. He was a man of integrity and honor. But what would she have to give up to forge a life with him?

Her job? Her plans to become sheriff? Her country?

Much more than she was willing to sacrifice. No. A future with Nathanial wasn't possible. More than a boundary line separated their lives.

The jangle of her cell phone was a welcome distraction. She glanced at the screen. Her mom. No doubt Mom was wondering where she was and if she were okay. Audrey hadn't checked in for a few days. She pressed the talk button.

"Hi, Mom."

"Listen carefully and don't say a word," a man's deep voice intoned into Audrey's ear.

Her stomach dropped, as if the earth had given way

beneath her feet. Her hand tightened around the phone pressed to her ear.

"If you want to see your mother alive again, you bring Longhorn to her cottage. You tell anyone, and I'll know. And then your mother will die."

The caller clicked off. Silence echoed inside her head.

Her mother was being held hostage.

By a man whose voice Audrey recognized.

Chapter Fifteen

"We can reconvene at the IBETs headquarters," Blake said. "I don't want to conduct interrogations out in the field. I'll need to study the schematic to ascertain those who would have been in position to have a clear view of the back alley."

Nathanial wanted answers now but understood Blake's concern. Questioning the other officers and agents on the fly could lead to confusion and show their hand before they were ready. "Any word on Chase or Luke?"

Bleakness entered Blake's eyes. "No. Nothing. No trace of where they are or what happened to them."

"We have to check the docks." Nathanial hated to think that the two men were floating in the ocean as he'd been. Thankfully he'd washed ashore and had been rescued by a beautiful golden-haired deputy.

He could only pray Chase and Luke were as equally blessed to not only survive but be rescued.

Though he doubted anyone could top Audrey as a rescuer. His gaze slid to where she stood on the sidewalk next to the building with her phone in her hand.

Though the day was overcast, her blond hair brightened up the gloomy weather.

But her pale, stunned expression wasn't what he'd expected to see. His stomach lurched. Something was wrong. He hurried to her side.

"Audrey?"

She lifted her blue gaze to his as she disconnected the call. Her pupils were blown wide. Her breathing came in small gasps. "They have my mom."

"What? Who?" He gripped her shoulders. "Talk to me."

She shook her head. "Not here. Will you come home with me?"

He tilted his head. "Tell me what's happening. How can I help if I don't know what's wrong? Who is *they*?"

Her gaze darted left and right as if afraid someone would overhear their conversation. "It's not safe to talk here."

Grabbing his arm, she tugged him into the shadows between two buildings. "I received a call from my mom's phone. Only it wasn't her. The man on the other end said he'd kill her if I don't bring you to the cottage."

The air swooshed out of his lungs. *Will you come home with me?* Did she mean to trade him for her mom? No. She wouldn't do that. She wanted his help. There was no mistaking the pleading in her eyes. It took a second for him to catch his breath. "Let's not panic. We'll get Drew and Blake and head to Calico Bay."

"No." She clutched at his arm. "He said we had to come alone."

"They always say that," he said.

"Listen to me," she demanded. "He said he'd know if we told anyone."

Nathanial frowned. "Did he identify himself?"

"He didn't have to," she said, her voice shaking. "I know who it is. I know who betrayed you."

He stilled as alertness stole over him. "What are you saying?"

"Nathanial, it was Chase."

He rocked back as if someone had slapped him. "Wait. You're saying *Chase* is the one who called you threatening your mother?"

"It was him. I'm certain. He's the one working for Kosloff."

Nathanial reeled from the news. That day in the sheriff's office had been a charade—Chase's show of rage and grief, blaming Nathanial for two deaths, had been an act, and he'd had his own men killed. Had he been the man on the rooftop? The man who'd repeatedly tried to kill Nathanial?

"We have to tell Blake," Nathanial insisted. "We'll leave the Kelleys out of it. Thanks to the toxic gas, Sami's in no condition to deal with this. And we're going to need help to get your mother back."

Audrey took a shuddering breath. "I agree. My great-uncle and the others will help us. But I'm not sure telling Blake is a good idea. If Chase has more traitors working with the IBETs team, he'll know if we talk."

Nathanial shoved a hand through his hair. "We have to get Blake away from here so we can talk to him."

"How?"

"I'll tell him my head is killing me," he said, which wasn't too far from the truth. He indeed had a splitting headache. "I'll ask him to take us to the hotel. We'll explain on the way."

"What if...if he's with Kosloff? He and Chase seemed tight."

Nathanial's mind rebelled at the thought of Blake being dirty. No way. He took Audrey's hands in his. "We have to trust someone. Everything inside me says Blake is a stand-up guy."

"I'm sure everyone thinks the same of Chase."

She had a point. But they needed assistance getting back to Calico Bay. Not to mention support, weapons, ammunition and manpower. Yes, Sheriff Crump and his deputies would be useful, but Nathanial doubted they had the experience to tackle a situation like this one.

The photo from Blake's wedding surfaced in Nathanial's mind. He'd trusted Blake in the past. He had to put his life, and those of Audrey and her mother, in his hands now. It would take a leap of faith. "Pray with me," he said to Audrey. "Pray that God will guide us and guard us and your mother."

She nodded and tugged him closer. "Dear Father in Heaven, please hear our prayer. We ask for Your wisdom, Your guidance and safety for my mom. For us as we rescue her."

Nathanial nodded his agreement and gave her a reassuring smile that they would succeed in rescuing her mother. Now that they knew who the bad guy was, they could put an end to this nightmare.

They found Blake giving orders to pack up and return to the IBETs headquarters in Washington, DC.

"Hey," Blake said as they halted at his side. "We're heading out. I'll have Phillips drive you to the hotel to pick up your stuff and then take you to the airport."

"No," Nathanial said. "We need to go with you."

He frowned. "I'm staying to wait for the crime-scene techs."

"Let Phillips do that," Nathanial said, holding his gaze steady and trying to convey the necessity through his stare. "We need you to take us to the airport. It's important."

Blake cocked his head then nodded slowly. "Okay."

Nathanial was a bit surprised by Blake's easy acceptance and grateful for it as well. He and Audrey climbed into the black SUV to wait for Blake as he gave Agent Phillips instructions. A few moments later, Blake joined them in the vehicle and slid behind the steering wheel. He remained silent as he fired up the engine and drove away from the harbor area.

"Explain," he said finally.

Nathanial nodded to Audrey. This was her story to tell. She quickly laid out the details of the call.

Blake pulled the SUV to the side of the road. "Let me get this straight. ATF agent Chase Smith is involved with Kosloff? He's holding your mother hostage?"

"Yes." Nathanial felt Blake's upset all the way to the soles of his feet. "It's mind-blowing."

"It's ridiculous," Blake stated.

"I know it was him on the phone," Audrey insisted. Nathanial folded his hand over hers, offering her his support. He believed her.

Blake started driving again. "We'll find out soon enough."

Two and half hours later, they rolled into Calico Bay. The sky was clear. Clumps of snow lined the streets. The Christmas decorations on the storefronts were a mockery of the anxiety filling Nathanial as they halted in the back parking lot of the sheriff's department.

The last time Nathanial had been here, the generator had blown up and men with guns had tried to kill him. He'd survived thanks to the woman at his side. Their trek through the tunnels to the cliffs would forever be ingrained on his brain.

Audrey jumped out and hurried inside the station. Nathanial and Blake followed in her wake. Before stepping inside, Blake put a hand on Nathanial's arm, halting him. "You trust this woman?"

"Funny, she asked me the same thing about you." Nathanial stared at the man he'd once called friend. "I trust her with my life. Just as I'm trusting you with all of our lives."

An interesting array of emotions crossed Blake's face. "When this is over, you have to come to Hilton Head. Liz will want a full accounting and to make sure for herself you're okay."

"Sounds like a plan." He took a deep breath and slowly let it out. "But first let's put an end to this ordeal. Kosloff and his minions are going down."

Nervous energy buzzed through Audrey's body, making it difficult for her to concentrate. A state she'd never experienced before. Nothing had prepared her for the fear of losing her mother to some psychotic rogue ATF agent and his Russian arms-dealer boss. She paced a short path inside her great-uncle's office as he, Nathanial and Blake strategized how best to execute a rescue of her mother. She listened, but her heart was busy praying.

She'd never had her faith tested so greatly before. She wanted to rail at the sky, shake her fist and ask God

why He'd allow her mother to be put in such a dangerous situation.

But Audrey knew that God wasn't at fault. He gave
men free will to do good and evil. But God also gave
strength and protection to His people.

She clung to the verse running through her head.
Have I not commanded you? Be strong and courageous.
Do not be afraid; do not be discouraged, for the Lord
your God will be with you wherever you go.

"What do you think, Audrey?"

Nathanial's question snapped her to attention. "I'm
sorry?"

He held out his hand. She closed the gap between
them, slipping her hand into his.

"I want to know what you think of the plan," he said.

His dark eyes searched her face. She flushed as she
realized she had no idea what they'd decided. That was
so unlike her. Usually she had to be in control, the one
calling the shots. But she was letting Nathanial take
the lead. She was putting her trust and her life into his
hands. "Can you run the plan by me again?"

"I approach the cottage from the front. Make sure
they see me coming. I will distract whoever's inside so
that you, Blake, Sheriff Crump and the deputies can
enter through the back and rescue your mother."

Dread clamped a steely hand around her throat.
"You'll be vulnerable to an attack."

"Yes. Can't be helped." He squeezed her hand. "This
is happening because of me. I need to end this."

"No. I won't allow you to walk directly into the line
of fire," she said in a strangled voice. She felt as if her
throat were collapsing on itself.

"The priority is your mother." He tucked a strand of

her hair behind her ear, his touch gentle and electric. "I'll do whatever it takes."

He was so generous and brave. His courage gave her the motivation she needed to pull herself together. She squared her shoulders with determination. "You're not going in alone. I'll have your back, while Uncle David and Blake rescue Mom."

"Thank you. But—"

She placed her finger firmly against his lips. "No *but.*"

His gaze softened and filled with something that made her heart pound and her blood race.

Despite the grim circumstances and the fear crowding her, Audrey realized how deeply she'd come to care for this man as she found strength in his dark gaze.

"Okay, now that that is settled," David said. "Agent Fallon and I will organize the troops. Audrey, take Officer Longhorn to the equipment room for a flak vest."

"Yes, sir." Keeping hold of Nathanial's hand, she led him to the back of the station, where they kept extra equipment.

They entered, but before she could reach for a flak vest, Nathanial tugged her close. The room was cold, but pressed up against Nathanial, she felt warmed from the inside out.

He cupped her cheek. "Whatever happens today, I want you to know that I—"

Flutters of excitement made her hold her breath. "You?"

"Am thoroughly, totally in love with you," he said. Then he kissed her.

Shock from his words vied with the magnificent sensation of his mouth moving over hers, chasing away the gnawing little voice that warned her not to believe it. Hadn't she made the mistake before of buying into a charming man's declaration?

But this was Nathanial. And, oh, his kiss made her knees weak. He was a good man. An honorable man.

A man willing to sacrifice his life for her mother's safe return.

A declaration born out of desperation and fear couldn't be trusted. She broke the kiss and stepped back. Her head was reeling, her heart groaning with longing and need. But she had to be smart.

"You are not going to die today. I forbid it. And when this is over, then…" Then what? She didn't know. Couldn't see beyond the immediate need to rescue her mother.

She grabbed a flak vest from the rack and shoved it into his chest. "Put this on. I'll get you a weapon."

"I have Drew's Glock still," he said as he donned the vest, his expression unreadable.

"Good." She opened a cabinet and took out a bolt-action Remington 700 sniper rifle used by police departments all across the United States. She grabbed a box of ammo. Catching the incredulous expression on Nathanial's face, she arched an eyebrow. "What? You're not the only one who can do overwatch."

He barked out a laugh. "You are a treasure, Deputy Audrey Martin."

"And don't you forget it." She walked out with the rifle tucked under her arm.

Nathanial held up his hands as he approached the front of the Martin cottage. He'd parked Blake's SUV at the end of the driveway. The sound of the nearby ocean drowned out the thrumming of blood in his ears. The place looked like something right out of a Thomas Kinkade painting.

A cobblestone path led to a large wooden door, where a green wreath sporting a red bow hung in welcome. The eaves were dusted white, and little colorful Christmas lights peeked through, reminding him that tomorrow was Christmas Eve. A fully trimmed tree with lush boughs dominated the front window and kept him from seeing inside.

But that didn't mean those inside couldn't see him. He prayed they couldn't see Audrey. Even though he couldn't see Audrey's perch, he could feel her gaze as surely as if she were standing beside him. She had his back. She'd had his back from the moment he'd washed ashore on the beach.

He stopped at the foot of three stone steps. "I'm here. Let Dr. Martin go."

The front door opened. A man hung back in the shadows of the darkened house. "We'll let her go when we're ready. Come in."

The heavily accented voice wasn't Chase's. Kosloff? Would he be bold enough to do his own dirty work? Nathanial couldn't make out the man's face—he stayed just out of the light enough to keep hidden.

"What assurances do I have that you won't kill her?" Nathanial called back.

The tip of a rifle poked out of the door. "You don't."

"I'm not coming in until I know Dr. Martin is unharmed," he said, bracing himself. It would be too easy for the man in the doorway to put a bullet between Nathanial's eyes. But then the shooter would also find himself on the receiving end of Audrey's bullet.

The man disappeared. When he returned to the door, he held Dr. Martin by his beefy hand. A ski mask covered his face, which was a good sign. If Dr. Martin couldn't identify him, there was no reason to kill her.

Nathanial turned his attention to Dr. Martin. She had a gag over her mouth. She wore her hospital lab coat, and her wide-eyed gaze locked with his. He saw her terror, but he also saw her strength. She was afraid, but she wasn't cowering. She was, after all, Audrey's mother, and Audrey had learned to be strong from the woman who'd raised her. "It's going to be okay," Nathanial assured her.

The man jerked her back into the house. "Now you come in."

"Sure." Nathanial stepped onto the first stair. "Where's Chase?"

"Stop stalling," the man yelled. "Get in here."

A loud bang from the back of the house distracted the man at the door. He turned toward the sound. Nathanial vaulted up the stairs and tackled the guy, taking him down to the cherry hardwood floor in a heap. Nathanial scrambled for dominance and landed a well-placed punch to the man's jaw, knocking him out.

Dr. Martin crouched down behind the couch as Blake, Sheriff Crump and Deputy Paulson came into the living room with another masked man with hands cuffed in tow.

The sheriff hurried to Dr. Martin's side and quickly released the gag from over her mouth and the rope binding her hands together. She hugged her uncle.

"We found this one in the kitchen," Blake said as he pushed the man to his knees. Gripping the edge of his ski mask, Blake ripped off the mask. Nathanial didn't recognize the guy. "Not Chase."

Focusing on the unconscious man, Nathanial stripped him of the mask. "Not him, either." Blake handed Nathanial a set of zip ties to cuff the man's hands together.

"I'll let Audrey know to come in." The sheriff pulled out his phone and stepped to the front window next to the Christmas tree.

Nathanial could only imagine the relief Audrey would feel learning her mother was safe. He wanted to go to her. He still had trouble believing he'd told her he loved her. The admission had bubbled up without forethought. But he didn't regret it.

That she hadn't expressed any similar sentiment stung. Though he couldn't fault her. There would be time enough later to discover if she felt the same. And if she didn't…he didn't want to think about how lonely and unfulfilling his life would be without her in it.

"Dr. Martin," Blake said. "Can you tell us what happened?"

"I was leaving the hospital when a man approached me," she said. "He had a badge and said he was here to protect me. He drove me home. Then he surprised the stuffing out of me when he tied me up and locked me in the bedroom so I'd be out of the way."

"Where did he go?" Nathanial asked.

She shook her head. "I don't know. It's been hours since I've seen anyone until that one came in and brought me to the door."

Blake addressed the man on his knees. "Where's your boss?"

The guy stayed stubbornly silent.

"What was the plan?" Blake asked. "Were you to kill Officer Longhorn?"

The suspect's gaze flicked to Nathanial then away. Nathanial took that as a yes. Disappointment filled him. This wasn't over, but at least Dr. Martin was safe.

"That's odd," the sheriff said as he turned from the window. "She's not picking up."

Dread crept up the back of Nathanial's spine. That was the one thing about overwatch—you had everyone else's back, but no one had yours.

He raced from the house, tore down the drive and scrambled up the hill that faced the cottage and the ocean. The place where he'd left Audrey was empty save for her rifle and flak vest. Eerily similar to what Drew had said Nathanial's disappearance had looked like. Terror clawed through him with razor-sharp talons.

He had to get to the ocean before they could throw her in as they had him.

Chapter Sixteen

Awareness came in spurts of sensation. Cold seeped through Audrey's clothes. Light filtered through her silted eyes and stung her retinas. The roar of the ocean in her ears. The salty taste of brine filled her mouth and nose. The gentle rocking of a boat buffeted by waves made her stomach roil. Her head throbbed, and her arms were pulled back in an awkward position and bound at the wrists by a thin rope.

Anger erupted within her chest, heating her skin and her mind. *Oh, no, you didn't just kidnap me!*

She held herself still, taking stock, assessing the situation. She needed to be smart, wait for an opportunity to escape. But first she had to know what she was dealing with. And whom.

After a recon of the area above her mom's cottage to make sure it was safe, she'd taken a position perched in the snow-covered V of a large paper birch tree that stood less than fifty yards from the cottage. She'd watched through the Nikon scope attached to her Remington rifle as Nathanial walked up the path leading to her mother's front door. There had been a noise behind her, just a whisper of sound. Expecting to see one of the white-tailed deer that were in abundance in Maine, she'd glanced over her shoulder at the exact moment that she'd been struck in the head with the butt of a rifle.

Just as Nathanial had been when he'd been taken from the rooftop in New Brunswick. Though in her case, she thankfully had her memories. A blessing, to be sure.

But why take her? They could have killed her or left her there unconscious. The answer washed over her with a sickening certainty.

To punish Nathanial. To use her as leverage against him. Chase had worked with Nathanial and for some reason must hold some ill will against him.

Well, little did her captors realize they'd messed with the wrong woman.

Slowly she shifted, hoping for a better view of her surroundings. The boat was the open picnic style of a local boat maker. She recognized the company logo on the floorboard. It wasn't a fast boat, nor one meant for choppy waters, which led her to believe whoever had her wasn't from Down East and had no idea how dangerous taking the small day cruiser into the winter ocean would be.

No doubt they planned to take her out to sea and dump her overboard the way they had Nathanial. She wasn't sure if her captors were cowards, unwilling to actually do the killing, or if they took joy from cruelty.

A foot appeared in her line of sight. Droplets of blood splattered the top and sides of the heavy black boot.

She ground her teeth together. But whose blood?

"Drop him over there," a man said. The timbre of his voice struck a chord within her. She'd heard it before. It wasn't Chase's. But it was American.

Oh, no. *Please, Lord, don't let them have taken Nathanial, too.*

The thud of a body hitting the floorboard jolted through her but was outside her field of vision. Unless she wanted to give away that she was conscious, she couldn't move to see who lay there.

"We've got a problem," another man stated. One of Kosloff's thugs, if the accent was any indication. "Ivan and Sven were captured."

"I should've known," the first man said. "Kosloff will not be pleased. But now that we have Longhorn's girlfriend, he'll come to us, and then we can finally get rid of him."

Audrey's stomach churned. She was correct. They planned to use her to bait Nathanial into a trap.

But if it wasn't Nathanial they'd dragged aboard, then who?

The boat's motor revved as they began to move.

"Halt! Sheriff's department!" Deputy Harrison yelled.

"Stop!" shouted a familiar voice. Nathanial!

Gunfire erupted over her head. She sent up a plea that God would keep those onshore safe. *Keep Nathanial safe*, she prayed.

Nathanial watched with helpless frustration as the boat taking Audrey away raced through the churning waves until it was a tiny speck. He held Drew's Glock in his hand, but he hadn't fired. He'd been too afraid of hitting Audrey, who had been lying unconscious on the deck. The sight made his blood run cold. There were no other boats on the private dock. Short of jumping in the ocean and swimming, there was nothing he could do.

He'd failed her. He went to his knees on the wet, slick dock. "Please, dear God. Don't let them hurt her."

Blake tucked his weapon into his holster. "We'll get her back. Sheriff Crump is on the line with the coast guard now."

The older man was hurrying back toward the cottage with his phone clutched to his ear.

"What if they dump her overboard?" Nathanial said. He couldn't take it if she died because of him. He never should have let her take overwatch. He shouldn't have let her come anywhere near the danger. He shook his head, knowing there'd been no way he could have stopped her. She was a brave, strong and stubborn woman who had proved over and over again that she was capable and good at her job.

And he couldn't fault her for letting someone get the drop on her. Not when the same thing had happened to him.

Blake held out his hand. "Come on. We need to figure out what these guys in the cottage know."

Nathanial grasped his friend's hand and rose to his feet. They hurried back to the house, where Deputy Paulson was standing guard over the two thugs. The sheriff was with Dr. Martin in the kitchen, explaining the situation. Nathanial's heart bled for her. She'd endured her own kidnapping and now her daughter had been taken. None of this would have happened had he not been beached on the sand like a whale.

Blake bent down so he was eye level with one of the men. "Listen carefully. I'm only going to offer this once. If you tell me where your boss's base of operation is now, I'll talk to the prosecutor about not deporting you. Because we both know you'll fare better in the US prison system than in your home country."

Nathanial crossed his arms over his chest, tucking his hands under his arms to keep from reaching out and pummeling the two goons until they gave up the information they needed to find Audrey.

"You talk, we're dead," the other thug said.

"Sven, we'll have a better chance of not being dead if they get Kosloff," the other goon argued.

"Not if we end up in the same prison," Sven said.

Antsy with the need to do something, Nathanial stepped closer. "We'll make sure you're protected." The offer grated on his nerves but he'd do, give, offer, anything to find Audrey.

"He has a warehouse on Moose Island." The thug in front of Blake gave him directions to Kosloff's hideout.

"Ivan!" His buddy groaned then pinned Nathanial with pleading eyes. "You'll protect us? Kosloff is not someone you want to cross."

"Tell me the name of the American who's working with Kosloff," Nathanial demanded.

The two men glanced at each other. "Which one?"

"The one in law enforcement," Blake specified.

Ivan shrugged. "Kosloff has many officers working for him in many countries. We don't know names. It's better that way."

Nathanial's jaw ached from the force with which he clenched it. "Call Director Moore. We need everyone on this."

Blake rose. "We'll call from the car. The sheriff and his men can handle these two."

Before Nathanial stepped out of the cottage, Dr. Martin stopped him with a hand on his arm.

"Please, find my daughter and bring her home safely," she asked him. Her blue eyes, so like Audrey's, dug at him.

He covered her hand with his own. "I will."

Even if he died trying.

The boat halted, the engine dying with a gurgle. Audrey tensed. Where were they? She'd tried calculating the distance in her mind, but chills had set in, distracting her. Was this the moment when her captors would throw her overboard? No. She remembered what the man in charge had said. They were going to use her to lure Nathanial into a death trap.

"Bring them." The command came from the American.

Rough hands grabbed at her. She couldn't afford to pretend any longer. She came to struggling. Kicking with her bound legs and twisting, turning.

A large hand slapped her across the face. "Stop it. Or I'll do worse."

She opened her eyes fully and met the angry gaze of a big and burly man with a mean expression on an otherwise bland face. He lifted her from the floor of the boat and flung her over his massive shoulder.

Mortified by the undignified position, she levered herself as high as she could and took stock of the location. The boat had docked at a lone pier. She could see Calico Bay in the distance. They had to be on Moose Island. Relief washed through her. She knew this place.

The lug carrying her set her unceremoniously on the hard concrete floor of a large warehouse, propped up against the south-facing wall. High windows let in light but blocked the view in and out of the building. Another thug dragged the other captive, still unconscious, across the floor and left him in a heap next to her.

Rage simmered low in her belly as she watched the men move to take a standing position along bench tables to clean their weapons. The scent of gun oil mingled with the dank smell of the warehouse. She had to find a way out of here. A way to warn Nathanial to not come for her, that he'd be walking into a trap. The roll-up door they'd come in through closed with a loud grating sound that stroked the hairs at the back of her neck to attention.

A staircase at one end of the warehouse led to an office. The lights were on, and she could see the silhouettes of several men through the closed window shade. Kosloff and his high-ranking minions. The only other exit was a side door that she prayed led to the outside. She worked the rope around her wrists, desperate to loosen its hold on her. The skin around her wrists burned, but she continued on.

The heap of a man lying on the ground beside her groaned. The back of his blond head was matted with blood. He lay facing away from her, so she'd yet to identify him. His hands and feet were bound like hers were.

"Hey," she whispered, hoping the man would come to so he could help her untie the cord around her wrists. "Wake up."

She shifted so she could push at him with her feet. "Come on."

He moaned as he flipped to his back, revealing his face.

Shocked rippled through her. "Chase!"

How could this be? He'd been the one to call her, threatening her mother's life if she didn't bring Nathanial to him. Had Kosloff turned on the ATF agent?

Chase's eyes fluttered open. For a moment he lay still, then his body jerked as he tried to rise but the binding holding his hands and feet together prevented him from doing more than flopping about like a fish on a hook.

"Stop," Audrey commanded in a harsh whisper, afraid he'd pull his arms out of their sockets, and then he'd be of no use to her.

He froze. His gaze zeroed on her. "What happened? Where are we?"

Darting a glance at their jailers to make sure they hadn't drawn anyone's attention, she hissed, "Shh. Not so loud."

Too late. One man left his place and came to stand over her. It was the same lug who'd carried her inside like a sack of potatoes. She bared her teeth at him with a growl of rage and frustration.

He hunkered down in front of her. His breath smelled worse than rotten fish on a hot summer day. "You're a little wildcat. We could have some fun."

He dared to skim his knuckles down her cheek. She pressed into his touch as if seeking his caress before jerking her head toward his fingers and chomping down hard on his pinkie.

He let out a yowl of pain and fell back on his behind. "Ow. She bit me."

"Try that again and I'll bite it clean off," she ground out, which his buddies found hilarious. They barked out laughter at the goon's expense.

He raised a hand to hit her.

"No!" Chase shouted and swung his legs in front of Audrey. Though she appreciated his attempt to stave off the blow, she braced herself.

The thug hesitated.

Audrey leveled her gaze on him in challenge. "You think your boss will be okay with you abusing me?"

He let out a disgusted snarl and jumped to his feet. Audrey let out a relieved breath as the lug stalked back to his weapon.

Chase shimmied to the wall and used it as leverage to bring himself to a sitting position. "Your mother?"

"Safe." Audrey narrowed her gaze on him. "You're working with Kosloff? How could you betray Nathanial like that?"

"No. I'm not. Absolutely not," he insisted in a harsh tone. "They forced me to make that call. He threatened to hurt my wife and daughter."

Her heart thumped. "We have to escape before Nathanial and the others walk into a trap."

Chase's gaze lifted to the office. "Kosloff and Wellborn are in there."

Surprised, she stared at him. "Wellborn? Luke?" An image of the baby-faced agent rose in her mind. He'd seemed so sincere when she'd met him. "The border patrol agent is the one working with Kosloff? The one who betrayed Nathanial?"

"Yes." The bitter tone lacing Chase's voice made her shiver. "He's the one responsible for the deaths of my men and the one who's been trying to kill Nathanial."

A fresh wave of fury infused her, heating her blood. "We need to untie these ropes."

He shifted so he was semisideways. "Put your shoulder against mine so they can't see what we're up to."

She maneuvered into position. Pressing close to him so he could work at the knot in the rope. She kept her gaze on the men, barely daring to take a breath, and sent up a prayer that none of the thugs would notice what they were doing. The seconds ticked by until she felt the rope loosen enough that she could slip a hand out.

"My turn," she said beneath her breath and began working on the cord binding Chase's wrists.

The small side door banged open, and one of Kosloff's men rushed inside. "They're here," he announced before racing to the office with his proclamation.

Audrey's stomach dropped. She plucked at the rope around Chase's wrists with renewed vigor. They had to get their hands on some weapons.

Four men filed out of the upstairs office. Audrey recognized Luke and two of the thugs. They'd been on the boat with them. But the fourth man she'd only seen in photos. Kosloff. He wore an expensive-looking suit beneath a wool trench coat and sported a furry Ushanka hat, the traditional headwear of Russia.

"Bring me the woman." Kosloff's guttural voice carried across the warehouse.

Ack. She wasn't done with Chase's rope.

"Leave it," Chase said. "Save yourself."

She had every intention of saving them all.

Giving up on Chase's cord, she pressed her back to the wall to hide the fact that her hands were free. A different thug hurried over, grabbed her by the biceps and forced her to her feet. He had the strap of a semiautomatic slung over his shoulder. The weapon bumped into her as he pushed her toward his boss.

"Kosloff, we have the place surrounded." Blake's deep voice sounded through the warehouse walls. "Come out with your hands up."

Kosloff snickered. "Not likely." He peered at Audrey. "Too bad you must die. I could use an amazon like you in my stable."

Audrey's lip curled in a sneer. Her hands fisted with the need to disabuse him of that thought. But she held herself still. The timing wasn't right yet for her to make a move.

Noise on the roof sent her pulse careening. Her body tensed. The sound of glass breaking as men swung through the windows was the distraction she needed. She whirled on the goon holding her arm. Using the side of her hand, she chopped into his throat. He doubled over. She slipped the strap off his shoulder and gripped the semiautomatic in her hands. Two thugs stepped in front of Kosloff, blocking her aim.

A team of men dropped into the warehouse with weapons drawn. Kosloff's men formed a circle with Audrey and Kosloff in the middle. They were at a standoff.

Luke held up his hands. "Whoa! Everyone take a breath. No one wants to die today."

Nathanial separated from the others. He had Audrey's Remington aimed at Luke's chest. "Wellborn!" The hurt in his voice made Audrey wince. "You're the traitor? Why?"

Luke shrugged. "I needed the money. Tell your men to lower their weapons or we all die."

"I don't think so." Nathanial pushed his way through the men to Audrey's side. "You're surrounded. Outmanned and outgunned."

Luke smirked. "You don't think I know your moves?" He made a sweeping motion with his hand. "These are only the men you can see. There are many more waiting to mobilize."

Audrey couldn't discern if Luke was bluffing.

"Enough of this," Kosloff said. "Kill them all and be done with it. I want to get home in time for Christmas Eve dinner."

Tension rippled through Audrey as a barrage of gunfire erupted around her. Kosloff and Luke ran toward the exit, followed by the two protective goons. She fired, hitting one thug in the leg. He went down. The other thug pivoted and turned the barrel of his weapon toward her.

"Audrey, look out!" Nathanial cried. He shoved her hard as the goon pulled the trigger.

Nathanial jerked and fell unconscious at Audrey's feet.

"No!" Audrey's scream bounced off the concrete floor. She sank to her knees and cradled him in her arms. His head bled from the bullet. "No, please don't leave me."

The roller door opened, and a swarm of additional federal agents stormed in and quickly subdued the few remaining thugs. But all Audrey could concentrate on was the man in her arms. The man she loved with her whole being.

"Please, Lord, let him live."

Nathanial awoke to the beeping of monitors and the white stucco ceiling of the Calico Bay hospital. A sense of déjà vu hit him with the force of a nor'easter. Only this time there was no void where his memories should have been. His memories were intact.

Including everything that had happened in the past week.

It all came rushing to the forefront of his mind. Being hit from behind while on overwatch. Being dragged onto a boat and seeing Luke Wellborn's familiar face. The icy shock of the ocean water when Luke and another goon had dumped him overboard. Then the beautiful woman who'd rescued him on the beach.

Audrey!

He had to know she was safe. He grappled with the bed to find the nurse's call button. Frantic with worry, he depressed the button repeatedly.

When Kosloff's thug had put her in his sights, Nathanial had reacted. He'd pushed her aside, taking the hit himself. That he wasn't dead was a blessing. He didn't know why God had spared him, but he sent up a grateful prayer of praise.

The door opened. Dr. Martin hurried in. "Are you in pain?"

"No." He gripped the bed railing. "Audrey? Is she okay?"

Dr. Martin's expression softened as she took his vitals. "She's outside with the others. I'll let them know you're awake."

He lay back with relief and became aware of the throbbing in his head. Worse than it was before. "I was shot."

She made a noise very reminiscent of one her daughter had made when he'd stated the obvious and she wrote on his chart. "The bullet grazed your forehead. You most likely have another concussion. I don't recommend any more."

"My memories came back," he told her.

"That's good news. It's been known to happen after a head contusion." She set the chart aside and pinned him with a sober look. "What are your intentions with my daughter?"

Taken aback by the blunt question, he blurted, "I'm afraid of love. Afraid of the hurt that can come with it."

"So is she," Dr. Martin said. "But the greatest blessings lie beyond your greatest fears."

He absorbed her wise words, thinking that was something his own mother would say. He searched his heart. He loved Audrey, but was he willing to risk it all without knowing how she felt about him? Especially now that his life was no longer in danger and she was no longer obligated to protect him?

The past pain of losing his child and the sting of Laurie's rejection lay on his heart. Though the wounds were not gone, they were healed. He'd always mourn the loss of the baby, but Laurie had been right not to marry him. He could see that now.

Their love had been young and flawed.

He thought of all the years he'd held on to his grief and pain as a shield from feeling anything like that again. But it took losing his memories and a beautiful deputy sheriff to make him see that the past shouldn't dictate his future.

A future he wanted to share with Audrey, if she'd have him.

He met Dr. Martin's gaze and spoke with earnestness. "I love your daughter and want to spend the rest of my life with her."

The older woman's eyes lit up. "I'm glad to hear it." She turned and nearly danced from the room.

A few moments later, Audrey came in, followed by Blake, Drew and Sami. Nathanial only had eyes for the uniformed deputy who stopped at the foot of the bed. Her gaze caressed him, and he wished they were alone so he could explore that look.

"Hey," Blake said, drawing his attention. "You scared us a second time."

Nathanial gave him a lopsided grin. "Well, apparently the second time is a charm, because my memories have returned. All of them."

"That's great," Sami exclaimed.

Drew gave him the thumbs-up sign. "Most excellent."

"I thought the saying was three times is a charm," Blake retorted with a grin.

"Please, God, don't let there be a third time," Nathanial quipped.

"That's great, Nathanial," Audrey said softly.

Blake withdrew a box from inside his coat. "I thought you might want this back."

Nathanial lifted his eyebrows. Blake opened the lid to reveal a lethal-looking steel knife. "My Becker Necker. Thanks, dude."

Blake set it on the eating tray by the bed. "Your government wants you back ASAP. And the director wants to debrief us all as well. It doesn't look good for one of our own to be an accomplice with Kosloff."

"Right. How's Chase?" Nathanial asked. His mind still reeled with the knowledge that Luke had betrayed them. For money. The root of all evil, or so they said.

"He's fine. Livid, as we all are," Drew said.

A moment of silence pervaded the room.

"We should let Audrey and Nathanial have a moment alone," Sami said, her keen gaze bouncing between them.

"That's subtle." Her husband laughed. "We'll check with Dr. Martin to see when she'll release you."

They filed out of the room. Audrey remained at the end of the bed. An awkward tension filled the space between them. He held out his hand.

She rounded the bed and twined her fingers through his. "I was so afraid I'd lost you."

Though he didn't like that she'd been scared, he couldn't keep a dopey grin from forming. "Lose me? Never."

"You remembered why you never allowed yourself to fall in love," she said. "Is that still the case?"

"No. The past is over."

Her big blue eyes were so full of love that he felt his own eyes welling up. Whoa. He wasn't a crier. "I love you, Audrey." He rushed the words out before he was too choked up to speak.

"When you said that before, I thought it was only because you thought you were going to die," she stated in a soft, uncertain tone.

"I said it because it's true."

"I know." She brought his hand to her mouth and kissed his knuckles. "I love you, too," she murmured against his skin.

His heart skipped a beat. "Come again?"

She lowered his hand, squared her shoulders and lifted her chin. His warrior bracing for battle. "For too long I've let fear keep me from accepting that anyone could love me for me."

He held up his other hand. "I do."

She gave a small laugh. "I know."

"A wise woman recently told me that our greatest blessings lie beyond our greatest fears." He squeezed her hand. "I want to be your greatest blessing."

She beamed at him. "I love you."

His heart soared with joy. But then crashed to the ground. "I have to go back to Canada."

"Not until after Christmas," she stated. "Mom won't sign off on letting you travel until next week."

"I like the sound of that, but…" He didn't want to think about leaving her.

"But we'll tackle the future after Christmas. I'm in," she said. "Whatever may come, wherever we end up, as long as we're together, I'm good."

Tears slipped down his cheeks. "Give me a kiss before I start blubbering like a baby."

She leaned in to place her lips against his in a kiss that made the world fade away.

Epilogue

One year later

The Christmas tree twinkled in the window of the cottage by the sea. Audrey stepped back after putting on the last decoration. "It's perfect."

"Not quite," her husband said as he slipped an arm around her waist and held out a box wrapped in red paper and gold ribbon.

"Nathanial, Christmas isn't for a few more weeks," she exclaimed but snatched the pretty box from his hands anyway.

He laughed and kissed the side of her neck. "I don't want to wait."

His impatience was one of his most endearing and annoying qualities. With a grin, she sank down on the plush rug covering the hardwood floor. He sat beside her. His eagerness for her to open the gift was so cute she sighed with contentment. She had everything in life she could want. A wonderful husband, a home and a community to protect.

After their summer wedding, her mother had gifted

them with the cottage, saying a young couple needed space to grow. The obvious hint at providing grandchildren wasn't lost on Audrey. Mom had moved into Audrey's studio in town and was dating the bank manager.

Nathanial had convinced the powers that be of the need for an IBETs presence Down East. Being married to a US citizen allowed him to live in Calico Bay. And when he had to leave on a mission, Bangor airport was only a few hours away.

She slipped the knot out of the ribbon and laid the gold material to the side.

Nathanial groaned. "You're torturing me on purpose."

She giggled then ripped through the paper to reveal a white box. Jewelry? She glanced at the marquise-cut diamond on her finger. That was all the decoration she needed. She opened the box. Nestled against cotton batting was a beautiful, shiny ornament in the shape of a star.

With a gasp, she lifted it up to catch the light and turned stunned eyes to the man she loved. "It's lovely."

He grinned, his dark eyes shining bright. "You don't remember, do you?"

Searching her brain and coming up empty, she said, "Can I claim amnesia?"

"Hey!" He laughed and shook his head. "What were the first words I said to you?"

She was mentally transported to that day on the beach when she'd found him lying on the sand. "'Betrayed.'"

"No, not that. The other thing."

She looked at him blankly.

"When I woke up in the hospital," he prompted.

The heat of a blush swept up her cheeks. "You said I looked like a Christmas ornament. Shiny. Pretty." Now the gift made sense. She hugged it to her chest.

He leaned in to kiss her. "Merry Christmas, my shiny, pretty wife."

HARLEQUIN
PLUS

Announcing a **BRAND-NEW**
multimedia subscription service
for romance fans like you!

Read, Watch and Play.

Experience the easiest way to get
the romance content you crave.

Start your **FREE 7 DAY TRIAL** at
<u>www.harlequinplus.com/freetrial</u>.

LOVE INSPIRED

Stories to uplift and inspire

Fall in love with Love Inspired—
inspirational and uplifting stories of faith
and hope. Find strength and comfort in
the bonds of friendship and community.
Revel in the warmth of possibility and the
promise of new beginnings.

Sign up for the Love Inspired newsletter
at **LoveInspired.com** to be the first
to find out about upcoming titles,
special promotions and exclusive content.

CONNECT WITH US AT:

Facebook.com/LoveInspiredBooks

Twitter.com/LoveInspiredBks